BBC
DOCTOR WHO

THE PIRATE PLANET

THE CHANGING FACE OF DOCTOR WHO
This book portrays the Fourth Doctor, whose physical
appearance later transformed as the Black Guardian finally
caught up with him.

This bo̶... Swansea Libraries ...ch has been

DOCTOR WHO

THE PIRATE PLANET

This novelisation is based on the first draft scripts by
Douglas Adams.
So it probably isn't what you're expecting.

James Goss

BBC
BOOKS

1 3 5 7 9 10 8 6 4 2

BBC Books, an imprint of Ebury Publishing
20 Vauxhall Bridge Road,
London SW1V 2SA

BBC Books is part of the Penguin Random House group of companies whose
addresses can be found at global.penguinrandomhouse.com

Penguin
Random House
UK

Doctor Who is a BBC Wales production.
Executive producers: Steven Moffat and Brian Minchin

Sound of the Underground by Brian Thomas, Niara Scarlett and Miranda Eleanor
De Fonbrune Cooper. Xenomania Songs Ltd (NS) and Warner/Chappell Music Ltd
(PRS). All rights on behalf of Xenomania Songs Ltd and itself administered by
Warner/Chappell Music Ltd. All rights on behalf of Xenomania Songs Ltd
administered by Warner/Chappell Music Publishing Ltd

First published by BBC Books in 2017
Paperback edition published in 2018

www.penguin.co.uk

A CIP catalogue record for this book is available from the British Library

ISBN 9781849906784

Commissioning Editor: Albert DePetrillo
Series Consultant: Justin Richards
Project Editor: Steve Tribe
Cover design: Two Associates © Woodlands Books Ltd
Production: Alex Merrett

Printed and bound by Great Britain by Clays Ltd, St Ives PLC

Penguin Random House is committed to a sustainable future for our
business, our readers and our planet. This book is made from Forest
Stewardship Council® certified paper.

MIX
Paper from
responsible sources
FSC
www.fsc.org   FSC® C018179

CONTENTS

PART ONE

"We Have All Systems Go for the Dawn of a New Golden Age of Prosperity!"

CHAPTER ONE
THE SKY WITH DIAMONDS

It rained diamonds that day, but no one cared. The people of Zanak simply held up their umbrellas made of gold and got on with their lives, which, for the most part, involved shuffling through streets already clogged with emeralds and rubies. No one looked up. No one wanted to see the rain of precious stones, far less get hit in the eye by one. But that wasn't the real reason. If you lived in Zanak's capital city and you looked up, you couldn't help but see the mountain. And no one wanted to see the mountain. So, their gold-leaf umbrellas dented with diamonds, the people of Zanak went about their business, looking dead ahead.

Crowning the mountain was the Citadel. It was a peculiar building, a haphazard mingling of ancient stone and burnt metal that looked pretty much as though a starliner had fallen into a mountain. Which, curiously enough, was exactly what had once happened.

The jutting heart of the Citadel was a room called the Bridge. Mr Fibuli was wanted on the Bridge. But Mr Fibuli wasn't coming. Not today.

Today, Mr Fibuli was crouched in a cupboard wiping his glasses with a dirty cloth. It was only making things worse. Every event in Mr Fibuli's life made things worse. At his feet lay a vast stack of paperwork. He had stayed up late the night before, clearing all of his paperwork away until his desk was empty. He had come in this morning, before anyone else, to find his desk full again. Crammed with documents, memos, counter-memos, circulars, and even junk mail assuring him that a long-lost friend on a distant planet had shares in a diamond mine. Mr Fibuli had found this last letter so absurd he had almost laughed. He'd stood there, staring at it, urging the sides of his mouth to move. They did not move, up or down. He swept away his thoughts about the vast pile of paperwork to concentrate on the piece of junk mail. It was so repellently ironic he just couldn't figure out how it had got there. Just for a moment he wondered if the Captain himself had placed it there. But no. No, he couldn't have.

He'd finally started sifting through the rest of the new day's relentless paperwork. Reports from the automated mines, diagnostics from the engines, and a set of Standard Termination Fee Orders for the latest victims of That Thing. Mr Fibuli signed those first. That Thing was getting hungrier.

Mr Fibuli then turned his attention to the last folder on his desk. It was a summary of Ancillary Personnel Displacements Caused By Manoeuvres. He opened it, grimaced at the total, and shut it hastily. This time someone had gone too far.

He wasn't sure what made him then go and crawl into a cupboard. It may have been the staggering total contained within the folder. It may have been that someone came in, smirked at him, and dropped a dozen more folders on his desk. He didn't know for sure. But Mr Fibuli went and hid in a cupboard anyway.

It did not make Mr Fibuli feel any better. For a moment, he curled up there, and felt almost safe. And then, to his horror, someone pushed more folders under the door. They knew he was here. They'd come and fetch him eventually. When the Captain had grown tired of calling for him. Aghast, Mr Fibuli watched the folders slide under the door one by one, kicking at them with his heels. Why was there so much paperwork? After all, they were supposed to be pirates…

The Doctor was also hiding in a cupboard. As he was an Ancient Lord of Gallifrey and the owner of an infinitely huge time machine it was a very large cupboard, but nevertheless it was still a cupboard. The Doctor was on a quest, and those always made him sulky.

The Key to Time may have been the most powerful object in the universe, but the Doctor found it boring. Yes, it was the supreme fragment of the previous universe, yes, it could restore the balance between good and evil in this one, but really… did there have to be six pieces of it?

The Doctor had been assigned the task of collecting the Key to Time by the Guardian, a glowing white figure who, if not exactly God was certainly happy to fill in for Him if He was busy. So far, the Doctor had collected one piece out of the six and was thoroughly over it.

Six segments. He kept on returning to that. He had enough trouble finding his hat. Now he had to find six whole bits of a thing. It required dedication and single-mindedness and all sorts of other things that the Doctor, frankly, was lacking.

He understood the idea of why the Key to Time had to come in a limited-edition collect-the-set format. After all, it was the most powerful object in the universe, and if it just lay around, anyone could get their hands on it. Therefore it made sense to split it up a bit. But really, two chunks would have been plenty:

'Hello, I believe you have the other half of the Key to Time. May I borrow it for the afternoon?'

'Any particular reason? Not planning on taking over the universe?'

'Not as such, no.'

All right, perhaps two slices was a little strict. But surely causality could scrape by with four segments. Having to hunt down all six was just vexing. It was like having to do a really important jigsaw with the danger that at any moment you'd find the missing bit of sky was in the hands of the Black Guardian.

The Black Guardian, by the way, was a rather ominous figure who was dedicated to all things evil. As he co-owned the Key on a timeshare basis with the White Guardian, he was theoretically entitled to gather it together himself if ever he decided the universe was getting too good and running itself too efficiently. In practice, however, he'd never really needed to bother. As the universe fell apart on a regular basis, the job of being Black Guardian was somewhat of a sinecure, and there were too few of those around nowadays. The Doctor would have had a soft spot for the Black Guardian, were it not that, with little else to do, he was bound to be terribly interested in the Doctor's attempts to reassemble the Key. The Black Guardian would hamper the Doctor's progress with all the obfuscating zeal of a middle manager at the British Broadcasting Corporation.

A further problem with the Key to Time was that the individual segments could disguise themselves as anything. The Doctor reflected on this. Notionally, this was quite exciting. What could the six segments be, eh?

- The continent of Africa, that would be fun – you'd need to buy a new one.
- Buckingham Palace? Also a laugh, but need to square it with Liz.
- The TARDIS? Tough.
- The Doctor himself? See. Now that would be a puzzler.

Instead the Doctor had the sinking feeling that the segments would be as lacking in imagination as 6-year-olds going to a fancy-dress party. The first segment had justified his pessimism. In its natural state, a segment of the Key to Time looked like a precious jewel. The first segment had been found in a display case, cunningly disguised as a precious jewel.

His hearts in his boots, the Doctor dreaded slinking around the universe, gradually turning his time machine into a trinket shop stuffed full of crystals, pendants and knick-knacks. It would be terribly embarrassing if he invited people round. Which was unlikely, because of the final annoying thing about the Key to Time.

The final annoying thing about the Key to Time was that the Guardian had given the Doctor a new companion. Had the Doctor been consulted he'd have produced a list of desirable attributes in a companion:

- human(ish)
- stupid and heroic (if male)
- wide-eyed and amazing (if female)
- good sense of humour
- likes long country walks through quarries
- knows one end of the kettle from the other
- plucky (no idea what plucky means, but will know it when I see it)
- pathologically unable to ask questions
- sturdy ankles

The Doctor would have also pointed out that he already had the ideal companion. It was a robot dog called K-9 who allowed the Doctor to cheat at chess and ran out of steam when faced with a steep hill. No yomping up mountains with K-9 around, which, considering the Doctor was now knocking at 750, was something of a blessing.

But no, the Guardian hadn't taken the Doctor's wishes, or the existence of his charming robot dog, into consideration. He had instead provided him with the Time Lady Romanadvoratrelundar, who, so far, was as much fun as a well-dressed telephone directory.

The Time Lady Romanadvoratrelundar was fresh out of Gallifrey's Time Academy and therefore life with her was one long giddy whirl of chit-chat about her A levels, or whatever they were calling them this week.

Instead of laughing at his jokes (the Doctor adored companions who did that), the Time Lady merely regarded the Doctor with barely polite amusement. Sometimes she did this little grimacing thing with her lips which implied that he'd fallen out of a Christmas cracker. Her expression was the total opposite of wide-eyed. The Doctor had travelled with giddier lizards.

Since Romanadvoratrelundar had arrived, the Doctor had noticed how dusty bits of the TARDIS were. This, he thought, was most unfair. It wasn't that he was untidy, just that there were more important things to do. He had, once, hired a cleaner, who had vanished inside the TARDIS with a duster and a bucket and never been seen again. He occasionally worried about that – after all, was he paying her by the hour?

Also, the Time Lady Romanadvoratrelundar seemed to have been at the thermostat. The TARDIS was now distinctly chilly. What had been his home for a considerable number of years now felt altogether less cosy. Even the TARDIS's once reassuring hum had changed to a less settled 'hmmm'.

The one thing the vast interior of the time machine lacked was a shed, so the Doctor had, for the moment, gone to hide in the Limbo Chamber. It was completely black, and had an ominous echo but, thanks to a plug-in three-bar heater, was nice and snug. In theory the Limbo Chamber provided a point of secure nullity in which to store the Segments of the Key to Time, but it had already accrued several half-drunk mugs of tea and a pile of *Times* crosswords.

The Doctor's previous incarnation had been a dashing silver-haired gentleman addicted to velvet and capes. His next incarnation would wear white linen which would remain miraculously stain-free. But this Doctor, the fourth, was a proud spiller of crumbs and defier of convention. Every morning, he advanced on the wardrobe as though he were seeking revenge. What did it matter what he wore, he figured. The Doctor's face radiated an impish kindness, as though he was about to share a joke about someone you didn't like. This Doctor was not a man for plans, schemes or quests. This was a man who woke up, grabbed a scarf, and went to laugh hard at the universe. And right now, the Doctor was hiding out in his den with K-9, polishing the first segment of the Key to Time with said scarf.

'There we are, K-9,' he announced, holding the segment up to the light. 'Five more of these and we'll be able to put up a "job done" sticker.'

The robot dog considered this remark dubiously. 'Query, Master: I have no record in my memory banks concerning such an object.'

'Never a boy scout, eh?' The Doctor flashed K-9 a dolorous grin.

'Scout?' the robot dog sniffed. He had been sniffing a lot since Romanadvoratrelundar had arrived. Perhaps he was allergic. 'In military terms, a scout is one who is sent ahead of a main body of troops. Query relevance to stationery supplies.'

'Quite,' replied the Doctor firmly, and left the room.

At the other end of time, the Old Queen blinked. This took longer than you would expect.

'You can't be here!' she croaked, her voice worn out from a life of shouting.

'But I am,' replied the figure in the shadows in a deep voice.

'How?' she roared as the figure stepped closer. 'You can't be here.'

Unusually for him, the figure shrugged, and then favoured her with a rather ghastly smile. 'No, don't get up,' it said. 'We have a lot to discuss…'

CHAPTER TWO
THE DEAD PLANETS

Let us talk of planets. Since this book is about planets, here are four of them. All very different, but their fates sadly exactly the same.

Temesis Beta had been the target of a long and arduous space mission. The capsule from Temesis Alpha had been primitive – little more than an optimistic tin bath that had somehow left its home world, crossed a formidable distance, and settled into a brief orbit with its neighbouring planet.

The crew had carried out careful observations of the world spinning beneath them. They were unable to land, but it was early days yet. As their craft lacked portholes, a series of remote cameras and radarscopes supplied them with a complicated data picture. One day their people would come back and they would land here. But for now, they were using the last of their fuel to return home to a hero's welcome.

Their most remarkable find had been the detection of radio emissions from the surface of Beta. Unintelligible, basic, but their eyebrows had risen when they had realised that some of the messages were pointed in their direction. The crew were returning home with news that there was intelligent life elsewhere in the universe and that it was friendly.

After a long, exhausting, but triumphant flight, the craft reached orbit around Temesis Alpha. Only something was wrong. Its crew were roused from dreams of long, hot showers followed by book deals and chat show appearances by the self-important ping-ping-ping of the craft's computer.

The readings on the consoles were astonishing, unbelievable. So utterly confounding that the captain of the ship immediately launched one of the remote cameras.

It confirmed the terrible truth to the dumb-founded, suddenly doomed, inhabitants of the craft.

Temesis Alpha was no longer there.

Nothing happened on Calufrax. But then it never did. It rained a little, but only really for appearances. From an evolutionary point of view, Calufrax was waiting for a bus. If a planet could be said to be slumming it while hoping for a better offer to come along, then that was Calufrax. Clouds drifted through the sky like thumbs being twiddled. Glaciers crept along with 'must we?' huffs. Such life as Calufrax had evolved mostly just clung listlessly to rocks. It would, it definitely would get around to growing vertebra. Just not today.

Actually, especially not today.

It has often been said that nothing good ever came out of a committee, but there is always an exception to this rule. On Sakunthala they had worked out the meaning of life by committee. Surprisingly, a politician suggested it. One day, on the spur of the moment, to avoid answering a difficult question, he just came out with it. 'I'm pleased you asked me that. It's a good question, a really good question,' he began, conventionally enough. 'But I'll tell you what's an even better question…' And, even then, that was what people expected politicians to say. But that was when the wheels came off. 'An even better question is what is the meaning of existence? What are we all here for, other than to fill in the gaps before we die? You know, we can sit around calling each other names, watching as things get progressively worse and blaming other people, or we could just, you know, find out what's it all for. And then we could work backwards from that and find out if we really need to build all those roads and houses and what not.'

Oddly enough, the idea caught on. Someone immediately suggested building a computer, but sensing he was on a roll, the politician pooh-poohed it. 'We'll just end up with a tendering process, a procurement contract, scope creep, and then blaming each other when the wretched thing is late, doesn't work, and has to be scrapped. Let's just talk this one through.'

And that's what the people of Sakunthala did. They kept the hospitals and the schools running, but apart from that, pretty much everyone sat down to form the Committee of What (this was partly to avoid getting side-tracked by naming the thing, and partly because that was, after all, what they were trying to find out). Countries broke off into various sub-committees to really think about such topics as 'Why do we have children?' and 'Does Death matter?' and 'Why toenails?'

The whole planet just talked. They talked the whole matter out and gradually, as the various groups came together, they reached a consensus.

'Oh,' they all said, and broke into cautious smiles.

And then the skies of Sakunthala grew dark.

The fleet had come looking for Bandraginus 5. They had voyaged long and hard across the quadrant. The last of their energy reserves were almost spent. They had lost many fine ships in their quest. But they were here. They had reached Bandraginus 5.

They had come, they insisted, not because the planet was wealthy. That was the very last of their concerns. Any Oolion they found would, of course, be placed in a secure trust to be administered in the interests of the people of Bandraginus 5. They had the planet's best interests at heart. This was, primarily, a Peacekeeping Mission.

They said so, in a nicely worded speech broadcast as they pulled into the solar system. Perhaps, yes, the speech did conclude with a few small threats about what would happen if their completely peaceful (and very well-armed) mission was met with even token resistance. But they were very firm on the matter. They were here for the good of Bandraginus 5.

There was only one problem.

Bandraginus 5 had gone.

CHAPTER THREE
LIFE FORCE

'Mr Fibuli!'

To describe the Captain would be to spoil the surprise. It's probably safest to describe his chair, which was very large and dominated the Bridge of the Citadel. From here, the Captain could look out through the vast domed windows, down the mountain, across the city of Zxoxaxax and over the plains of Malchios. The cities were easier to see than they were to spell.

The Captain (who cannot yet be described) was sitting in his chair (which can). The Captain's Chair was large and black and could spin round very quickly if its occupant needed to do some angry glaring. As he needed to do this frequently, it was kept very well oiled.

Today it had developed a squeak, which was bothersome. But it was not for this that the Captain was calling for Mr Fibuli.

The Captain's voice echoed across the Bridge in a full-throated roar. The Captain's Nurse (who was young, small, pretty and adept at keeping herself out of the way) heard it and made a note to check his blood sugar. The Drive Operators heard the shout and were glad it was not aimed at them. The Sifting Technicians shrugged. The Extraction Specialists wondered if today old Fibuli would get what for and declared the miserable goat was long overdue for it.

'Mr Fibuli!' repeated the Captain, really and truly finding his voice. His previous shouts had been little more than a warm-up, in the same way that a volcano can be said to be warming up. 'Mr Fibuli! By all the X-Ray storms of Vega where is that nincompoop?'

The Summoner leaned over a microphone and said in a very precise voice that was relayed over the entire Citadel, 'Calling Mr Fibuli. Mr Fibuli required on the Bridge immediately.'

There was a pause. A few people glanced over to the cupboard in the corridor. Someone would have to go and tap on it in a bit, wouldn't they?

The Captain continued to shout from his large black chair. 'Send Fibuli to me! Send him to me now or by all that's degenerate in a neutron star I'll have the lot of you past the next event horizon faster than a positron in a hadron collider. Moons of madness, why am I encumbered with incompetents?!'

No one answered this. The Captain rarely expected an answer to that sort of question. The Captain spun away to look out of the window, allowing the cupboard door to open. Mr Fibuli stepped carefully out, gathered together his paperwork, took a deep breath, and then came running onto the Bridge.

'Captain, sir!' he announced. As he came running past, people pushed more reports and printouts into his hands. He sighed to a halt before the back of that large black chair, which looked, it had to be said, fairly ominous.

'Ah…' The soft voice that emerged from the chair was silken in its purr. 'I am obliged to you for your alacrity. Your report, Mr Fibuli?'

Mr Fibuli ran a tongue around his mouth in a fruitless search for moisture. 'Yes… I have it…'

'It's thirty seconds late.'

'Yes sir.'

'My qualities are many, Mr Fibuli,' rumbled the chair. 'But I'm afraid an infinite capacity for patience is not one of them.' A pause. And then, simply because he liked saying it, a final, threatening 'Mr Fibuli.'

The Captain turned around in his chair and, since he did so, we may as well finally describe him. If his chair was large, ominous and covered with wires, then the Captain was rather more so. It was hard to tell where the chair ended and the Captain began. Somewhere in amongst it all were the remains of a very large man. There was still enough left over to make a reasonably sized one if you started from scratch. But whoever had worked on the Captain had vowed to keep the scale intact, if nothing else. The overall impression was still of a large, sinister, bearded man with a piercing gaze. But half of his face was covered with a metallic plate. A green eyepatch glowed dangerously, metal lips sneered, and even half of his beard was iron. Things got worse beneath the neck. A vast robotic arm, two artificial legs, synthetic lungs that hissed with effort, and, at the end of a velvet-covered sleeve, the rather pathetic remains of a human hand twitched occasionally as it tugged at the immobile wrist it was sewn to.

There really wasn't very much of the Captain left, but there was more than enough to be absolutely terrifying. What did not help was the smell. Wafting around the Captain, especially when he was angry, was the entirely disagreeable whiff of slowly cooking meat.

At the various consoles, sporadic bets were taking place as to whether or not today would be Fibuli's last day. The old goat had had a good run, but the Captain really did seem to have it in for him right now.

Something was scuttling across the Captain's shoulder, shifting its weight from one claw to another. It too was glaring at Mr Fibuli. That Thing.

Mr Fibuli had decided that, if today really was his day to die, then so be it. He wasn't sure he could take much more of it. He wasn't sure what was the most unbearable. The paperwork, the horrid statistics in his folder, the glare of the Thing, or the constant shouting. But if it all ended today, then fine. He'd stared death in the face so many times he could recognise its smile.

From somewhere foggy he could hear his voice oozing away: 'I apologise most abjectly Captain, sir, but I do believe I have good news, sir.'

And the Captain replied almost genially: 'By the Seven Suns of Orion, I should hope you do, Mr Fibuli!'

The Captain reached up to the Thing on his shoulder and stroked it. It made a chirrup and glared at Fibuli. Fibuli didn't really care, not any more, but was rather surprised to see that the Captain tipped him a wink.

'Well?'

Mr Fibuli accidentally opened the folder of Ancillary Personnel Displacements Caused By Manoeuvres, saw the figure of three billion, and closed it again. He instead pulled open a manila folder and began to read from it in a fussy tone.

'Sir, all deposits of the minerals Voolium, Galdrium and Assetenite 455 have now been mined, processed and stored, sir. We have lots of silicates, alumina, the usual sir, carbon isotopes, etcetera, etcetera, and the residue has, you will be pleased to hear, been processed.'

'In the normal way?' The Captain's voice was soft, keen, eager. He risked a furtive glance over at his Nurse but, if she noticed his excitement, she let it ride.

'In the, er, normal way, sir.' The Captain's seemed a strange preoccupation, but then again, theirs was a strange life, and every man must have his hobby. 'Oh, and here is a list of the minerals, sir.'

The Captain took the list, barely glanced at it and let it slide from his mechanical grasp. 'Ha! Baubles, baubles, dross and baubles!' With a grunt of pistons, he leaned forward in his chair, his diesel breath wafting over Mr Fibuli. 'We must find Vasilium. We must find Madranite 1-5. Mr Fibuli, by the ancient fires of Rigel!'

'But sir…' Mr Fibuli, flicking through his printouts, smiled. 'I think we've found some.'

'You have located a source?'

Mr Fibuli stared at the printout in some surprise. 'Yes sir.' He actually was bringing the Captain some really good news.

'Excellent.' The Captain clucked with delight. As did the Thing on his shoulder.

Having described the Captain's chair, and the Captain himself, we may as well go the whole hog and describe his pet. The crew called it 'The Thing' or 'That Thing'. They didn't dignify it with a proper name, because its name was actually very silly and the Thing was not. The Thing killed people. It killed them quickly (sometimes) and painfully (always). The Thing was a small robot parrot. Its eyes were bloody diamonds, its sharp plumage a spread of precious metals, its claws and beak titanium. At first glance you might have said, 'How cute,' but then you wouldn't have got a second glance. The gimlet eyes of the Thing drilled into Mr Fibuli and told him quite plainly that he was about to die. Mr Fibuli hated much of life, with a dull, weary hatred – he hated paperwork, motion sickness, the Sifting & Extraction Engineers, but most of all, he hated the Thing. Because, whenever it was on the Bridge, wherever he was, whenever Mr Fibuli looked up, the Thing would be glaring at him.

Yet it still had not killed him today.

'In fact,' Mr Fibuli pressed on, feeling his confidence grow. Perhaps, yet again, it would all work out fine. 'In fact, that's what caused the delay. I wanted to be absolutely certain… You see –' temporising, he consulted the printout, which was still warm – 'the source is in a very unexpected sector. Let me show it to you on this chart.' Mr Fibuli fished around uncertainly among the papers in the crook of his arm, and pulled out what he hoped was the correct map.

The Captain squinted at it with his one good eye and sighed gloriously. 'Ah, we'll mine it! Make immediate preparations.'

Across the bridge came a flurry of activity from the Drive Operators, but Mr Fibuli continued to look at the star charts and frowned. The one slight problem with the source was that it really shouldn't have been there. 'There's something rather curious, sir. Here's a detailed description of the sector…'

The Captain stood with a hydraulic growl. 'I said we'll mine it, Mr Fibuli!'

'But—' Mr Fibuli often wondered if that would be his last word.

The Captain's mechanical arm swung out, heaving Mr Fibuli off his feet. 'Molest me not with trifles, or I'll have your bones bleached. Is that clear?'

'Aye, aye, Captain,' whispered Mr Fibuli as he landed in a heap.

The Captain sank heavily back down in his chair, spinning away to look out at the city beneath them. 'Oh, and Mr Fibuli…' his voice murmured as softly as an avalanche. 'You have done well. But I would advise you against being late again. After all, you wouldn't like to become known as the late Mr Fibuli now, would you?'

Mr Fibuli was just about to agree with a dutiful laugh when That Thing on the Captain's shoulder spun round and glared at him. A single blast radiated from its eyes, singeing Fibuli's fingers and completely incinerating the Ancillary Personnel Displacement folder. Well, of course it would.

A point had clearly been made.

'My qualities, as you know, are many,' the Captain muttered casually, 'but tolerating incompetents is not one of them.'

Mr Fibuli thought that a little unfair. But then again, nearly everything in his life was unfair. He hurried away to make all the necessary preparations, aware that handfuls of cash were exchanging hands at the realisation that the First Mate had survived again. The Nurse, carefully filling the Captain's hot-water bottle, gave Mr Fibuli a tiny, reassuring well-done grin.

The one fact that no one on the entire bridge knew was that the Captain kept Mr Fibuli alive mostly because he just liked the sound of his name. It made him smile.

Speaking into a microphone, the Captain bellowed across the bridge. 'This is your Captain speaking. I want the following announcement made in all Cities. There is to be a New Golden Age of Prosperity. I repeat, a New Golden Age of Prosperity.'

Somewhere a tinny fanfare sounded, and Mr Fibuli looked up from the master computer as reports filtered in from the various decks. 'I can confirm. We have All Systems Go on a New Golden Age of Prosperity.'

The Captain chuckled and reached out with the crude stump of his artificial left arm. A large hook flicked out of the end of it and he reached up to the Thing that crouched on his shoulder. It was the Captain's confidante, soulmate and one true joy in life. The Captain's claw ruffled the parrot's metal feathers, each one twanging like piano wire.

'Who's a pretty Polyphase Avatron, then?' cooed the Captain.

'Pretty Polyphase Avatron, Pretty Polyphase Avatron,' croaked the parrot happily.

Even a charitable observer would say there hadn't been many jokes in Pralix's life. By and large, people who've watched their father killed don't tend to be jolly.

The last thing that Pralix's father had said to him had actually been a joke, of sorts. It just took Pralix a long time to see the funny side of it.

Pralix's father lay dying in the streets, blood seeping into a mound of discarded emeralds. He looked up at his son, and at the Captain's Guards who were closing in to shoot him again. And then he took Pralix's hand and whispered to him, 'Try not to let things prey on your mind.'

After that, Pralix had become a quiet child. He'd then become a quiet youth, a quiet teenager and was now a quiet young man. He lived in his grandfather's unremarkably opulent house. Zanak's problem was that it was choked with wealth. As everyone had all the money they could possibly want, no one could afford to buy anything.

The First Golden Age of Prosperity had been the last time anything had been worth something. When it had first started to rain gold from the skies, it had mostly fallen on the slopes of the mountains and out in the fields. By sheer fluke, not too many people died, but, for some reason, the crops died overnight. Consequently the cities had suddenly been overrun by farmers, staggering under their new-found riches. With nothing else to do, they promptly bought everything in sight.

The people who had lived in the city could suddenly no longer afford to, but didn't really fancy moving. Gradually, things evened out, but by this point the countryside was barren, the cities were overcrowded, and no one could buy any house larger than a shoebox. Everyone was so rich they didn't feel like working, so spent all their time cladding their tiny houses with precious metals, patching their clothes with rubies, and wondering what to eat on their platinum plates.

The answer was, soon enough, nothing. The farmers were rich and idle, the fields were stubbornly empty of all but the least exciting mineral deposits. The entire population of Zanak learned overnight that one cannot eat rubies, and began to starve.

It took a long time, and a fair few brutally quelled uprisings before things reached a truculent status quo. The Captain's Guards would march troublemakers off to do the odd bit of manual labour, and in return, there would be the occasional declarations of a New Golden Age of Prosperity. These would be greeted with mild excitement at best. The people of Zanak had grown bored of wealth. No one really needed any more of it.

There were a few exceptions to this calm boredom. Pralix was about to become one of them.

He stood in the market square, watching people kick aside some unwanted gemstones.

One of the Captain's Guards marched into the square. People paid him less attention than the gemstones. On the one hand, they did sometimes shoot people. On the other hand, the more attention you drew to yourself, the likelier they were to shoot you. The people of Zanak had come to terms with their tyranny by largely ignoring it.

The Captain's Guard mounted a platform and held up a loudspeaker.

'People of this City!' he proclaimed dutifully. 'I have here a piece of paper. It is signed by the Captain!'

The crowd drew to a grudging standstill.

'I am to announce to you,' shouted the Guard grandly, 'the Dawning of a New Golden Age of Prosperity!'

'Oh,' shrugged the crowd. Well, this wasn't *bad* news, they supposed. It wasn't a compulsory work order.

The Guard produced his gun and fired it into the air. 'A New Golden Age of Prosperity!' he repeated.

This time the cheers were a little louder.

Only Pralix did not join in. He remained quiet. But that wasn't unusual. He was a quiet young man.

Deep underground Pralix was being watched.

Hundreds of pairs of eyes crowded into the Mourning Chamber. The chamber had not been there yesterday. On the floor someone had drawn with chalk two circles, one inside the other. And the dust of the inner circle started to glow, the motes drifting up into the air.

A picture formed in the glowing dust, glinting in the low light. The picture hung there for an instant, and then was replaced in a rapid, shifting blur. The dust picture seemed to flit across the surface of Zanak, over the barren fields, the empty plains, from city to city, down to the mines, and even, fleetingly, up to the Bridge. It was as though the dust was hopping between the eyes of everyone on the planet.

The dust picture steadied slightly, showing the market square of the capital city of Zxoxaxax, moving more slowly around it, surveying the crowd from amongst it, caught in the gaze of a stone sweeper, and finally seeing things from the Guard's point of view.

The Guard rubbed his eyes, which stung slightly. His speech was printed out for him, but he knew it off by heart. He looked down at the crowd, just in case there was a troublemaker. They were always fun. He liked a public shooting.

'Under the benevolent leadership of our Captain, a period of unparalleled wealth and affluence will begin!' he intoned nasally. 'The mines will once again be full of riches! Rarer jewels! Finer clothes! Gruel! Nothing will be denied the loyal, industrious servants of the Captain! Wealth beyond the dreams of avarice will be yours! A few seconds from now the omens will appear in the skies to signify that the new Age has indeed begun.'

With a bored coo, the people of Zanak glanced up into the sky. Some even had their gold umbrellas ready as more stones began to patter down around them. A common cause of death on Zanak was being hit on the head by an uncut diamond. It was not a particularly dignified way to go, knowing that someone would be rifling through the remains of your brain to see if the stone that had done for you would polish up and be worth keeping before deciding that, on the whole, it probably was not.

The crowd stood, waiting for the omens, that dazzling moment when the mountain began to shimmer, lights spreading up from it until the heavens danced. Despite their jaded nature, the crowd never grew tired of the sight.

All except for one quiet young man, who let out a sudden moan.

Down in the heart of the planet, the shifting circle of dust focused in on Pralix, standing at the back of the crowd. He was caught in the glances of several worried people, as he mouthed the word 'No' over and over again. The dust jumped to show the Guard squinting curiously down at him.

Finally the dust leapt to show the world as Pralix saw it.

His whole world was spinning.

His world was not flat. His world was a giant globe hurtling through a vast dark void.

Hurtling so quickly that he was desperate to get off it.

Pralix ran hurriedly from the square, clutching his head, running to get away from the spinning world. But there was nowhere to go.

A voice rang out through the Mourning Chamber, silencing the growing whimpering.

'The day grows dark and the omens sing. The time of evil is once more come. We must prepare. We have found another one...'

Chapter Four
Have You Ever Seen an Arcturan Mega-Chicken?

She could hear the Doctor coming. Romanadvoratrelundar flinched slightly at the sound of those muddy boots, the out-of-tune whistling, and the faithful whirr of his robot dog. She was trying ever so much not to find the Doctor intimidating, but it was really very hard.

On her (already much-missed) home planet of Gallifrey, people respected each other's intelligence. Her tutor had never tired of pointing out how annoying he found her, but couldn't help but concede that she was often right. Romanadvoratrelundar had spent her entire life being right. Only, in the last couple of days, it had stopped mattering. Her life had, for the very first time, stopped making sense.

Ever since she'd met the Doctor she'd felt out-of-sorts. It wasn't that she wasn't saying the right thing (she was always right); it was just that, whatever she did, no matter how hard she tried, being right seemed to go over rather badly with the Doctor. She had spent the last century in a world of rigid order that really knew how to reward brains. Yet the Doctor looked at her as if she'd just been generated yesterday. It was all so solidly unfair.

The Lady Romanadvoratrelundar chewed daintily on her lower lip and made a decision. Today she and the Doctor were going to get on well. She had drawn the line at working out how to use the TARDIS kettle, but she'd spruced the place up, tidied a few things away, and made a rather jolly discovery. She looked at the book and smiled. He would, she calculated, be ever so, ever so pleased.

The Doctor swept into the central control room of the TARDIS. It was white. Suspiciously whiter than white. Had Romanadvoratrelundar been cleaning? The only thing whiter than the control chamber was Romanadvoratrelundar's dazzling gown. Wherever the Time Lady went, the gown flowed behind her with a slithering grace that tended to scare furniture. Right now, she was perched gracefully on top of a stepladder, reading from a large, heavy book. She was studying it with fierce concentration and occasionally pursing her lips.

For a moment the Doctor didn't recognise the book. Then he did, and he groaned. It was the TARDIS's technical manual. If a copy of it had fallen into the clutches of the Kraals, the Zygons, or even the Daleks it would have been curtains for creation, but, as it was, Romanadvoratrelundar was reading it with the casual pleasure of an I-Spy book. Wherever had she got the wretched thing from?

'Romy!' he called out.

The Time Lady glanced up at him, winced, and shook her head.

This was another problem. Romanadvoratrelundar had a fiercely impractical name. You couldn't shout it at moments of danger, and you certainly couldn't get them to write it on a cup at Starbucks. The Doctor had gamely suggested a few shorter alternatives, and Romanadvoratrelundar had countered by insisting it was either the full scrabble bag or nothing.

'Romana,' the Doctor ventured again.

Romana considered, then nodded. 'Yes?'

'What, er, what do you think you're doing?' Trying to reassert himself, he pointed to the book.

'Oh, this?' Romana used the airy tone of someone who'd reached Ladybird Easy Reader 7C and wondered what all the fuss had been about 4B. 'I've found your ship's manual, and am just familiarising myself with the technical details of this time capsule.'

'Capsule?' The Doctor winced. 'If you mean the TARDIS, why don't you say so?' Wherever had she got that book from?

Romana surveyed the control room of the Doctor's time machine dubiously. 'Well, I suppose it is a TARDIS, more or less,' she conceded. 'But the Type Forty Capsule wasn't on the main syllabus.' She turned a page of the manual very carefully.

'Oh, that's disgraceful.' The Doctor patted a chunk of the control console proudly. 'I can't think what the Academy is coming to these days. Leaving out the Type 40. Why the old girl's a classic.'

'The study of veteran and vintage vehicles was an optional extra,' Romana conceded. She frowned. For some reason it was all going wrong again. Here she was trying to show an interest in his antique and he just seemed cross with her. Whatever had she done? She pressed on. 'It was hardly an essential subject. I preferred—'

'Something really useful, like the lifecycle of the Gallifreyan flutterwing, I suppose?' the Doctor harrumphed.

Ah, he really was in one of his moods. Romana smiled gently at him. 'Now we're being frivolous, aren't we?' she chided.

The Doctor was, he realised to his horror, being nannied.

'Instead,' she continued, 'why don't you tell me what the next segment of the Key to Time is?'

'Tell you? I thought you might like to work it out for yourself when we arrive.' The Doctor yawned elaborately. 'I know how frustrating it must be for you going round with someone of my ability. You never have to think for yourself. Terrible waste of a ... what was it... Double First?'

'Triple First,' corrected Romana automatically, a trifle less composed.

'Ah-ha!' From out of nowhere, the Doctor flashed her a winning smile. He was teasing her. 'You know what, I think you're going to turn out very well.'

'Thank you Doctor,' Romana beamed.

'Ye-ess,' he continued, lethally. 'When you have a few hundred years' experience under your belt.'

'When I'm like you, you mean?' Romana met his gaze and didn't blink. She kicked up her legs and slid down the stepladder. 'When I'm middle aged.'

The Doctor went very quiet. Was Romana all right? She seemed to be teasing him back. Worse, she was winning.

He heard a tiny whirr. K-9 appeared to have turned around, just a little, to stare pointedly at one of the walls.

The Doctor suddenly felt alone in a big, cruel universe, where his companions were younger, smarter and altogether better turned out than him. His last companion had worn a loincloth, the one before had sometimes dressed like a *Play School* presenter. But Romana? Clearly, he was going to have to up his game. Did he even have an iron, he wondered? Or could he get K-9 to trundle back and forth over his shirts?

'Romana,' he said eventually, 'Why don't you go and talk to the dog for a bit? I'm trying to programme the TARDIS. Big work for grown-ups.'

The Doctor busied himself around the TARDIS console. The Guardian had given him a magic wand for finding the six segments of the Key to Time. He and Romana had discussed what to call it. He'd said the Tracer, and of course, she'd plumped for the Locatormutor Core. The Tracer would feed him a series of coordinates, allowing the ship to zero in on the next segment. It was a disappointingly efficient process.

'Hmm,' he said, plugging the Tracer into the console and waited until it booted up. In practice this meant going from not glowing at all to sparkling. Exactly like a magic wand. The Doctor found the Tracer deeply embarrassing and handed it over to Romana at every available opportunity. Let her look like a fairy-tale princess.

The Tracer glowed, sparkled, shimmered, and then began to emit coordinates.

'Oh,' the Doctor tutted. 'How very dull and boring.'

'What?' Romana looked up from fussing K-9.

'Our next destination.' The Doctor affected his Seasoned Traveller's tone. 'It's a planet called Calufrax. On second thoughts, why don't you come and watch me set the coordinates on this vintage veteran of mine? You might just learn something.'

'All right.' Romana nodded a touch too seriously and glided to loom over the Doctor's shoulder. As she was wearing heels, this was rather easy and the Doctor refused to let it annoy him.

'Now,' he said, 'The first sequence of numbers…'

'Doctor,' Romana breathed into his ear. 'I am sorry. I didn't really mean it when I said you were middle aged. You're not so terribly ancient.'

'That's all right,' the Doctor replied evenly. 'I didn't really mean it when I said you were an ignorant meddlesome cloth-eared student.'

'But you didn't say that,' Romana retorted brightly. 'Perhaps you're becoming forgetful.'

'Didn't I say that?' The Doctor beamed at her. 'Oh, well tact is something that comes naturally with experience.'

'Oh, touché.' Romana bowed elaborately to him.

Like a cloud passing from the sun, the two grinned at each other.

'What is that first sequence of numbers?' Romana prompted, squinting at the readout on the Tracer.

'They're the coordinates of the horizontal galactic grid.'

'Fancy.' Romana sighed. Those hadn't been used since the days of the printed Galactic Ordnance Survey.

'0963-625-27,' the Doctor announced as though it answered everything. He pressed some buttons with a small flourish. Romana crossed to the technical manual, and ran her finger down a page.

'What about setting the synchronic feedback-checking circuit?'

'What about it?' The Doctor looked worried as she checked the manual. Suddenly his shirt collar felt a little tight.

'You never seem to programme it.'

'Waste of time. Never bother with all that.' He rubbed the back of his neck. His shirt really was pinching terribly.

'But on page 673 it says that it's essential.'

'Well it would.' The Doctor glared at the TARDIS Manual with suspicion and annoyance. Ever since he had first borrowed his time capsule, he'd operated it pretty much by instinct. More often than not, he'd got away with it. Well, there had been that unfortunate time when he'd left the doors open and shrunk everyone to the size of mice.

Immediately after he'd sorted that one out, the TARDIS technical manual had made its first appearance. It had been waiting for him, placed on a beautifully carved lectern. He'd been tempted, of course he'd been tempted, but the Doctor had left home to get away from being told what to do. So he'd turned his back on the book, and pottered off to get the food machine to whip up duck-flavoured ice cream.

The technical manual had sidled back from time to time. When fleeing a Dalek Death Squad dispatched to Lord's Cricket Ground, or when he'd tried to stop the Master escaping in a filing cabinet. Shortly after both these incidents, the technical manual had reappeared. It always seemed to be frowning at him. If a book could cough, it would have cleared its throat meaningfully.

But now, the book was back again, and it was pointedly ignoring him. It clearly regarded Romana as the sensible adult. He looked up at the ceiling of his time machine and shook his head at it sadly. Well, fine. Let Romana learn all about the secrets of the Moog Drone Clamp. He had a universe to explore.

The Doctor decided to concede a point. 'Romana, have you any idea how long I've been operating the TARDIS?'

'Yes. Lots and lots of hundreds of years.' Romana was leafing through the manual.

'Five hundred and twenty-three years. Time really does fly.'

'That's a common delusion among the middle aged.' Romana looked up from her book and smiled at him gently. 'It's known nowadays as the Mandrian Syndrome. According to Professor Halcron—'

'Never heard of him.'

'He happens to be the leading authority in the universe on hyper-psychological atavisms.'

'Can he fly a TARDIS?'

'I hardly think that's relevant.'

'Well, I do and I can.' The Doctor chewed his thumbnail. 'And just between ourselves I'm really rather good at it.'

Romana raised her eyes reluctantly from the book, prepared to give him the benefit of the doubt. She was in time to catch the Doctor flicking a switch that she was fairly sure shouldn't be flicked. 'Only –' Romana looked back at the book, worried – 'it says in here that—'

'Oh, don't worry about the book!' The Doctor waved a hand dismissively. 'If you followed everything it said in that book you'd end up finding it was quicker to walk. It's all just handbook twaddle for beginners. I'll let you into a little secret.' He seemed to be addressing both her and the ship itself. 'The man who wrote it was being paid by the page.' The Doctor tapped the book's fat spine. 'I know that for a fact. I once met him, told me he'd never been near a TARDIS in his life. Nice chap, used to breed chickens.' He let that nugget sink in. Romana wondered if he was fibbing outrageously. 'Now, what were the second group of figures? They give us the vertical galactic coordinates.'

'But what about the multi-loop stabiliser?' Chickens or no chickens, that had seemed very important. It had had a whole chapter devoted to it.

'Trust me. You. Don't. Need. It.' The Doctor was plugging away.

'But…' The more Romana read, the more worried she became. 'It says here that it's impossible to effect a smooth materialisation without activating the multi-loop stabiliser.'

'Give that here.' The Doctor plucked the book from her hands, glanced at it, then tossed it over his shoulder with a satisfying thud. 'Utter tripe. It's perfectly possible. I've done it a thousand times. Silly man was obviously thinking about egg laying.'

'With a multi-loop stabiliser?'

'Have you ever seen an Arcturan Mega-Chicken?' The Doctor waited for a response. Of course she had not. 'Now then, I'll show you a smooth materialisation. Calufrax, here we come!'

Impressively, the Doctor threw a switch.

The TARDIS immediately fell wildly out of control, emitting a terrible grinding noise as the ship plummeted alarmingly down the Time Vortex.

Curiously, the Captain's New Golden Age of Prosperity had developed a calamitous hitch.

Up on the bridge, pandemonium raged. Hardly had he declared an age of unparalleled luxury, hardly had he got ready to enjoy the lights spilling out of the mountain, than the entire Citadel shook. For a moment he wondered if something had gone wrong with their grand plan, if the mountain they were on had exploded, or if they were under attack. But something was definitely wrong.

So wrong that Mr Fibuli had dropped all of his paperwork and was scurrying from console to console frantically trying to find out what was happening. No one was giving him an answer.

The Captain lurched to his feet, the Polyphase Avatron whirling around his head.

'Imbeciles!' he roared at the terrified crew. The one person who was not panicked was his Nurse. She kept her balance without effort, keeping a cool eye on him. The wretched harridan was no doubt planning to check his blood pressure. At a time like this. There really was no escaping the woman's tyranny.

The Captain staggered forward, the magnetic clamps of his feet finding a purchase on the deck as everyone around him slid helplessly.

'Fools! Thrice worse than incompetent idiots! What pernicious injury have you inflicted on my precious systems?'

Mr Fibuli literally flew past, and the Captain grabbed hold of him, casually preventing him from dashing his brains out on a control panel.

'Captain!' Mr Fibuli, even dangling in his master's grasp, somehow managed to shrug helplessly.

What the Captain said next was rather strange.

'Mr Fibuli – are you trying to scuttle this planet?'

'What's happening?' yelled Romana over the din. This brought the Doctor some small measure of comfort. Well, if she didn't know what was going on, then he couldn't feel too bad about not having a clue.

'Oh, nothing very much,' he said, clinging to the hat stand as nonchalantly as possible. He managed a sort-of-sauntering fall onto the controls, and flicked a few switches with the aplomb of a pianist who finds his baby grand wired to a ticking bomb. 'The old girl just won't materialise for some reason. I'll have to back her off.'

One does not back off a TARDIS. The vast, interdimensional and frankly incomprehensible vessels of the Time Lords of Gallifrey are like cats: bad at reversing. It shows a loss of face. Still, the Doctor did his best. He'd learned a few things in half a millennium of flying his TARDIS, and one of them was a little trick he'd learned while chasing the Master up the M1 in a Mini Metro. He jammed on the handbrake.

With a loud whinny of protest, the TARDIS came to a very abrupt stop, one edge of it poking into the universe next door. The elaborate wording on the craft's outer door rearranged itself from the baffling but welcoming 'Officers And Cars Respond To Urgent Calls' to the rather curter 'Not Today, Thank You'.

The Doctor was lying flat on the floor. Carefully, he opened his eyes. Romana was standing neatly on one leg with her arms tucked under themselves. With a terribly straight face and not quite looking directly at him, she was making chicken noises.

Romana flapped her arms and, very gently, clucked.

'Bgerk,' she said.

The Doctor had never been clucked at before.

'I,' began the Doctor with all the dignity he could manage from the floor, 'am quite capable of admitting when I'm wrong.'

'Oh?' Romana looked at him with the widest, most innocent of eyes.

'It just so happens that on this one occasion I am not wrong.' He smiled winningly up at her. 'There was something external actively jamming our materialisation field. That's all.'

Romana's eyes became even wider, even more innocent. 'Ah, so that's what it was, was it?' She nodded gravely.

'Yes,' the Doctor scrambled awkwardly up. 'It certainly had nothing to do with that wretched multi-loop stabilising thing you keep going on about. Trust me.'

'Of course not,' Romana cooed sympathetically. She laid a gentle hand on his arm, stroking his elbow. The Doctor frowned.

His companions did not normally do this. Leela of the Sevateem was many things, but not reassuring. Sarah Jane Smith would have lifted him out of his mood by sticking her tongue out at him, and the Brigadier would perhaps have checked his watch, muttered something about the sun being over the yardarm, and suggested they adjourn to the pub. No one had patted him before. It was curiously pleasant.

'Doctor?' Romana purred casually.

'Yes?'

'May I have a go?'

'At landing?' So that's what all this was about. Hah! 'You want to land by the book?'

'Oh yes,' Romana vowed solemnly. 'Just so I can learn the error of my ways.'

'Be my guest.' The Doctor gestured to the console. What was the harm? In the three hours it'd take her, he could do a crossword or two in the Limbo room. 'Flying that way won't make any difference, you know. The old girl will probably just think I've gone mad and blow herself up, won't you, you dear old thing?' He rubbed a favourite bit of the console fondly. 'But all right. Do it your way and see for yourself. There's definitely a jamming field in operation and we're going nowhere fast.'

'I'm sure you're right,' Romana agreed.

K-9 obligingly trundled over with the manual somehow neatly propped open on his back. Romana glanced at it and chewed her lip. One thing she had not told the Doctor was that she had never actually landed a TARDIS before. Oh, she'd had a go on plenty of simulators in the Academy, but never tried her hand at the real thing. Also, the newer models were automatic. Still, in for a penny. 'Right then,' she announced coolly, flicking a switch. 'Synchronic feedback…' She carefully adjusted a lever. 'Multi-loop stabiliser…'

The Doctor opened a panel on the console, pulled out a belt, and harnessed himself to the console.

'Don't worry!' he smiled as he strapped himself in. 'One can never be too careful, that's my motto. You see how fiddly it all is, don't you? Sheer waste of time. And it won't make a jot of difference, I promise you.'

'Hush,' said Romana, and activated the materialisation switch.

For a very long moment nothing happened, and then the TARDIS landed with a very gentle sigh. The sigh somehow summed up the buttering of a perfectly toasted crumpet.

'Oh,' said the Doctor after slightly too long a pause. 'Very good.'

'Really?' asked Romana eagerly.

'Very, very good.' The Doctor was impressed. 'Wouldn't you agree K-9?'

The robot dog considered. 'Very, very, very good.'

Hiding his disappointment, the Doctor unclipped the harness, and made an elaborate show of folding it away. Then he cuffed the temporal geometer fondly. 'See, old girl, it wasn't that bad, was it? You are a silly old thing, making all that ridiculous fuss.' He wagged a stern finger. 'I've a good mind to put you in for your fifty billion year service.'

Romana grinned. The Doctor was many alarming things, but he was rather charming.

The Doctor leaned in to the console, and lowered his voice, just a little. 'Of course, old girl, it was pretty easy really, now that that beastly jamming field has obviously been turned off. Of course, it would be churlish to say so out loud, wouldn't it? Yes, rather spoil her fun, not good.'

He leaned back, spun round, and looked at Romana as though surprised to find her listening. He jerked a thumb over his shoulder at the console. 'Just, ah, a little pep talk, you understand. She needs a little reassurance from time to time.'

'Don't we all,' Romana said slowly and evenly. 'I am going to take a look at Calufrax.'

She turned on the TARDIS view screen and looked out at the world she'd landed them on. All in all, she felt rather proud.

The Doctor didn't give the planet a glance. He was trying to get a response out of K-9.

'Come on autopooch,' he coaxed.

'Master?' The robot dog, insofar as he thought about these matters, decided to tread carefully. He was reluctant to take sides. The Doctor-Master was many things, most of them erratic. The Mistress-Romanadvoratrelundar had shown herself to be careful, thoughtful and thoroughly logical.

'K-9, you don't think I'm getting middle aged do you? I'm still quite a sprightly 750, don't you think?'

K-9 was about to respond in a careful, thoughtful and thoroughly logical manner when something very strange happened to him.

Mr Fibuli knew they weren't going to die. Not now. The shaking had subsided. The alarms had quietened. The awful shuddering view out of the window had settled down. There was still a persistently awful noise from the engines grinding away far below him, but overall, things were getting back to normal. People were handing him damage reports, spare part requisitions and the odd sick note. Where there was paperwork, there was life. He looked at it all, helplessly, and then up at the Captain who stood glaring out of the vast window at the shimmering sky beyond.

'I do like a new view,' the Captain muttered softly, seemingly to himself. He gave a contented little sigh. Suddenly aware of Fibuli's presence, he swung round. 'Fools!' he began, his voice still soft. 'Thrice worse than incompetent idiots!' His voice raised a little. Clearly he was warming up. 'May the star sickness assail you! The whole mountain shook like a leaf in the hand of the Sky Demons! By my electronic arm, you'll answer me for this! Explain, Mr Fibuli, explain!'

Mr Fibuli remained rooted to the spot. Partly through fear and partly through a simple inability to care any more.

The Captain raised his arm, and the giant metal hook flew out, grabbed Fibuli by the scruff of the neck and reeled him up the podium. Mr Fibuli found himself dangling next to the Captain. He tried to say something but managed only a faint croak.

'Can't face me, eh, Fibuli?' the Captain whispered. 'Know how you feel, know how you feel.' And then the hook dropped Fibuli's feet gently to the ground.

For a moment the two of them stood there, gazing out at the new vista washing into view beyond the dome.

'Two suns, Fibuli,' the Captain continued in his kindly murmur. 'I do like an extra sun, don't you?'

'A, uh, notable novelty,' Fibuli concurred, sensing the tightness in his chest relax.

'This one seems to taint half the sky purple,' the Captain continued. 'Very catching. I've a good mind to paint it.' He shook his useless metal claw and, with as much of a mouth as he had left, grinned. 'Ready to go on?' he whispered.

'Yes,' said Fibuli.

'All right then.' Wearily, the Captain drew in his breath. 'Well?' he roared.

'Captain, sir,' Fibuli began, 'I've run a quick inspection and the actual damage isn't as bad as we'd feared—'

'Not as bad as we feared? I tell you Mr Fibuli, you would do well to fear considerable damage for by all the flaming moons of hell I am of a mind to administer it!' The Captain strode in front of the window, the gentle purple of the new sky lending an infernal pallor to his face.

The Captain's Nurse had slid back into the room. Fibuli noticed she had made herself scarce when there were real injuries to attend to. Her only concern seemed to be the Captain's health. Here she was, small, mousy, a tiny, professional smile, her prettiness carefully hidden under her mint-green uniform. She hastened silently to the Captain's side, her eyes glancing at an upside-down watch pinned to her jacket.

'The problem is very slight indeed,' Fibuli reassured them both. 'Just a few minor circuits shorted, there's nothing we can't quickly—'

'Do not trifle with me,' the Captain grated. 'I need to know what happened!'

Fibuli glanced helplessly at his reports. Nothing. 'Well, some freak local disturbance. Probably electromagnetic. It passed very quickly.'

The Captain swept Fibuli's papers to one side, lurching over to a wall. 'The idle prattlings of a fool! A caveman with his first rock could tell you that was no mere electromagnetic disturbance. I will know the truth!'

He drew his arm back and punched the metal wall. Three prongs emerged from the tip of his stump. The Captain was interfacing directly with the ship's systems, symbols and diagrams glowing across his forearm. He flapped the limp remains of his organic hand at them. 'See! Warp oscilloscope readings. There – there's your local electromagnetic disturbance. What do you make of those readings?' The Captain's one eye glared at Fibuli with a fierce intelligence, willing him to work it out.

Fibuli slid his glasses off his nose and peered at the readouts on the Captain's arm. 'But that… that's extraordinary!'

'Isn't it?' muttered the Captain gently, before swinging round to bellow at the Nurse. 'Do you hear me?' he raged. 'For ten seconds the entire fabric of the space-time continuum was ripped apart!' He punched his fist into a different socket. 'See? Etheric saturation readings, critical overload, and every system jammed solid,' he said in a dazed gabble. 'And here,' he plunged into a third socket. 'Gravity dilation readings. What do you make of that? Can you explain that?' The Captain raised a heavily scarred eyebrow.

'I can't explain it,' gabbled Mr Fibuli. 'Not off the top of my head.' He clutched at his reports, squeezing the little cardboard folders together tightly.

'No…' mused the Captain. 'And why not? Because those figures show that for those ten seconds the whole infrastructure of quantum physics was in retreat. It was running scared! But from what, eh? I tell you, in all my years navigating the uncharted currents of the ether I have never encountered the like!'

The Nurse came over, a look of professional concern on her face. She gently eased the Captain's robotic arm from the socket and checked a couple of settings on it.

Brusquely, the Captain brushed her away, the rage back in his voice. 'Find out what happened Mr Fibuli, and find out fast, or by all the fires of night I'll have that skull off you!'

Meanwhile, aboard his affront to the laws of physics, the Doctor was dealing with his dog.

He was used to K-9 reacting to most things with a rather librarian prissy calm. And yet, right now, the dog was growling and spinning uncertainly around.

'His hackles are up!' he called to Romana.

'What are hackles?' she answered.

'Well…' He gestured to the dog, only to find K-9 had subsided into immobility. Clearly he'd be getting no help from there.

'Doctor,' Romana said gently. He did get distracted ever so easily. She'd landed them on a planet and he didn't even want to look at it. 'Do come and have a look at Calufrax.'

'Must we?' The Doctor continued to prod his robot dog gingerly. 'Calufrax is a horrible place. Cold and wet and icy and – Oh.'

He had glanced up at the scanner. Which showed a rolling desert landscape. The TARDIS seemed to have landed on the slopes of a mountain, at the very edge of a shining city basking in the suns.

'What's the matter?' Romana felt suddenly defensive about the view. 'I got you to Calufrax, didn't I?'

'Calufrax? Don't make me laugh. You students, thinking you know it all. That isn't anything like Calufrax. You've probably missed it by a couple of million light years. Tell you what.' The Doctor winked at her generously. 'I'll give you two out of ten for effort.'

Romana was hurt. She hadn't realised that the Doctor was secretly pleased that the TARDIS manual was as useless as he'd suspected.

Seeing the crestfallen look on her face, the Doctor was ready to apologise for having, perhaps, been a trifle over-emphatic, when K-9 lurched back into life, once more snarling and trundling around in neurotic little circles.

'I wonder what's biting him?' the Doctor said, jumping out of the way.

Clearly they were all having a bad day.

Chapter Five
Mourning Sickness

Deep beneath the planet's surface, the Mourning Chamber was flooded with emotion. The cavern echoed to wails of sadness, the figures inside it crawling and writhing piteously in the dirt. Inside the two chalk circles, the dust still danced and glowed, but the picture it showed was just of darkness. Exquisitely rendered, somehow awful darkness.

Occasionally one of the mewling creatures on the floor would glance up at it and recoil, backing away. But there was nowhere to go. For the duration of their misery, these people had sealed themselves in with their terrible sadness.

An old lady stood. Her robes had once been the finest of hues, encrusted with amethysts. Now they were plain rags, soaked in grime. She was the oldest of them, and she had suffered the most. She stepped forward, unflinching as she reached out and stroked the glowing black circle.

'Life force dying,' she sighed.

*

Mula had brought Pralix home. He was a disgrace, but it's what sisters do.

She'd been carrying home the shopping when she'd found him curled up, squirming in a pile of glittering dirt in the market. He'd twisted away from her, his foot knocking over the week's food. She'd picked it all up first and then grabbed hold of his wrist.

'Life force dying!' he'd shrieked.

'Not again,' Mula had said and dragged him home.

Because Pralix was older, he'd got all the attention. Even before their parents died, it was Pralix who people stared it. 'He's such a worryingly quiet child,' they'd say, while at the same time telling Mula not to make so much noise.

When their father had died, people had said to Pralix, 'You're the head of the family now,' which had immediately seemed an insane decision, and they'd all worried about it.

No one had ever asked Mula how she felt about things. She was the younger sister. She was the one who would cope. Whenever any of her relatives addressed her, they normally started by saying 'Mula, you must…' That was all she ever heard. Mula was there to fetch and carry, and manage the household while everyone got on with worrying about Pralix.

There simply wasn't the space for her to get any attention. It had become remarkably worse once their grandfather, Balaton, had taken them in.

Balaton looked like Pralix left out in the sun for fifty years, an anxious grape shrivelled to a really worried raisin. Balaton spent so much time worrying that Mula found she had even more housekeeping to do. Balaton was even less practical than Pralix. On a good day Pralix would lie moping on a couch while Balaton would pace around worried about whether or not to get the couch reupholstered.

In truth, the couches were remarkably uncomfortable. A few Golden Ages of Prosperity ago, the streets had been littered with lumps of a soft, pliable metal. As no one bothered weaving cloth anymore, a craze had sprung up for cladding your soft furnishings with this metal, riveting the sheets in place with diamond pins. It had swept through the city before anyone dared admit that the results were both ugly and painful.

Mula's father had always insisted that, threadbare or not, a sofa should be comfortable. When she'd moved in with Balaton she'd been dismayed to realise that his whole house mercilessly obeyed the fashions of Prosperity. The sofa was metal, the cutlery gold, the plates diamond, the walls papered with rubies. Every surface shone, every corner was hard. It was all so cold and unwelcoming. Feeling hideously alone, she had immediately run to her bedroom, thrown open the bronze-clad door, and dived under a bedspread with only a handful of emeralds sewn into it.

She had waited for someone to come and comfort her. Perhaps Balaton, certainly Pralix. But neither of them had come. Eventually she'd emerged, found a shopping list pinned with opal to the table, and stomped off to the marketplace to scare the few remaining traders into providing something like dinner.

Ever since, Mula had simply got on with things. When Pralix had grown quieter, everyone had expressed even more concern for him, while she'd chewed her cheeks and thought, 'When, when have you heard me say anything?'

That was the problem, Mula thought. I could, actually could, just set myself on fire and everyone would only worry about the impact it would have on poor Pralix.

She'd once tried suggesting he go for a walk among the sand gardens, or up into the mountains but he'd explained he just couldn't face it. She would have loved to see him try. Instead, Pralix just lay on his silly metal couch and occasionally slumped dejectedly through the streets.

She'd once asked what he was doing.

'Thinking about mortality,' he'd said.

Well, she'd thought, that just about figures.

Recently, Mula had decided: 'You know what, I just cannot stand any more or this. Literally, one more thing. Pralix's sulking and Grandfather's worrying. Enough. I'm full.' At around about this time she had met someone. Completely coincidentally, at exactly this moment, Pralix's behaviour had got much worse.

His descent had started during a Golden Age of Prosperity. She'd just introduced Pralix to Kimus in the Market Square. Pralix had let out a loud groan. 'Great,' Mula had thought, vowing to make sure that Pralix got the woody bits of root in tonight's stew. It wouldn't make any difference, as he never seemed to notice what he was eating, let alone thank her for cooking. But it would matter to her.

That night it had rained, really rained, a shining silver mist that turned out to be Mercury. The whole sight had been breathtaking (if a little dangerous) as the droplets sparkled in the suns (they'd had three then) before gathering into quivering metal bubbles that golloped satisfyingly down the drains. The sunset had been magnificent, but Pralix had gone to bed and cried loudly. It had, coincidentally, been the first time that Kimus had come over for supper, and their small talk had been punctuated by whimpers coming from the door to Pralix's room.

He had only got louder with every subsequent Golden Age, as though he took them personally. The more prosperous everyone got, the more miserable Pralix became. So far, they'd been lucky not to have had a visit from the Captain's Guards.

Today Pralix had clearly pushed things that little bit further. Crying in the streets was, if not precisely punishable by death, at the very least considered to be extremely suspicious behaviour.

Mula had dragged him home, telling a couple of slyly concerned neighbours that he'd been hit on the head by some Prosperity, and hustled him inside. Where he'd proceeded to shout the house down.

*

While Grandfather Balaton had fussed, Mula had hurried round the house, closing the windows, pulling the shutters to and running a muffler across the door. This was, she was determined, going to be a purely private grief.

She came back to find Balaton trying to comfort Pralix by shaking him. 'Calm yourself! You must calm yourself!' Grandfather said in that fussy little whine of his.

Pralix writhed on the couch, shaking, his eyes wide. Even Mula was worried. 'He is much worse than last time. Pralix – can you hear us? Tell us what's wrong, please?'

Balaton put out a tremulous hand to stay her. 'No, no, no! It is a mistake to ask too many questions.'

'That's your answer to everything isn't it?' Mula snapped.

The worried little man did not take offence. 'I have no need of answers,' he simpered. 'For I seek to ask no questions. I ask only for a quiet life.'

At this point, of course, Pralix let out an ear-piercing shriek.

'Oh Pralix.' The little man winced. 'You must calm yourself. Please…'

Pralix arched up on the couch, spitting the following phrase through his clenched teeth:

'Life force dying.'

Inside the TARDIS, K-9 was spinning. Romana added this to the list of curious things about the day. Nothing in the Doctor's life seemed to be entirely straightforward. Prior to her arrival, he'd appeared to have no system in place for exploring infinity. There wasn't even a list. They couldn't even get something as simple as landing on the correct planet quite right. The Doctor's robot dog was equally baffling – in theory K-9 was simply a computer on wheels, but in practice the Doctor appeared to have constructed a fussy, charming toy. Yes, it could answer direct questions with a straight answer, but it was also endowed with several baffling behavioural quirks.

Such as, at the moment, the spinning.

The spinning thankfully stopped, only to be replaced with a strange electronic growling.

'Defence mechanism?' she asked.

'I haven't a clue,' the Doctor admitted. 'It's very strange.' He reached out towards the dog, but snatched his hand back as the growling increased. He backed away, deciding to try and solve the problem of where they'd landed.

Romana was also trying to solve it. The coordinates read Calufrax, therefore what was on the scanner had to be Calufrax. Perhaps the Doctor had last visited on a rainy day?

'Are you quite sure that's not Calufrax?' she asked.

'Well…' The Doctor double-checked the coordinates and then triple-checked them. A lot was on the line here. His dignity, for a start. But no. Romana hadn't made a mistake. Of course she hadn't.

'Where are we then?' Romana continued to stare out at the desert. The one thing right about the planet was that it did have the right number of suns. That had to count for something.

The Doctor didn't seem to hear her. 'That can't be right. But it is right.' Muttering, he produced a felt-tip pen and then started writing on the console.

Romana went over to where K-9 was now staring fixedly at a wall. 'Do you think I made a mistake, K-9?'

'Uh?' said the dog, rather unusually. He slowly turned to focus on her, his little neck twitching as though he was trying to smell something.

'I said I think I got it right. Don't you, K-9?'

'Oh… Affirmative Mistress.' The robot dog did not seem to be giving her his full attention. He growled again to himself.

Romana had never tried to make friends with a robot before. She'd grown up surrounded by them, but had, up until now, treated them with the same affection she had for kettles and hair dryers. The thought had never even crossed her mind to try and anthropomorphise them. Then she'd met the Doctor and had realised that, firstly, she needed an ally and, secondly, with his lovely little shiny nose, waggy tin tail, and tartan collar, the robot dog was just painfully appealing.

Clearly the dog was in some distress, so she made a ghastly attempt to bond with him.

'Wassa matta little doggy?'

The Doctor, buried in a service panel, grunted.

Strangely, K-9 completely failed to bristle. 'I cannot tell Mistress,' he replied, with a thoughtful waggle of his ears. 'I am experiencing an instinctive feeling of fear and aggression.'

'But you're a robot,' albeit a terribly pattable one. 'Robots can't have instinctive feelings.'

'Affirmative Mistress,' K-9 agreed heartily. He lowered his voice, confidentially. 'I can only conclude it must be a programming error.'

'Programming error?' The Doctor slammed shut the service panel, stuffed a stray spring hurriedly into a pocket, and strolled over. He tapped the robot gently on the snout. 'I think it's very peculiar.'

'Have you found out where we are, Doctor?' asked Romana.

The Doctor held up a small thermal paper printout he'd managed to coax from the console. 'According to these space-time coordinates we have come to precisely the right point in space and precisely the right point in time…'

'There!' Romana beamed. 'What did I tell you? I got us to Calufrax.'

The Doctor shook his head and continued. 'But we have definitely come to the wrong planet.'

'What?' Romana couldn't help smiling.

'Right place. Right time. Wrong planet. This is not Calufrax.'

Earlier this morning Romana had been chased through the catacombs of Ribos by an intergalactic war criminal and a conman from Hackney Wick.[1] Yesterday she'd aced a tripos

---

[1] See *Doctor Who and the Ribos Operation*

on sidereal time. She made an effort to get used to her entirely unpredictable new life.

'Then where are we, Doctor?'

For a moment, the Doctor looked as though he was about to say something terribly clever. Then he opened his mouth and announced, 'I really haven't the faintest idea. The only thing I have managed to prove is that this isn't the same planet that was here when I tried to land.' He held up another printout. Even at a dot-matrix glance, Romana could see two completely different sets of readings for mass, gravity and orbit. 'So, shall we see what this planet's doing here?'

The Doctor opened the TARDIS doors and went to get some answers.

Up on the Bridge all seemed more normal than it had for some time.

The Captain sat back in his chair surveying the bustle with something approaching calm. His claw raked among the metallic feathers of the Polyphase Avatron.

Bank after bank of machinery came back online, filling the Bridge with the sounds of vast industry and a gentle, almost imperceptible vibration began to build up. The Engine Team were already at work on their latest report, and the Extraction Team were arguing over a few surprising readings they'd encountered. Mr Fibuli scurried between them, uncertain of what was going on.

The Nurse had unobtrusively slipped over to the Captain's shoulder and was carefully monitoring his vital signs. He flinched, trying not to show his annoyance as she fussed around him. The Nurse favoured him with her tight little smile as she made a minute adjustment to her little black box.

'We're doing well today, aren't we, Captain?' she said, giving him a small, approving smile.

The sound of the engines grew louder and the Polyphase Avatron began to sing a rasping sea shanty.

Pralix's moans had become screams. It had never been this bad before thought Mula, finding herself both very concerned and also utterly helpless. She turned to her grandfather, hoping that, for once, he would say something useful.

Balaton pressed his hands over his ears and wailed, 'We have to move him! People will hear! Oh dear, oh dear me, I don't suppose we can put him out in the streets? Can we?'

'No,' said Mula firmly.

'Well then, I'm fairly sure the kitchen window is open. Is it? I'm sure it is.' It was not. 'We must move him to his room. We shall have to carry him, I suppose. Oh dear, it's all so very inconvenient. The Captain has declared a Golden Age of Prosperity and I shall hate to miss the celebrations.'

Mula began to suspect that her grandfather was the mad one, rather than Pralix. Her brother was writhing, shaking and shrieking in agony. This was quite beyond anything she'd seen before. 'Grandfather, we cannot move him. Can't you see he's very ill? We should be getting help for him, but all you can think of is what will happen if the neighbours hear. Have you no feelings at all?'

Suddenly Balaton was standing right in front of her, his shrivelled little face drawn as tight as could be. 'You know very well what will happen if this is reported.'

Mula's defiance crumpled as Pralix gave out another piercing howl.

She didn't say anything, but grabbed hold of his twitching ankles and lifted him off the couch. Balaton sort of took hold of his wrists, and sort of let Mula drag Pralix to his room. She was bitterly aware that soon she was trying to ease her brother into bed while her grandfather stood to one side, fretting uselessly. He went to fetch more blankets, which seemed thoughtful, until she realised he was hanging them over the windows, to blot out the sound.

'I first did this, you know, many years ago,' confided Balaton cheerily, 'when your grandmother was in labour. Worked a treat.'

Mula gave up tucking Pralix in. He was thrashing about wildly, throwing the quilt off as soon as she put it on him. 'Why is this happening to him? Why?' she asked.

'Why?' Balaton muttered, perching on the end of the bed and resting a hand on Pralix's burning forehead. 'Why must you ask these things? I've lost a son, and I'm now going to lose a grandson. Possibly you as well. Why can't you youngsters just settle down and enjoy what life gives you freely and abundantly, rather than snarling it all up with questions? Questions all the time! Oh you'll know what you've lost when you've lost it right enough, you mark my words. And then where will you be?'

Mula sat limply down on the bed beside him. 'I don't know, Grandfather, where will I be?'

'Oh,' wailed the old man, miserably. 'Still so many questions. Why must you ask these things?'

Pralix gave out a piercing shriek of agony and there was a sudden, urgent knock at the door.

CHAPTER SIX
THAT NEW PLANET SMELL

There is a joy to taking one's first steps onto a new planet. How it looks, how it smells, the general planety feel of the planet, the pleasingly imminent threat level. These were all things the Doctor tried to calculate on the threshold of his ship by the beloved scientific formula of throwing open the door and having a gander.

Two suns, a rather steep hill, an appallingly designed citadel above them, a desert to the left and a very, very shiny city to the right.

The Doctor sniffed (whenever changing bodies he always made sure to get a remarkable nose) and considered the results.

This planet was wrong. It looked wrong, it smelt wrong, it felt wrong. Very wrong indeed. Splendid. He strode forward. He, K-9 and Romana were off for adventures new.

'Excuse me.' Romana's voice was pained. 'This won't do at all.'

'What won't?'

Her foot was hovering over the door, and moving not an inch. 'Well, my last hope had been a scanner malfunction. You know, old vehicle, these things can happen.'

'Well, it's not is it?' The Doctor tried not to take offence.

'No,' Romana agreed. 'I give up. This planet is not Calufrax. And the thing is, well –' a shrug and a disarming smile – 'I'm just not dressed for it. Back in a tick.'

The door slammed shut and the Doctor was left standing on the edge of a desert. He leaned against the TARDIS, which on the outside looked like a small, sad wooden shed, and certainly not the most remarkable craft the universe would ever know.

He addressed the reassuring blue door. 'Not dressed for it? What can she mean?'

The Doctor briefly considered his own outfit of boots, coat and flowing scarf. It worked for every occasion. He'd stopped giving the matter a moment's thought.

He bent down to K-9. 'I don't suppose you need an outfit change, do you?'

'Negative, Master.'

'Good dog.'

The Doctor straightened up and surveyed the desert stretching before him. He squinted up at the suns. It was a little chilly, which was rather wrong for a desert. An obvious explanation presented itself.

'I blame the Black Guardian,' the Doctor announced, and immediately liked the sound of it.

Yes. That made a lot of sense. The Guardian was a being of terrible power. He'd simply swapped Calufrax around with another planet like a pea under a cup. The Doctor was standing on a feat of cosmic sleight-of-hand. Despite himself, he was seriously impressed.

Mula's relief that the Captain's Guards weren't on the doorstep was replaced by annoyance that it was Kimus.

Kimus was the best thing in Mula's life. Where Pralix was quiet, Kimus was energetic. Where Balaton was worried, Kimus was cheerful. Most bafflingly of all, he put up with her family because he genuinely seemed to like her. Then again, perhaps Kimus was just that sort of person. Kimus was a man of action and the only person she'd ever met who just seemed to like her.

Mula really did think, however, that Pralix's latest screaming fit might be one step too far for him.

Kimus sailed into the house. He ignored Balaton's look of thunder, just as he always did, and seemed not to notice Mula's anguished expression. He was a very handsome young man, his features spoiled only by a little, wry twist to his mouth.

'Well, Mula, have you heard the news!' he called to her. 'Oh, hello there, old man!'

'Show some respect, Kimus, respect,' growled Balaton, forgetting his troubles at the chance to be cross.

'Beg your pardon, just overcome by the good news.' Kimus glowed with ironic enthusiasm. 'Haven't you heard? We're all going to be rich. Again. The Captain, our great and benevolent leader who we've never even seen, has announced… oh guess what? A New Golden Age of Prosperity. Again. Omens in the sky. The Works. Everyone's out celebrating in the streets trying to look as if it's the greatest thing that's ever happened and they haven't even cleared up all the jewels and stuff from the last one. For heaven's sake, the last Golden Age of Prosperity was only weeks ago. What's it all about, I ask you?'

'That's the modern world for you, isn't it?' For once, Kimus had struck a chord with Balaton, as it gave the old man a chance for a grumble. 'In my day, they only used to come every few years or so. And we really appreciated it, I can tell you. Not like you youngsters.' Warming to his subject, Balaton waggled a cautioning finger. 'Questioning things all the time. You're just spoilt, do you hear? Spoilt. Too many Golden Ages, that's your trouble.' Having delivered this definitive edict, the old man folded his arms.

Mula worried about the faint air of challenge in Balaton's stance. The sour mood Kimus was in. The two of them enjoyed nothing more than a good argument. She suspected it was the only reason Balaton let him come round. And, in its own strange way, it was entertaining enough. But she really wasn't in the mood for it today. Please, she thought, please don't take the bait.

Mercifully ignoring Balaton completely, Kimus flopped into a chair. Or at least, he tried his best to. All the furniture on Zanak was so hard that flopping took a bit of effort. 'So, anyway, that's my news. Where's Pralix?'

Mula coughed with embarrassment. It was, she thought, time to tell him the truth. 'Kimus,' she began gently. 'You know how we don't need to be told when the new Golden Ages are announced?'

'Oh.' Kimus's face fell, and he looked genuinely concerned. 'You mean…?'

'Yes,' sighed Mula. 'My brother's gone stark raving mad again.'

She threw open the door to her brother's room, filling the house with a shriek of 'Life force dying! Life force dying!'

Romana had joined them. She'd presumably changed her clothes, but the Doctor couldn't really tell. She seemed to have coaxed the TARDIS wardrobe to provide an endless supply of glamorous, dashing dresses. Which was odd. Whenever he went there it was all waistcoats, velvet and venerable moths half the size of Menoptra.

The Doctor explained his remarkable theory that the planets had been switched around by an ancient force.

'Um,' conceded Romana dubiously. 'Well, this certainly isn't an uninhabited, ice-coated planet.' She pulled the Tracer from the sleeves of an elaborate coat and waved it around. The device sniffed the universe for the second segment of the Key to Time and crackled excitedly. 'And yet… it appears to be the right place.'

'Fascinating.' The Doctor liked that as a word. It was a safe bet.

Romana waved the Tracer around, trying to get a bearing. The wand's crackle advanced to an alarming electronic roar. Romana switched it off.

'Even if you are right,' Romana pocketed the Tracer swiftly, 'and I'm not saying you're wrong, of course I'm not, but even if you are right and something has switched the planet, then the Tracer still thinks the second segment is around here somewhere.'

'I told you not to trust gimmicky gadgets,' said the Doctor. 'Didn't I, K-9?'

For once, the Doctor's robot dog said nothing.

The Doctor was used to being the centre of attention. If you'd asked him about it, he would have said he hated it, especially when giant green slugs stopped him for an autograph. So embarrassing.

And yet, he'd entered the mysterious city on the mysterious planet and not made much of an impression.

He and K-9 were free to wander as they pleased. People walked past, by and large ignoring him. 'But I don't even get ignored in Paris,' thought the Doctor, scuffing his way through a pile of quartzite like it was autumn leaves. It was very odd.

He tried stopping people, but they just swerved around him, absolutely and utterly determined not to make eye contact with him. He leapt at one hapless man, who simply staggered backwards, stumbling against K-9 and scrambling away, eyes still downcast.

'Hey, watch out!' the Doctor called at him. 'That's my dog you've just dented.'

The path of people seemed to be leading them to a large square where they were all celebrating. Well, sort of celebrating. Mostly they were milling around under the golden gaze of a heroic statue, trying to look happy, and holding up golden umbrellas. Occasionally someone would issue a lacklustre cheer which would be sheepishly taken up, before fading quickly away. It couldn't have looked a more awkward gathering if you'd got together a group of Englishmen and ordered them to declare what was great about themselves.

The Doctor and K-9 drew to a halt at the edge of the square.

Romana peered dubiously at the crowd. 'I wonder what it is they're all celebrating?'

'Not our arrival, that's for sure.' The Doctor puffed out his cheeks. He stepped forward and tapped a hurrying stranger on the shoulder. 'Excuse me, would you take me to your leader, please?'

The man took no notice, apart from hurrying away a shade more hurriedly.

The Doctor looked at K-9 and huffed. 'Not doing very well, are you, K-9?'

To say that K-9 never had a sensible suggestion is inaccurate. The robot dog often offered the Doctor advice. His master very rarely listened to it, however.

'May I suggest, Master, that you let the Mistress make contact with the local population?'

For once, the Doctor had heard him. 'Maybe one day. But not just yet. First contact with an alien race is an immensely skilled and delicate job. What can she possibly know about it?'

'She is prettier than you, Master,' announced the dog.

'Pretty?' the Doctor boggled. 'That's got absolutely nothing to do with it. Has it?' He looked around for Romana. 'Oh.'

Romana was some distance off, chatting away to a small group of young men.

Romana had decided to show some initiative. She had once been to a lecture on Initiative, and it had seemed a nice enough concept, but she'd never really needed to try it out. Now seemed just the occasion to give it an airing. Second planet they'd landed on, and she was determined to impress the Doctor by getting some results. While he was striding back and forth demanding to be taken to someone's leader, she stepped neatly over to a small group of young men and turned on a smile as

THE PIRATE PLANET

dazzling as her gown. It turned out, they were only too happy
to talk to her.

'It's a New Golden Age, you see,' one of them was telling her
eagerly. 'A Golden Age of Prosperity.'

'I must say,' one of his friends cut in quickly, 'I still get terribly
excited by it all.'

'We have them rather often, though,' the first man said in an
attempt at wry cynicism.

'But that's because of the Captain's great goodness, you see,'
his friend countered.

'The Captain?' From this distance, the Doctor could have
sworn that Romana fluttered her eyelashes. Surely not.

'Oh yes,' a third youth babbled in an attempt to mask his
shyness. 'The Captain does it all for us. And it was terribly
spectacular this time. Oh yes, the omens! The skies shook like
lightning. And you know what that means?'

'No, I'm terribly afraid I don't.' Romana appeared to be using a
strange, breathless tone. Perhaps she was having trouble adjusting
to the planet's atmosphere. But that wouldn't explain why she
was twirling a finger in her hair.

'Oh, well…' The first man rallied gamely. 'It means we're going
to be very rich!'

The group burst into laughter, chanting 'Rich, very, very rich!'
over and over again.

'What, just like that? Rich! Because of lights in the sky? Fancy!'
Romana's wide eyes looked terribly impressed.

'That's the way it always happens,' the second friend said.
'Here, let me give you some diamonds—'

'I've got rubies – they're heaps better!'

'Here, have some emeralds!'

'Oh, thank you,' Romana managed as the men pressed handfuls
of precious stones on her.

The Doctor was baffled by all this and had important questions.
He stepped over to them. 'Er, excuse me! Hello there!'

No one noticed him.

Romana slipped the stones into a pocket and brought out a small paper bag. 'I say, would any of you like a jelly baby?'

The men helped themselves while the Doctor boggled at the scene. Being ignored was one thing. Now the new girl was stealing his best material. This was only day two. Give her a fortnight and it would be 'Hello! I'm Romana and this is my assistant, the Doctor.' He glanced down. K-9 had trundled over to Romana's side.

The first man ignored the dog, holding a jelly baby up to the light. It glowed a strange green and was rather like a squishy precious stone. 'What are they?'

'Sweets,' announced Romana grandly, then faltered. 'I think you have to eat them or something.'

'Oh, I'll try that,' announced the man uncertainly.

His friends examined theirs equally dubiously.

'Excuse me,' the Doctor tried again.

The bravest of the men popped the jelly baby in his mouth and made an effort to chew it with a weak smile.

'We'd better go,' one of his friends announced. 'Or we'll be late for the Triumph. Nice to have met you.'

They sauntered off. One turned back to her. 'Hope the Mourners don't get you.'

'What?' the Doctor shouted after them. 'The who?' As there was no reply, he turned on Romana. 'Where did you get those jelly babies from?'

'Same place you get them,' she announced. 'Your pocket.' And she dropped them neatly back into his coat with a pat.

Standing on a mysterious alien planet feeling thoroughly outwitted, the Doctor felt it was time to impart a piece of serious moral wisdom. 'Good looks are no substitute for a sound character, you know.'

Romana took the reproof with a nod that was just a shade too grave to be serious. She appeared to be chewing slowly on a jelly baby.

The Doctor changed the subject. 'Didn't those men say something about omens?'

'Yes, omens in the sky.'

'Hmm.' The Doctor pulled a small brass telescope from his pocket, extended it and peered up at the heavens. He made a succession of his very best Thinking Noises. Romana tried to see what he was looking at.

'Ahhh,' finished the Doctor, lowering the telescope. 'You know, I can't see a thing. Just ordinary sky. Nothing unusual. Do you see any omens, Romana?'

The Doctor handed her the telescope and prayed he hadn't missed anything. He jammed his hands in his pockets and looked around the square. He peered at the golden statue. It was of a distinguished, noble figure, bedecked in a glorious uniform. The handsome face twinkled with kindly authority. Hmm, the Doctor wondered. Was this the mysterious Captain? He looked again around the previously crowded square. It had suddenly emptied. 'Hello, I wonder what scared them all off?'

The young men stood in a group, regarding their jelly babies doubtfully. One had assured the others that his was 'quite nice actually', and the rest were considering their options. Which is when the Guard found them.

The Captain's Guards were excellent at spotting unusual things.

Today a New Golden Age had been declared. A Golden Age was not celebrated by lurking behind an awning hesitating over food.

The Guard loomed over them. 'Where'd you get those?' he demanded.

The three men pointed without hesitation in the direction of Romana.

Romana was still squinting through the telescope.

The Doctor was examining the stones Romana had been given.

'Do you know, I think these things are genuine.' The Doctor held them out for K-9. 'What do you think?'

The dog considered them, his ears whirring. 'Affirmative, Master. The clear ones are the diamonds and the red ones are the rubies,' he added helpfully.

'Why thank you.' The Doctor beamed proudly at his dog, and slipped the stones into his pocket. You never knew when they'd come in handy. After all, these things were rare and…

The Doctor had noticed how untidy the streets were. Only now did he realise what they were untidy with. Glittering stones lay in little heaps at every corner. 'Now, there's an extraordinary thing. The whole ground seems to be littered with jewels.' He picked through them. 'Diamonds, rubies, emeralds, Andromedan bloodstone, gravel, more diamonds. Don't they have street cleaners here? Maybe they've all had to go into tax exile.'

'I expect these stones just aren't valuable here,' Romana offered.

'Not valuable?' Oh, she was so green the Doctor couldn't help but smile. 'They're valuable anywhere. They're not just shiny – they're useful.' The Doctor picked up a stone. 'Diamond is one of the hardest substances in the universe. The only thing harder is the crystalline tooth of an Algol Suntiger, and no one's ever got close enough to one to tell what it's made of, and, as soon as the beast dies, the crystal structure disintegrates.'

'But…' Romana was puzzled. 'How do we know the teeth are so hard?'

'Because, the Algol Suntiger traditionally uses diamond toothpicks and they don't seem to last very long.'

'Ah.' Romana filed this away. No doubt it would never come in handy some day.

'Rubies…' The Doctor picked up another stone. 'These are still needed to make any halfway decent laser beam. Have you seen the ones they're making now with plastic crystals? Horrid shoddy things. I wouldn't shoot my worst enemy with one.' He held the ruby up to the light. 'Apart from which, they're terribly pretty. Don't you think?'

Objectively, Romana supposed so. The thing was, there were just so many stones lying around them. The first time she'd seen the Time Vortex, she'd thought, 'Well, that's going to take some getting used to.' But she had. More or less. And in many ways, this was the same thing. She couldn't quite describe the sense of wrong casualness that had crept into her reaction to being surrounded by so many, many precious stones, but then she caught the Doctor juggling with them. And that summed it up perfectly.

They were only precious, only pretty, almost by accident. The gestation of planets is such a tediously long process that, in amongst all the formations of land masses and volcanoes and cores, you're bound to get the odd statistical outlier. A tiny pocket of geological pressure here, a fluke of worried carbon atoms there, and some interesting things were bound to happen, and some of them were bound to be shiny.

Perhaps, she postulated, this planet had simply been geologically very lucky? 'Maybe they just occur naturally here? Perhaps the ground's full of them.'

This did not go down well with the Doctor. He stopped juggling, letting three fist-sized emeralds skitter across the pavement. 'Don't they teach you youngsters any astro-geology these days? You poor thing, I really must pop back and have a word.' The Doctor made a mental note: 'Add an Air of Wonder to the Academy's teaching'. Poor Romana was standing on an impossible planet next to a pile of objects so remarkable she should have been pulling the feathers from her boa. Instead she looked so casually aloof. 'The precise combination of minerals, pressures and heat needed to make these stones has to be very rare, just on the Law of Averages. You've heard of the Law of Averages?'

'Yes, Doctor,' said Romana drily. 'It is on the syllabus.'

'I'll tell you something about it that isn't on any syllabus. You can break any law you like and, if you're clever, you can get away with it.' The Doctor stopped and smiled to himself. 'But if you break the Law of Averages then sooner or later someone will smell a rat. For instance...' His shoe combed idly through a pile of abandoned abundance. 'For instance!' He plucked up an object rather like a duck egg, only the colour seemed to be hiding somewhere deep inside. 'This is really rare. Oolion. One of the most precious stones in the universe. And, when I say precious, I mean scarce. It occurs naturally on only two planets I know of...' The Doctor hoped he'd got that right, or, at the least, that he was pulling it off. 'Qualactin and Bandraginus 5. Bandraginus 5...' He stopped, worried. 'Where have I heard that mentioned recently?'

Romana was more impressed by the stone. She cupped it gently in her hands, tilting it slowly to watch as the colour shifted somewhere intangibly inside it. 'It's beautiful.'

'You just hold it up to the light,' coaxed the Doctor, pleased by her reaction. That was more like it. 'See the green flame blazing in its heart? People have killed for that beauty, hoarded it, worshipped it, ravaged empires for it. And lying about in the street is almost exactly where I wasn't expecting to find it.' The Doctor took the stone from her, suddenly worried. 'I wonder where Calufrax has got to?'

He wandered away, becoming increasingly worried. What was happening around him wasn't just breaking the Law of Averages, it was jumping up and down on the pieces while being rude about its mother. The whole situation was so dazzlingly unlikely it felt like someone was interfering in the universe.

Romana watched the Doctor go. She was worried.

She'd been delighted when told that she was going on a quest for the Key to Time. She'd also been just slightly baffled. The Key was the most important object in the universe. By logical extension, her selection to locate it had to mean that she was, in

72

some way, special. On paper, she had to admit, she was an excellent candidate. But that was only on paper. She had graduated with distinction, but she had *only just* graduated from the Time Lord Academy. Why pick a novice when there were surely equally qualified and rather more experienced people – someone from the College of Paradoxes, or the Institute of Infinite Possibility?

In fact, why not all of them? If finding the Key was so important, why not send everyone you had? Rather than just her? Still, nagging doubts aside, Romanadvoratrelundar had swelled with pride that she and not someone more experienced had been selected for the mission. Someone had recognised her potential and selected her for a quest to save the universe.

Then she had met the Doctor and begun to feel very worried. She'd heard about him, of course. For one thing, he was theoretically President of the High Council of Time Lords, although, since he'd only attended the one meeting, everyone kept quiet about that. That was the Doctor's problem – he couldn't stick to anything. If Romana were ever elected President (delighted to be considered, a great honour, etc., etc., but she currently had no ambitions in that area), well, she'd jolly well sit it out. Not immediately dash off out into the universe again. Everyone knew about the Doctor. Lectures about the General Theory and Practice of Careful Time Intervention famously began with a picture of the Doctor and the command 'Not Like This'.

But that was the Doctor. Everyone knew about him. He was an exception, a warning. 'Been off observing the Celestis Wars again, have we? Careful you don't get a taste for it and end up like the Doctor.'

The way of the Time Lords was strict, austere and dignified. On formal occasions they appeared wearing ornate robes and a vast ceremonial collar moulded on a fragment of the First Clock. On informal occasions they just wore the ornate robes. 'You lot don't dress for running or getting through doors sharpish,' as someone had once remarked. That someone was the Doctor.

The Time Lords of Gallifrey observed, they discussed, they debated and they reached a correct, considered decision. The Doctor hared across the universe knocking over governments like dominoes. Being paired up with him on a quest was a disastrous choice. For one thing, she'd get none of the credit (not, of course, that she sought any, not for herself). And for another, the Doctor would only get distracted by trivia. Their mission was simply to find the segments of the Key. They'd already thwarted an intergalactic coup and that had been their first outing. That was how things went with the Doctor.

Romana found him intimidating but also puzzling. She even chose her clothes with the correct consideration. The Doctor never gave anything a first, let alone a second thought, and yet, she had to admit, he seemed to be doing… all right so far. It just wasn't… well, it wasn't what she would have done. Chaos followed him like his robot dog. Only the Doctor could head for a simple planet and end up on one that was in the right place but, in all other aspects, so impossibly wrong that she felt dizzy just trying to make a list.

But that was the thing about time travel. When you stepped outside a time machine, life had a habit of becoming complicated. Inserting yourself into a non-determined causality required the careful tread of generations. (As she thought this, she watched the Doctor playing hopscotch among the diamonds.) In fact, it had long ago been decided that the most dangerous thing a Time Lord could possibly do was leave their TARDIS, so it was, on the whole, best avoided.

And that was when the dreadful penny dropped. The reason why a fleet of War TARDISes hadn't been sent roaring through the stars after the Key to Time. The reason why the Doctor had been selected for the mission was because his TARDIS was one of the last built with a door.

*

The Doctor was also worried. He kicked up a cloud of random stones and watched them skitter across the gilded pavement.

The segments of the Key to Time were shiny stones. He was on a planet full of shiny stones. He kicked sadly at a lump of Oolion big enough to start a war. And he sighed. Sorting through this lot was going to take an awfully long time.

CHAPTER SEVEN
HAS ANYONE SEEN CALUFRAX?

'Life force dying!'

Pralix was still screaming. Mula had started off worried and was now heartily wishing he'd just shut up. Previously he'd passed out after only a bit of shrieking. Today there was no stopping him.

'But what does it all mean?' she'd asked.

'Mean? It doesn't mean anything!' Balaton had his hands clamped over his ears and was pecking around his house like a worried old bird. 'Why should it mean anything?' He took his hands from his ears, shrugged, and then clapped them back. 'It's just the way life is, and very pleasant it is too, if you'd only learn to accept what's given to you. You can have anything you want, you know that.'

'Except answers,' retorted Kimus, and Mula smiled at him gratefully.

'Answers, answers!' the old man sneered. 'Who ever dressed himself in answers, eh? Or filled his stomach with them? I remember when I was a lad… If I'd said *Why?* every time my father put a plate of food in front of me, I'd have had short shrift, I can tell you. "Because otherwise you'll just go hungry my lad," he'd have said, and boxed me round the head, I shouldn't wonder. And deservedly too.' Balaton finished this stream of nonsense with a self-satisfied nod. But that was just how he was. Mula guessed she loved him, despite all his strange fussy ways. The old man was always worried but never concerned. He was worried about upset, about change. But he seemed to almost deliberately ignore what was wrong with the world. All the old people just didn't want to talk about it.

Mula adored Kimus because he did nothing but. He shared her concern that something was very wrong with their planet. A lot of the young people thought the same.

'Now, I remember what it was like before the Captain.' That was a clear sign that Balaton had started up again. 'My grandfather, he told me. "You think life under the Captain's bad," he used to say. "Why, you should have tried living under the reign of Queen Xanxia." You think there's no freedom now? It was a different story then. You youngsters don't appreciate what's given to you. That's your trouble, always wanting something just because you can't get it. And what are answers worth, eh? Nothing, just unpleasantness. Throw your lives away for an answer, would you?' He strode to the dining room, banging empty golden plates down on the solid silver table. 'Answers? I don't know, I never heard such stupid nonsense.' Plate after plate slapped down, and then he rattled the cutlery drawer viciously.

'But it doesn't add up!' protested Kimus. Balaton thrust a handful of forks at him, and Kimus dutifully began to sort them. 'Can't you see that, old man? What are you, blind or something? Deaf? Just plain dumb?'

Balaton said nothing. All his concentration was on inspecting an inadequately polished spoon.

'No, you're scared silly and you don't know what of. Is that a way to live?' Kimus waved a fork at him. Balaton ignored him. 'Listen! If we are getting richer and richer for generation after generation, then someone or something, somewhere, somehow must be getting poorer.'

Mula had heard Kimus expound this theory before. She almost got it. She found it rather politically racy, herself. Surely everyone could just get richer – perhaps not to the excess they were currently enjoying, but just a little bit, and then no one would come to any harm? She noticed a dent in the gold handle of a diamond knife and, with a sigh, threw it away.

Balaton greeted Kimus's outburst with a snort. 'Nonsense!'

'Really? Well, I'd just like to know three things,' demanded Kimus. 'Who is getting poorer? Why? And is it all worth it?'

'I'm sick of all the endless diamonds and gold and stuff,' Mula said. 'What's the point of it?'

'The point?' Balaton started banging a plate on the table. 'It's wealth! Wealth in its purest, most absolute form!' Young people just didn't understand. How little they'd once had. How much Xanxia had taken away. And how much the Captain had given back. 'Wealth symbolises the success of our people!'

'Success? Success at what?' Mula asked him.

'Success at... success at...' Balaton felt momentarily worried, then brightened. 'Success at being wealthy!'

'Success at being wealthy?' Kimus sneered. 'But what about Pralix? What about your grandson? What's all this success doing to him? Every time we have a new Golden Age of Prosperity, he throws a screaming fit and half dies. Very prosperous I must say. Very Golden.'

Balaton said nothing. He went over to the tureen and started to ladle a thin soup into the ruby-studded bowls. He'd hoped for bread, but there'd been none today.

Mula sat down and glared at the soup furiously. It was as bad as ever. Her hand sneaked automatically over to the salt cellar, but it had been empty for weeks. 'Pralix must be the key to it all. He must know something. He must.'

'Really?' The old man stood up, and strode over to the door of Pralix's room, throwing it open again.

'Life force dying! Life force dying!'

'Does that really sound as if it's worth knowing?' he asked them, closing the door gently.

'Yes,' said Mula and Kimus. They smiled at each other.

A few streets away, the Doctor was still looking for the Planet Calufrax.

'Excuse me.' He had taken to knocking on doors, calling through letterboxes and was now, seemingly, bellowing to an eerily empty street. 'Hello! Has anyone seen a place called Calufrax? It's a sort of planet thing. It's ooh… about 14,000 miles across, you couldn't miss it. Oblate spheroid, cold, covered in ice… Well, except at the equator, which is more sort of tundra-y.'

The Doctor finished speaking and cocked a hand to his ear, listening for any reply.

None came.

'Does it ring a bell at all?' called the Doctor. His perpetual cheeriness was starting to fray. 'Bit like Maidstone. No? Oh well. Just asking.' He turned to Romana with a madman's shrug. 'They haven't seen it.'

Romana looked around the street. It was terribly, terribly quiet. The kind of quiet that assured you that people were home but ignoring you very hard. She shivered. 'No one's in,' she said. 'Perhaps they're all out enjoying themselves.'

'Maybe…' The Doctor didn't seem that convinced.

A window at the far end of the street was flung open and the figure of a man threw himself scrabbling out. He stood uncertainly on the sill, weaving back-and-forth in the air. 'The Life Force is dead!' he screamed. 'The Life Force is dead! We are all murderers!

Murderers!' His eyes fixed the Doctor and Romana with a glare of fury. 'Murderers!'

For a moment the young man wavered. Perhaps he was going to jump. Maybe he was going to launch himself at them in a furious attack. Instead, with a sudden cry, he was pulled back into the room and the shutters hastily slammed shut.

Romana turned to look at the Doctor.

'Well, at least someone's at home,' the Doctor said, heading towards the house.

Far underground, the strange, sad group had fallen silent. They had only stopped crying and screaming because they were exhausted. They lay, draped across rocks and each other.

Hovering in the air above them was the figure of Pralix, being wrestled onto his bed. The image jumped to his anguished face and then faded away, the glittering cloud of dust dimming as it drifted to the floor.

The Chief Mourner propped herself up, her voice a hoarse croak. 'The vigil of evil is accomplished. And now…' She sighed. She sighed very well. 'The one called Pralix must be harvested. In my bones, I sense that soon shall be the Time of Knowing.'

'The Time of Knowing,' sobbed her audience.

'And fast upon that shall follow the Time of Vengeance.'

'The Time of Vengeance.'

'Vengeance for the crimes of Zanak!'

'The crimes of Zanak,' the exhausted crowd repeated loyally.

They picked themselves wearily off the ground. There was no rest for them. They were the Mourners and their grieving never ceased.

Balaton finished closing the shutters, and pushed the door to the room firmly shut. Then he went over to the bed that Pralix lay in, and sat gently on the edge of it. Certain he was alone, he allowed his face to drop, his posture to slump.

He picked idly at the jewels sewn into his threadbare jacket, pulling one loose and hurling it into a corner. Then he turned back to Pralix, his hand resting on his grandson's forehead. When he spoke his voice was gentle and tender and so terribly sad.

'Sleep, sleep, son of my dead son. Let these evil visions slip from your mind, they are but dreams. Sleep Pralix, you are safe, no one will harm you, if you will only sleep.'

They appeared in the streets. No one saw where they came from, probably because people found themselves suddenly looking very pointedly in another direction. The Mourners had that effect on people, creating little ripples in the world wherever they went.

When it had all started, the Mourners had defiantly wanted to be noticed. They'd wished to be objects of attention, with their tattered cloaks shorn of all jewels, their gaunt faces and worn-out eyes. The Mourners wanted the world to know that they were its conscience.

At first the people had stared in horror, puzzlement and shame. Some had even drifted from the crowds to join their silent ranks.

No one was quite certain when people started looking away from them. Was it before or after the Guards started shooting them? But one thing was now certain – people now no longer looked them in the eye, and the Guards shot them on sight.

The City Criers claimed this was because the Mourners carried a terrible disease. And in some ways, Guilt was a disease. At first the Mourners took their executions stoically, as though it was precisely what they deserved.

Over time, that shifted. Now people tended not to even notice the Mourners, as though they deliberately placed themselves beyond thought. Perhaps they had grown bored of being shot, or simply felt that it was too easy a way out.

Whatever, they could enter the Cities silently, unobserved. As now, when they swept past the throngs packed into the squares, the Mourners' dragging tread taking them steadily, sadly, towards Pralix.

Chapter Eight
There Are No Other Worlds

Balaton had sampled a lot of life and had decided that he was happiest when he was asleep.

He'd not been able to save his son. He'd not been able to save his son's wife, who had died from grief. Now he doubted he could save Pralix. But perhaps there was a chance for Mula. If only she would, could, realise.

'Mula.' He clasped her hands, pleading. 'We must shelter Pralix from the Mourners. Remember what they did to your poor father.'

Mula dropped his hands and stared at him. Was that really what he thought? 'My father was shot by the Captain's Guards.' She was so angry now.

'Only to save him from the Mourners!' protested Balaton. He remembered the scene. He had fully intended to watch when the Guards opened fire, but the moment came, and he found that he'd clamped his eyes tightly shut and never wanted to open them again. It is a terrible thing to ask of one's eyes: to open and look at the body of your son. Much better to just keep them shut. But that was the way of this world. 'At least my son died a clean death. It was an act of mercy. The Captain is merciful.'

'Thank you, oh merciful Captain, for so kindly having Mula's father shot down in the street like a dog.' Kimus made a nasty little mock bow, and Balaton really hoped that a Golden Age of Prosperity landed on his head. 'Oh Captain! Your benevolence is clearly too great for my simple brain to comprehend. Where do I kneel?'

Loud words were all very well. But Balaton knew how this would end – with a lot of people dead and Kimus strangely untouched by things. People like Kimus just didn't understand – you couldn't change the world. The best you could hope was to quietly navigate your way through your waking hours.

'Kimus,' Balaton sighed. 'I let them kill my son. And I would let them kill my grandson if it saved him from those zombies.' He patted Pralix's sleeping shoulder.

'The Mourners?' Kimus was as dismissive as ever. 'Of course they're not zombies!'

Mula adored Kimus. He had a wonderful voice, a quick wit, and friends who shared his cynical opinions, laughing and banging the table at whatever he said. But sometimes he did say the most terrible rubbish. He acted as though the Mourners were just another protest group – like the Unprosperous and the Old Agers – just a forlorn bunch of people who you could argue about, broadly champion, explain that you would, of course, join with them immediately, only they had one or two regrettable policies you could not quite get behind. Protest groups were all very well, until they got mown down in a storm of gun fire and were never mentioned again. But the Mourners were different. The Mourners were a lot older. They'd been around for a very long time, for so long they were almost a myth. 'Sleep tight, or the Mourners will come for you,' mothers would whisper as they gave their children nightmares. Everyone knew the Mourners existed, some swore they lurked around the corner, an extra shadow following them home, a whisper on the wind, but no one had ever seen them.

'I've seen them,' said Mula defiantly. 'Once.'

Kimus stared at her. The way that Balaton was shaking his head and muttering 'No' convinced him that she was telling the truth.

'The Mourners? What did you see?'

'I just know that they are evil... They hate us. All of us.'

'Enough!' Balaton held up a hand, commanding. It didn't help that he was clutching a pillow.

'Who are they, Grandfather?' The questions started to pour out of Mula. 'Why do we never know who they are? Are they people? Why are they? Why do they hate us so? What do they want?'

'All these questions.' Balaton lowered his miserable head. 'You want to know what they want?'

Balaton pointed a shaking hand at Pralix.

The Mourners walked through a crowd. Around them the celebrations continued without anyone even noticing them. A chill spread through the crowd, smiles faded, and the joyful mood dissipated. The people fell silent, staring emptily at the jewels in their hands, with no idea why they felt so sad.

'They will take Pralix.' Balaton's bluster and anger left him. 'Just as they took Brandmar, just as they took Tralakis, just as they wanted to take your father.'

'But is it as the Captain says – will they eat him?'

'They will take him.' Balaton was defiant.

'We can hide him,' announced Mula. 'We can save him from the Captain and from the Mourners.'

'Where?'

'I'll work something out.' Mula advanced on the bed. 'We'll hide him.'

'Hide him?' Kimus reasserted himself. It was time to make a stand. He was very good at them. The thing was that, just at the moment, Mula was dragging Pralix and he was rather heavy, and the fact that Kimus would rather make a speech than lend a hand was grating on her a little.

'Are we going to hide all our lives?' Kimus was declaiming. 'Let the Mourners come! We shall face them!'

Balaton caught Mula's eye. They both smiled weakly at each other.

At this point, rather impossibly, the very locked front door swung open.

Kimus recoiled in horror and ducked instinctively behind a pillar.

Mula and Balaton froze, Pralix slung between them.

All three of them stared at the figure silhouetted in the door.

'Excuse me,' called a voice, 'but are you quite sure this planet's meant to be here?'

Romana hadn't even noticed the Doctor had gone. She was staring up at the sky through the telescope and learning. She liked gathering facts together and giving the world around her shape and order. For a start, there was something amiss with the ozone layer. For a binary system, she would expect both the thermosphere and exosphere to be slightly distorted, and yet, as far as she could tell, this hadn't happened. That was one curious thing.

Another curious thing was the cloud formation, which suggested some remarkable upheaval had happened. Also, it was clearly broad daylight and yet the flowers appeared to be trying to behave as though it was night.

Then there was the citadel on the distant mountain. An attempt had clearly been made to merge the ancient and more modern parts of the structure, but the overall structure refused to have any unity. It looked so wrong that she could have accused the Doctor of making it.

She brought the telescope down slightly and then squinted. A face was filling it, staring at her. It was ugly, curious, and very angry. She lowered the brass instrument. Standing in front of her were two figures. Romana might not have been travelling with the Doctor for very long, but she had already learned how to recognise A Guard.

The Guards both looked pretty identical. The one on the left was piggier, the one on the right grumpier. But honestly, where did the universe find them?

One of them snatched the telescope from her. 'This is a forbidden object,' he snarled.

'Oh, really?' Romana's reply was cool. She supposed she was in a certain amount of danger. These men had weapons. They were probably going to try and imprison her. She worked through the probabilities. This planet was a mystery. The most useful thing about it was the Citadel. The best way to acquire answers was through an authority figure. The Doctor would probably try and elude these people but, yes, Romana thought, assessing them carefully, they could most definitely be of use to her. 'A forbidden object,' she prompted. 'Why?'

'That is a forbidden question,' snapped the piggy Guard on the left. 'You are a stranger?'

'Well, yes,' conceded Romana. She managed not to roll her eyes.

'Strangers are forbidden,' growled Piggy, of course he did. 'Where are you from?'

'I'm from another world.' Romana grinned at them.

Their answer was surprising. 'There are no other worlds,' said Grumpy. 'It is a forbidden concept. How did you get here?'

Romana resisted the temptation to point out the logical flaw in his statement. 'Oh, I came with the Doctor,' she breezed as though that answered everything, and then, as Piggy started to say something, she held up a hand. 'No, no, don't tell me – Doctors are forbidden as well?'

Grumpy turned to Piggy. They nodded at each other and then turned back to Romana, smiling their very nastiest smiles. They then said the words guaranteed to reduce anyone to whimpering, begging, hysterics. 'I think we'd better take you to the Captain.'

'Splendid,' Romana beamed and rubbed her hands together.

There was a stunned pause.

Romana raised an eyebrow and waited for them to tell her where to go.

They stared at her, confused, and then, with a lacklustre attempt at aggression, seized her by the arms and started to drag her away. Even being dragged, she seemed to glide.

As they rounded a corner, a small grey object shot forwards. Before the Guards had noticed it, Romana's leg shot gracefully out, and hastily nudged the object back into the shadows.

'No, you mustn't,' the prisoner cried.

The Guards smiled. Finally, she was begging for mercy. Good.

'You dare speak?' Piggy growled, feeling rather more enthusiastic about his prisoner.

'No, no, wouldn't dream of it,' she assured them graciously. 'Do leave me be and fetch the Doctor.'

'What?'

Their prisoner somehow folded her arms. 'I would like to be taken to the Captain,' she announced. 'I'm looking forward to being interrogated by him terribly.'

The Guards, with the annoying feeling that they were being led, continued to drag her away.

From the shadows, K-9 watched Romana go. 'Affirmative, Mistress,' he said dubiously. K-9 would not dream of correcting anyone, of course he would not. But, if he'd been asked his opinion, he would, gently, have stated that getting captured was not necessarily a wise move. Certainly not for the Mistress Romana. It was, after all, only her second trip.

If a pirate is any good, then he will, over time, acquire quite a hoard. The Captain was taking a walk through his collection. It was the one place in his empire where he could be guaranteed privacy.

As each artefact drifted past him, it lit up, unveiling a treasure that would have made any sane being flinch. He would stand in front of it, smiling benevolently until it danced away into the air. Sometimes the Polyphase Avatron would react as well, uttering an admiring, thoughtful chirp. Away from the crowded bridge, both Captain and pet seemed to be behaving quite differently.

The robotic parrot's gentle notes formed a singing catalogue, a careful report of each object's status. The Captain stroked its alloy wings thoughtfully, nodding. His gallery always put him in a soft, reflective mood. Even his voice here was quiet.

'We're surrounded by incompetents, Polly, you and I,' the Captain sighed wistfully. 'Incompetents and fools. You're my only true friend.' The parrot purred. 'The only one I can really trust. Out of the whole lot of them, eh, imagine that?' He caught a reflection of his dreadful face in the front of a cabinet and his entire body slumped heavily against it. Only when he was completely alone, could the Captain allow himself to feel tired and sad, to really wallow in how miserable things were. His art gallery brought him some comfort, some hope, but it also made him even sadder. In here, in this beautiful, mournful place, he just wanted to die. It was all he had wanted for quite some time.

Sensing the shift in his mood, the parrot uttered a little coo and nudged him with its beak. It began to warble a gentle song, one the Captain had taught it long ago. Over the hundreds of years, though, the bird had elaborated the song, enhancing, improvising, expanding. Woven into it was the music of a hundred planets, all celebrated in a piece of music that was haunting in its complexity.

As the parrot sang, the Captain's mood shifted with the song. To think something so exquisitely complicated had come from a simple shanty he'd hummed to himself once while working to build the parrot. He rubbed the creature under its tin chin, and the bird rubbed a knuckle with a claw. It had learned that this was the one part of the Captain's hand that had any sensation.

'Never mind, Polly.' The Captain managed a weak smile. 'Not long now. Not long before it's finished. And then you and I… we'll be free.'

'Free!' the bird repeated in a metallic rasp, and the Captain's sad smile increased.

Mr Fibuli, breaking all rules of protocol and precedent, came running into the Gallery.

'Captain! Sir!'

For a moment, just a moment, the Captain wondered about killing Fibuli. Charmingly silly name or no silly name – there and then, the man was an annoyance.

'What is it?' he groaned with annoyance.

Sensing how wrong he was, Mr Fibuli stopped. He was puzzled by the Gallery, by the Captain's posture, by the soft cooing of that wretched bird. The Thing was still singing, but its eyes had turned in his direction, and it was looking at Fibuli hungrily.

'It's, ah…' He licked his lips and really wished he had some comforting paperwork to clutch. The whole situation felt dreadfully embarrassing. He'd once had to arrange his mother's execution, and that had been similarly mortifying. 'Well, sir, the Mourners are marching.'

The Captain drew himself up.

The bird stopped singing.

'Ghouls! Vultures of Death!' The Captain was himself once more, his voice shaking the chamber. 'They must have located another rogue telepath.' He lurched out of his gallery, the lights around the exhibits snapping off as he went. Borne on the Captain's shoulder, the Polyphase Avatron favoured Mr Fibuli with a poisonous glare as it passed him. 'This is all your fault,' its look said.

The Captain punched the wall, plugging himself into a data port, pulling information from a rush of screens, his voice filling the Citadel. 'This is your Captain speaking! Sector Five! The

Mourners are moving towards Sector Five of the City. Mobilise all Guards! Their quarry must be found and destroyed. They must not be taken by the Mourners! Why –' the Captain unplugged himself from the port and lurched towards the Bridge – 'by the great Death Ship of Magron, when will we ever rid ourselves of these ghosts? These mind zombies!'

The parrot spun its head around to glare at Mr Fibuli once more.

'Mr Fibuli!' The Captain issued a final threat as he staggered away. 'Find the subject and destroy them or, by all the suns that blaze, I'll tear you apart, molecule from molecule!'

Guards poured into the City, searching for the Mourners. It was not an easy job. The security cameras told them where they were, but they'd rush to a square and find nothing but rocks and frightened peasants.

The Mourners had made themselves very good at only being seen when they wanted to be seen. If you were quick, you could catch a glimpse of them out of the corner of an eye, but that was it. That was your best hope. Your one chance of a shot.

One Guard had fallen back from his squadron, and was alone in the square. Something wasn't right. It seemed innocent enough – a few old men bickering over a pile of stones, some others sharing a bowl of soup. But there was something. A bitterness to the air that didn't belong to a hot, dry day.

Curious, uneasy, the Guard spun round quickly, and found himself surrounded by the Mourners. Row after row of empty, downturned faces, pale and gaunt, their tattered cloaks hanging off their spare frames.

He'd already fired at them before he understood that they'd allowed him to see them, because he was alone. The blasts from his gun fizzled harmless away in mid-air, and the Mourners just moved closer towards him.

The Guard called out, shouting at the old men, at the people by the food stall. But no one noticed him. Not any more. Suddenly, the Guard didn't matter.

The sense of misery increased, pressing down on him. The Guard, wailing now, hurled his gun away and ran at the Mourners.

For a single moment, they stopped in their march and turned to stare directly at him. Little more than a passing glance. But it was enough.

Suddenly, the Guard knew how desperately pointless the universe was, how obscenely sad the act of living was, and decided not to.

The Captain watched this from the screens on the bridge. He wasn't sympathetic. 'The brainless fool, he deserved to die. All Guards,' he roared, bouncing up and down in his chair. 'They are moving through to Sector Six. Find the subject before they do!'

He glanced over at the Nurse. The wretched woman was advancing on him. She didn't like it when he got excited. But he didn't care. He knew how important it was to stop the Mourners gaining in strength. 'Find their quarry and destroy it!'

The Doctor had surveyed the living room containing three guilty people and one unconscious lunatic and very swiftly taken charge. This, he felt, was definitely much more like it. You didn't need Romana to get this lot's attention.

The old man and the young girl were clearly frantic with worry. The arrogant young man was clearly afraid someone would tell him he didn't matter, and the lunatic was clearly very much in need of help.

The Doctor could lay on help faster than the White Guardian could whip up cucumber sandwiches and a pitcher of crème de menthe. The Doctor had long ago learned that the best way to win over complete strangers was to instantly help them. He'd seen midwives do it, and it was only the trouble that some planets had with kettles which stopped him from wandering into rooms and automatically demanding blankets and boiling water.

He'd had Pralix removed to a remarkably ugly couch and was tending to him whilst trying not to object to the furniture. He'd often passed the furniture shops on Edgware Road and wondered, 'Well, yes, fine, but who buys this stuff?' It seemed that Balaton had bought all of it – every diamond chandelier, marble stool, gold couch and silver salver – and crammed it all into a tiny living room that was so opulent the Doctor wanted to kick it. No wonder the young man was in a coma. His sense of taste was probably trying to kill him.

Now that Pralix was receiving some proper care, the three other people in the room sifted themselves nicely. The old man began to gibber worriedly about the dangers of letting strangers into one's home. The arrogant young one started posturing while checking to see if there were any other exits. The girl, however, he liked at once. A touch grumpy, slightly surly, but full of compassion, common sense, and she possessed that rare ability to provide a good answer to a simple question. In about three minutes he'd learned pretty much all he needed to know about the planet from her. Also, she was managing to wear a dress woven from platinum and emeralds gracefully, and the Doctor just knew that Romana would have been jealous.

'So,' he was saying to her, 'your brother Pralix has fallen into a state of shock. And you say he does this every time the Captain who rules you announces a New Golden Age of Prosperity?'

'Certainly the last two or three times. But never this badly before.'

'Hmm.' The Doctor labelled this as significant, felt Pralix's forehead and made his next statement appear as though it was directly related to the patient's health. 'I'd like to meet this Captain of yours. Pleasant chap, is he?'

'We've never seen him,' said Mula. And, for the first time in her life, this struck her as odd.

Her grandfather caught the mood and dropped it like it had burnt him. 'And why would we want to? The Captain is great and good! His statues are everywhere! The Captain looks after us and makes us rich.'

'He makes us his fools,' announced Kimus.

He struck a tiny bit of a pose, and the Doctor noticed a trifle sadly that Mula glanced at him with admiration. The Doctor often found love baffling. Along with fondue, jigsaws and skiing, it was on his list of things to try one day. Clearly Kimus fancied himself as a rebel leader. The Doctor noticed Kimus had altered his posture a little after checking it in a mirror. Well, now. Clearly Kimus just fancied himself.

The comatose Pralix suddenly sprang to life on the couch, twisting himself up. His eyes were wild and his voice hoarse. 'The Mourners! They are coming!' he shrieked.

'The Mourners?' echoed the Doctor. That did not sound good.

Up on the Bridge, the Captain was coordinating the search, pulling information from the myriad of security screens faster than any of his crew could hope to. Even the Nurse was standing back and admiring his efficiency. 'Find the subject and destroy it! Search Sector Seven!' he was bellowing. Suddenly the Captain came to a juddering halt, panting with exertion. The Nurse rushed to his side, but he pushed her away.

'What was that?' he groaned. Something had glided past one of the cameras. Barely in shot, little more than a shadow. But the Captain did not miss it. And neither did his pet. The Polyphase Avatron threw itself from the Captain's shoulder, its beak pecking furiously at the screen. 'Enhance!' roared the Captain. 'Make sense of this madness now!'

The images jumped, rolled back, and the camera angles changed.

The Nurse blinked. Today had been quite a strain, but even she was surprised to find the Captain confused. She was not quite sure what effect this would have on his health.

'What the planet's bane is that?' demanded the Captain, his one eye boggling.

The Polyphase Avatron was hopping anxiously on the Captain's shoulder, screeching with rage. The screens of the bridge were filled with the remarkable image of a small robot dog, gliding neatly into a house. 'Search that house!' the Captain thundered. 'That house! Search it and kill everything inside!'

Unaware that he'd just betrayed them all, K-9 entered Balaton's house with a gliding saunter. The robot dog was very fond of his Master and pleased to be reunited with him. He enjoyed the disorder that the Doctor created. He also (although he would have drained his batteries rather than admitted it) loved making an impressive entrance. The humanoids reacted very favourably to his arrival. The Doctor-Master beamed, the others expressed wonder and amazement:

'Captain save us!' wailed the ageing male.

'What is it?' asked the younger male.

'Is it a machine?' suggested the female.

And the clearly ill humanoid male emitted an involuntary psychic distress call on some difficult frequencies across the Vantalla scale.

'Don't worry.' The Doctor patted K-9 on the head. 'He's a friend of mine. Right K-9?'

'Affirmative, Master.' The dog risked waggling its tail. 'I am a friend.'

As far as K-9 could ascertain, they were in danger of imminent attack. The robot dog quickly checked its weaponry banks and found them most satisfactorily charged.

'So, who are these Mourners? And why are they coming here?' the Doctor asked. K-9 awarded him points for two unusually pertinent questions.

'They are evil zombies! They have terrible powers.' The old man began ranting with a mixture of ill-informed superstition and mystical terms that K-9 found distracting. He had an important mission of his own.

'Master,' he announced. 'Important. The Mistress is in danger.'

The Doctor was about to react to this. K-9 could see that his Master was running at full capacity. He was:

- On a quest for the second segment of the Key to Time
- Trying to find the misplaced planetoid of Calufrax
- Trying to determine the name of the planet that was seemingly occupying the coordinates of Calufrax
- Attempting to understand and assimilate this planet's customs, economy and governance before lethally assaulting at least two of them
- Trying to heal a clearly wounded young humanoid male

Perhaps, concluded K-9, the news that the Mistress was in danger was more than his Master needed at the current time. But he had also learned that it was always best to keep the Doctor abreast of all available facts.

The Doctor-Master emitted a strange groan and was about to say something when, luckily, they were attacked.

The door to Balaton's dwelling burst open.

'The Mourners!' pronounced Kimus before throwing himself behind a metal couch.

'No! It's the Guards!' wailed the old male, throwing himself to the floor in surrender. Judging by the appearance of the group of people, the elderly male's diagnosis was correct. The figures wore body armour, helmets, carried guns, and behaved with a belligerence typical of the genus Guard.

'Where is the subject?' demanded one of them angrily, proving K-9's theorem. 'Find the subject. The subject must be destroyed.'

'Shoot them all! Kill them now,' another agreed. Clearly humanoids of low intellect.

K-9 liked simplicity and quiet. He shot them all. Inasmuch as he was ever bored, Guards bored him. The stunned figures crumpled to the floor. A rapid scan informed him that they would be unconscious for 2.3 hours. However, something worried at the dog's circuits. Something was missing.

It was not that he had not made an obligatory attempt to reacquaint the Doctor-Master with the Mistress's abduction. Although the Doctor-Master was overdue for a reminder.

'Master—' he began.

'Not now, K-9,' came the reply.

That was fine. K-9 was aware that it took a median average of four separate attempts to alert the Doctor to new information. The universe immediately went on to prove K-9 right.

'The Mourners!' shrieked Pralix from his couch. 'The Mourners are coming!'

'Ah yes,' the Doctor said, leaning close to him, staring into the empty eyes with concern. 'Who are they, why do they want you?'

'The Mourners!' Mula, Balaton and Kimus all started talking at the same time, babbling with alarm and with a flood of alternative suggestions.

'Don't get me started on the Mourners!' Balaton was clearly warming up. He wanted to hide Pralix before he could come to further harm. 'We must hide him, we must hide him! They must be nearly here... Oh, the Captain's way is better... Why can't you see?'

Kimus, ever eager for a fight, and strangely empowered by the sight of a small robot shooting some of the Captain's Guards, was standing on a footstool, posturing. 'You're cowards, all of you! We must fight! We're not going to be pampered, frightened vegetables any more! Let's take this fight out into the streets, let's take it to the Bridge!'

Despite all the noise, Mula was listening carefully. 'There's noise of firing out in the street. Pralix is right. The Mourners are coming. There's no way we can save him now.' She bit her lip, and then looked at the Doctor. 'Is there?'

The Doctor was shaking Pralix gently. The boy was shivering in fear. 'Pralix? Pralix? Can you hear me? Can you hear my voice?' He listened for a response. Nothing.

The Doctor noticed how quiet the room had become. 'What's happening?' he asked, feeling the hair stand up on the back of his neck.

'Query,' asked K-9 in the silence. 'Are these the Mourners?'

The Doctor turned around. It was never a pleasant sensation to discover that It, whatever It was, was indeed, behind you.

He turned slowly, working out which grin to try out on them.

The Doctor found himself confronted by an unpromising collection of empty-faced figures, clad in grey, tattered robes. Their faces were pale, drained of all emotion, contentment and joy. Their eyes were large, and grimy tears fell over their cheeks. The room seemed suddenly desolate.

The Doctor's attempt at a grin utterly failed to catch light. So he settled for 'Hello.' That normally worked quite well.

The Mourners did not acknowledge him. They stared at Pralix. Almost in passing, just for a moment, they glanced at the Doctor, their eyes that little bit wider.

The Doctor, normally the cheeriest of souls, suddenly found himself aware of the utter crushing futility of the universe. The misery of life, the agony of existence, the unstoppable spread of death all rushed screaming into his brain. For just a moment, the Doctor felt like arguing with the tidal wave of thoughts. 'Now steady on—' Thoughts of a cup of tea, the smell of grass clippings all rallied to his cause, followed by silver sunsets on distant shores and the merry pop of self-destructing battle fleets. Then the cloud of despair overwhelmed him. His brain gave up completely and surrendered.

For once, the Doctor faced the universe and found it so unbearably sad that his mind simply snapped off.

PART TWO

'Water's running in the wrong direction.
Got a feeling it's a mixed-up sign.
I can see it in my own reflection…
It's the sound of the underground.'

Girls Aloud

CHAPTER NINE
THE 5,000-MILE TEACUP

Mr Fibuli wished he was anywhere but the Bridge. He'd tried the door of his favourite cupboard, but found it locked. By all accounts, the relatively routine mission to wipe out the target of a Mourners' Hunt had not gone well, and now the Captain wanted to have a 'debrief'. Even though Mr Fibuli had been nowhere near the operation, he still felt an ominous sensation sliding into his stomach and prodding at his breakfast.

As he entered the Bridge, Mr Fibuli saw the Nurse hovering anxiously around the Captain. For a moment the tin pirate looked absurd, with a blood pressure monitor around his arm and a thermometer in his mouth. A look of intense professional concern on her face, the Nurse anxiously fussed at the medical kit she had slung around her shoulder. It kept a constant check on the Captain's life signs, and she was often to be seen adjusting a dial here and a setting there.

Mr Fibuli would have loved to have had a look at her device. Not – obviously not – to switch the thing off, but just to be able to see how the Captain was doing. Mind you, right now, he didn't need a monitoring device. The remaining lumps of the Captain's face were purple, and the Polyphase Avatron was marching along his shoulders like they were ramparts. Occasionally the bird would pause and swivel its head round to glare at one of the assembled crew. Everyone looked thoroughly miserable. And the killing hadn't even started yet.

The Captain stood up, waving the Nurse off as she tugged the thermometer from his lips. She backed silently away, smoothing her uniform down, patting her mousy hair into place. She seemed completely at rest, calmly packing away her testing kit. For a moment, a look of alertness flashed over her eyes, one taking in the Captain, the crew and, finally, Mr Fibuli. He blinked, but then she gave him her watered-down smile and melted into the background.

The Captain strode over to the windows, looking out at the two suns, and folded as much of his arms as he had behind his back. For a long time he said nothing.

'Gentlemen, the rogue telepath has not been destroyed,' the Captain began, low and dangerous. 'I ordered that he should be. Instead he has been allowed to fall into the hands of the Mourners. I ordered that he should not be so allowed.' The Captain spun round from the view and glared at his crew. 'Failure is something I find it very hard to come to terms with. Is that not right, Mr Fibuli?'

When someone coughed, Mr Fibuli realised that this was not a rhetorical question. 'Yes sir, that's very true, sir, you do have that difficulty.' Mr Fibuli wished he wasn't quavering quite so much. There was a big smear on one of his glasses and he was fighting the urge to clean the lenses.

'By all the flaming moons of hell, I do suffer from that difficulty. You and I seem to have been having a lot of difficulty today.' The Captain paused to flash a dangerous smile.

Oh dear. Mr Fibuli suddenly realised he was cleaning his lenses without even thinking about it.

'It is not two hours since you very nearly blew up every engine in the mountain and the entire planet with it whilst performing a very straightforward operation which should be second nature to you by now.'

Mr Fibuli placed the glasses back on his nose, and peered through them at the Captain. He really had to protest and very hard. 'Yes sir, but the cause was external. You yourself said that.' He frowned. He seemed to be gibbering. In terms of defiance, this really wasn't that good. 'Something extraordinary happened to the whole fabric of the space-time continuum.'

The Captain was having none of these excuses. 'And have you discovered the cause of that yet, Mr Fibuli?'

'I'm working on it.' Along with a thousand other things.

'Then you have failed to find it, Mr Fibuli?' The Captain flashed a delighted little smirk. 'Failed, failed, failed! We have just discussed my attitude to failure. We decided it was something I had a lot of difficulty accepting, didn't we? Mr Fibuli, when someone fails me, someone dies!'

Mr Fibuli wondered why he'd spent some of the last minutes of his life cleaning his glasses. He could have spent them running away. Or, at the very least, he could have had an altogether smearier view of his impending doom. The people around him didn't exactly all take a step back, but there was a definite shuffling. Distance was being placed between Mr Fibuli and them. One of the Drive Technicians even gave him a rather nasty little smile. I find all this really rather unjust, thought Mr Fibuli, miserably.

With great difficulty, Mr Fibuli stood his ground. The Polyphase Avatron shifted its weight from left claw to right and back again, before taking sudden screeching flight, eyes glowing a vicious red. The Thing was finally coming for him. Mr Fibuli screwed his lids tight shut and hoped that would be the end of it.

He heard the blast, heard himself scream. It seemed curiously detached. His soul had clearly left his own body and was floating away, off to a realm where there were no more orders, demands, paperwork or shouting. A peace washed over him. He had felt no pain. Dying had all been rather pleasant. In fact, he wouldn't mind another go.

Mr Fibuli opened his eyes expecting heaven, and instead saw only disappointment. The body of the smug Drive Technician lay at his feet, the robot parrot squatting on the blasted remains of its face. The creature was even singing to itself. Mr Fibuli had never heard Psalm 23, but if he had, he'd no doubt have appreciated the parrot's rather jaunty take on 'The Lord's My Shepherd'.

Mr Fibuli continued to stare aghast at the body. Were bits of it still twitching? Was the parrot really winking at him?

Reluctantly, he dragged his eyes up from the body to the distant figure of the Captain. The Captain nodded just once.

'So anyway,' he began, as though embarking on the punchline to an anecdote. 'I hope you find the cause of our engine problems very soon, Mr Fibuli. I do hope you will not fail me again.'

'No sir.' Mr Fibuli felt an urgent need to swallow. 'I wouldn't dream of it. Thank you, sir.'

'No, thank *you*,' the Captain purred. The parrot flew back onto his shoulder, and the Captain ran his fingers along its wings. 'Who's a pretty Polyphase Avatron?' he clucked, striding away from the corpse and his aghast crew to settle down in his chair, spinning it around to admire the view.

'Pretty Polyphase Avatron, Pretty Polyphase Avatron,' the bird repeated with a chuckle. It spun its head round to stare at the crew balefully.

Edging quietly back into the room, the Nurse crossed to the Captain's side, smoothing him down. She seemed such a tiny little thing, Mr Fibuli thought. He really didn't know why she put up with him, but she fussed over the Captain like he was a beloved uncle. The Nurse gently took a pulse, checking it against the black box around her neck. Her voice was a low, hesitant whisper that carried across the entire Bridge. 'Captain, if I may offer some advice, I do think you'd find your crew worked better in a more relaxed atmosphere.' She pulled a little face. 'Also, you really must watch your blood pressure.'

The Doctor woke up and for once didn't feel like springing out of bed. He slept rarely, but when he did so, it was purely for the sheer fun of it and the delight of the breakfast that would follow. Sleep helped him cope marvellously with a lifetime of being stunned, rendered comatose or knocked unconscious. He always woke up with the expectation of scrambled eggs.

Instead, just this once, he woke up and felt utterly dejected, as though he was sinking into the nasty silver floor of this wretched little house. The universe felt like nothing more than a desperately unfunny joke, a place that had seen so much suffering it would be the act of a madman to try and count it. It all seemed so cruelly pointless.

K-9 was extending a probe from his forehead, jabbing him with an intensity which the Doctor found an exquisite misery all of its own. The whining of the probe was just horrid. 'Master?' the dog asked.

'What happened to me?' groaned the Doctor. He tried to look around the room, but could barely stand it. Those three fussy natives were standing over him. Also there were a couple of sleeping Guards on the floor. There was no sign of Pralix, poor Pralix, the one person in this whole world who could understand how he felt. 'What hit me?' he asked again, wearily.

Kimus, the arrogant one, spoke. 'It was the Mourners, they did something, I don't know.' Like life, everything Kimus said was pointless.

'I'm not asking you,' the Doctor dismissed him. 'K-9, what hit me?'

'According to my instruments, Master, it was a gestalt-generated psychokinetic blast on a wavelength of 338.79

micropars with interference patterns on 317.06, 259.13 and 15.41 micropars, reaching a peak power level of 5347.2 on the Vantalla Psychoscale.'

'Yes, that's exactly what it felt like,' the Doctor said ruefully, making an effort to sit up and then deciding he'd just look at the ceiling. It was about as miserable as anything else here. He noticed the girl, Mula, was trying to help him, but she looked equally beaten up by existence. Poor thing, he thought, why not come and lie down on the floor next to me and just wait for the ceiling to fall on us?

'What's the Vantalla Psychoscale?' asked the pointless boy pointlessly.

'A measurement of psychokinetic force.' The Doctor flapped a hand and hoped he'd fly away.

'Psychowhat?'

Oh dear. Would it be too much to land on a planet of moderately intelligent people?

'It's the power to move physical objects by mental power alone,' the Doctor muttered. 'Not much is known about it, but 5347.2 on the Vantalla Scale represents the power that will move a single teacup 5,347.2 miles. Or 5,347.2 teacups one mile. Or an entire Gallifreyan ceremonial dinner service 25.462875 miles...'

K-9 made a whirring noise. He was about to dispute the last figure. There were, for a start, 210 teacups in a Gallifreyan tea service, and the Doctor had left out the spoons. The Doctor clamped a hand over the dog's mouth and concentrated on the ceiling very hard. He really was feeling terribly low and needed to find the right trigger to get things started again. Somehow, not even thoughts of buttered soldiers and a three-minute egg were going to cut it this time.

'Pralix is gone!' wailed the old man. 'The Mourners have taken him! My poor grandson.'

Oh, right, that did it. The Doctor sprang to his feet and clapped an arm around Balaton's shoulder. 'Don't worry, old man. We'll find him.'

'If he's alive,' murmured Kimus unhelpfully, provoking fresh groans from Balaton.

'Sure he's alive,' the Doctor beamed, only a little wearily. 'Now, do you have any idea where these Mourner coves hang out?' Perhaps overplaying it just a little there, but never mind. He'd got their attention, and that was all the Doctor needed.

'Well, no,' admitted Kimus. 'They're like ghosts. They just arrive in the city and depart. They're all too frightened to follow them.'

'They? Who's they?'

'The cowardly people of this city,' sneered Kimus.

'You mean you're not too frightened?'

'No! Definitely not!' Kimus struck a defiant pose.

'I see,' the Doctor nodded. 'So, you just never got around to it, is that it?'

Caught, Kimus stopped looking the world in the eye. 'I mean that I will follow them. Today.'

Adoringly, Mula sprang to her feet. 'And so will I!' she shouted, nicely scotching Kimus's plan of saying he was only staying to look after her.

Balaton found this all a bit too much. 'No, Mula, no! Haven't we lost enough already? Pralix is gone, lost, nothing will bring him back from the Mourners, curse their zombie souls.' He sank down onto a couch, and just for once, wished it didn't have solid bronze cushions. 'Oh, don't you understand, Mula. Pralix is dead! Eaten, I shouldn't wonder.'

The Doctor interceded. 'No, he won't be dead. They wanted him too badly to kill him. They needed him. I felt that in the pyscho-blast, a very strong sense of need, of purpose, of trying to find a meaning to the terrible, nagging futility of life…'

Mula didn't hear the last bit. 'If Pralix is alive, then we'll find him. Kimus and I!'

Kimus looked just as alarmed at this as Balaton. 'No,' the old man wailed, 'Do not go after him, Mula. You will only lose your own life.'

'No, I must go, Grandfather.' Mula felt very determined about things. Life had changed in the last hour. She'd realised that Pralix wasn't an annoying, selfish layabout – well, wasn't *just* an annoying, selfish layabout. She was also, for once, being listened to and was making plans. She wasn't going to let this opportunity go. Also, it really wasn't wise to let Kimus actually enact one of his grand ideas. She cared for him very much, but wouldn't let him out alone.

Balaton had, of course, plunged into an epic of mourning. 'Stay, Mula. Isn't it enough for me to lose a son, and then a grandson? All I have left to me is a granddaughter. Must I lose that little too?'

Well, that made Mula's mind up very firmly.

'Listen to the old man,' laughed Kimus, nodding to an entirely imaginary crowd. 'He's afraid he's going to have no one to pamper him in his old age.'

'Oh, Kimus,' sighed Mula. He could be such a pill.

'Respect, Kimus, have some respect,' begged Balaton. 'You don't know what it was like. In the old days…'

The Doctor right then and there, vowed never to go on a long country walk with either of them. And that was before Kimus strutted his way through his next speech. 'Respect? What for? A lifetime of taking the path of least resistance? I'd have more respect for half a pint of water. At least it wouldn't grovel as well. Go hang your respect, and hang your old days.'

Crikey, thought the Doctor. If you invited Kimus round to dinner, he'd forgo bringing a bottle and just turn up with some pamphlets and a wearying list of dietary requirements.

'Master,' prompted K-9. Ah yes. He'd been on about something, hadn't he?

The Doctor decided to take control. Initially of the room, but probably the entire world before the day was out. 'Look,' he began. He'd learned how to say a very firm 'Look'. 'Are you lot going to stand around shouting at each other all day, or are we going to find Pralix?'

'I'm sorry,' said Kimus, abashed. 'Doctor, we're with you.'

'Well, I'm not.' Balaton stood up. 'I don't want any part in this madness. I don't want to hear it.' He favoured them all with a look that managed to balance misery with contempt. 'Mourners! Guards! Madness!' He began the slow, sad shuffle to his room, waving Mula away. The poor girl stood in the hall, not knowing where to turn – to this stranger, to Kimus, or her grandfather.

There was a reason the Doctor avoided domestic drama. It was all so terribly complicated. No, give him a shouting idiot with a diabolical plan any day.

The Doctor watched the old man go to his room, and heard the very firm slam of a heavy lead door. There were some people he could do nothing for. He tried to shake off the terrible despondency thrown over him by the Mourners. Utter despair, and yet also a feeling of regret. How very odd. It was rare that people who attacked him apologised.

'Master,' K-9 announced again.

'Not now, K-9, not now,' the Doctor said automatically. Splendid dog, really spurring him on to action. 'Now, wait a minute – could you track the Mourners by their psychospoor?'

'Affirmative, Master. Psychokinetic energy on that level leaves considerable disturbance in the ether,' the dog replied, and then, for the third time. 'But Master—'

'Good, good,' thundered the Doctor as a splendid plan formed in his head right there and then. He was feeling more himself again. 'Who's coming? Kimus, Mula, Romana…' He frowned. 'K-9, where is Romana? I thought I left her with you.'

'She has been arrested, Master,' K-9 said.

'What?'

'She sent me to inform you of this fact.'

'Then why didn't you?'

An electronic cough. 'This is my fourth attempt.'

'Oh.' The Doctor sucked at the end of his scarf.

Mula laid a gentle hand on the Doctor's shoulder. The poor man – if his friend had been taken by the Captain's Guard, that would be the last he saw of her. This land was terrible. If he really was a stranger then it would be a lot for him to take in. She realised that their chances of rescuing Pralix had suddenly dwindled. This stranger would be prostrated with grief. 'Who is Romana?' she asked the Doctor gently.

'Oh, my assistant,' the Doctor sighed, the exact sigh that Pralix used when asked to tidy his room. 'She's new. Imagine that – getting herself arrested. That's normally my job. Ah well, I suppose we'd better go and bail her out.'

'Bail?'

'When people are released from captivity?' the Doctor prompted.

'No one ever comes back from the Citadel,' Mula said as kindly as possible. There. She'd told him the worst. She waited for the disaster to break.

'Splendid!' The Doctor clapped his hands together. 'Then it looks like we'll have to mount two rescue operations. Romana's very important,' he said.

Mula nodded.

'Well, she has some very important equipment of mine on her as well,' the Doctor added.

Mula eyed him narrowly. He had a very odd relationship with his friend.

'This Citadel…' began the Doctor, a new plan forming already. 'No one ever comes back from there?'

'No one,' Kimus sneered. 'Except the Guards.'

'Splendid!' The Doctor smiled. 'Then let's get some Guards.'

*

110

Meanwhile, Romana was several hundred feet up in the air and unconscious. The way it happened was roughly thus:

The Guards who had arrested her had dragged her through the town, and they had enjoyed this immensely. The Doctor had warned her that 'regular drubbings were only to be expected in our line of (haha) work', but Romana had put that down to there being something about the Doctor that just made aliens want to hit him. That kind of thing would, she thought, never happen to her.

As she was bumped and pushed through town she found herself thinking of words like 'manhandling' and 'roughhousing' and wondering what kind of treatment the postal system on this planet meted out to its parcels.

They reached a square where a rather quaint air-car sat atop a pile of emerald gravel. One of the Guards shoved her towards it.

'Stop that at once,' commanded Romana.

The Guard stopped that at once.

'I am perfectly capable of getting in myself, thank you,' she said. 'And don't expect a tip.'

She stepped lightly up and settled herself onto the bench at the front of the air-car, and patted the cushion beside her. One of the Guards clambered in, glowering at her.

'Now then,' offered Romana pleasantly. 'Will you drive or shall I? I assume you know where we're going?'

The Guard looked at her and then at his companion on the ground, whose shrug clearly said, 'She's all yours.'

The air-car lifted off and slid towards the mountain.

'Ah,' sighed Romana happily. 'Antimagnatronic propulsion. I had an air-car rather like this once. It was a present for my 70th birthday. Do you know that if you realign the magnetic vector and fit a polarity oscillator you get twice the speed for half the energy?'

The Guard blinked.

His prisoner smiled at him, ever so sweetly. 'You should try it some time,' continued Romana. 'It's really quite simple when you put your mind to it.'

The Guard pushed the comms system. 'Guard 3…' his voice crackled. '3VX to Bridge. Come in, please.' His voice sounded pleading. 'Please come in…'

'Of course,' continued the prisoner, 'if it's beyond you, then I'd be thrilled to have a go at it for you, if you'd like?'

The Guard realised his hands were gripping the steering control very hard. He frowned, and casually clubbed Romana across the shoulder.

Failing completely to flinch, Romana narrowed her eyes. 'You're quite obviously suffering from an excess of unsublimated aggression, do you know that? Tell me, do you have potatoes here? On Gallifrey now, that's where I come from, I'm a sort of Time Lord you see, they've just started a new law that anyone who has to carry a weapon as part of their normal work has to spend at least forty minutes a day punching a sack of potatoes to work off their surplus aggression – and do you know it works terribly well? Of course some of them cheat by shooting the potatoes but—'

At this point, there was a thud, a sigh, and the air-car flew on in silence.

CHAPTER TEN
THE KINGS OF ALDERBARAN III MAKE A DECISION

The Doctor and Mula had dragged the stunned Guards into the street. 'They'll be better off there. You don't want them cluttering up your living room, do you?' the Doctor had said.

He now stood in the hallway, watched closely by Kimus and Mula. He pulled a coin from his pocket.

'What's that?' asked Kimus.

'A coin. It's a… well, it's a unit of currency. Some planets are terribly boring and demand that you pay for things. You can do it with a coin. It's a token of value made of cheap alloys.'

Kimus nodded. 'I see. We simply give each other lumps of gold.' He sounded rather proud of that.

'Well yes,' the Doctor nodded. 'But the really handy thing about coins is that they have a head on one side and a tail of sorts on the other. Great for making your mind up. Heads we go after

Romana first, tails we go after Pralix.' He flipped the coin. 'Ah. Heads. Romana it is.'

Mula wasn't impressed. 'But that was a very serious decision. How can you leave it to chance like that?'

The Doctor shrugged. 'They have two kings on Alderbaran III.' He flashed the coin. On one side the head of King Eshak Prim, on the other King Balash Quoir. 'They ruled a hemisphere each for 320 days, then swapped, taking care not to meet as they crossed.'

Mula didn't seem terribly interested in the politics of distant star systems. She seemed rather more outraged about the fate of her brother. 'That's not fair,' she said.

'Oh yes it is.' The Doctor spun the coin a few more times. 'If my guess is right, Romana is in far greater danger than Pralix, and I am *in loco parentis* for her, you see, so I have to start acting more responsibly. If anything happens to her, the White Guardian will be terribly cross with me, and then the universe would probably end. So, how do we get to the Citadel? Can one just walk?'

'No!' Mula looked him firmly in the eyes. 'I'm going after Pralix. I'll find my own way.'

The Doctor tried to tell her about the dangers she'd face, the risks she'd have to take, but she just carried on looking at him. Odd, really, the way that she just refused to blink. Her entire face shone with determination and general splendidness. The Doctor risked a look at her ankles. They were encouragingly sturdy. Excellent.

The Doctor harrumphed, and bent over K-9. 'Dog, now listen to me carefully. I'm putting Mula in your charge. Take her to the Mourners. Look after her, is that understood?'

K-9 wagged his tail seriously. 'Affirmative.'

'Good dog.'

K-9 trundled over to Mula, his nose pointing firmly towards the door. He was clearly keen to be off.

Mula smiled gratefully at him.

'I'm going with Mula as well,' announced Kimus.

Mula's smile faded a little.

'She needs me!' he said. 'She needs protecting.'

The Doctor and Mula pulled a face at each other.

'Ah, Kimus, if only I could spare you.' The Doctor shook his head. 'But I need you more,' he intoned very, very seriously, with only the tiniest of winks in Mula's direction. He steered Kimus out into the street before he could protest. 'Don't do anything I wouldn't do!' the Doctor called back to Mula. 'I'll follow you later.' He turned to Kimus. 'I hate people who say things like that, don't you?'

'Like what?' asked Kimus.

'"Don't do anything I wouldn't do."'

'Then why do you say it?' Kimus was baffled.

'I don't know, really. Just to see what it's like. Come on, let's go and rescue Romana.'

Mula stood watching the figures of the Doctor and Kimus vanishing into the city. Now it was up to her. If she had the courage.

The door to Balaton's room opened and he poked a worried, desolate head out. 'Oh, Mula! Mula! Don't go!' he called in a piteous wail.

'We'll be back soon, Grandfather,' she said firmly, and, with K-9 at her side, went off to rescue her brother.

Out on the streets, Kimus the Revolutionary became Kimus the Mumbler. The Doctor had met his fair share of rebel leaders, and Kimus did not, it had to be said, look promising. Some required a fair deal of coaching, and the Doctor was normally only too happy to lay on a wide-ranging syllabus taking in speech-making, the importance of not executing your enemies, and even logo design. Che had just needed a pep-talk and some T-shirt printing. But Kimus was at the other end of the scale. Really, at heart, Kimus just wanted a nice second-hand bookshop that would provide him with shelter from the rain, and free mugs of tea. Perhaps, if he was lucky, they'd even let him hand out flyers for the rebellious slam poetry event he curated in their basement every third Tuesday.

The Doctor smiled to himself. Kimus did not look promising material, but the young man had to do something before Mula saw through him. He decided to take Kimus under his wing. That never failed.

As the Doctor strode whistling through the city, Kimus skulked. The Doctor would point out interesting architecture, or guffaw at some really ill-advised bit of ostentation, such as the house pebble-dashed with diamonds. The latter was a curious feature – surely in a binary system, by mid-afternoon the light from both suns would be concentrated through the gemstones and start a small fire in the living room.

'How very odd,' he said.

Kimus kept staring at his feet.

They reached an empty square. The whole of the city felt empty, like a Spanish town in the middle of the afternoon. If people were awake, they were pretending not to be.

From here, you could get a nice view up the mountain to the remarkably strange castle on top of it.

'That's the Citadel,' said Kimus, confirming the Doctor's suspicions.

'How do you get up to it?' The Doctor looked around, hoping for a funicular railway. He loved those.

'You don't,' Kimus mumbled firmly. 'At least anyone who's been there hasn't come back.'

'I see.' The Doctor regarded the building severely. 'One of those jobs, is it? So how does anyone get up there in order to not come back?'

'Well, the Guards go up in their air-cars of course…' conceded Kimus.

'Air-cars!' The Doctor loved an air-car even more than a funicular railway. He'd once owned an air-car, mostly for the sheer delightful jealousy it evoked on the North Circular Road. 'What air-cars?'

'There's one over there.' Kimus pointed to an opening at the end of the next street.

They walked on, drawing into a little courtyard. There, resting on a pad made out of completely impractical lead, was a small, very shiny air-car. A Guard was dozing gently inside it. It was an almost bucolic picture.

'Ah,' the Doctor smiled. 'That looks like the answer. I think we'd better steal it, don't you?'

'Steal it?' The sheer heresy nearly dropped Kimus on the spot. 'It belongs to the Captain!'

'I know,' grinned the Doctor. 'Aren't we being wicked?'

The Guard woke up. The worst thing about a New Golden Age of Prosperity was that there was an awful lot of standing around to do. First you had to stand around telling the populace the good news, then you had to stand around and ensure that they were sufficiently happy about the good news, then you had to stand around while they sorted through the piles of Prosperity arriving on the streets, and make sure that no fights broke out over a particularly rare mineral.

Then there were the food riots. Some bright spark was always standing on a street corner saying, 'We can't eat gold, can we?' Once the Captain had made one of the protesters do just that. He'd afterwards claimed he'd meant it as a joke and had been horrified that it had been carried out, but then the Captain was always like that.

One of the few relaxing bits about a Golden Age of Prosperity was the chance to look after an air-car. They were always needed to ferry protesters high up into the air, taking them all the way to the Citadel. Or sometimes not quite all the way.

A thud woke the Guard up. Something had landed on the front of the air-car. He glanced up automatically, ready to protect himself in case there was another shower of Molybdenum. But the skies were clear. Whatever it was that had landed on the bonnet, it wasn't what he was expecting. It seemed to be small. The Guard watched it slowly slide along the air-car and then drop to the floor. Only at this point did he realise that it was probably an impact grenade. He flinched, but there was no explosion.

Curious, he clambered down from the air-car and went to look at the ground, trying to find the package. On closer inspection it looked like a small paper bag. This was new. The Guard was not entirely sure he cared for new things. Even if a protest group had learned how to make a grenade, they'd be unlikely to wrap it in paper.

He reached for the bag, and poked it. Nothing happened. He picked the bag up. As he did so, its contents scattered in a rainbow-coloured array across the metal platform. The Guard flinched in bafflement and then threw himself out of the way as the air-car suddenly roared off from the landing pad, with a long scarf trailing behind it.

Inside the air-car, the Doctor gave the puzzled Guard beneath a cheery wave. 'You know that actually makes me feel guilty? Poor fellow, shouldn't be out on the streets by himself. I never like shooting fish in a barrel.'

As the air-car flew higher, Kimus felt his whole world spinning away. 'What was that you threw? Some deadly weapon?'

'No.' The Doctor rifled in his pocket, throwing them into a small spin. 'Just a bag of jelly babies. Don't worry. I've got plenty more. Would you like one?' Clinging on for dear life, Kimus took one of the sweets, but was just too terrified to swallow it.

Mr Fibuli knew that today he would die. Right now. Within five minutes he would be dead. Finally, certainly dead. He knew this because the next words out of his mouth were: 'Captain, sir. I'm afraid I bring bad news, sir!'

A hush fell across the bridge, one so complete you could hear the thermometer dropping from the Captain's mouth. It rolled away, to be picked up by the Nurse with a tut. She favoured Mr Fibuli with a particularly icy glare as she pocketed it. He felt a sudden, silly urge to stick his tongue out at her back. Why not? To his own amazement, he did.

A stifled chuckle rewarded him. He looked around. It seemed to have come from the Captain. But that was impossible. The Captain was glaring at him, thrashing around furiously in his chair.

'Bad news? Bad news! By all the… all the…' He was roaring. The Nurse hurried over to calm him, but his flailing shoulder nudged her back. He staggered to his feet like a drunk, leaning forward so quickly that Mr Fibuli worried for a moment that he'd topple onto him and crush him. He wasn't the only one – the Polyphase Avatron flew up to the ceiling, squawking. It did not help that it was squawking, 'You're dead, you're dead.' But then again, nothing that Thing ever did helped.

The Captain rocked to an unsteady balance, his face flushed, sparks fizzing from his eyepatch. The cold metal tip of his stubby squared-off nose pressed against Mr Fibuli's. He could smell the Captain's breath, which was an odd blend of cloves and diesel oil.

'By the horns of the Prophet Balag, speak, Mr Fibuli,' grated the Captain. 'Speak! Tell us your latest Bad News.'

'Well sir, we have not yet… not yet discovered what it was that caused our accident, sir, but we think it may—'

'May?' the Captain snorted.

'May well have been an unidentified materialisation within our own field.' The words poured out of Mr Fibuli like blood. 'That would be very much consistent with the evidence, even just a meteorite slipping out of hyperspace at that moment could have caused it – but the point is, sir, that we have discovered some more damage.'

The controlled iciness of the Captain's stare pulled him up for a moment, but he licked his lips and carried on. 'The Macromat Field Integrator has burnt out, sir.'

The Macro Materialisation Field Generator & Integrator had been bought off-the-shelf, much against the Captain's advice. But, as he had been told, time was running out, and corners needed to be cut. So, the heavy lifting of creating a field allowing the stable integration of a very large object into normal space was handed over to a bunch of engineers the Captain wouldn't ordinarily have bothered to toss into the Fires of Rigel. The same bunch of cowboys had also taken care of three other bits of work: the air-conditioning system; the inertial dampeners; and the frankly unsatisfactory Wi-Fi. Having taken a vast amount of the Zanak's money, the company promptly vanished.

Mr Fibuli confirmed the Captain's worst suspicions. 'I'm afraid the Macromat Field Integrator is one of the four components we can't replace ourselves.'

Mr Fibuli finished his speech and was rather surprised to find himself still alive at the end of it. He just couldn't understand how he'd managed to get so far. He decided to be rather fatalistic about these things and just plod on.

'We are faced with two alternatives, Captain. Well, three alternatives. We can try to find a new Macromat Field Integrator, though I can't envisage how we would do that, at this present time, sir. Alternatively there is a very rare mineral, PJX18, which could conceivably do the same job as the Integrator if we could find any. Either way, sir, in our current condition we could only possibly make one more jump, and even that would be risky in the extreme, sir, so it would have to be The Right Jump.'

The Captain stiffened with alarm. The Nurse rushed to his side. Fibuli noticed she seemed equally alarmed. As well she should.

Fibuli knew his news was a stinker. He'd be amazed if the Captain was satisfied with just his body. He'd always thought the Nurse's survival remarkable. Maybe, just maybe, Fibuli would get to see her go before him. That would be something.

'And what is the third alternative, Mr Fibuli?' asked the Captain, his voice echoing across the Bridge. 'By the seven suns of Orion man, the third alternative?'

Mr Fibuli took his last breath. 'It is for Zanak to settle where it is, sir.'

The Captain roared at Mr Fibuli. 'No by the Sky Demon!' His arm roared up to strike. 'No by the eleven moons of madness!' His arm sliced down towards Mr Fibuli. 'No by the Skies of Hell, I say no!'

The blow connected. There was a loud pop.

Mr Fibuli opened his eyes. The Captain's arm had buried itself in a console, his remaining human hand jumping limply around among the sparking electrical components. The pain should have been, must have been excruciating, and yet the Captain continued to drive his hand further into the mess.

Mr Fibuli stared in horror.

Very oddly, instead of rushing to help, the Nurse stood rooted to the spot, checking her little black box. She almost seemed to smile.

Mr Fibuli rushed to help, but the Captain's other shoulder shoved him to one side. The Captain roared as his arm thrashed about amongst the electrical fire, sparks flying from the circuits around his body. The shout echoed with frustration, fury, and complete pain.

The arm reared up and smashed further down into the smoking wreckage, and the Captain roared again.

It was at this point that the door opened, and Romana encountered her very first diabolical mastermind.

'Hey, this is marvellous!'

The one dog-like thing that K-9 sadly never did was stick his head out the window. The Doctor thought that was a shame. The TARDIS spinning on its way somewhere or other it wasn't supposed to be, and K-9 poking his head into the Time Vortex. And probably sniffing disdainfully. Ah, K-9.

Instead, the Doctor was sharing an air-car with Kimus, and the young man was a giddy riot of enthusiasm.

'This is freedom at last!' he cried, his head swaying, leaning over from one side of the air-car to the other, chewing happily away on the last few jelly babies from the bag the Doctor had given him.

'You're not free yet, not by a long way.' The Doctor found it all rather distracting while he was trying to steer. Kimus's feeling of independence was probably mixed with a sugar rush.

'I'm free to think!' Kimus wriggled himself over the windshield, leaning down to look at the City beneath them. He looked back at the Doctor, desperate for approval. 'Everything looks small and pretty from up here. The city and, oh look, the mines, the processing plants... Oh this is living, this is really living! Do you know how claustrophobic life is down there?' He pointed at the little buildings, twinkling away in the sunlight. 'We're being stifled with a rich silk pillow. Do your bit of work, operate the mines, the processing plants, the factories, and everything is yours, fine houses, rich clothes, jewels, plenty, plenty, nothing but relentless plenty.' The Doctor got the feeling that Kimus had aired this material before. 'But you'd better keep smiling, oh yes, because if you once stop to ask where it all comes from they take you away and kill you. What kind of life is that for a growing lad? And yet, ohhh...' He pointed delightedly at a little street. 'Isn't that something? Just something. Have we traded in our freedom for that? Is it worth it? Ooh, look at the pretty mountain.'

The Doctor wondered if the suddenly thin atmosphere was making the young man lightheaded. He wondered if the air-car could go any higher. It was all rather like stumbling into a student bar. 'Now listen to me Kimus, and listen to me carefully,' declaimed the Doctor. 'There is evil on this world…'

'Evil?' the young man asked dazedly. 'But what is it? What's happening?'

'That's what I've got to find out, with your help. These mines –' the Doctor picked the word that had interested him – 'tell me about the mines.'

'Well, we extract all the raw material we need from the mines. It's all terribly efficient.'

'Who goes down them? Do you?'

'Us! No fear. It's all automated, we just run the equipment.' Kimus looked frankly horrified at the thought of getting his hands dirty. 'They never stop going.'

'And what happens when the mines run empty?'

'Oh well…' Kimus shrugged. 'The Captain just announces a new Golden Age of Prosperity, and they fill up again.'

The Doctor nearly plunged the air-car into a tailspin.

'Whee!' exclaimed Kimus.

'They fill up?' The Doctor spoke slowly. 'Just like that?'

'Well yes.' Kimus frowned. 'Are you saying that's wrong?'

'Wrong? It's an economic miracle. Of course it's wrong.'

'Oh, and then, of course, the lights change,' muttered Kimus dreamily.

'Of course?' The air was cold, they were flying in a nice straight line towards the mountain, the suns beat down around them and the Doctor was experiencing a terrible chill which had nothing to do with the atmosphere.

'There'll be new ones tonight,' Kimus said happily.

'What lights?' The Doctor's hand gripped the steering wheel tightly.

'Oh you know.' Kimus frowned, baffled. He pointed up. 'The ones in the sky at night time, the little points of light.'

'You mean the stars?'

'Uh-huh,' said Kimus vaguely, confirming the Doctor's worst fears. 'Stars, eh? Is that what you call them? Fancy,' Kimus continued. 'Yes, they keep putting up new ones. Seems pointless to me but the old people do seem to like it.'

'Do they indeed?' sighed the Doctor. 'Does no one in the galaxy take any interest in the worlds around them?' An advanced, Level 4-ish civilisation with no concept of astronomy. Bonkers. The Doctor decided he should make quite sure. 'Kimus, have you the remotest idea what stars actually are?'

Kimus looked around, a little bit bored by the question. 'Well, they're decorations of some sort aren't they? I'd never really thought about it. Is it important?' A thought struck him. 'Can we zoom up and touch one?'

'Oh never mind. I'll send you a planetarium some day.' The Doctor angled them towards the approaching Citadel.

'What's a planetarium?' Kimus wrinkled his nose.

'A museum for studying planets,' said the Doctor.

'Planets?' Kimus asked. 'What are planets?'

The thin purply clouds passed above them.

'What you're saying,' the Doctor concluded, 'is that you've never been allowed to think about these things. And that's worrying.'

'In what way?'

'Well, it's a matter of joining up the dots. In this case, the little dots in the sky. Every time they change, all your mines miraculously refill themselves with raw materials…'

'So?' shrugged Kimus.

They flew on in silence for a bit. When the Doctor spoke, he sounded very old. 'I've just had a very, very nasty idea. If I'm right, Kimus, you are living on top of the greatest crime the galaxy has ever known.'

'Oh really?' Kimus politely tried to listen to the Doctor, but was distracted by the view again. 'Look, down there. There's some sort of entranceway in the side of the mountain! I think that's the way to the Bridge.'

The Doctor, without even seeming to notice, angled the air-car into a smooth dive.

'Hey, you're very good at that.' Kimus bounced in his seat. 'Do you drive these things for a living?'

'No.' The Doctor was grim. 'I save planets mostly. This time I think I've arrived here too late. Far, far too late.'

CHAPTER ELEVEN
THE FASTEST CORRIDOR

Romana's first impression was that the Captain was something a madman might have made. Given a pile of body parts, half an hour, and an old cyborg or washing machine, and he'd have pulled back a dust cloth and with a cheery 'ta-da!' unveiled the Captain. The creature looked absolutely disgusting and terribly pathetic.

The Time Lords of Gallifrey were lucky. If they were injured or maimed, they didn't have to bother with replacement limbs. They could simply regenerate their entire bodies. Romana was rather looking forward to the process (she was already wondering what she'd do with her hair). On the other hand, the rest of the universe wasn't so lucky.

When ordinary people broke, they were forced to make do and mend, patching themselves up with all sorts of spare parts and synthetic limbs. This was normally done with a great amount of sensitivity, or by the Cybermen. But even the Cybermen had retained some aesthetic sense. What was most appalling about the Captain was the shambolic end result.

Anyone, surely would have looked at this and gone, 'Perhaps we'll have another go?' But no. Someone had decided that this would do. Worse, someone had decided that this grisly, piebald concoction of man and machine was both functional and frightening. Romana found her eyes both wanting to look away and also to look more, to try and work out where the joins were. Her main worry was about the occupant of the suit – the Captain wasn't so much a body as a shell. Anyone who'd suffered the kind of injuries he'd suffered would need an intensive amount of therapy, even if he'd been gifted with an immaculate set of artificial limbs. But whoever had done this had clearly not given a hoot about what the Captain felt. He must be in constant pain and anger.

Someone had just thought, 'Well, this'll do.' Romana innately despised people who thought that.

The Captain pulled his burnt hand from the sparking console. He strode over towards her. As he walked, she detected the whining, mistimed servos of his leg, the fizz of loose wiring, the smell of dirty grease, and a whiff of bacon wrapped in septic surgical dressings. The Captain came to a shambling halt in front of her. Romana was terribly aware that this creature could have immediately crushed her, but her fear was mixed with something else.

The Captain pointed a horridly burnt hand at her. 'Speak, girl!'

'Yes?' Romana said politely. 'What about?'

The ghost of a smile twitched at the half of a mouth. 'Who are you that you dare to intrude upon my ship?'

'Your ship?' Romana's suspicions were confirmed. 'You mean this Citadel is your ship?' Her brain formed a hypothesis – the Captain's ship had at some point crashed into the mountain. Both the ship and the Captain had been rebuilt. Sort of. By people who did not necessarily know what they were doing. Such people were, Romana knew from looking long and hard at the Doctor, potentially very dangerous.

'The Citadel?' The Captain hissed a hydraulic sigh. 'By the mountains of Hell, I will not ask you again, but obliterate you where you stand. Your name, girl.'

'Romanadvoratrelundar.'

'You jest with me.'

'No, really it is. Actually, it's the Lady Romanadvoratrelundar,' Romana announced grandly. She glanced around at the Captain's crew. Disappointingly, no one clapped. 'Well, you did ask. My friends call me Romana, but I think you're going to have to call me Romanadvoratrelundar. Tell me, have you had an accident?'

'Silence!' the Captain seethed.

'I only ask because whoever patched you up obviously didn't know anything about the new developments in Cyboneutralics. Or the old developments, for that matter. Do you get a squeak when you move your arm?'

'Silence!' screamed the Captain, pointing his arm furiously at her. It emitted a squeak which echoed across the Bridge. 'Silence, or the silence of death descends on you in the winking of an eye.'

Oh really? Romana was beginning to see why the Doctor couldn't take these types entirely seriously. I mean, clearly, they were capable of doing terrible things and causing immense cruelty, but all the shouting was quite tiresome.

The silly robot bird on the Captain's shoulder opened one of its glowing red eyes and chirruped. Romana paid it not the slightest bit of attention. She had thinking to do.

The Captain took Romana's cool consideration for silent capitulation. 'Now, child, how have you come to this planet?'

'Child? I'm older than I look.'

'Aren't we all.' The Captain's voice softened, almost twinkling with mystery. 'How have you come here?'

'I rather think that's my business.' Romana smiled sweetly.

A beam blasted from the robot bird's eyes, destroying a chair beside her. Romana affected not to pay it any attention, although the smell of burning foam was rather disagreeable.

'How came you here? Speak or die!'

The problem with the Captain, Romana posited, was that he was both literally and figuratively lacking in gears. An endless juxtaposition of syntagmatic binary absolutes with little leeway as to practical compromise boded rather badly for his project management skills. On the other hand, there seemed no point in dying just because of a syntax error.

'I came by TARDIS.'

'TARDIS? What is this TARDIS? By the ninety names of hell!'

'It's my craft.' Romana hadn't yet had the Doctor's lecture on saying as little as possible. 'I'm a sort of Time Lord, you see. Not actually a proper Time Lord yet because I've still got some exams to take, and all the dinners as well, which are terribly dull, but…'

'By the mealy-mouthed prophet of Agranjagzak, speak plainly! For by the Alpha Storms of Cygnus, obliteration is at hand.' He gestured at her with his arm again. It squeaked once more.

Romana winced sympathetically. 'See, it does make a frightful noise, doesn't it? Now, if you got a handsome set of the new frictionless bearings, well…'

'I will not ask you again!' The Captain cradled the mechanical arm protectively. 'What is your function?'

'Sorry, yes, plain speaking. Of course.' Romana's apology was so abjectly sincere that three of the watching Drive Technicians had to turn away and look very hard at an oscilloscope. 'Well, I, as a Time Lord, or a nearly Time Lord, travel around in space…'

'Ah,' declaimed the Captain. 'Just a common space urchin. Pah! You will die.'

Pah? Thought Romana. Really? She played her trump card. 'And I can also travel in time. Hence, Time Lord.'

'Time?' laughed the Captain. 'You expect me to listen to such nonsense? Travel in time? How is this possible?'

Romana clucked with sympathy. 'Yes, it is a difficult concept, isn't it?'

Had he been watching and scoring proceedings, the Doctor would have applauded while being worried that she'd overplayed her serve.

The Captain tottered towards her with badly oiled fury. 'The insolent breath of idle fantasy! Death Comes Now!'

The robot parrot launched itself from the Captain's shoulder, circled and then dived towards Romana, squawking, 'Death! Death! Death!' with a malignantly tinny delight. Romana debated whether to face death nobly or duck behind a desk. She also figured it was hard to be dignified when you were about to be executed by a robot parrot. What would her tutor have made of it?

The thing bore down on her and she grimaced.

A fussy little man came running forward at a crouching run, flapping a clipboard at the parrot, and clearly keen to convey his point while keeping out of the line of fire. 'Captain, sir, if what she says is true, then perhaps she will have knowledge that can help us?'

'True?' the Captain roared. 'What can a puny slip of a girl know of such matters?'

Thanks a million, thought Romana. 'Do you know, that's exactly what my tutor used to say. He didn't enjoy giving me a Triple First at all.'

The Captain snapped his metal fingers. 'She's just a trespassing urchin. Kill her!'

The Avatron finished its circle and then dived.

At this point, the figure of the Captain's Nurse appeared on the Bridge, smoothing down her crisp, pale green uniform and wagging a stern finger. The bird stopped in mid-air, and perched on the Nurse's shoulder.

Romana regarded the new arrival with some surprise. The starched uniform, the meek attitude, all seemed strangely out of place, and yet very welcome. How nice to find the Citadel wasn't just full of shouting men.

The Nurse spoke gently, but with authority. 'Captain,' she said in very soothing tones. 'Captain, do forgive me interrupting but the excitement of more than one execution in a day is bad for your blood pressure, and I really think you should consider postponing it till tomorrow for health reasons.'

'Postpone?' The Captain's voice was that of a sulky child sent to bed without any supper. His lip quivered.

'I really do think it best,' the Nurse said.

'Purulent pulsars,' the Captain muttered.

'Besides...' The Nurse seemed to actually notice Romana for the first time and favoured her with a surprisingly charming smile. 'A time travelling visitor from beyond the stars? I think her story sounds quite interesting even if it is idle fantasy. Why don't you ask her how this machine she mentions travels?' She turned back to Romana, coaxingly. 'You will tell him, won't you?'

On the whole, Romana rather thought she would. Romana approved of the Nurse. She was a model example of how bullying and bluster was no match for logic and courtesy. The Nurse gestured with her hand, and the robot bird fluttered back to its perch on the Captain's shoulder. Finding herself reluctantly the centre of attention, the Nurse grimaced meekly, and stepped to one side.

If the Captain had been cowed by the Nurse's well-meant intervention, he was clearly too magnanimous to show it. 'Speak your fantasy!' he snapped at Romana.

Ah well, she thought. 'Roughly speaking, and putting it terribly simply, the TARDIS dematerialises in this dimension, passes through the Space-Time Vortex and then rematerialises again in a new location.'

She waited for her words to sink in. The Drive Technicians were staring at her. The man with the clipboard was gaping. The Captain appeared to be trying to frown.

'Ooh.' The Nurse's voice came floating through the quiet. 'I think that sounds jolly interesting. Don't you, Captain?'

The Captain glared at the Nurse with barely suppressed fury. The Nurse lowered her eyes and stepped back into the shadows. As she did so, the fussy little man rushed forward excitedly. 'Captain! That might mean that—'

The fury snapped from the Captain's face, and he suddenly favoured the entire Bridge with a radiant, smug little grin. Again, Romana was reminded of a little child offered a sweetie.

'Mr Fibuli, I am light years ahead of you,' glowed the Captain. He patted at the burnt-out chair, gestured for Romana to take a seat on it. 'Space urchin, do sit down, we have much to discuss.'

'You mean you're not going to put me to death just yet?' asked Romana brightly, perching on the least charred bit of chair.

'Your reprieve is conditional on the truth of your story,' the Captain shrugged with a clank.

'Oh good.' She straightened out the folds of her dress, looking in vain for her rescuer. 'I happen to agree with your Nurse. Executions are bad for you. I would hate to be the cause of increasing your blood pressure. One of those joints might blow at any moment.'

K-9 had led Mula out of the City and into the desert. The two of them walked quickly and silently. Mula did not bother K-9 with questions, and K-9 did not offer her his opinion. Both were, as much as either could enjoy anything, rather enjoying the walk.

Yes, Mula thought as she trudged over a dune, Pralix may have been kidnapped, but she had every faith that K-9 would help her find him. Let Grandfather rot in his golden house. She was going to rescue her brother, and the Doctor and Kimus had actually gone to the Citadel for a showdown with the Captain. Kimus had been right – change was coming to Zanak.

K-9, meanwhile, was simply delighted at how efficiently he was traversing the sand. Perhaps, if the occasion arose, he would compliment the Doctor-Master on his new traction engine. It was proving forty-two per cent more effective than the previous version. They carried on into the desert in silence.

The air-car had landed a long way up the mountain on a smooth plateau dotted with snow. Far beneath them lay the desert and the shimmering city. Ahead of them was a door, painted the same colour as the rock. That was as far as camouflage went because it was a very secure door.

Kimus was pleased to have knowledge to advance, or, at the very least, quite exciting hearsay. 'This is it!' He tapped the door, neatly proving to the Doctor that it wasn't electrified. 'This is definitely it, I remember hearing it mentioned now, the Doorway into the Forbidden Mountain. Some of the citizens have found it whilst wandering on the slopes.' He paused, relishing delivering the punchline to the story. 'It's quite impossible to open, of course.'

'Impossible? Oh dear.' The Doctor's face fell. 'That means it's probably going to take at least 73 seconds, 73 seconds which we can ill afford.' He rapped the door firmly and resoundingly.

Kimus tried hard to hide his disappointment. They'd already come quite far enough for a good, heroic anecdote. *'My brothers – we are not alone. Aliens came to free us. The Captain imprisoned them, but I went to lead the storming of the Citadel. Sadly, to no avail – the Great Doorway into the Forbidden Mountain (yes, I have touched it with my fingertips) cruelly thwarted us. We could do no more than listen as the screams beyond it grew fainter. But one day, ah yes, one day, we shall prevail against the Captain. Is there a drop more in that bottle of turnip ale?'*

The Doctor had ruined all that. 'You mean you can open it?' Kimus asked doubtfully.

'Open it?' huffed the Doctor. 'Of course I can open it, it's just a question of how.' His fingertips ran gently across the door's surface.

'How?' asked Kimus.

'I've no idea.' The Doctor shrugged, not at all worried. He'd managed to open a very tiny hatch which contained a stubborn-looking lock. With a grin, he produced the sonic screwdriver, which had opened everything from Henry VIII's dungeons to an MFI wardrobe. He waved it over the lock. Nothing happened.

'Nothing happened!' exclaimed Kimus, with unnecessary glee.

The Doctor had been on the receiving end of several lifetimes' worth of distinctly un-wide-eyed amazement. Kimus had a lot to learn. Seemingly improvising wildly, the Doctor dug about in his pockets and pulled out a small bit of metal that, if you'd asked him, he would have claimed had once belonged to Marie Antoinette.

'Bent hairpin,' he announced and plunged it into the door. With a click, the door slid back into the rock face.

Kimus stared at him with amazement. 'How did you do that?'

The Doctor shrugged. 'The more sophisticated the technology, the more vulnerable it is to primitive attack. People always overlook the obvious. That's why the cleverest thing to be is simpleminded, like me. Shall we go in?'

Kimus wanted nothing more than to run off down the mountain, but the Doctor had already stepped inside. With little choice, he trotted glumly after him.

Inside the doorway they were confronted by an endless corridor.

'A corridor!' exclaimed Kimus, excitedly.

'Um,' said the Doctor. He'd seen loads.

'Gosh, there must be miles of it!'

'Yes I know,' grunted the Doctor. He really couldn't get worked up about an abundance of corridor. Especially one that went on in such a rigidly straight line with no doors. It looked thoroughly boring.

Sadly, Kimus had found a burst of radical enthusiasm. 'Guess we'd best get a move on.' He smiled nervously. 'No point in hanging about, is there? We'd better get running.'

The Doctor was rarely in the mood for running down corridors. 'Wait a minute,' he cautioned. 'I'm thinking about it,'

'Oh, think, think, think!' sneered Kimus with all of his new-found courage. 'I thought you wanted to rescue your friend, and I want to have a go at the Captain. You can catch me up!'

He plunged off down the corridor, running very fast.

The Doctor watched for a while, pulling a paper bag from his pocket, unwrapping and then sucking slowly on a boiled sweet.

Kimus was running very fast and going nowhere. His feet kept moving, but completely failed to gain any friction on the surface. He was, in effect, running on the spot, if not a couple of microns above it.

Kimus realised that something was wrong. He looked at his pedalling feet and then back at the Doctor. 'Hey, what's happening? This floor doesn't work.'

The Doctor reached out and pulled Kimus out of the corridor. He stood, panting at the edge of it, as perplexed as a family pet. The Doctor admired enthusiasm, especially misplaced enthusiasm, but really felt he had to step in.

'What's wrong with this corridor?'

'Kimus, I want you to do something very important for me.'

Kimus, distracted by the gravity of the Doctor's tone, nodded glumly.

'You like guns, don't you?'

'Do I!' Kimus brightened.

'Good. I want you to go to the air-car, fetch one of the guns…'

'Yes?'

'And stand guard at the doorway. We're probably going to need to get back out of here in a hurry.'

'You're going down there without me, aren't you?' Kimus's face fell. 'But, Doctor, can't I come with you?'

The Doctor toyed with explaining to Kimus the fundamental problem that it was practically impossible to use a method of transport you didn't believe in. Then he simply appealed to his ego. 'I'm sorry Kimus, but it's the most valuable thing you can do at the moment. There are many things here you cannot possibly understand. And a linear induction corridor is one of them.'

'You can explain it to me.'

The Doctor shook his head. 'Later. They also serve who only stand and wait, you know.' He rapped at a button on the wall and then strode into the corridor.

Kimus watched in amazement as the Doctor was whisked away from him at a remarkable speed. He darted after him but nothing happened. He jabbed at the button, but again, nothing happened. The Doctor had by now receded to a distant point of light, waving vaguely.

Kimus sighed, went to find a gun, and practised shooting rocks.

Inside the corridor, the Doctor was trying to keep his calm. The linear induction corridor was really very, very efficient. 'Fascinating,' he wobbled. 'I've never come across as smooth a ride as this before. Or as fast. Hmmm, it is actually terribly fast. I think I'd better have another humbug, just to steady my nerves.' He reached into his pocket, which was rather more difficult than he'd expected. His hand pinioned to his sides, he fumbled for the humbug and was dismayed to watch the boiled sweet tumble and ricochet off the corridor walls.

The Doctor nearly lost his balance, which, at this velocity, would probably have been lethal. Holding on to his hat, he worked out his speed from the flapping of his scarf. Yes. Definitely lethal. He was starting to feel rather giddy.

Much to his distress, the Doctor accelerated again, pinging towards a wall. He cried out in alarm, only to find himself swerved sickeningly around a previously hidden corner.

The Doctor zoomed off into the heart of the mountain.

CHAPTER TWELVE
THE ASTROMOBILE ASSOCIATION

Some way above the Doctor, and considerably more slowly, Romana was examining a large, very burnt-out component. The Captain and Mr Fibuli were watching Romana closely. The Nurse was keeping a wary eye on the Captain. He was shifting from side to side with loud impatience.

'Well? Space urchin, tell me, do you know what this is?' There was an element of terribly forced pleasantry to the Captain's tone that Romana found as discordant as his elbow joints.

Romana turned the cube around once more. 'Oh… it's a… no. Wait a minute it's a… no, it isn't that either. I failed my part one paper in Astro Engineering, I'm afraid,' she grimaced. 'It's terribly embarrassing. Give me a clue. Whatever it is, it's obviously burnt out.' She popped it back onto the table and dusted the soot from her hands.

'A whining infant could tell me that!' the Captain roared, his tone rather less honeyed. 'Your time is once more running out.'

'Ohhhh.' Romana ducked her head. 'I'm sorry, I didn't realise this was Beat the Clock. I think I'd better give up before I make a fool of myself, hadn't I?' With a shrug she picked the cube up and threw it to Mr Fibuli, who made a dreadful attempt at catching it. It landed on the floor with a thud and a tinkle. Romana looked at it sadly. 'It was probably something like a Macromat Field Integrator or something.'

An approximation of a warm glow lit up the Captain's ruined face. 'Ah! She does know! By the beard of the Sky Demon, girl, the jaws of death were hot about your neck, you know.' He flung an arm around her shoulder in an attempt at camaraderie which nearly dislocated her collarbone.

'You don't normally see them that large, though,' Romana opined. 'It'd have to be part of a massive dematerialisation circuit.'

She was suddenly aware of the Captain and Mr Fibuli and even the Nurse looking at each other and grinning, like they were in on a private joke. With a creaking giggle, the Captain leaned forward, his voice a ghastly echo of Romana's earlier tone.

'Roughly speaking, and putting it terribly simply, it is part of the system which transports us instantly through space. We dematerialise in this dimension, and then rematerialise again in a new location.'

'What? You mean the whole mountain?' If the Doctor had taught Romana one thing, it was how to boggle. 'You take this mountain with you through space? What are you, some kind of ski-freak?'

Talking of ski-freaks, the Doctor was currently hurtling through, rather than down, the mountain. He was crossing skiing, hastily, off his list of things to try. While logic was telling him that all would be well with the inertia-less corridor, his every instinct was telling him to curl up into a ball and howl. The Doctor had abandoned his earlier *sang froid* for a rather less dignified crouch, his hands thrown over his face. He was now very alarmed, and the science he knew wasn't helping. At this speed, and without a very large and comfy net at the end, he was going to end up as a bohemian chutney.

As the walls whipped past at a blur, he made a solemn vow: 'I'll never be cruel to an electron in a particle accelerator again!'

The corridor took another dizzying, sickening, Planck-irritating turn, and a very solid wall loomed up ahead. Unable to disguise his alarm, he let out a loud shriek of fear and outrage. He'd overcome mega-villains, battle fleets, and evils from the Dawn of Time. But now public transport was about to be the death of him. Oh, the indignity of it all.

With an abrupt, yet subtle, halt, the Doctor stopped moving. He was simply standing at the end of the corridor, its quiet hum gently mocking him. He peeped out from between his fingers, finding his nose millimetres from a wall.

'Good lord,' he said eventually. He patted himself gently all over, just to make sure he was still all there. 'Ah! Of course, this isn't a linear induction corridor, it must work by neutralising inertia. How fiendishly clever. I must tell Newton about this next time I see him. No, it'll only depress the poor fellow.'

He looked around the end of the corridor. There was no door. Well, it had to happen some day. He'd run through lairs with lots of doors, tunnels with rather sporadic doors, and now he was up against someone who'd only built corridors. He had to admire the minimalism, while also feeling a little trapped. A steel shutter slammed down behind him, making him feel even more isolated.

'Oh dear, more sudden death, I expect.'

The Doctor was starting to calculate his escape options when he spotted the control panel on the steel shutter.

'Oh, I beg your pardon, you're a lift.'

He pressed a button and, without the reassuring benefit of a platform, shot up into the mountain.

*

141

In case you were wondering, K-9 and Mula were still gliding through the desert, Kimus was stood on the plateau looking bored, and Balaton had gone back to bed.

K-9 had found something to irritate him about the desert. His knowledge of habitations was such that he knew that it was illogical to build a city in the middle of one. He also knew that, given projections of even modal average rainfall, there really shouldn't be a desert at the foot of the mountain.

'Query,' he began. 'This desert is incorrect.'

'Is it?' Mula said. 'Well, I suppose it is. My great grandfather farmed here. All this used to be fields.'

K-9 rolled through the barren fields, querying this further.

'Well, we were once ruled by a wicked Queen and when she died the crops began to fail.' Mula pointed around the shimmering hot sand. 'This used to be a lush planet, but we were terribly poor. Then the Captain arrived, and the Golden Ages of Prosperity began. We all became very rich, but every time there was an Age of Prosperity, the crops withered, and the fields retreated.'

K-9 nodded, filing this information away. It was certainly curious.

Meanwhile, Romana was again examining the ruins of the Macromat Field Integrator. The very anxious little man (who seemed to be called Mr Fibuli, of all things) was most insistent that perhaps she might be able to do something.

'Well, yes, I might be able to throw it away,' she'd retorted. That had not gone down well.

The Captain had hissed menacingly, his tin bird had glowered, and even the Nurse had tutted. Mr Fibuli had simply looked wretched. So Romana had picked up the wrecked component and given it a squint.

'Well, what's happened is that you've shorted out the multicorticoid whizzbang—'

'Whizzbang? What nonsense is this?' The Captain's response was rather more professional pride than outrage.

'Whizzbang, yes.' Romana was definite. 'Short for whittlezanticron hyperbandrigic maxivectometer. We call it a whizzbang because that's the noise it makes. I think this one's banged its last whizz though. You'd be lucky to get a phut out of it. You also seem to have blown the metagallic tribo whatsit – that's not short for anything, I just can't remember what it's called – which in turn means you've probably deformed the microcircuits in these pieces of silicate…'

'Pieces of silicate, pieces of silicate,' squawked the Polyphase Avatron. Only the Captain laughed.

Romana continued to ignore the parrot. 'Ah, now this is interesting. You've wired an ambicyclic photon bridge across the field terminals as a stabiliser. I always wanted to try that, but my tutor just said it would fuse, silly old goat. I'm glad to see that someone else has a little imagination.' Her face fell. 'Oh. This one's fused.'

At a clanking snap of the Captain's fingers, Mr Fibuli drew close.

'Do you think she can repair it, Mr Fibuli?' the Captain hissed curiously.

'Well, sir, she obviously knows what she's talking about, but I maintain that it's irreparable.' Mr Fibuli licked his lips and offered up just a little cunning. 'But it occurs to me, Captain, that she must have something similar aboard her own vessel, and perhaps we should…'

The Captain's rare and unusual smile widened, showing off a row of unconvincing metal teeth.

'Mr Fibuli, as ever, I am light years in advance of you…' His laughter was soft, and he proceeded to curse almost genially. 'By the evil eye of the Sky Demon, she will not be needing it again, for clearly she can never be allowed to leave Zanak. However, if she can repair our Macromat Field Integrator as well, I think it will be useful to have a spare. Will it not?' There was almost a twinkle in the Captain's human eye.

'Agreed, Captain.'

Nodding to Mr Fibuli, the Captain strode over to Romana. For a moment, it seemed as though he was itching to reach out and examine the Macromat Field Integrator for himself. Instead he stopped himself and glared at her. 'So, girl! What is your diagnosis? Can it be repaired?'

'Repaired? Oh yes, I should think so,' Romana offered.

'Then do so! Now! Instantly!' the Captain roared.

Every urge she had to help expired then and there. 'Ah, well, I don't think I'd be able to manage it myself. It's fairly advanced stuff, after all, and I am just a space urchin.' She gave him a simpering smile. 'You'd have to ask the Doctor.'

'Doctor?' The Captain rumbled away like a smoke stack. 'By all the stars of evil, who is this Doctor of which you speak? Are there further intruders upon this planet?'

'Well, yes, the Doctor's definitely an intruder. He's far more experienced in this sort of malarkey than I am. He's the one you should be talking to. Or rather listening to, if you have the stamina.' Romana paused, checked the Doctor wasn't within hearing range, and then bubbled. 'You see, I'm only his assistant.'

She bit her tongue.

Excited, the Captain snatched up a microphone and began barking orders into it. 'All Guards on alert! All Guards on alert. There is an intruder, he must be found! His name is the Doctor, repeat the Doctor, he must be found and brought to the Bridge instantly!'

The main door to the Bridge opened, and the Doctor strode in. That, thought Romana, will do nicely.

A squadron of the Captain's Guards rushed past the Doctor without noticing him. That, thought the Doctor, will never do.

He'd had quite enough of this planet dismissing him. He grabbed a Guard by the hand and shook it.

'Hello! I'm the Doctor.'

The Guard stopped, blinked, and rushed on. Snubbed, the Doctor marched further onto the bridge, took it all in, and smiled. This was decidedly more like it. A crazed cyborg, a group of terrorised technicians, a frightened henchman, a nurse (mental note: must win her over in case things go wrong and I end up being locked up and / or sacrificed), Romana looking at her most Romana, and joy of joys, a robot parrot. Home ground at last.

'Who are you?' yelled the swaggering cyborg, and the Doctor could have kissed him.

'Hello, I'm the Doctor!' He ignored the Captain completely and descended on Mr Fibuli. He was at his most affable, genial and charming. 'How can I help you today?'

The Captain emitted a roar which caused Mr Fibuli to yelp and the Doctor to turn on him with open arms. His face lit up with delighted surprise, as though noticing the Captain for the first time.

'You must be the Captain, I expect, delighted to meet you, heard so much about what a splendid chap you are from your terrified population. Now then, I see you've met my assistant Romana, I expect you've been getting on like a house on fire, lovely girl, brains of a goose.' Cheery wave. Romana stuck her tongue out at him. 'Marvellous place you have here, gather you've been having a spot of trouble. And I am most certainly here to help.'

'Seize him!' thundered the Captain.

To the Doctor's ears this was the equivalent of 'I'll just pop the kettle on.' 'Ah, such hospitality,' he grinned. 'I'm underwhelmed.'

He happily let himself be seized. You can tell a lot about an adversary by the quality of their seizing. He made no attempt to resist, but just as he gave every appearance of being tightly grabbed, he easily freed a hand and casually flicked up a Guard's lip and inspected his teeth.

'I'd have that gum seen to, could turn nasty, you know,' the Doctor said before the hand was pinioned behind him.

It is dangerous to go inside the Captain's brain. A lot was going on in there. Calculations, computations, and equations. The machine half of the Captain's brain ensured that all this work took place at a frantic rate. On the outside, he could twitch, shout and curse, but on the inside he was gliding gently across the board, intent on capturing the most powerful piece. He regarded the Doctor and Romana as simply a part of his great game. He had allowed them both a chance to show off. Now he needed to teach them that they were little more than a noisy distraction.

He strode over for a bit of towering and glaring. 'Doctor, I regret to inform you that your line in insolence appeals only to the homicidal side of my nature.'

'Oh, well, I shall have to watch it then, won't I? Don't want to end up dead before I've had a chance to place my full services at your kind disposal.' He beamed and made a little chirruping noise, jerking his nose towards the Polyphase Avatron. 'I say, what a nice parrot. I've always been fond of parrots, haven't I, Romana, and so clever to have a mechanical one, saves all that nasty clearing up. Who's a pretty Polly? Who's a pretty Polly?'

Romana had never seen a robot parrot roll its eyes before. Ah well, she thought, this was turning out to be quite an interesting week. She wondered if the Doctor ever took a holiday, and if so, what happened to the resorts after he'd left.

The Captain was used to having things go his way, one way or the other. Today seemed to be stacked against him. 'Doctor, I assure you that my Polyphase Avatron carries death in its eyes…'

'Then take it to a vet.' The Doctor was so wonderfully fatuous that Romana giggled.

'If you would avoid its deadly gaze, perhaps you would enlighten me as to these services you speak of.'

'I'd be very glad to. We, that is Romana and I, are patrolmen for the Astromobile Association, and our job is to hop around the universe doing on-the-spot repairs for stranded spacecraft. We happened to notice a disturbance in this area of space and just popped along to see if we could be of any assistance. Our rates are very reasonable, particularly if you carry a Galactibank Credit card.'

The Captain considered the Doctor very carefully. His eye bulged until the Nurse took an anxious step towards him. 'Doctor,' he growled, 'you are correct in assuming that we need assistance. I do not carry this credit card you speak of. How would it be if in return for your services I offered to spare your miserable life?'

'More than generous.' The Doctor clapped his hands together. 'Excellent. I wonder if I may inspect the damage?'

With barely an effort, he shrugged himself free of the Guards and strolled over to Romana. She handed him the remains of the component.

'I think this is the root of the trouble, Doctor.'

The Doctor surveyed it as regretfully as a slice of burnt toast. 'Was that a Macromat Field Integrator? Whizzbang gone wrong?'

'Yes.' Romana was a little impressed. 'And the ambicyclic photon bridge is fused.'

The Doctor sniffed. 'And they've blown the metagallic tribo whatsit. Tut tut.'

'Quite.' Romana clucked with mock sympathy, and, just for a moment, the two Time Lords looked each other in the eye. It was, Romana thought, good to have the Doctor here.

'Scrap,' sighed the Doctor dolorously. 'But I wonder if I could examine it in situ? It would help me diagnose what actually happened so you know how to avoid it in future. All part of the service.'

'Oh yes.' Romana brightened. 'They've apparently got frighteningly powerful engines. Do you know, they fly the whole mountain around?'

'The whole mountain? Golly.' The Doctor feared there was rather more to it than that. 'How exciting. Yes. I'd love to have a peep at those engines.'

'No one sees my engines,' seethed the Captain, writhing in anger. The Nurse gave him a look of alarm.

'Oh, that is a pity. Well, then, I'm afraid that's all we can do.' The Doctor dropped the component to the floor with a clang. 'This is a paperweight. There's nothing more I can do for you. Unless you let us have a look around, you're going nowhere. Sorry not to be of more use. Come on, Romana. We'll be off. There's a breakdown on an intergalactic bypass we really should look in on.'

He grabbed Romana by the shoulder and swept her towards the exit.

For once, if this manoeuvre worked, they could be out of here and on their way and, honestly, that would be the best outcome for all concerned.

'I think not,' snarled the Captain. He was examining a console. 'My computer suggests that you could be of rather more help than you are currently willing to offer me.' He smirked with half his face. 'My computer has suggested you require persuasion.'

'I suggest your computer is wrong,' the Doctor said.

The Captain stood, shouting. 'Guards, take them to the Knowhere.'

One of the things that Mula liked most about K-9 was how much he was based in facts. He (and it was definitely a he) had very definite opinions, but, unlike all the other men she'd ever known, those opinions were derived purely from facts.

For one thing, K-9 really knew his way through a desert. Pralix would have refused to try, burst out crying and eaten her lunch. Kimus would have said they were only lost because of the Captain's cruel tyranny. Balaton would have wailed they were only lost because the desert wasn't as good as it used to be.

'How are you doing that?' she asked.

'Query: Define "that".'

Mula pointed backwards and forwards at the sand around them. 'Just… you know… making your way around.'

'This unit is following a path laid down by telepathic psychospoor,' the robot dog offered.

'Well, yes,' Mula said. 'But you seem so certain about it.'

The dog tilted its head at her. If it had been capable of admitting 'I do not understand,' it would have said that. But K-9 didn't.

'It's just… well, we have… the mountain and things further away from the mountain. And there are other cities but we don't go there. Not really. Not any more.' Mula found herself struggling with words.

K-9 adjusted the following of the psychospoor and then queried Mula. 'We are heading due magnetic north. What is in this direction?'

Mula frowned, annoyed at herself. 'I don't know. We used to be great wanderers, but these days everyone stays very close to the cities.'

K-9 found that curious. 'Is it because of your primitive supernatural mythology?'

'Not really.' Mula shook her head. 'We just tend to get very lost.' She looked around the sand. 'It's very hard to explain, but I couldn't tell you what direction the city is. No one could. People say it is another curse of the old Queen's.'

K-9 dismissed this explanation. The phenomenon certainly merited further exploration. An entire planet's population lacking a sense of direction? What could cause that? And how could it be tied up to the crops dying? K-9's analysis told him that this wasn't just a mineral-rich planet that was slowly starving to death. There was something far worse wrong here.

Chapter Thirteen
Try Not to Think of Anything Annoying

The Captain stood outside the very edge of the white box, the bird on his shoulder singing quietly.

'My computer is capable of devising a variety of fascinating and unusual torments,' he remarked as Romana and the Doctor were ushered inside. 'This is perhaps one of the most interesting. It pits a man against himself. His own weaknesses plague him. Why waste processing power devising tortures when you will provide them all by yourself?'

'How efficient, but this really isn't necessary, you know,' said the Doctor, genially. 'Failing that, do pop Romana outside. She's awfully squeamish and she's far more likely to crack just by watching. Aren't you?'

'Oh I'm fine right here,' breezed Romana, pacing the confines of the white cube. 'I once did a seminar on Primitive Interrogation Techniques and it all seemed rather jolly.'

'Jolly?' began the Doctor as the door was slammed shut.

'Yes,' sighed Romana. 'I presume this is some sort of imaginarium or psychoscope? Pity there's not a chair.'

'You've never been inside one before.' The Doctor tried to adopt a worldly-wise tone while also being encouraging. He didn't want the new girl losing her head and screaming. That was always terribly unhelpful.

'The Captain has,' offered Romana. 'I think he's been in this machine. Or one very like it.'

'What?'

The walls were starting to glow and the air was getting dense.

'Did you notice he stood outside and was very reluctant to come inside?'

'Interesting.' The Doctor was impressed.

'Isn't it?' Romana said. 'There's something odd about the Captain. If I didn't know better I'd say his combative psyche was subject to a controlling animus resulting in an extroverted imbalance hiding a sinister introversion.'

'Well yes, I agree,' said the Doctor. The pulsing of the walls was starting to make him giddy. 'Here it comes. I've a tip for you. If you want to come out of this unscathed, try not to think of anything annoying.'

'I'll try,' said Romana, very deliberately not looking at the Doctor.

The white walls dimmed, and they were in almost total darkness.

'And here we go,' said the Doctor.

The machine glided at them out of the darkness.

'Oh heavens,' sighed Romana. 'One of yours, I'm guessing.'

'Yes.' The Doctor was grim.

The machine glided a little closer and then stopped, suddenly aware of them.

'Dok… Tor…' it grated, its eyestalk lit up and glaring at them.

'Coo,' said Romana.

The Doctor's tone was grim. 'It's a Dalek,' he said.

'I can see that,' said Romana. 'I often wondered what they'd be like up close. I've read about them, of course. Rather smaller than I'd have expected.'

The Doctor found himself in the unique position of being defensive about the Daleks. 'This is the nastiest, most evil creature in the universe.'

'Well, yes,' said Romana. 'If it were real. The Knowhere is simply skimming off your fears to create a projection of one.'

'You wouldn't be so cool if you actually met one.'

'Maybe, maybe not.' Romana considered. 'But it's useful to see one up close.' She stepped forward. 'Fascinating.' She waved a hand in front of the creature's eyestalk, and it followed the movement.

'Romana.' The Doctor's tone was grimly serious. 'Do not touch the Dalek. It is not a toy.'

Romana's hands paused in mid-air. 'It's jolly convincing,' she said. 'But it's not real. This room would make a great teaching aid at the Academy. My tutor would hate it.'

'And mine would have adored it,' the Doctor offered, trying to change the subject. 'Remarkable fellow. Come over here and I'll tell you all about him.'

'Well, I'm not sure I fancy you conjuring up your old tutor. He's bound to be a nervous wreck.' Romana crouched down to look at the twitching mechanical limbs of the Dalek. 'I'm inferring that the top thing is some kind of eyestalk. These other two limbs are fascinating, though. I'm guessing this allows for digital manipulation through vacuum technology, but this...' She pointed to the shorter, stubbier arm. 'Well, what does this do, eh?'

'No,' cried the Doctor as the arm angled up to point at Romana. He leapt forward, but he was too late.

The Dalek shot Romana.

*

'Ow,' she said.

The Doctor stopped running and stood very still. 'Ow?'

'Yes.' She rubbed at the arm. 'How very tingling.' She looked at the Dalek accusingly. 'There was no need for that.'

The Dalek wheeled around to face the Doctor. 'Exterminate,' it croaked and shot him.

'Ow,' the Doctor winced.

'See?' said Romana. 'Static shocks. I once had a gown that kept doing that.'

The Dalek shot the Doctor again. This time he let out a slightly louder yelp.

'Don't be a baby,' said Romana.

'I'm not.' The Doctor staggered slightly. 'It's getting stronger. It may just be a projection now, but it's definitely getting more forceful. Give it another few blasts and it'll be up to full strength.'

'Really?'

The Dalek shot Romana again and she fell back against the wall. 'Oh, I see what you mean,' she gasped as she pulled herself back to her feet. 'It's calibrating the nature of the threat against our perceptions of it. Hmm. We should probably get out of here.'

She backed away. The Dalek glided after her. The cube really wasn't very large and there was nowhere for Romana to go. The arm with the lethal sucker extended, pinning her to a wall. The Dalek slid down the arm, closing on her. The single eye glowed as it approached her face. The eye had no pupil, no expression. It just fixed on her face. It wasn't looking at her, it was surveying her. Cataloguing, figuring, calculating, utterly, inhumanly unreadable. It drew closer and closer to her. Romana felt a moment of complete terror.

'Doctor,' she announced, her voice rather less calm. 'I don't like this.'

The Dalek vanished as water started to pour in from the walls.

'I thought of something else, very hard,' said the Doctor over the rushing water. 'I've never cared for drowning.'

Romana gasped, the torrent cold and inescapable. 'I wish you'd thought of something gentler.'

'I've just saved you from a Dalek!' Really, she had no gratitude.

'Which wouldn't have turned up at all if you hadn't thought of it,' she retorted. The water was at waist height now, dragging at their clothes. It was rising rapidly.

'Not especially my fault,' said the Doctor. 'This room is—'

He vanished under the surface for a moment, fighting his way back up, gasping.

'There's something in the water with us!' he called out.

Rationally, Romana thought this a terribly unhelpful thing to say. Irrationally, she felt something slither past her legs and started to panic.

Which was how they found themselves neck-deep in a desert.

'Sorry,' said Romana. 'First thing I could think of.'

'Right,' said the Doctor. He was sinking fast. He tilted his head back to try and keep his mouth above the sand.

'The good thing about all this –' he could hear Romana's voice, a little muffled by the sand, but still very assured – 'is that the Gallifreyan respiratory bypass system should allow us to survive for quite some time without anything more than slight discomfort.'

The sand crept over the Doctor's chin. 'You're missing the point,' he couldn't resist saying. 'The projection is not about the actuality of drowning. It's about the fear of it.'

'Oh,' said Romana.

The Doctor heard no more. But that was quite nice actually. He was encased completely in sand and it gave him a lovely bit of peace.

The Doctor opened his eyes and found himself in the TARDIS.

Home.

That was something. He'd wondered how easy it was to game the computers behind the Knowhere. Clearly he'd managed it.

Leave a few gobbets of thoughts about the TARDIS floating around in the stew of his thoughts and they'd get picked up eventually. Ah yes. Here he was. It was tremendously reassuring being back in the TARDIS. It would give him a chance to regroup and rebuild his strength, and to work out what was going on.

Romana was dead right about the Captain. Or was she? She'd certainly said something about him which had made the Doctor pause for thought. Now what was it? He looked around for Romana, but there was no sign of her. She'd be along in a moment. Probably reordering the library or something.

No, nothing was right about this planet. Its people rich, ignorant, and starving; its houses gilded and completely lacking in comfort; the despot in his castle playing at being a tin-pot general and that nagging sense that something was very wrong. Like the planet had no heart.

He'd ask K-9. He looked around for the robot dog but could not see him.

He strode around the control room of the TARDIS, just in case the dog was hiding behind a chair. He threw open the door to the rest of the ship, blew on the whistle, and waited but the dog did not come trundling up.

No K-9. Disappointing.

He turned back into the room and stopped. The control console had gone. The TARDIS was now an empty box. He went to open the doors, but couldn't even get a bitten fingernail in to prise them apart.

The Doctor had no way out. No companions.

The gravity of the situation sank in. The Doctor was alone and going nowhere for ever.

The Knowhere had done its work. Finally the Doctor knew what he was really afraid of.

*

It's not that Romana was less caught up in the Knowhere, nor that she had less of an imagination than the Doctor. To the Knowhere, the Doctor's mind was a rich, cloying meal. But when it threw itself at Romana's mind, it found things it just couldn't calibrate by comparison.

Yes, Romana feared academic failure enormously. But also, she had just graduated with a Triple First, so this was no longer a problem for her.

Yes, Romana vaguely worried that she wouldn't make her way in life. But she also firmly believed that Gallifrey was an egalitarian society where her merits would be firmly recognised. After all, if the Doctor could end up as President, then why not her?

Sometimes, Romana worried that she was a little naïve and too self-confident, but she had met the Doctor. Someone who simply refused to take her seriously and resolutely delighted in showing her new things. When the Time Lords spoke of the universe, they emphasised how delicate it was. How it needed their protection, guidance, and nurturing. At no point had anyone ever told her it would be so thrilling.

And yet. Perhaps… just perhaps, there was the tiniest chance that they would not succeed in their Quest for the Key to Time. As she thought this, the shadows at the edge of the room rippled in slight excitement. For a moment, a figure seemed to be watching her. She shivered. But no. The Doctor would win. It's what he did.

Unware that the Knowhere had given up, Romana sat neatly on the floor, waiting for the psychic assault to begin. She started to hum to herself.

The Doctor was on his own for ever. Only there was a noise. He left the empty centre of the TARDIS and walked its empty corridors.

'Hello, Doctor!' Romana was sitting on the floor. Humming to herself.

'You're clearly a projection,' he muttered grimly.

'And you're clearly in one of your moods,' she said, standing up.

'Still a projection,' said the Doctor firmly.

Romana arched an eyebrow. 'Oh really? How so?'

'Answer me this – how did you escape the Knowhere?'

'I'm not sure I did,' Romana said frankly. 'I think it got bored.'

'Poppycock.'

'I'm sure it just found you much more interesting,' she said, and the Doctor frowned.

'Then there's the voice,' the Doctor muttered. 'They never get it quite right with duplicates.'

'I see.'

'Yes, it's always just that little bit flat, unemotional and dull.'

'Do go on,' said Romana, gathering her cloak around her.

'And then there's the clothes – no one's clothes ever behave that neatly. I mean, just look at mine.'

'I am,' said Romana witheringly.

A long silence passed.

The Doctor produced a paper bag from his pocket.

'Humbug?'

'Certainly not.'

'It really is you, isn't it?' said the Doctor. 'Knew all along, of course. Um, the clincher was when I said about your voice being all... ah... anyway. Your face! Ha-ha! Sure you won't have a sweetie?'

Romana said nothing. She gestured to a door.

'Shall we go?'

The Captain's Nurse unsealed the Knowhere and was surprised to find the Doctor and Romana sat patiently on the floor. Romana had her back to the door and was doing light callisthenics. The Doctor was playing with a yo-yo. The Nurse had seen the Knowhere produce a lot of extreme reactions, but never before insouciance.

Almost as though they hadn't noticed her, Romana was saying, 'Of course, it's not a torture device at all.'

'Not as such, no,' agreed the Doctor, looping the loop. 'More a way of making its subjects malleable.'

'Which is a total waste of time in our case, of course, Doctor,' said Romana. 'On two counts. For a start, it doesn't work on us.'

'And for another thing,' said the Doctor, springing to his feet, 'we are only too happy to help anyway.'

The Doctor grinned at the Nurse and bowed with elaborate courtesy. She gawped at him, startled to be looked directly in the eye. No one ever did that to her. The Doctor smiled his most charming smile. He did so admire shy people. They could come in so very handy later.

'Hello!' he waved. 'Have you come to fetch us off the Naughty Step?'

The Nurse led them down a corridor.

'You're not very chatty, are you?' the Doctor put in. He was still hoping that, with a bit of charm, she'd prove a useful ally at some point. Romana had already told him how she'd interceded to save her life. The signs were promising.

'I've never really had a chance to thank you,' said Romana.

The Nurse shrugged bashfully. 'My duty is to look after the Captain's welfare. I did not believe that your death was in his own best interests.' She tapped the black box hanging from its strap around her shoulder.

'I say, is that his chart?' the Doctor enthused. 'I'd love to read it.' He leaned forward towards the box, but the Nurse jumped back.

'Patient records are confidential,' she said.

'Absolutely,' said the Doctor. 'But he's a fascinating... er...'

'Survivor,' put in Romana.

'Exactly. And quite the character.'

But the Nurse would not be drawn. She simply marched them down along the corridor to a lift.

'In here,' she said. 'The Captain has relented and will, after all, allow you to look at his engines.'

While the Doctor and Romana were battling with their souls in the heart of a hollow mountain, Kimus was still trying to look heroic by the air-car. He heard a noise, and whipped round, startled. It was just a stone, dislodged by the wind.

It would be poetic to say that, somewhere out in the desert, Mula heard the same wind. But she did not. She and K-9 were still following the psychospoor of the Mourners, and Mula was beginning to feel rather tired and wished she'd packed something to eat.

The entire mountain was hollow and mostly engine. Pistons the height of towns surged up and down, heat blazed from dozens of outlet vents, and the air was full of shouts and calls as countless systems were engaged.

If the Knowhere had been meant to subdue the Doctor and Romana, then it was the sight of the Engine Room that actually succeeded.

Standing on a distant gantry, a nervous Mr Fibuli watched them. The Captain stood at his side, watching as the Polyphase Avatron flitted between the massive silos.

'Why do you trust them, Captain?' Mr Fibuli often found his master's motives hard to work out.

'Trust them? Ha!' The Captain continued to watch his pet, enraptured. His voice was surprisingly genial. 'By the evil winds of Gizak, do you take me for a fool, Mr Fibuli? I am simply giving them a long rope to hang themselves with. They will do no harm.'

'But they defeated the Knowhere...'

For a moment, the Captain's geniality faded. 'It is of no matter. Clearly, whoever they are, they have been well trained. Perhaps they are playing for time; they will even buy time by assisting me. If they choose to mend my engines whilst playing for time, then so be it.'

'But what are they playing for, Captain?' Mr Fibuli tried to see the bigger picture. 'What are they after? What do they want here?'

'That is what we have to find out.' The Captain held out a hand, and his pet settled onto it, purring happily. 'They have come here somehow. We must let them lead us to their vessel, so my Guards can gain entry to it. So we allow them a little rope. At all events, I hold the trump card, don't I, my pretty?' The Captain ruffled his pet's feathers again.

'What trump card?'

'The Ace of Death. It will be played, Mr Fibuli, it will be played.'

The Nurse joined them on the gantry. As often happened, she appeared silently, almost as though she'd slipped out of thin air.

'You think of death too much, Captain,' she admonished. 'Life is to be cherished, preserved.'

'The Ace of Death will be played,' insisted the Captain firmly and proudly.

'Don't forget…' The Nurse risked a cautious smile. 'The Queen is the highest card, Captain. Aces score low.'

Romana was finding the Engine Room magnificent but also pointlessly inefficient. If it existed to move the mountain through space then it was also an utter folly, as so much of the mountain was engine. You may as well just try moving something smaller rather more efficiently. On the other hand, she'd never tried mending a mountain before. The sheer scale of the endeavour was staggering.

'Whoa!' the Doctor had said as they'd walked in, his exclamation echoing off the walls.

'Amazing,' Romana had said.

'Something like that.'

The Doctor stood rooted to the spot in the centre of the vast hall, feeling the whole space echo with power. Standing inside a vast wrist watch, with cogs the size of cars and pendulums the size of buses, all turning, ticking and spinning away. A vast machine that moved and ground remorselessly around them. Right now the engines were just idling – the scale of it all when it was active must be utterly awe-inspiring.

Romana nudged the Doctor. She'd been expecting a quip from him, but he'd just fallen silent. 'I suppose you're going to tell me you've seen it all before.'

'No, actually. Not like this.' True to form, the Doctor tried to look casual, but it was curiously ghastly.

'Really?'

'Really. Although I suspected something of the kind. Something…' The Doctor's sentence ended in a long and pained sigh. He turned around on the spot once, and then again, at a loss for thoughts, let alone words. He flashed a cheery wave up at the watching Captain and then sauntered over to a row of glowing glass valves. 'Come on. Let's look busy.' The Doctor peered at the valves. 'Magnificent. Well I never,' he said.

'What do you mean you suspected something of the kind—'

'Shsssush!' hissed the Doctor. 'Look at this.' He was absorbed in the readings from underneath the valves. 'What do you make of this lot?'

'Well…' Romana squinted. The valves were, at first glance, completely alien. And yet, if you thought about them, just a bit laterally… 'These are remarkably similar to early Time Lord technology.'

'Very good.' The Doctor nodded, but he didn't seem happy about it. 'That Macromat Field Integrator was crude but big. There's nothing crude about this lot.'

'But the scale is fabulous.'

'Isn't it? I mean, look at this.' The Doctor pulled a spanner from his pocket and tapped a vast bronze dome with it. 'This could be a Gravitic Anomaliser.'

'With an input of 9.5?' Impressive, thought Romana. What a staggering concept. The whole mountain was basically a TARDIS. She changed tack. 'Doctor... When you say you had your suspicions. You knew that this mountain was actually a spaceship and it had broken down?'

The mountain? The Doctor blinked. Was that really what she thought? Ah well. 'More or less, yes.'

'But how? How did you know? What does this mountain have to do with the displacement of Calufrax?'

'Well...' The Doctor turned the valves one way and then another, then tossed the spanner into a corner. 'Well, let's just say, I just put 1.795372 and 2.204628 together, that's all.'

'What does that mean?'

'Cleverness, Romana, pure cleverness. Now listen...'

'Yes?'

The Doctor continued to murmur, low and severe. 'Things are much more serious than you can possibly imagine. We are in very, very great danger...'

'What! From the Captain? He's just a terrible old bully. All you have to do is play dumb and his fury burns itself up in frustration. All that *By the evil nose of the Sky Demon* stuff. It's just bluster. And as for that parrot—'

'It's a highly sophisticated killing machine. The Captain is a very clever, very dangerous man, and he's just playing with us.'

'What?'

There was a pause. The Doctor looked around at the vast engines, at the remorseless, vast perpetual motion of a machine setting itself against the universe.

'The thing you need to remember is that the Captain is very keen to know what we know and why we're here.'

'The reason why we've come here is to find the second segment of the Key to Time, in case you've forgotten.' Romana slipped the Tracer quietly from her jacket and waved it around as though scanning a computer. How odd. 'Getting involved in all this is a bit of a sideshow. Can these engines somehow have interacted with the segment of the Key to Time?'

'Hmmm…' The Doctor tightened a screw. 'What does the Tracer say?'

Romana stared at the Tracer and shook it gently. It fizzed. She waved it subtly over the engines as though inspecting them. Surprisingly the Tracer continued to fizz. 'I just don't understand it. If Calufrax has been displaced somehow, then why are we still detecting the segment? It just seems to give out a continuous signal wherever we go.'

'What?' The Doctor listened to the gentle fizzing from the Tracer and frowned. 'That's it, then.'

'What?'

'The answer.' Ashen, the Doctor sank back against a pipe, his hands deep in his pockets. 'Romana, if I'm right we have stumbled on one of the most monstrously wanton crimes ever perpetrated in this galaxy.'

'What?' Romana hissed. 'These engines?'

'Quite.' The Doctor waved a hand around the chamber at the enormous cogs ticking and spinning slowly around them. 'Our next task is to get out of this Citadel and back down to the City somehow. That's where we'll find the answer. I've learned all I want to know from this…' He stared at the engines and tried to say something. But the more he thought, the fewer words he had. He just looked disgusted. 'We've got to get away from here and get away from here quickly.'

Mr Fibuli's thin voice called down to them from the gantry. 'I say, is everything all right down there?'

The Doctor looked up, suddenly jaunty. 'Yes, yes. You know, I think we've got to the root of the problem here. Can we have a chat about it?'

'By all means!' Mr Fibuli nodded. He looked around for the Nurse, but she had gone. Instead he asked a Guard to bring them up. He turned to the Captain and whispered: 'Do you think he seriously believes that the mountain is a spaceship?'

'No,' the Captain said after some consideration. 'He suspects the truth. But the truth will be of no assistance to him.'

The Captain smiled, watching as a huge pendulum swung back and forth, with each swipe moving lower down.

Kimus was becoming bored of being an ever-alert rebel leader. He'd struck several heroic poses, settling on one leg on the air-car, with the gun resting on the crook of his knee. This was both strident and determined. He practised shooting some of the scrubby bushes dotted around the plateau. He then went through the air-car storage lockers and found some food rations. Eventually he settled down into a posture best described as the Heroic Leader Takes a Nap.

'Your Magnefactoid Eccentricolometer is definitely on the blink.' The Doctor delivered his diagnosis, standing on the gantry overlooking the great engines. From up here it looked even more like the insides of a vast clock, pendulums swinging between huge copper tanks, vast chains threading slowly between huge spindles. The Doctor became aware that the platform he was standing on was gradually moving – almost as though it was a hand of the clock. This giant, dreadful engine inside the mountain, ticking inexorably away.

The Doctor nodded to it all, and sucked the air through his teeth as though he saw this thing every day.

'Yes, Captain, we can repair your engines for you, and also replace one or two other components that were going to give you a spot of trouble before long.'

'You are aware of what will happen if I even begin to suspect you of sabotage?'

'Sabotage, Captain?' The Doctor looked hurt. 'It's more than my reputation's worth.'

'Or your life.'

'Or indeed my life, as you say,' conceded the Doctor. He played the next move carefully. 'We will, of course, need to return to my own ship now to prepare some special equipment.'

Romana nodded seriously.

'The girl stays here,' the Captain rumbled.

'Much as I'd love that, I'm afraid that won't be possible.' The Doctor looked truly regretful. 'You see there is a special lock on the TARDIS door. It needs the physical presence of us both to open it.' For just a moment the casual amiability dropped. 'Rather clever, don't you think?'

The Doctor winked at Romana. Romana, who had never winked before, winked back. It looked like something was in her eye.

The deception did not play well with the Captain. 'By the Triple-Headed Hound of Death, you lie!'

'Oh no, no, no, it's an obvious precaution, wouldn't you say? The Astromobile Association has to be very careful. What with all that valuable equipment lying around inside our craft. Why, otherwise, practically anyone could stroll inside and help themselves to it. Couldn't they?'

The Captain nodded, his lip twitching. 'There is a flaw to your argument. One which we will discuss... should you return.' He motioned to a couple of Guards. 'Guards! Escort these two to their ship. Any attempt by them to escape is to be met with instant obliteration! Go now!' He turned back to the Doctor, a ghastly smile on his face. 'Just a precaution, you understand.'

'Quite,' the Doctor agreed. 'It's turning out to be such a pleasure to work with you, Captain. Bye now.' He turned to the Guards, waving them to lead him from the room.

Romana found it all very complicated. She came from a world where people just said what they were thinking and quite often told you what you were thinking as well. Was this really the Doctor's world? A world where everyone constantly lied to each other and knew that they were lying and steadfastly refused to trust each other? It was all so complicated. She wasn't even sure which bluff the Doctor was playing currently. Mind you, she was fairly certain neither did he. All she knew was that they were leaving the Captain's Citadel alive, which seemed something of an achievement. Coming here had been very informative but also really rather dangerous.

There were aspects of the trip which recommended itself. Scientifically, the chance to see such a vast dematerialisation circuit was one thing. She had also learned that a vital component of it was not working. Anthropologically, she felt she'd learned a lot more about the way the society they were interacting with functioned. Psychologically, the afternoon had also presented a fascinating opportunity to observe a deranged egomaniac in action. Actually, make that two deranged egomaniacs in conversation.

'What are you smirking about?' whispered the Doctor.

'Nothing,' said Romana, and walked on.

The Captain watched the Doctor and Romana go and, just for a moment, exulted in the view of his beloved engines. 'Death's Asteroid, Mr Fibuli, it will be a pleasure to kill them. Won't it, my pretty?' He stroked the beak of his pet, and the parrot cooed in agreement, flying out among the eternally churning cogs. Soon the Doctor and Romana would be unlocking their craft and its secrets would be his. And then, then the Captain could finally unleash his masterpiece.

CHAPTER FOURTEEN
THE WATERS OF CALUFRAX

Kimus had so nailed the pose of the Heroic Rebel Leader Taking a Nap that he failed to hear the air-car skimming over the plateau and then landing softly nearby. As Kimus gallantly snored, a Guard slid from the car and started to creep towards him.

'You know, I wouldn't have your job for the world.' The Doctor nudged one of the Guards escorting them in the lift.

The Doctor could and would talk to anyone. Romana was only really used to conversing with people once she'd established their qualifications. But not the Doctor. Oh no. Here they were, being marched off by two faceless people who had, in all probability, been ordered to kill them, and the Doctor was being infernally chatty.

The Guards were having none of it. The Doctor had even whirled around to look one of them in the eyes, which could just be glimpsed through the leather mask.

'Standing around all day, looking tough. Must be very trying on the nerves.'

The lift bumped to a halt, the shutter slid open, and the Guards prodded them onto the inertia-less corridor. It whipped along. Romana found her hand grasped by the Doctor – was it to steady himself, or to balance her? Behind them, the Guards stood impassive.

They reached the end of the corridor.

Romana stepped off smoothly. The Doctor blinked. His face seemed ashen.

'Are you all right, Doctor?' she asked.

'Perfectly.' The Doctor swallowed, and leaned against a wall.

'I found it an exhilarating proof of concept.' Romana turned to the Guards behind them. 'Did the Captain invent this?'

The Guards did not answer.

'I'm sure he did, you know,' she enthused. 'It really is terribly clever. Although,' she considered, 'a trifle slow.'

'Hum.' The Doctor delicately let go of the wall and wobbled gingerly towards the exit.

Kimus was under attack. He heard the footfall, ducked, and the blast missed him. He scurried around the side of the air-car. The Guard continued to fire. Kimus ran for the cover of the doorway. The Guard ran in pursuit, blasting away.

'Your job's terribly hard.' The Doctor had rallied. 'The long hours, the violence, no intellectual stimulation…'

They turned a corner. There was Kimus, running. He slammed into them. The Doctor dropped, taking Kimus and Romana with him. As he went down, their two Guards raised their guns and fired. So too did the Guard chasing Kimus.

The air crackled with electricity.

The three Guards fell to the ground.

The Doctor stood up sadly. 'And now this happens. I'd give it up, if I were you.'

Romana looked at Kimus cowering on the floor. 'Doctor, who's that?'

'Romana, meet Kimus. He's the fearless rebel leader who's going to overthrow the Captain.'

'Ah,' said Romana. 'Nice to meet you.'

Kimus scrambled uncertainly to his feet and boggled at Romana. His face was wreathed in a sudden smile. Oh dear, thought the Doctor, here we go.

'Kimus,' he asked, 'have we still got that air-car?'

'Yes.' Kimus kept on staring at Romana, a lopsided grin on his face.

'Well then, that's something. We've got some travelling to do.'

The Doctor led them out to the plateau.

'Where are we going?' Kimus asked Romana.

'To investigate your mysterious mines,' the Doctor replied firmly. 'Come on.'

The Doctor found Romana had already slid into the driving seat. 'I'll drive,' she announced, revving the engine.

'Don't you ever grow tired?' Mula asked the robot dog.

It had been a long slog through the desert.

'Negative,' the dog replied. 'I am currently recharging using solar energy.'

'Solar energy?'

'The sun,' sniffed the dog.

'Oh, the great big light in the sky.'

For a moment, the dog hesitated. 'Yes. I am operating at optimal efficiency, since your planet has two of them.'

'I'm pleased about that,' said Mula. 'We had just the one yesterday.'

'Negative,' said the dog firmly.

'Oh, I know,' Mula said. 'Very handy, isn't it?'

K-9's world was a binary one. He liked absolutes and he appreciated order. He did not care for statements which were clearly preposterous. One drawback to the Doctor-Master was that he excelled in extraneous input. Despite gentle schooling, the Doctor-Master would, rather than clarifying his initial statement, instead insist on further obfuscation of syntax. Sometimes K-9 just longed to meet a robot like himself. He was certain they would get along most satisfactorily.

In the meantime, he had Mula. He found her commendably straightforward. He would normally have challenged the statement that this planet had recently gained an extra sun. But Mula seemed a very honest individual and also had had important information to impart.

'We have reached the end of the psychospoor,' he announced. 'This is where the Doctor-Master needs us to be.'

They were at a small cave.

K-9 had been quietly formulating a suspicion that the Doctor-Master had had an ulterior motive in sending them following the psychospoor. The Doctor frequently relied on the correct people being in the correct place at, as near as possible, the right time. Because he often needed rescuing at the last possible moment.

Mula entered the cave, and, after a moment's hesitation, K-9 followed after her.

Romana was making admirably smooth work of flying the air-car. Kimus was directing whilst itching for a go. And the Doctor appeared to be slumbering across the backseat, his boots slung over the side. But Romana knew that he wasn't dozing. Something had deeply troubled him, and he did not want to talk to them. This suited her fine.

'What did you make of those engines, Romy?' The Doctor's voice emerged from under his hat.

Romana ignored it. He had to be taught that Romy was not a thing and never would be.

'I said—' the Doctor began.

'Is this a test?'

'If you like.'

Good. Romana liked tests. 'The engines were surprisingly similar in principle to an old F-type TARDIS engine but with no temporal dislocation facility...'

'What?' The Doctor sound annoyed.

'It can't travel in time.'

'It's much simpler like that, isn't it? Long Words were only invented to confuse the enemy and make your Professor feel wanted.'

This really was too much. If there was one thing the Doctor loved more than the sound of his own voice it was a long word. 'Really? First you tell me we're in terrible danger then you stop to give me a lesson in semantics.' The Doctor was also missing the significant bit about how surprisingly familiar the great engines were.

And he continued to miss it. 'Well, I think we're safe enough for the moment, it's just the safety of the rest of the galaxy I'm worried about now.'

'Oh Doctor, you always seem to be worried about that.'

'Do I?' The Doctor sat up in his seat, and yawned.

'Yes,' said Romana, swinging them out across the desert. 'You're forever going on about it.'

'Oh, and I'd always seen myself as the irresponsible type.' The Doctor settled back in his seat and pushed his hat across his face. He yawned.

'Pure affectation,' Romana said firmly.

'All right, clever clogs, what else did you notice about those engines?' The Doctor was proving he'd not missed a thing. And also that Romana was right. Try as he might to protest otherwise, the Doctor had an air of bumbling competence. 'Tell me Romy, didn't you think they were very…'

'Hyperdimensional?'

'No.'

'Analogically cross-matricised?'

'No.'

'Needed dusting?'

'Yes, but no.'

Romana thought again. 'Tangentially aligned to the STC curve?'

'Oh no,' the Doctor tutted. 'Definitely not.'

'All right, what then?'

'Give up?'

The Doctor grinned at Romana, and Kimus suddenly felt utterly excluded from their world. He desperately wanted to say something clever that would impress Romana but all he could think of was 'We're a long way off the ground.' So he said nothing.

Romana lifted the Doctor's hat. 'All right, then,' she said. 'I give up.'

'Not only were those engines suspiciously familiar. They were also Big. B. I. G.'

'Well of course they're big, he's flying that entire mountain through space. Heaven alone knows why, it's not even a particularly nice mountain.'

The Doctor frowned. 'Did the Captain tell you he was flying the mountain?'

'Well no, but… Ohhhh.' Romana frowned and the air-car's course wobbled, just a bit.

'Quite,' agreed the Doctor. 'The power of a transdimensional mat / demat engine increases exponentially with its size.'

'Well, of course.'

'So…' The Doctor waited for her to work it out.

Romana gasped and stalled the air-car. They plunged like a rock. Kimus let out a squeal, the Doctor grabbed his hat and worried about Galileo dropping things out of his bedroom window.

Romana flicked the engines back on, the words pouring out of her in astonishment. 'You mean those engines are shifting something much bigger than a mountain?'

'Much much much bigger,' intoned the Doctor. They were hundreds of times larger than a TARDIS's engines and a TARDIS was, more or less, a pretty large thing.

Now Romana was worried.

Kimus pointed at a patch of scrubland at the edge of the desert. 'Doctor, we're very close to the mines now. Down there, do you see? They'll be closed down, it's nearly nightfall.'

'So it is,' said the Doctor, and they paused, for just a moment, to admire the binary sunset.

Then the Doctor motioned them down. 'Good. We should be able to land undetected.'

'Doctor, what are you expecting to find in the mines?' asked Romana, bringing them in to a remarkably smooth landing. Had she realigned the magnetic vectors? Of course she had.

The Doctor sprang from the air-car and looked up at the deserted mine works. 'Romana, if we find what I think we're going to find... then I'm afraid I can hardly bear to contemplate it.'

He made short work of the locked gate and strode on into the mine.

That the cave was very big didn't seem to trouble K-9. He led Mula to the back of it, finding traces of the Mourners' psychospoor leading to an ever-narrowing tunnel. They crept down it. Mula felt the walls of the planet pressing in around her. Claustrophobia gripped her, along with a terrible sense of sadness. She caught herself in a sob and stifled it quickly before it didn't stop.

'Can't you feel it K-9?'

'Negative.'

'It's a feeling of terrible misery, like it's seeping from the rocks.'

K-9 extended a sensor probe. 'Suggestion: I am detecting a variety of residual wavelengths on the Vantalla Psychoscale.'

'What does that mean?'

The robot dog considered its reply carefully. 'There is sadness in the air.'

They crept further down the tunnel.

Mula felt it start on her back. A tickling, cold sensation. As though someone was breathing on the nape of her neck. She turned around. There was no one there. She carried on walking into the tunnel. The prickling sensation increased. She wondered – why had the Doctor sent them there? And what would be waiting for them?

For a moment, just a moment, she thought about turning around and going home. It was too late to save Pralix. Grandfather had been right. The unknown did no one any good.

No. She was tired, hungry and frightened. But she wanted to know what was at the end of the tunnel.

The Captain had returned to the Bridge and he was not in a good mood. In fact, thought Mr Fibuli, he was in his worst mood all day. And today had been a peachy pippin.

'Escaped! They've escaped!' the Captain was roaring. 'Your incompetence beggars the imagination! There will be blood for this, teeth of the Devil, there will be blood! Every Guard must be mobilised instantly! If those two are not found within fifteen minutes then, by fury, one in ten of you shall die! Find them! Find them! Bring them back alive if possible, but find them!'

Having delivered himself of that lot, he sank back in his chair and, oddly enough, grinned at Mr Fibuli. 'An irritation,' he whispered, 'but an amusing one.'

As the suns set, Romana reflected it had been quite the day. Although this was only the second planet she'd landed on in the TARDIS it had already presented her with a rich seam of experience. The first planet she'd visited had been Ribos, where a lot of men had shouted at each other until there'd been a loud explosion. She was now on another planet of shouting men. She wondered if this was what the universe was really like? How disappointing. No wonder Time Lords so rarely interfered. Where were all the interesting women?

The mine workings were remarkably plain. So far she'd seen an ugly city of gold, and a citadel of stone and steel. The mine buildings were made of ancient, solid concrete. No architect had been involved. These buildings simply worked for a living.

But no one was around. There was a constant hum in the air, of automation.

'We used to be miners, a lot of us did. Good, hard, worthy men of toil,' Kimus was declaiming loudly, as though trying to get her attention. 'But then, well, once we became rich, we became idle, and so the mines were automated. We occasionally have to come and check – but for the most part, we grow fat on the Captain's indulgence.'

'Hmm,' said the Doctor. 'And you'd rather work down the mines, then?'

'Well, no.' Kimus was completely unaware he was being teased. 'I mean, I know that there are many decent sons of toil who are dying to. I simply hanker, like most of my brothers, for the noble feeling of an honest day's work.' He came to a metal door and, with an effort, opened it. 'This leads to a lift shaft. No one's used it for years.'

'Why not?' asked the Doctor.

'Well,' said Kimus. 'The penalty is death.'

'I can see there wouldn't be much incentive,' the Doctor agreed.

Romana found the lift itself. It was a rather unenchanting metal box, significantly plainer than the invisible gravity platforms in the Citadel. 'It looks as though it's maintained in working condition,' she said. She did not, however, fancy a go in it. The box hung on a metal chain, swaying in the breeze coming from a deep, dark shaft.

'Let's see if it still goes, shall we?' the Doctor said, leaping a small gap into the box.

Right then and there, Romana decided she'd stay behind.

Kimus scrambled into the lift.

Romana, with her eyes firmly not looking down, stepped in as well, feeling the cage sway beneath her feet.

The Doctor pressed a button and the lift began to slide downwards. The walls of the shaft passed by them. Romana felt she could reach out and touch them, but then realised that the rocks were blurring into one another.

'It's going terribly fast,' she said.

The Doctor nodded. His sombre mood hadn't really lifted. 'I expect we've got a very long way down to go.'

An alarm went off on the Bridge. Mr Fibuli went over to check it. 'The mineshaft?' he queried. 'Someone's in the mineshaft.'

The technicians on duty all shrugged. No one was due to do any maintenance down there for ages.

Mr Fibuli switched on a camera, hoping to avoid attracting the Captain's attention, but already he could hear the voice ringing in his ears. 'The mineshaft?'

A screen showed the Doctor and Romana and a native in one of the lifts. The Captain started roaring. 'Moons of madness, they waste no time! Alert! All Guards to the mines immediately. The intruders must be caught! Mr Fibuli!'

He grabbed Mr Fibuli by the shoulders and squeezed so tightly, the man couldn't even draw his last breath. 'I don't care what excuses you come up with. You will have to find a method of breaking into their vessel without their help. We can take no more chances on them. Look at them – look at what they're doing! The Mine, Mr Fibuli, the Mine!' The Captain's mood seemed strangely close to panic. 'Once they have seen what lies at the bottom of the mineshaft they must never leave alive. Never! Guards! The intruders in the mineshaft are no longer to be captured. They must be killed on sight! They must be obliterated!'

K-9 and Mula reached the end of the tunnel. They were in a chamber, covered with markings.

'Explain the function of this space?' queried the dog.

'I can't,' said Mula, thoroughly baffled. She had never seen anywhere like this before.

At the centre of the cavern was a pile of dust arranged in two circles. Mula knelt down to touch it. As she did, it glowed.

'Diamonds?' she wondered. At first she'd been excited, but now it all seemed rather humdrum.

'Negative,' K-9 reported.

The dust glowed even more, and then started to shift, spinning up into the air.

'That's impossible,' exclaimed Mula.

The robot dog started to explain precisely how possible this in fact was. And then the dust did something remarkable. It showed a picture of the Doctor.

Guards ran into the deserted mine. The Captain's words relayed through speakers. 'Find the strangers! Kill them on sight! They must be obliterated!'

Romana was still not enjoying the lift. Of all the various kinds of transport she'd been in that day (including the TARDIS), this seemed both the most simple and the most dangerous. There was something marvellously reassuring about a lot of science and buttons and safety protocols. This was simply a metal box on a cable. The cable could (probably would) snap at any moment, and then they'd fall to their deaths. The cable didn't even need to break to kill her. Romana could see the walls sliding past – she merely had to reach out and touch it to be dragged out of the cage. The other thing about the cage was that it was not taking them anywhere good. The Doctor leaned against the side of the cage, staring at the ceiling and humming. He was clearly very, very worried. He wasn't even trying to make any small talk, or say anything even the slightest bit annoying. This was very unusual behaviour indeed. It did not make Romana feel any more reassured about what they'd find when they reached the bottom of the mine. Even Kimus was looking subdued.

The lift juddered to a halt.

'Well, we're here,' said the Doctor grimly. He gestured to the darkness beyond.

'Attention,' K-9 remarked. 'We are no longer alone.'

Mula stared in alarm at the giant dancing dust picture of the Doctor. Figures stepped through it. Coming towards them. Mula backed away, crying out in horror and fear. She turned to run, and more of the cowled figures emerged from the shadows, stepping silently towards them.

'Shoot them, K-9,' she begged. 'You have to shoot them.'

One of the figures pointed at her, and Mula recoiled. 'I'm warning you!' she gasped as the sad figure shuffled towards her. 'Stay back!'

But the Mourners just kept walking towards her, their sad faces pressing in on her.

'K-9,' she begged. 'Fire on them, please!'

The dog's reply was baffling. 'Negative.'

One of the figures stretched out a hand, gripping her wrist. She felt the cold flesh against her own, and she flinched. She stared up into the empty, weary face of what had once been a woman.

'Tell me,' Mula demanded. 'What have you done with Pralix?'

The withered face of the woman almost smiled.

Romana peered out into the gloom. It was freezing. Did this world have an ice core?

'Doctor? Where are we? It's so cold!'

The Doctor breathed into the gloom. 'It's cold, wet and icy!' He produced a torch and waved it around. There was a small jump down from the lift platform onto the ground below. 'Mind the gap,' he intoned. He landed with a crunch. 'We're about three miles beneath the surface of the planet, I'd say.'

He waved the torch above them – there appeared to be a gigantic lattice of ironwork above them, stretching out in all directions. The torch gradually picked out the space they were standing in. It was huge.

'But it's a vast cavernous space…' breathed Romana. 'Why's there so much empty space so far down? It's beautiful…'

'Beautiful?' The Doctor splashed across the ground, finding a rock and sinking sadly down onto it. He shook his head. 'Romana, I was right. This so-called planet is entirely hollow.'

'Hollow?' Romana stared at the cavern. 'What do you mean Doctor? How can it be hollow? What are we standing on, then?' The absurd wrongness of his assertion contrasted with a terrible suspicion. 'A torch! Give me your torch, Doctor!'

'Here.' The Doctor handed it to her without enthusiasm. 'You'll find it's just ordinary ground.'

Romana looked at what was beneath her feet. There was something wrong about it. Something terribly wrong. Water ran over it. Cold water.

Kimus peered uncertainly over her shoulder. He was curious, but he couldn't see anything remarkable. He'd never been inside a planet before. Why shouldn't there be rivers down here? 'These things are beyond me,' he admitted. 'I don't know where I am.'

'Kimus,' said the Doctor with gentle savagery. 'You are no longer standing on your world.'

Romana ran her hand through the cold stream and then straightened, splashing over to the bank. Flattened blades of grass poked up through the snow. She stopped.

'It *is* just ordinary ground,' she gasped. 'It shouldn't be here. The water, yes, but not the mud, not the plants.'

'Where are we?' asked Kimus.

The Doctor reached over to him. 'Listen, Kimus, the reason the stars in your sky keep changing is that, when the Captain's engines start up, it's not just the mountain that moves – your whole planet jumps through space. Those engines are huge enough to dematerialise the entire planet, flip it halfway across the galaxy and rematerialise it round its selected prey…'

'Other planets.' Romana was appalled.

'Wrapped around them like a huge fist.' The Doctor clapped his hands around one of Romana's. It was not a reassuring gesture. The light from the torch went out.

'This entire planet is a huge hollow mining machine. It mines other planets, extracts all the valuable minerals and leaves the rubble behind.'

He shone his torch again, playing it up into the vaulted ceiling above them. The light petered out, only just glimpsing the vast lattice of iron above them. In every direction, as far as the torch beam could wander, the crust of Zanak was braced together. Romana was, quite literally, looking up at the roof of the world. Her eyes wandered down to the icy stream pooling around her ankles.

'Then what we're standing on now is the planet we originally came looking for?' Romana stared around her. 'Cold, wet, icy Calufrax.'

The Doctor's voice echoed through the emptiness. 'She's buried inside Zanak, the Pirate Planet, having all the goodness sucked out of her by the Captain.'

Kimus pulled a pebble from the bed of the stream. 'You mean whole other worlds have died to make us rich? Whole other worlds like ours?'

The Doctor nodded. 'Whole other worlds.'

'But Doctor! Supposing some of them were inhabited planets – I mean, they can't have been. Calufrax wasn't,' Romana reasoned. 'It's bizarre. But there's probably no harm to it. Really.'

'Remember the Oolion stone I picked up in the street?' The Doctor took the rare gem from his pocket. 'From Bandraginus 5. I knew I'd heard the name mentioned recently. A hundred years ago it disappeared. Vanished without trace. A planet of a thousand million people. Captain fodder.' He dropped the gem into the river. 'I've seen enough,' he said and stormed back to the lift.

Left alone, Kimus's only light was the soft glow of the Oolion stone glowing through the water. He looked down at it. For a moment he nearly reached out to touch it. Then he let go of the pebble he'd picked up, watching it drift down to the bed. Someone should say something, to mark this moment.

'Bandraginus 5. By every last breath in my body, you will be avenged,' vowed Kimus. It seemed to be what a hero would say, but his heart just wasn't in it.

The Doctor was about to scramble up to the lift, but Romana paused. She took the Tracer from her pocket and switched it on. 'I have a hunch,' she said. To start with, the Tracer just went *click-click-click*. And then it began to roar, a rush of static echoing back off the distant walls of Zanak and the forlorn surface of Calufrax. 'It's going mad!' cried Romana, fighting to turn it off.

'As well it might,' sighed the Doctor.

'The Second Segment of the Key to Time must be around here somewhere.'

'Pick a planet, any planet,' sighed the Doctor. 'How many has Zanak devoured? It could have been on any of them.'

Kimus came running. No doubt with even more good news.

'Doctor—' he began, and then the blast knocked him flat.

The Captain's Guards were standing in the ironwork above them, blasting at them. Steam rose from the waters of Calufrax, splinters of rocks flew through the air. The cacophony was deafening.

The Doctor and Romana grabbed a dazed Kimus and pelted across the slippery, icy surface. There was a mining corridor ahead of them. If only they could make it. They slipped and scrabbled through ice, their way lit by fire.

The Doctor was fishing in his pocket, reaching around for his sonic screwdriver. If only he could get the bulkhead door open. Otherwise they'd be sitting ducks. He reached out for the door.

It was locked tight.

'Doctor,' called a voice.

Lights snapped on.

He looked up into the vaulted eaves of Zanak. Figures emerged from behind iron struts, standing looking down on the Doctor's group. Each figure was wrapped in a grim shroud.

The Guards, only a few paces behind, were levelling their guns when they saw the figures. They stopped and gasped.

One of the figures above them spoke again.

'We have come for you,' he said, his voice weary.

The figure threw back his cowl.

It was Pralix, his features pale, his eyes dark. He looked at them with utter desolation.

'The Mourners have come for you all.'

PART THREE

The music of the spheres!
… It nips me unto listening, and thick slumber
Hangs upon mine eyes: let me rest.
William Shakespeare, *Pericles*

CHAPTER FIFTEEN
BAD OMENS

On the surface of a dead planet there was an impasse.

Romana considered her position, and she did not consider it favourably. Standing inside a hollow planet. Behind her, men with guns. Above her, a group of menacing people in cloaks. She was realising that the main reason why the Doctor was unable to take the universe entirely seriously was that things like this just kept happening to him. Life regularly presented him with unenviable and unlikely choices and he somehow kept surviving. He had been travelling the universe for several centuries and it had never got the better of him. Not yet. That was, in its own way, rather marvellous.

She looked at the Doctor, hoping he'd flash her a quick, reassuring grin. He was too busy staring at the Mourners in amazement.

Kimus was slightly surprised to find himself still alive. Normally the Captain's Guards didn't hesitate to shoot fleeing people in the back. In fact, they were excellent shots when people were running away. But they were not firing their guns. Perhaps because they were used to seeing a small, easily executed group of Mourners, heads meekly bowed, welcoming the end. Instead the Guards were facing a considerable force of them. These Mourners looked different. Their shoulders were back, they weren't slumping. They were staring down at the Guards, and they looked powerful.

Kimus wondered if the Guards would shoot the Mourners first and then turn on them. He didn't really want to die, but then again, if he lived, he would have to explain to Mula that her brother was now a Mourner. She probably wouldn't take that well. All the rumours about what they did to their victims were wrong – they hadn't killed or eaten him. On the contrary, he actually seemed somehow better for the experience. Pralix was standing taller. He'd pulled the jewels from his robes, and stood there, plainly dressed, his face drained of colour, and yet, sadly serene. The horrible transformation somehow suited him. Yet Kimus doubted Mula would ever see it as good news.

The Guards paused to assess the situation. The Captain didn't tend to appreciate people who thought too much, especially not about the consequences of their actions. A smart tactician would have wondered what the outcome of shooting at a group of aliens and telepaths would have been. But the Captain did not employ smart tacticians.

'Kill them! Kill them all!' one of the Guards shouted, and the others agreed.

They sprayed blaster fire through the cavern.

And that would have been the end of that, only Pralix smiled. It was a very slight smile, and rather wan. The blasts fell out of the air sadly. It really was the only way to describe it. It was as though all of the beams suddenly realised the miserable futility of existence, sighed, and dashed themselves to the ground.

The other Mourners echoed that same flicker of a smile at the Guards. The Guards staggered back, crushed by a despair that they couldn't bear, let alone describe. They fell back under it, moaning, trying to shoot at the air. Men who had never once questioned a decision or regretted an action, now bitterly regretted breathing. Confronted by how awful the universe was, they unanimously decided to have a lie down and see if that would make things better.

Silence came again to Calufrax.

'Oh my,' said the Doctor.

The wan smiles on the face of the Mourners all twitched upwards, just a little, as though existence had become slightly more bearable. Then they turned to face the Doctor.

'Come,' said Pralix. 'Follow us.'

The Mourners clambered down from the struts, stepping softly onto the surface of Calufrax. Pralix motioned for them to follow, and then they marched away in a silent line.

'I rather thought that would happen,' remarked the Doctor as soon as he dared.

'Oh, come off it!' Romana stepped daintily over the whimpering body of a Guard. 'You always say that.'

'No, honestly, I did. The Mourners are treated by the citizens as devils, zombies, pariahs, but when they attacked me with a mental blast a few hours ago...'

'They attacked you?' Romana somehow wasn't that surprised.

'Yes, they thought I meant to harm Pralix – but I could tell by the wavelengths on which the blast hit me that they were not evil. Frightened, confused, but not evil. They weren't kidnapping Pralix, they were rescuing him.' The Doctor's boots crunched neatly through the slush of a frozen meadow.

'So who are they?' Romana had felt the edge of their telepathic emanations. They weren't traditional telepaths – they seemed to be acting as the conduit for some great and awful power. A force which had just flickered past her mind and made her shudder.

'I haven't a clue who they are!' the Doctor beamed, and hopped over a stream. The Mourners stood waiting for them in a patch of light, at the top of what had once been a small, icy hill. 'But I think it's all terribly exciting.'

*

A little way across on the surface of Calufrax, one of the Guards woke up. He felt completely miserable and that life was crushingly unfair. Staggering to his feet, he fled to the Citadel. He had to see the Captain.

The dust hung in the air, glowing and dancing.

The small group of Mourners stood to one side. They did not seem to be guarding them, or threatening them, or even holding them prisoner. The old woman had simply said one word to Mula. She had pointed at the cloud of dust and she had said, 'Watch.'

It kept forming patterns and shapes which Mula could almost recognise and vaguely, nearly identify. For a moment she saw a tree. Then an ocean crashing on a shore. Then a wonderful, strange city.

Even though there was a sensation of sadness to the chamber, Mula found the room curiously hopeful. As though it were, in an odd way, celebrating something. She had asked K-9 to help her clarify this, but the robot had remained truculently taciturn. He was, he insisted, analysing the dust.

Mula reached her hand into the glowing cloud, surprised it did not even tingle. In her hand was a tiny hopping bird made out of dust. She drew her palm back and, for a moment, the bird lingered there, its plumage ruffling. And then it fell apart into the air.

'How sad,' she said. 'It was a very pretty bird.'

'Master?' K-9 looked up.

'What is it?' asked Mula.

'The Mourners have located the Doctor-Master,' K-9 informed her. 'They are approaching.'

'How can you tell? I can't hear anything.'

K-9 considered his answer. 'The Doctor has a very distinctive heartbeat. I can detect it through half a mile of rock. At the current rate of ascent, they will arrive in 23.9 seconds.'

Mula glanced at the large rock door carved into the wall of the chamber, and then over at the imposing figure of the old woman, her head bowed as though in shame. 'I can't get over it. All my life I've been taught to fear and loathe the Mourners. Now it seems they are the only honest people on this planet. Can they really be trusted?'

'Sixteen seconds to arrival.' K-9 was both ignoring her question and instructing her to wait for the Doctor's arrival. 'The Doctor-Master would not have programmed me to lead you to them if he had not thought it safe.' The robot dog paused, and his ears twitched. Mula suddenly wondered if he had just caught himself in a massive fib. 'Twelve seconds to the Doctor-Master's arrival,' he said firmly.

'Safe? But how could he possibly know that?' protested Mula.

'I supplied him with analyses of their brain-wave patterns when they attacked him,' K-9 informed her, as though that answered everything. 'The frequencies they chose conveyed a considerable amount of emotional complexity, but they indicated no malice.'

'No malice?' Mula remembered her mother sending her to sleep with terrifying tales of the evil Mourners who wanted to wipe out the world. 'You mean they slammed him to the wall with good vibrations?'

'Affirmative,' K-9 reported. 'Arrival in one second.'

The great rock door slid away, and Pralix walked in.

Mula stared at him, at first in horror, and then in relief. At least her brother was alive. But so terribly changed. 'What have they done to you?' she cried.

Pralix paused on the threshold. He looked momentarily ashamed, and then he shrugged. 'I have joined the Mourning,' he announced.

Well, that was so typically Pralix, thought Mula. He'd gone off to join a bunch of people who would indulge his self-pity. They could sit around in their sparkling cave of sadness feeling sorry for themselves all day. Well, fine.

And yet, Pralix looked... he looked at peace. She ran to him, and he held her hands, gently. His hands were so awfully cold. A wave of something broke over her – the gentle regret of the end of a pleasant festival day, the tiredness at sunset on a long summer evening, the darkness just before dawn.

'Oh, Pralix,' she sighed. For the first time in ever so long, her brother smiled at her, just a very little. It was the saddest, slightest smile she had ever seen, but it was a smile.

The Doctor broke the mood by sliding delightedly across the floor to K-9. 'K-9!' he bellowed happily. 'Bet you're surprised to see us, eh?'

'Amazed, Master,' the dog said.

'There you are!' the Doctor nudged Romana in the ribs. 'Didn't I say he'd be amazed?' He tapped the dog on the nose. 'Can you guess where we've been?'

'Affirmative,' K-9 announced.

'You're lying,' the Doctor said, and then forgot all about teasing his pet. He was staring up at the dust cloud. It showed a wonderful park, its trees, flowers and grass all ordered into neat, perfect lines, lines completely ignored by the children running between them as their laughing parents watched.

'Well,' the Captain demanded, 'are they dead?'

The Guard hadn't stopped running until he'd reached the Bridge. He stared at the Captain. He opened his mouth to say something, and then, to everyone's surprise, burst into tears.

The Doctor was sitting cross-legged on the floor, the cloud of glowing dust dancing around him. The Mourners had drawn closer around him.

'Pralix.' The Doctor's eyes were closed. 'You're looking better. How are you feeling?'

Pralix shrugged. 'I am no longer alone. I no longer bear the weight of this world upon my shoulders.'

'The weight of this world and so many others.' The Doctor refused to look at the cloud of dust. He instead surveyed the sea of pale, blank faces. His foot tapped the ground.

Finally Pralix spoke. 'Doctor, do you bring us the understanding we seek?'

'When you... ah... thought at me, you presented me with a challenge.'

'For generation upon generation our planet has been assailed by a nameless evil. We would know its name.'

'Pshaw,' the Doctor scoffed. 'Its name is the Captain, you know that. Why haven't you got off your bottoms and kicked him out? Surely it can't be a surprise to you?'

'It is the Captain,' conceded the ancient female Mourner. She was so very old, holding herself up with the aid of two gnarled wooden sticks. Her face was screwed up, as though thoroughly sick of life. 'The Captain's evil is beyond our comprehension. Strange images haunt our brains. Hideous death agonies wrack our bodies, weird powers of the mind descend upon us and yet we know nothing. When a new Mourning soul appears amongst the people we know we must find them and gather them to ourselves to protect them before the grief becomes too much.' The old woman's wrinkled face screwed itself up further, and she shuddered. 'Beyond the Mourning all is dark confusion, images and pain. Really we know nothing, have nothing, apart from our burden.'

'They found me in time,' said Pralix. 'They were too late for my father. He was shot down in the street like a dog.'

'With each new generation, with each new soul who joins us, we grow stronger, the images grow clearer, the pain bites deeper, but still the understanding evades us. Finally, in Pralix, is one untainted by the past, one strong enough to channel the Life Force. But...' The old woman sighed. 'We just don't know what to do with it.'

The Mourners all nodded, and the dust glowed and danced, forming more and more shapes. Romana wondered what they made of these glimpses of the landscapes of worlds long ago devoured? How could the Mourners know what was inside Zanak when they didn't even know what a planet was?

The Doctor, naturally, had started goading the elderly female Mourner. 'And you've just hidden away, feeling sorry for yourselves?'

The Mourner sighed, a deep and long sigh. 'We are powerless. The people hate us so much it constricts us – we cannot see into their minds, let alone change them. We cannot fight back. We can do nothing.' And now the entire group sighed. 'What are we?'

'You're a telepathic gestalt,' said the Doctor. 'Fuelled by an enormous reservoir.'

'A what?' asked Kimus.

K-9, sensing a definition was required, glided forward helpfully. 'A telepathic gestalt, a community of the mind. Many minds combined together telepathically to form a single entity. The whole is greater than the sum of the parts.'

'And Pralix is part of that?' Mula stared at her brother in alarm.

Pralix brushed her hand gently, and she felt the first days of autumn.

'I am of Us,' Pralix said. 'But I do not know what it means.'

'I hope one day you shall.' The old woman moved to stand in the glowing pillar of dust. 'Without understanding our nature, we are lost in our own misery. We can do nothing.'

'Nothing?' the Doctor scoffed. 'Nonsense. No one can do nothing.'

'Then you are the one, Doctor,' the old Mourner pleaded. 'Make us aware, that we may throw off this evil. Speak to us of your understanding of Zanak.'

The Doctor began carefully. 'The planet Zanak…' He snapped his fingers, and the cloud of dust sprang to form the image of a planet, spinning in space. 'This is your planet. It is completely hollow.'

'Hollow?' The sea of faces stared at him.

'Oh yes.' The Doctor snapped his fingers again, and the surface of the planet faded away, showing the emptiness inside Zanak.

'The shell of a planet. Hollow but rarely empty. You see, Zanak is always on the move for its next meal.'

'But how?' the old Mourner asked, the crowd muttering.

Romana chipped in. 'Hidden in the Captain's mountain are vast engines. They can make the entire planet suddenly vanish, drop out of the space dimension…' As she spoke, the planet faded neatly away.

'Vanish?' Mula was having trouble with the concept. Why would they vanish? Where would they vanish?

'Oh yes,' continued Romana, warming to her theme. 'You don't notice it, of course, because you are part of the transmat field, you stay with it. But in the same instant Zanak vanishes, it materialises in a different part of the galaxy.'

Inside the dust cloud a small dot formed. The dot grew in size, as though the dust cloud was growing closer, until the watchers could see the surface of a world, continents and seas spinning gently away.

'Very good.' The Doctor cut across her. A shadow formed around the spinning world. 'Zanak reappears and encloses the precise point occupied by another, slightly smaller planet—'

'Most recently Calufrax,' added Romana.

'So your planet—'

'Zanak.'

The Doctor stopped. He could see that Romana was trying to be helpful. It was taking some getting used to, having a companion who had more answers than he did. 'Romana, am I telling the story or are you?'

'You are, of course, Doctor.' Romana smiled sweetly. 'I'm just helping it along.'

'Romana, could you help me by mentally revising your seven hundred and ninety-eight times table?'

Romana considered the proposal seriously. 'All right.' She frowned in deepest concentration.

With her taken care of for a few minutes, the Doctor resumed his explanation. 'So, your planet—'

'Finished!' Romana beamed.

'Oh, very good.' The Doctor tried not to look impressed. 'Now, hush.' He started to pace around the room. 'So your planet, Zanak, entirely surrounds the smaller planet, smothers it, crushes it, and then mines all the mineral wealth out of it, sucking it dry like an enormous leech. And the only way this is discernible to you is that at the moment of the jump the mountain lights up and the sky flashes.'

'The omens!' Mula realised.

'Yes.' The Doctor nodded sadly. 'The omens your people rejoice at herald the death of another planet.'

Kimus looked about to say something, and then went very quiet. Mula went over to her brother. Finally she understood, realised the pain Pralix had been enduring. She touched his cheek and felt the cold of a winter's night.

The Mourners were staring at the cloud of dust. It had shifted again, forming into two rings, one inside the other. The outer ring swelled, the inner ring dwindled away to little more than a speck. 'That explains the images that haunt us,' the elderly Mourner groaned. She made a weary gesture towards the two concentric circles on the floor.

'That's the image of the Pirate Planet,' the Doctor agreed.

'And so that is where our grief comes from?'

The Doctor nodded. The entire society was paralysed. Those above the surface unable to notice what was going on, lacking the scientific skills or desire to question the world around them, happy with their endless baubles. Those beneath the surface were equipped with a vast and terrible power, but one that made them so sad they were unable to use or understand it. Lording it over all of them, the strangely broken figure of the Captain.

As he thought this through, the Doctor noticed the Mourners staring at him. A brief sensation crackled in his brain, flames catching at the first fire of autumn. They had shared his thoughts.

'Then the truth is known,' the Mourners chorused.

'Yes. I am sorry for you,' the Doctor concurred. 'The truth is known. And it's not a pleasant one. It so rarely is. Now, what are you going to do about it?'

The Mourners turned to each other. The old woman stepped back into the crowd and Pralix stepped forward. When he spoke his voice was firm, definite.

'We shall find a way to harness our power properly. To avenge the crimes of Zanak.'

The Captain regarded the Guard.

He really was behaving very oddly. He'd just stood there, crying as the Polyphase Avatron attacked him. He hadn't even run, which was really most disappointing. The bird had produced a set of claws and then proved how good they were at raking, tearing and shredding. The Guard was so sunk in his own misery, he'd barely noticed.

Aware that the mood on the Bridge was getting strained, the Captain had called the bird off and led the Guard over to a hole in the floor.

The man stood there, quavering at the edge.

When the Captain spoke to him, his voice was soft, coaxing. 'What's happened? What can you tell me?'

The Guard shook his head, shaking with misery.

For a moment the two of them stood there, considering the darkness of the pit. Then the Captain's boot nudged the Guard and he tumbled forward into the hole, vanishing with a cry that went on for a while.

'You didn't bring me good news, so I'm sending you back down to try again,' the Captain said softly.

He waited until the cry cut off abruptly, and then turned back to his appalled crew.

'Why must I be surrounded by incompetent fools?' He laughed. 'Any ideas?'

He hoped they'd learn from this.

The crew just stared back at him in horror.

Chapter Sixteen
Guilt Futures

Mr Fibuli wondered if death was yet again on its way. The Captain had been very cross all afternoon. All the Guards had been brought up from inside the planet. All of them seemed utterly, wretchedly miserable, and had only cheered up slightly when killed by That Thing, which now sat watching him hungrily from the Captain's shoulder.

The Nurse was in attendance. Multiple executions in the same day had been, she said, dangerously fatiguing, and, if she hadn't been on her break, she would certainly not have allowed it. She was carefully checking the readings on her little black box while the Captain ranted uneasily.

'Do you know what my problem is, Mr Fibuli?'

'Well no, sir. Of course not,' the First Mate ventured cautiously.

'It is that I have been too lenient.' The Captain glared out of the window until the twin suns backed away a little. 'By the blood of the Sky Demon, but we have been queasy fools! Why have we not obliterated the Mourners years ago and rid ourselves of their sickly power?'

'But Captain,' Mr Fibuli pointed out reasonably, 'we have tried many times in the past…'

'And failed Mr Fibuli, and failed!'

'Well, yes, but…' Mr Fibuli's eyes wandered over to the pile of corpses and then switched back to the sky. 'Captain, you said yourself it was a question of priorities…'

'I said? You dare to lay the rotting fruits of your own incompetence at my door? You shall rot in death in an instant!' He staggered to his feet, pointing furiously at his hapless aide. The robot parrot perked decidedly up.

The Nurse laid a gentle, restraining hand on the Captain's shoulder. It rested just out of reach of the bird's beak.

The Captain glanced up at her, pleading for another go on his favourite ride. The Nurse shook her head.

Aware that he was not going to die right this instant, Mr Fibuli pressed home his advantage. 'Captain, in your wisdom you observed that whilst the Mourners lay dormant with no leader and no purpose we were well enough protected, and they performed a useful psychological function as a focus for the fear and aggression of the people, and that very hatred, which you have so ingeniously channelled, has contained them. The stalemate was in our favour.'

'But now they will not be leaderless!' the Captain rumbled furiously. 'Now they will have a clear purpose. If they can't work it out for themselves, then the Doctor will happily give them one.'

'But Captain,' began Mr Fibuli with a clear and delighted twinkle. 'Now the means to destroy them is at last within our grasp. The planet of Calufrax which lies in the bellyhold of Zanak is rich in Voolium and Madranite 1-5. That is, after all, what we came here for.'

'Voolium and Madranite 1-5?' The Captain awkwardly stroked his own chin. 'That is true, that is true. What of them?'

'Well, I was just thinking, we could harness the vibrations of the refined crystals to produce interference patterns in the ether, which will neutralise the mental power of the Mourners.'

The Captain gurgled with delight. 'That will leave them defenceless, as weak as ordinary men, obliterable! Oh, excellent, Mr Fibuli, excellent!' The Nurse gave Fibuli an encouraging smile. 'Oh yes,' the Captain continued. 'Mr Fibuli! Your death shall be delayed.'

'Thank you again and again, sir.' Mr Fibuli hoped he didn't sound too dry. 'Your goodness confounds me.'

'We don't have time to discuss my goodness or the confusion it causes you!' The Captain was up and out of his chair before the Nurse could stop him. 'We have time only to destroy the Mourners! But by the ninety-three names of the Demi-God of Night, how soon can you be prepared, Mr Fibuli?' He was making an odd gesture as he tried to thump his metal fist into his dead palm. 'How soon will the crystals be ready?'

'Ah, well, that's difficult, sir…' Mr Fibuli started to sketch on a scrap of paper. The maths were really very complicated, but perhaps a little could be done. He noticed the Nurse arch an eyebrow.

'Difficult?' The Captain tapped the parrot on his shoulder awake. 'Why, the gnarled finger of the Sky Demon beckons you, Mr Fibuli…'

Mr Fibuli barely noticed the malicious glare of the robot, scribbling away on his pad. 'Well, if we put all the automated mining and processing equipment on the planet onto full power, sir, we could reduce the entirety of Calufrax within hours, but the machinery will be dangerously overloaded…' Finished, he tore out the scrap of paper and handed it to the Captain.

'That matters not a quark, Mr Fibuli!' The Captain screwed the paper into a ball. 'Speed is of the essence! The Mourners will be moving even now, do it on the instant and this time there shall be no escape for them, or for the Doctor!'

The Captain swung round to stare down at his kingdom. When he spoke again his voice was soft, almost pleading. 'Crush that planet! Hurry, Mr Fibuli.'

Mr Fibuli glanced over at the Nurse. She nodded with soft encouragement, and he scurried over to the computer. The Extraction Team rushed to obey, throwing the second greatest engines on Zanak into action.

Pralix was about to make a speech. Kimus perked up. He was clearly on familiar ground here. He liked a speech. Something to cheer loudly about and then bicker over afterwards. But still – Pralix the Chief Mourner? Fancy that.

Pralix stood in the cloud of dust. 'The Time of Knowing is come upon us. The Evil is named unto us. There shall be no more waiting. We go to destroy the Captain. Come, Doctor. Come, brothers!' He swept his arms up unto the air and the great rock door swung open.

Kimus led the surge towards the door, but the Doctor did not move.

'There's no point in being in too much of a rush, you know. There's something more I want to know about the Captain first.'

Pralix paused, conjuring up the Captain's face in the dust. 'Yes? Tell us, Doctor.'

The Doctor walked slowly around the sparkling effigy. 'Well, who exactly is the Captain?'

Zanak started to shake. On the planet's surface the waters rippled and the sands stirred. The shaking increased as you went up the mountain until you reached the Citadel. The entire Bridge was in turmoil as the engines threw their full force into the planet Calufrax. A noise filled the Bridge. The sound of a world screaming.

The Captain was on his feet, somehow keeping his balance as his crew gripped on to their desks. The Captain was driving on progress, and it could never be fast enough.

'Hurry, by the Sky Demon! By the hot breath of Death himself! I tell you, hurry! Calufrax is to be rendered! The Mourners will be obliterated.'

Deep underground they sensed the vibration, like the distant roar of a faraway engine. K-9's head turned to one side, curious. Romana felt mildly travel sick. The Mourners looked from one to the other, anxious, impatient to be gone.

But the Doctor stood his ground in front of the glowing figure of the Captain. Which rippled slightly. He may be in charge of a small rebel army of very angry telepaths, but this was one occasion on which he was not to be hurried.

'Where did the Captain come from? Not from Zanak, I bet.' He turned to a Mourner. 'Do you know? Does anyone know?'

The Mourners looked confused. The Doctor had explained the cause of their sorrows. Surely that was enough. Pralix looked anxiously over to the old woman who had, until recently, led them. She shook her head. It was clear that she wanted no more burden.

Romana could see the look of impatience and worry on their faces. She rather fancied she could read a crowd better than him. 'Does that matter, Doctor? Surely now is the time to move!'

The Doctor would not be budged. 'Of course it matters. Preparation is always terribly important, isn't it, Romana?'

Romana blinked.

'If you're deliberately setting out to destroy somebody, it's only decent to know a little bit about them. Anyway, the Captain may provide the answer to where the second segment is. Had you forgotten what we came here for?'

'Even so…' Romana looked again at the crowd.

The Doctor adopted his 'be reasonable' tone. 'And if he's been unable to destroy the Mourners so far, I hardly think he's likely suddenly to come up with a way of doing it this afternoon, now is he?'

203

The Doctor, as it happened, was very wrong.

Mr Fibuli gave a shout of joy that startled everyone on the Bridge. Even the Nurse blinked.

Mr Fibuli was waving a sheet of paper. 'The Extraction Team report the plant is now working at maximum capacity. The engines are holding! We will soon have the entire Voolium and Madranite crystal harvest!'

'Excellent, excellent.' The Captain staggered over and clapped Mr Fibuli affectionately on the back. Winded, Mr Fibuli decided he'd rather his master was just angry with him. 'You know, it would give me great pleasure to prepare the Psychic Interferometer myself. I would like to feel personally responsible for the final obliteration of the cursed Mourners. Fetch me some equipment!'

The Captain rubbed what passed for his hands together and sat down at a desk. He loved a project.

Pralix had eventually started to speak. He had prefaced his tale with a heavy regret. What he had to say was little more than a fairy story. 'The coming of the Captain is a matter of legend. Zanak was once a teeming, prosperous world, full of green and pleasant things… until it fell under the cruel yoke of the cursed Queen Xanxia of Zxoxaxax, may her spirit never rest.' The glowing pillar of dust formed into the figure of a regal, beautiful young woman. Her face was cold, and cruel, her eyes empty. The Doctor found her oddly familiar. 'It is thought Queen Xanxia was possessed of evil powers, for the legend says she lived for many hundreds of years.'

The Doctor interrupted Pralix. 'Now come on, that's not necessarily evil, you know.'

Pralix, annoyed at the interruption, glared at the Doctor. He opened his mouth to begin again.

'Master!' called K-9, suddenly alert.

'Hush, K-9,' commanded the Doctor. 'Please carry on, Pralix. I do so hate interruptions.'

'By the end of her reign, the whole of Zanak had been sacrificed to her evil caprice. She squandered and plundered her way through every resource that Zanak had. Her passion was extravagance, opulence, cruelty – vain wars to satisfy a whim, wild parties that would lay waste a continent – she amused herself whilst Zanak burned.'

'Sounds like Ancient Rome all over again,' the Doctor mused. He'd visited a few times. It had always ended badly.

'May Xanxia be accursed,' Pralix continued as though the Doctor hadn't spoken. 'It was to a desolate ruined land inhabited by only a few miserable nomad tribes that the Captain came.'

'How did he come?' Romana asked.

'The legend speaks of a giant silver chariot that fell from the sky one night with a mighty crash like thunder. It fell onto the Citadel of Xanxia. The people thought themselves free of their tyrant, but little realised that a worse curse had fallen on them. Most of the ship's crew died. But the Captain lived, may he be accursed.'

'With the aid of some pretty elaborate surgery by the look of him,' the Doctor suggested.

'Elaborate? Hardly.' Romana snorted. 'It's the kind of auto-surgery you'd get if you didn't bother to read the manual.'

'Well,' the Doctor coughed. 'What's important is that I wonder who did that?'

'On that the legend is silent,' snapped Pralix a little tartly. 'The Captain enlisted the aid of our ancestors to undertake years of mysterious construction work, at the end of which he pronounced himself satisfied and promised the people a new Golden Age of Prosperity…'

'They were stupid fools to listen to his promises,' thundered Kimus, striding in front of the Mourners, confronting them. Every now and then he shot a look at Romana, as though seeking her approval. It did not go unnoticed by Mula. 'Golden Age of Prosperity? Pampered slavery more like.'

'Maybe,' said Mula. For some reason she no longer hung on every word that Kimus said. 'But you'd have done just the same yourself. Particularly when the wealth turned up. And you did, didn't you?' She pointed to Kimus's richly adorned robe.

Kimus reddened and went very quiet.

Pralix coughed. 'And then, the legend says, for most of the people the wealth flowed…'

'And I'm sure everyone was deliriously happy!' snapped Kimus.

'Most were. Unthinkingly so. But for a few of them started the terrible agonies of the mind.'

'The dying Life Force of each pirated planet…' the Doctor mused.

'The Life Force…?' Romana queried. Oh hello, he thought she'd raise that one.

'Master…!' began K-9 again.

The Doctor noted this. This was the second interruption from K-9. That meant something bad was happening and / or coming their way. He knew that he had two more interruptions to go before it became serious and worth doing anything about. He had to act quickly. 'Just a minute, K-9. Do go on with your fascinating legend, Pralix.'

'But…' insisted Romana. She had to draw a line. They were standing on the site of an intergalactic crime and the Doctor was teaching its population theories from lurid spaceport paperbacks.

The Doctor made sure he had everyone's attention, declaiming grandly: 'Every planet in the universe, whether populated or not, carries within it its own unique Life Force. Every atom in the universe has a certain amount of energy locked inside it. With something the size of a planet, of course, there's an enormous quantity. The Life Force. And this dies when Zanak smothers it.

'Some of this energy will be on psychic wavelengths. So every time Zanak extinguishes a planet, it releases a fantastic blast of psychic energy, enough to smash open the neural pathways of anyone with latent telepathic ability, unlocking vast secret areas of the mind…' He was, he realised, making half of this up.

But Romana seemed impressed. 'And so… the Mourners were created?'

K-9 whirred dangerously. He was about to say something.

'The Life Force,' the Doctor continued quickly. 'It's an etheric reservoir. The more worlds Zanak destroys, the mightier it grows.'

'Each dying planet has bequeathed the power by which it will be avenged!' Kimus declared grandly. 'Mourners! This is your gift, your destiny – the power to crush the Captain.'

The Doctor wished people wouldn't put things like that. Kimus was right, of course. But he just sounded so pompous, throwing round fancy words without any idea of what they meant. He narrowed his eyes and considered the young man, and an idea formed. Before this was all over, he would take Kimus on an adventure. Show him a thing or two. It had already worked wonders with Romana. He looked over at her. She was examining her fingernails.

'This legend of yours,' she said to the room. 'Does it say how long ago it was the Captain arrived?'

'Two hundred years.'

'Two hundred years? Now that is interesting.' Romana looked up from her fingertips and favoured the room with a polite smile. The Doctor wasn't sure why, but he felt a little unnerved.

'Master?' prompted K-9 for the third time. Fair enough. Give him a chance.

'What do you want, K-9?'

'My seismograph detects enormous increase in mining operations across Zanak.'

The Mourners twitched at that. The Doctor really should look at K-9's tact circuits. But that did explain the tiny vibration in the air.

'Every mining plant is working at full pressure,' the dog continued. 'The planet beneath us is being totally consumed.'

The Mourners bowed their heads in silence.

'It ends again,' the Chief Mourner sighed, sinking to the floor.

Was it his imagination, or could the Doctor hear the grinding of enormous drills?

'Poor Calufrax,' said the Doctor. 'It means the Captain must be up to something.'

The Mourners looked distraught, but the Doctor reassured them. 'No, no, no, this is a good thing. We've given him a fit of the Panics. Well come on, what's everyone sitting about for? How do we get out of here?'

Pralix wearily pointed to the rock door. 'This way leads back to the city.'

'Right, shall we go?'

Kimus leaned over him. 'But what are you going to do, Doctor?'

'Oh, haven't I told you my plan?' The Doctor's grin lit up the room, casting shadows on the agonised faces of the Mourners. 'You really ought to hear my plan, it's terribly good. Now…'

At first Mr Fibuli thought that the Captain was whistling while he worked. Then he realised it was the Polyphase Avatron, chirruping as it hopped across the table, eagerly pecking its way through the circuit boards piling up around the Captain. Both man and pet seemed strangely content, almost happy.

It had been a long time since Mr Fibuli, since anyone, had seen the Captain this happy. While everyone else rushed around the Bridge, monitoring the devouring of Calufrax, their fearsome master was sat in a corner, crouched at a workbench, devoting himself to his project. He was using what remained of his hands with dexterity and skill. Mr Fibuli watched as the Avatron hopped across the table with a solenoid in its beak, one which the Captain welded neatly into place with the tip of a metal finger. It hopped away to find another component, almost like it was helping him build a nest. The equipment that was taking shape was both powerful and strangely elegant. The Captain tapped the edge of it with another thumb, taking readings.

'Alpha suppression signal triggering 338.79 microbits. Neuro Wipe-down circuit operational, Lobal Derangeamatic feedback parallel with the corticoid simulator. Oh, this is excellent!' The Captain leaned back and smiled as much of a smile as he could. His voice was almost a contented sigh. 'Why, by the left frontal lobe of the Sky Demon, Mr Fibuli, I was one of the greatest hyper-engineers of my time. And I still have it.' His face lit up with childish enthusiasm.

'Indeed Captain, your reconstruction of this planet is proof of that.' Mr Fibuli's flattery was sincere.

The Captain dismissed this nobly. 'Oh, that was a makeshift job Mr Fibuli, the best that could be done with what little was to hand.' And yet his smile broadened. 'Sine wave arlingtometer level 2267709...'

'But Zanak must be one of the great engineering feats of all time, surely,' marvelled Mr Fibuli, rubbing at his glasses. 'To build a hollow, space jumping planet...'

The Captain shook his head with gentle admonishment. 'It is not scale that counts, Mr Fibuli, but skill. Now, the ship from which most of the major components were salvaged, the *Vantarialis*... Now there was a ship...' He pushed back the circuits and stood up. Motioning Mr Fibuli to follow him, he crossed to the enormous window, gazing out at the world beneath the mountain. If he was looking at anything, it was at somewhere a long way beyond the view. 'The *Vantarialis* was the greatest raiding cruiser ever built, and I built it, Mr Fibuli, I built it!' The Captain glowed with pride. 'I made it with technology so far advanced from anything you have ever seen you would not be able to distinguish it from magic.'

The Captain paused, a small tic twitching on his right cheek. All that remarkable technology. Had he really invented all of it? And yet, what was that in his head? The echo of a deep, rumbling voice, whispering to him? He dismissed it. Mr Fibuli was speaking of the time when the Captain had been happiest.

'Yes, Captain, I heard my great grandfather speak of it with awe in his voice and tears in his eyes.'

'Your great grandfather?' The Captain gripped the deck rail and sighed admiringly. 'Why, he was a fine First Mate on the *Vantarialis*, daring, loyal and vicious...' If either was remembering that the Captain had slain him, neither mentioned it.

'And he was proud to be so,' Mr Fibuli concurred. 'As I am proud to be First Mate on this planet. First Mate on a planet. A considerable honour.'

It was, bafflingly, the wrong thing to say. 'This planet!' hissed the Captain. 'This vile lumbering planet! You presume to compare this ugly lump of blighted rock with the greatest, sleekest, most deadly ship that ever dared the starways?'

'Well, it probably doesn't have the sporty performance sir, but...'

The Captain's fist smacked into the railing, splitting it in two. 'Devilstorms, Mr Fibuli, you are a callow fool!' The Captain's rage was curious. It wasn't just angry – it was somehow miserable. 'Do you not see how my soul is imprisoned, how my heart burns for the dangerous liberty of the skies, plunder, battle and escape, savage acts of personal violence... And here I am, bound to this rock, beset with zombie Mourners and meddlesome Doctors.' The Captain reached out, tapping the shattered railing, prodding it regretfully as it swung back and forth. 'They shall all die, you know, Mr Fibuli.'

The Nurse appeared at the end of the gantry, and looked at the Captain with concern. Seeing her approach, he sighed, and turned on his heel. He marched back to his workbench. He sat down, picked up a circuit board and began to solder it together.

He considered his next curse carefully. 'By all the flaming moons of Hell, they shall die! I must complete this machine. Bring me the crystals, Mr Fibuli!'

'As soon as we have them.' Mr Fibuli went off to check a progress report from the mines.

'I shall be avenged! Avenged!' As the Captain worked, he continued to mutter about vengeance. A spasm had developed in his shoulder. His fingers twitched uselessly, dropping the soldering iron. The Captain roared, his thundering rage causing the parrot to back away.

A softly restraining hand landed on the Captain's shoulder. It was the Nurse.

'Ah, there you are,' she said. 'There's no getting away from me, you know.'

'I shall be avenged,' the Captain snarled.

'Of course you will,' the Nurse reassured him. She coolly took his temperature, tested his pulse, and then monitored his blood pressure.

The Captain shrugged her away, but she carried on inflating the cuff around his elbow. She looked with bored curiosity at the half-built machine and said with dry politeness, 'How lovely! I see you've found some occupational therapy. It's a good thing not to let your old skills die.'

The Captain nodded, and muttered sullenly, 'Oh, I assure you, my old skills are very much alive…'

On the lower slopes of the mountain was a blue box.

It had taken the Captain's Guards some time to find it, mostly because, for some unaccountable reason, they kept passing it and going, 'Oh, that.'

Perhaps it was because the blue box looked so very little like an advanced spaceship. Or perhaps it was because the blue box just did not want to be found.

But eventually, the Captain's Guards noticed the blue box, and when they did, it got all their attention. The Captain had ordered them to find the visiting aliens' craft and to get into it on pain of death. This did not, on the face of it, seem that much of a challenge. The blue box was made out of wood – it definitely was, as, when they tried shoulder-charging the door, they got splinters. They tried to force the lock, but then got the impression that the box was somehow laughing at them. So they unholstered their guns. The rays, focused by the finest real diamonds, should prove a match for anything.

The Guards got to work.

The Chamber of Mourning was a hive of activity. There was an air almost of excitement among the Mourners. To the Doctor it all seemed rather curious.

Many billions of creatures lived their entire lives without ever quite knowing what it was for or why things kept happening to them. Up until a few minutes ago the Mourners had simply known that they were literally stricken by grief, possessed of a mighty strength but with no idea of how to channel it, or what it was for. Now they knew the terrible source of their great power and they were hungry to use it.

Mula and Kimus looked rather less happy. This was understandable. They had just learned that all their wealth came from the deaths of other planets. Pralix was holding Mula's hands gently, a soft, sad expression on his face.

'The Life Force?'

Pralix nodded. 'Every time a planet died, I felt it.'

'Were you in a lot of pain?'

Pralix let go of her hands, rubbing against the torn patches of his robe. 'It was unbearable. As the Captain's hunger accelerated, so did my agonies. But now I am with people who can share the burden. Who can help me understand it.'

Mula wondered if he'd thrown that barb deliberately, but his hands reached out for hers again.

'Do you know what? I feel worse,' said Mula, not looking into his sad eyes. 'Because while all that was happening, I couldn't feel anything at all.'

Romana was still not entirely certain that planets themselves had souls and was conferring with K-9 on the matter. Between the two of them they were reaching a mutually agreeable framework based around Bocca Variables on the Vantalla Scale.

The Doctor listened to their conversation and smiled. Romana still had a lot to learn about the universe. How could a planet have a soul? Well, she had yet to see an English country garden on a summer's day.

He looked at his troops. Yes. It was time to go save a planet.

CHAPTER SEVENTEEN
NOTHING LIKE A PLAN

'This,' said the Doctor, fully aware that he was showing off, 'is like taking fish from a baby.'

Crouched by a pillar in the square, he neatly bowled a bag of liquorice allsorts arcing through the air. They scattered across the bonnet of an air-car, causing the Guard inside to leap out. Glaring around at the square, he drew his gun and headed off into the shadows.

The Guard didn't realise that the Doctor had already slipped into the air-car, dragging Kimus with him and depositing K-9 on the back seat.

Kimus was bouncing in the seat. Clearly, if the revolution was going to involve air-cars, he was all for it. Still, that was partly why the Doctor had brought him along. It was time Kimus learned what real life was like.

The Doctor flicked a few switches and the air-car lifted off. 'I really must stop doing this, you know,' he sighed, 'It's like shooting candy in a barrel.'

As they soared out into the desert, he waved down at the Guard beneath them.

The Guard waved back.

Then, realising he should do something, he shouldered his gun and fired.

The Doctor staggered from the smoking ruins of the air-car. His hands were already up in the air in surrender. He spat some sand dune from his mouth and grinned sheepishly at the Guard.

'Oh, I'm terribly sorry.' He jerked his head towards the wreckage behind him. 'Is this yours?'

The Guard hit the Doctor over the head.

Mr Fibuli found the Captain in his gallery, looking at his trophies. Their light flashed past the Captain's face, but he seemed almost asleep. Mr Fibuli wondered if the Captain ever slept. He started to feel awkward. Had he been standing there too long? He scraped up what courage he could.

'Captain?'

'Mr Fibuli?' The Captain jerked awake, his voice soft and thoughtful. 'Good news or bad?'

'Well…'

'Do go on.'

'I've just had a report. The Guards have been making fresh attempts to break into the Doctor's vessel to seize his Macromat Field Integrator…'

The Captain paused. It was both a dangerous pause and also a quietly amused one. Everything about his body language looked angry, but he seemed to be smiling as well. Mr Fibuli wondered if the last thing he ever saw would be that strangely angry smile.

'And?'

'Well, sir, nothing they can do to the craft will even mark it. There's no way of breaking it open.'

'Fools! Incompetent cretins!'

Mr Fibuli had learned to always have something up his sleeve. He produced a chart. 'But we have located a potential source for PJX18. I have determined that we can manage one more jump under our present conditions. If we made it to this planet, we could mine it for PJX18 and then make our own repairs to the engines.'

The Captain waved the chart away and strolled up onto the Bridge, deep in thought.

'We will mine this planet,' he announced to the crew. 'Prepare to jump as soon as the Voolium and Madranite 1-5 crystals have been produced. You know, it's all coming together marvellously, Mr Fibuli.'

Mr Fibuli had a small note to make. 'I feel I should point out, sir, that it is a heavily populated planet...'

The Captain's baleful stare shut the First Mate's mouth. 'You must remind me to catch up on my weeping one day, Mr Fibuli,' he yawned.

For a moment, Mr Fibuli was appalled. The loss of life, the paperwork. 'In other words,' he stammered, 'go ahead, sir?' Perhaps he was toying with him.

The Captain paused, as though about to reconsider. Then he snorted. 'By the blood-red eye of the Sky Demon, we will mine it, whatever and wherever it is!' He snatched up Mr Fibuli's chart and unrolled it across a workbench.

Mr Fibuli wafted a hesitant finger at a small blue-green dot on the chart. 'It is here, sir, in the planetary system of the star Sol. The planet Terra.'

'Ah yes, a pretty planet.' Was there a trace of regret in the Captain's voice?

Mr Fibuli handed him a mineral report, his tone coaxing. 'It looks a pleasant world, Captain.'

The Captain studied the report slowly, and Mr Fibuli could see his brain working.

'Yes, very pleasant,' the Captain announced eventually. 'It shall be a pleasure to atomise it!'

'Yes, sir,' Mr Fibuli sighed sadly. 'I shall make arrangements.'

He folded up the chart neatly, pocketed the mineral report, turned around and left the Bridge. The Polyphase Avatron watched him go and then clucked.

The Nurse appeared with some medication. She smiled at the Captain. 'Ah. Are we having another planet so soon, Captain?'

'Yes,' the Captain grated irritably. 'Another planet.'

'Then your objective will soon be reached, won't it?' she said soothingly as she started to check the Captain's vital signs against the readings on her black box.

The Captain snorted with laughter. 'It shall. It shall indeed.'

'How very nice for you,' said the Nurse, popping a thermometer between his teeth.

The Captain grimaced.

'And then what will you do?' she asked, ignoring the Polyphase Avatron's furious gleam. 'When you've finished that little project, what next?'

The Captain looked suspicious and worried, but then he rallied. 'What next indeed? Perhaps I'll find another hobby.'

The Nurse and the Captain regarded each other, the Nurse holding her little black box. Then Mr Fibuli came racing excitedly back onto the Bridge.

'Captain! They've caught the Doctor! They're bringing him here!'

The Captain bit through the thermometer and spat it out. 'Excellent Mr Fibuli, excellent! Fire up the torture computer! I foresee another little pleasure for us to enjoy!'

Kimus was enjoying being held prisoner almost as much as he'd enjoyed the air-car ride. He was, for the first time in his life, the centre of attention. Admittedly, the Doctor was unconscious, but Kimus was more than happy to deputise for him. 'I am Kimus. I speak with the True Voice of Zanak,' he had told the Guards. They had jeered at him, which felt marvellously satisfying. It was all glorious. Why he'd heard the Captain's own voice ordering him strapped down to the table.

Kimus had enjoyed denouncing the Captain as a monster, a parasite, and a tyrant. The Captain, for his part, had almost fondly ordered him beaten.

The Captain's voice had then, slowly and carefully, begun to explain to Kimus how he was going to be tortured.

'You are in the Knowhere,' the Captain had told him. 'The Doctor has already sampled its delights. It is an ingenious device,' he said, a touch ruefully. 'It reads from your mind an image of whatever it is you fear the most, and reproduces it in front of you. It's only an image, of course, but it will seem in all respects to be magnificently real to you and anyone else in the vicinity. The only way you can get rid of it is to turn off the machine. But first, of course, you have to get to it. Enjoy yourself!'

The voice shut off. The white walls of the room began to pulse.

'Ha!' laughed Kimus. 'I'm not afraid of anything.'

'I'm so glad to hear it,' groaned the Doctor, waking up. 'Oh good, chains.'

Kimus strained against his bonds and laughed. This was glorious. He was tied up next to the Doctor, about to be tortured to death by the Captain. This was living.

'And you won't be afraid of anything either, will you, Doctor?' he exclaimed. 'You are, after all, a hero, an adventurer. You fear nothing.'

'Actually, I fear a good deal of things. It's healthy.'

'Don't worry, my brother, I shall protect you.' Kimus stiffened himself as the pulsing increased. 'Oh.'

'Yes,' said the Doctor.

They were in space. Planets span all around them.

'What is this?'

'The last time I was in here –' the Doctor's voice was measured – 'I hadn't been clubbed unconscious for at least half an hour. My mental shields were in tip-top shape. Now they're not.'

'But this! This… it's beautiful!' Kimus marvelled. 'What are they?'

'Planets,' said the Doctor. 'Like Zanak. Only there are a lot of them.'

'But they're… round. Are all worlds round?'

'Yes.'

'And there must be dozens of them.'

'The universe has a lot of planets in it.'

'A hundred?'

'Considerably more than that. These aren't all of them.'

'So why these?'

'These?' the Doctor sighed miserably. 'These…'

The planets started to burn.

'What's happening to them? Is this what will happen as the Captain voyages to them?'

'Oh no,' the Doctor groaned. 'This has happened already. These are all the planets I failed to save.'

Kimus watched as each world was consumed and winked out. The Doctor, the laughing hero at his side, fell silent.

'Oh,' said Kimus. His confidence in the Doctor had ebbed.

'I tried my best,' the Doctor whispered. 'I always do. But I don't always succeed.'

'Surely not,' Kimus frowned. 'I mean, if there was a chance that you failed… you wouldn't risk it, would you?'

'Look at all these.' The Doctor slumped back against the slab. 'These are my failures. No man should have planets on his conscience.'

Kimus huffed himself up. 'Well, I can assure you…' He faltered.

'Yes?' The Doctor arched a weary eyebrow.

Kimus was staring at the cinders floating through the void. 'How many worlds has Zanak devoured? How many worlds are on my conscience?' His hand slapped at the jewels on his robe, plucking them out. 'How many more before we can stop it? Can we even try?'

The ruined planets whirled around him in a dizzying display.

'It's a wretchedly effective machine,' the Doctor sighed. 'Close your eyes if you can.'

They lay there for a bit more, watching skies burn and explosions bloom.

'What's that one?' asked Kimus.

'No,' said the Doctor. 'I'm not naming them. I can't face that.'

'Another of the Captain's brilliant inventions,' snarled Kimus.

'Do you think so?' said the Doctor. 'I notice this isn't a room he likes. Curious.'

'Curious?' laughed Kimus bitterly as another planet blew up. He'd heard quite enough of the Doctor. He'd believed in a fool, and now he was going to die for nothing.

They lay there in angry silence as planets burned around them.

K-9 perched uncertainly on a dune in the desert at an angle of precisely twenty-three degrees. He emitted a few very wrong-sounding grinding noises. He tried performing an elementary sensory diagnostic, but the procedure barely got thirteen per cent through the start-up before stopping and trying again.

The robot dog was merely able to tell that he was damaged. This was not, in and of itself, good. Or bad. He surveyed the wreck of the air-car and realised it was far enough away from them to avoid being further damaged when it blew up in approximately 7.2 minutes.

He slid with difficulty down the slope, bumping up against the side of the air-car.

K-9 wondered if anything could be done, and if so, in what order. It searched the proximity for the Doctor-Master, or, in an emergency, Kimus.

There was no sign of either of them.

'Master?' he called hopefully.

There was no reply.

K-9 was simply on his own, in the desert. Well, this simply was not good enough.

Balaton sat in his cold, gold house and did some worrying.

The house felt so terribly empty and quiet now. Night was settling in, and he'd never felt more alone. They'd all gone.

He heard a footstep outside and barely even whimpered. If it was the Captain's Guards come for him, then very well. They'd already slain everyone else. Well, why not him? He deserved it. He'd never understood the world, why it did such terrible things, he had simply made his peace with it. And that just hadn't worked out. He hoped it would be quick. When they had shot his son, it had seemed relatively quick.

The footstep came again and the silver door opened. The Captain's Guards had come for him.

'Pralix, Mula.' He whispered his farewells to the grandchildren who'd never understood him.

'Pralix! Mula!' he cried, overcome with joy, flinging himself at the two figures in the doorway. He barely even noticed how strange Pralix looked, or the curious, haughty woman who strode in with them. He just held his grandchildren close.

'Pralix! Mula! Are you back from the dead? How are you here? Alive? How have you escaped the Mourners? Did they try to eat you? What have they done to you? How did you get away? Oh, but do I detect the benevolence of our Captain in this? I think I do! Praise the Captain!' He looked quickly, eagerly, from one to the next, hungry to hear them confirm it. But my word, Pralix did look very strange.

'No, Grandfather.' His grandson shook his head as though it were very heavy. 'The Captain is an evil man; he is responsible for all the evil crimes of Zanak.'

Balaton wasn't entirely pleased by this. Had Kimus been at him? It was one thing to scream with misery, it was another to turn on the only being that gave the world order. 'Evil? What crimes? It's very nice here if you don't ask questions, you know. Clearly, those terrible Mourners have addled your poor brains.' He tugged at Pralix's clothes. 'And these rags… a disgrace. How can you show yourself like this? Come. We must have something better, some gossamer-spun platinum for you to wear…' He headed off for the bronze trunk at the back, but Mula gently reached out a hand to stop him. She was holding on to him tightly, and he would have chided her, only he was grabbing on to her just as firmly. For some strange reason, he was shaking all over. He found himself glancing nervously at the newcomer, the cold young woman who was, even now, uncertainly prodding at the solid cushions of his sofa.

'Grandfather, you don't understand,' said Mula. Oh, she would begin every speech like this. 'We have been with the Mourners, and they are good people.' Her smile broadened as she uttered this shocking heresy, and Balaton wished the roof would fall down. 'The Doctor has explained everything to us, everything that is wrong with the world. We must, oh, we must destroy the Captain.'

This was just too much. He wouldn't have even tolerated this from Kimus. 'What? Destroy the Captain? What wicked nonsense is this? I knew that Doctor fellow was going to cause trouble and distress. Listen to me, to your grandfather, the Mourners are loathsome sick zombies.'

Pralix chuckled. It had been a long time since Balaton had heard him make that noise.

'Grandfather.' Mula employed the same gentle voice his wife had used to sing to the children. 'Pralix is a Mourner.'

She was speaking poison now. 'What…? Who…? What is this?' He stared at Pralix in horror. His clothes were very shabby. His face was rather pale. His eyes so strange. Surely… surely it wasn't that bad. He just needed some soup and a lie down.

Pralix laughed again, and this time Balaton heard the sadness in the laugh. 'It's true, Grandfather, the Mourners are just ordinary people like me. We have been damaged by the Captain's crimes, but that damage had given us the power to fight back.'

'The Captain has committed no crimes!' Balaton squinted at him defiantly. Dressing up was one thing. Even joining the Mourners. But to accuse the Captain, well! 'Be reasonable. What is a crime if it is not an act against the Captain? How can the Captain commit crimes?'

Up until now, Romana had observed the family reunion with intellectual interest. Gallifreyans did not really have families. They did not stand around in small units shouting at each other. The closest thing she'd ever really had to a parent was her tutor, a small, incredibly old man who was, if you asked her, well overdue for a regeneration. She had been terribly fond of her tutor. Even though she had found him intellectually limiting. He was so rigidly rule-bound she occasionally wanted to break a rule to see how the dear thing would react.

The contrast these people provided was fascinating. So this was what a family was. It appeared to be a group of bickering people who had very little in common and constantly annoyed each other. It amused her how they defined themselves by their relationship to external authority figures. The old man delighted in obeying the status quo. The children exulted in coming home to show off their defiance to it. She guessed that reaching an accord was how they demonstrated affection. It was all so very different to the way the Doctor behaved. He was, by this definition, a child, never happy with any authority figure. Did this make her his parent? She rather hoped not. This poor Balaton had become so rigid as to appear foolish. She rather hoped she was not like him. In which case, who aboard the TARDIS was the grown-up?

She thought about this for a moment more. Ah yes. K-9. He would do. He'd like that.

Having solved that one, she addressed herself to the problem of Balaton. She figured some good solid plain speaking would work wonders with him. In situations like this, anyone could be won over simply by stating your case. She was sure this fundamentally kind-hearted old man would be persuaded by a statement of facts. 'Listen, the only reason the Captain is able to supply all your needs and make you rich is that everything you have is stolen from other worlds.' She restated her last point emphatically. 'Old man, your world is eating other worlds!'

Balaton simply blinked at her and looked rather puzzled. 'What wickedness is this? Zanak is the world, there are no other worlds...'

'Then where did the Captain come from?'

'Well, he came from the sky, that's different...' Gods should not have to explain themselves.

'Listen to me.' Romana adopted an insistent tone that was not at all cross. 'I am from another world, from the sky if you like, and I promise you that the Captain...'

'You're from the sky?' Balaton considered her and then dismissed the idea with a richly deserved snort. 'Then you lie! Only the Captain comes from the sky. If you say you come from another world you lie, and thus everything you say is lies.'

That had, Balaton considered, dealt with her.

Romana found herself confronted with something of a logical tangle. Was she really going to have to convince this gibbering old fool of the existence of other worlds and of life on them before she could challenge his dogmatic acceptance of an imposed patriarchy? Well then. She rolled up her sleeves.

Pralix stepped forward, his voice so very tender.

'Grandfather, the other Mourners and I have come to explain to you and the people of this City that the Captain has made dupes of us all, made us collude with his crimes. We must destroy him.'

'Other Mourners? What? Where?' Gibbering, Balaton looked around him in panic, and then out of the door.

Standing silently in the street outside was a large group of Mourners, watching him. They all tried their best to smile at him.

Balaton let out of a scream of pure terror. 'The Mourners? You brought them here? Oh my poor children! I preferred you dead to mad!' And with that he ran out of the room. A distant door slammed.

'Well,' tutted Romana. 'Are all the people going to react like this?'

Pralix shrugged. It was a strangely normal gesture. 'I fear so.'

Mula glanced apologetically at the Mourners. 'Sorry. I said winning people over would be difficult.'

'Even so,' Romana sighed. 'We have to try.'

It appeared people did not like being told what to think. No matter, she thought. She was just going to have to be terribly persuasive. If the Doctor could do it, so could she.

Out in the desert, K-9 had extricated himself from the sand bank.

That done, he had spent some time working out what to do next. This was normally not a problem, but there were, he had to admit, a fair few things that needed taking care of. He made a list, ranked in order of priority.

Firstly, the universe needed saving.

Secondly, the second segment of the Key to Time needed to be located.

Thirdly, the world-eating engine at the heart of the planet needed to be disabled.

Fourthly, the entire system of governance of the planet of Zanak needed to be overthrown.

(There was a short pause at this point while his systems shut down and restarted. His auto-repair circuits reported a satisfying leap in performance. He worked out where he was. Ah. 57.14 per cent through a list.)

Fifthly, the Doctor-Master required rescuing.

Sixthly, the engines of the air-car needed repairing before they exploded.

Seventhly, the Mistress Romanadvoratrelundar needed...
K-9 paused. There at last was someone who frequently required
nothing of him. That was something.

Having considered his list, K-9 decided that rescuing the
Doctor-Master was, if not of the most importance, probably
the most pressing on his list of concerns. The Doctor-Master
was probably located in the Citadel on the top of the mountain.
The easiest way of reaching this was to use the air-car. The air-
car that was currently on fire.

So, K-9 put out the fire, using a few controlled blasts from
his gun to cascade the sand dune down onto the conflagration.
He then, with a little difficulty in gaining traction, rolled across
the dunes, and managed to access the engines. He effected a
few limited repairs, before going around to the side. As the craft
hadn't landed evenly, it was reasonably easy for K-9 to glide inside
and reach the controls.

Unlike the Doctor's repairs, K-9 was pleased that the engines
started first time.

'Master,' said K-9 to himself as he took off for the Citadel.

CHAPTER EIGHTEEN
THE SKY DEMON CAN WAIT

When the Captain came for them, the planets had all burned away. There were just the stars and the Captain walking across them.

The Doctor had long ago passed out. He was mumbling to himself. 'Haven't I told you my plan? You really ought to hear it, it's terribly good. I've worked it all out.'

His eyes drifted open.

He saw the Captain standing over him. He tried to sit bolt upright but was still tied down. Vexing.

'Oh well, back to being spontaneous. Good morning!'

He glanced over at Kimus, who was still a long way out of it. Probably for the best. When there had been just one planet left, the Knowhere had zoomed in to it. Allowing them to watch the continents burn, and then, moving closer, the cities, the buildings, and then the people.

That had been pretty hard going.

The starscape faded away, and they were alone in the empty white room.

'I thought you didn't like it in here,' remarked the Doctor.

The Captain managed a ghastly shrug, and changed the subject. 'So, Doctor, you have learned the little secret of Zanak?'

'Yes.' The Doctor's voice was cracked. This would never do. 'You won't get away with it you know,' he began. Good opening gambit.

'And what makes you so certain of that, Doctor?' the Captain said.

'At the moment, nothing at all, but it does my morale no end of good just to say it,' the Doctor smiled. 'I've been strapped down on slabs by better men than you.'

'Possibly, Doctor, possibly.' The Captain drummed his dead hand playfully on the slab. 'But I dare guess you have encountered few more vicious than me.'

'Vicious?' The Doctor laughed, but it was hollow. 'That, I admit, is a depressing thought.' He turned to the unconscious Kimus. 'Don't panic, Kimus, don't panic.'

Kimus did not panic. He remained heroically asleep.

The Captain had very carefully unplugged the computer at the heart of the Knowhere. He moved methodically. The Doctor craned his head on the slab to watch him at work, and found something marvellous about the caution the Captain employed. He may have looked as wieldy as a forklift truck but he moved with the precision of a surgeon. He seemed terribly concerned to do a good job of disabling the system. Interesting. Underneath all that shouting and impetuous rage, the Captain moved with a steady, imperturbable thoroughness.

Having deactivated the machine, the Captain wheeled over a chair and sat down on it. The Doctor was glad he couldn't see this bit of the proceedings terribly well, as he feared he would start giggling. This never went over well.

The Captain opened with a rather ghastly attempt at being convivial. 'By the fetid liver of the Sky Demon, Doctor, you have enraged me.'

'Who is this Sky Demon fellow, eh?' the Doctor asked. 'He doesn't sound at all healthy to me.'

The Captain's clawed hand reached out to tap the Doctor's nose very gently. When he spoke his tone was still terribly even. 'The penalty for causing me annoyance, Doctor? It is death. The penalty for enraging me is death of a very special kind.'

The Doctor tried not to yawn. He had been here before. He rather hoped that, hundreds of years from now, he'd still be strapped down to slabs being threatened by maniacs. Routine provided such a marvellous sense of stability.

'While you have been suffering down here, I have programmed the torture computer to devise a suitable manner for you to leave us, and believe me Doctor, my computer has a wicked imagination.' The Captain smiled proudly. 'By the horny elbows of the Sky Demon, I shall enjoy your death, nay, I shall relish it.'

A thought struck the Doctor, and he would have slapped his brow if his hands hadn't been manacled. 'The Sky Demon! I've got it. The Pirate Fleets of Agranjagzak used to terrorise and plunder the whole western sector of the galaxy, raiding the interstellar heavy haulage cargo ships by materialising around them, selling your services as mercenary warriors. The Sky Demon was the mythical devil that the souls of dead pirates were supposed to go to, like Davy Jones's locker. You know –' the Doctor considered his history – 'I thought you fellows were all destroyed in the Dordellis Wars. You were certainly meant to be. That's what the Dordellis Wars were all about.'

The Captain's ghastly geniality vanished in a moment. He sprang noisily to his feet. 'Devilstorms, Doctor, you do ill to trample in my past!' His arms flailed around menacingly.

The Doctor paid him no attention. He was on a roll. 'No, now don't tell me, you must be the Captain of the *Vantarialis*...

presumed destroyed, but the wreckage was never actually found. So, let me see, you crashed here on Zanak and started operations on a totally new scale. Just a guess, but is that it?'

The Captain was furious now. 'Silence, by the skies of Hell, silence! You know nothing of these things.'

'Oh, don't I?' The Doctor risked a smug grin. 'I thought I was doing rather well.' I have just, after all, worked out exactly who you are and where you come from, from just one casually invoked deity. Well done me.

Meanwhile, in his stolen air-car, K-9 glided over the city, noticing a small crowd in a square, kneeling before a golden statue of a noble, benign man in a grand uniform.

'Engage full forward thrust,' K-9 said to himself. 'Course, three two zero.'

He was making shaky but reasonable progress. K-9 was on his way.

The Captain was throttling the Doctor. His choked gasps were almost loud enough to wake Kimus.

The Captain let go of the Doctor's neck, and the Doctor was rather surprised to find it still intact.

'Tell me,' he croaked. 'Something that's been puzzling me is how come you're still with us. Without wishing to be rude of course – it's all right for chaps like me who are Time Lords to knock around for hundreds of years, it goes with the job, but a pirate?' The Doctor grinned. 'Two hundred years and more is overstaying your welcome. The gnarled fingers of the Sky Demon will be tapping a little impatiently by now, don't you think?'

The Captain tried to ignore the Doctor's grin and just couldn't. 'Doctor, I see you do not care to wait and experience the death my computer is preparing for you, you wish to die now.' He raised his robotic arm, powering up the pistons. 'So be it.'

The Doctor composed his face carefully. His hunch was that the Captain wouldn't go through with it. But that heavy hydraulic arm could split his head like a lettuce.

The arm swung down.

There was a cough.

Lounging in the door of the Knowhere was the Nurse. She gave every indication of having wandered past on her way elsewhere, sticking her head in to ask if anyone wanted a cup of tea.

The Captain's arm paused, centimetres from the Doctor's face, the servos whirring nastily.

'Doctor,' said the Nurse sweetly. 'The Captain does not respond well to being provoked. I think you're being a little tactless now, don't you?'

'I know. I'm terribly good at it, aren't I?' The Doctor squirmed around to look at the Nurse, and waggle fingers at her in a wave. She gave him a smile of complete and utter innocence. He did not care for it one bit.

Up on top of the mountain, K-9 brought the air-car in to land on the plateau with grace and skill. He detected its sigh of regret as he unplugged himself from the flight computer, and then faced the next problem: there was no easy way out of the air-car.

The Nurse continued to stand in the doorway. For a moment, the Doctor wondered whether she was going to come and take his pulse, or check on the worryingly comatose Kimus. But she walked over to the controls of the Knowhere. Her hands made as if to turn the machine on.

Did the Captain flinch as she did this? Was the Doctor imagining that? He could well be. He imagined so many things.

The Nurse checked a setting, nodded to herself, and then smiled at them. 'Well,' she announced. 'I'll leave you boys to it.'

She walked crisply away.

Once she had gone, and having made comically sure that they were alone, the Captain kicked over his own chair, and glared at it with satisfaction.

The Doctor was beginning to have his doubts about what was going on. The Captain's rage was undoubtedly formidable, and yet, also, curiously classifiable. Sometimes he seemed genuinely furious, sometimes he seemed not to give two hoots about who, what or why he was shouting, and sometimes his rage was that of a thwarted little boy. His insecurity was oddly cheering – the Captain was, by definition, one of the most powerful maniacs in the galaxy, and yet even he didn't feel happy with his lot.

The Doctor, by contrast, was perfectly content. He may have been chained up in a torture cell with a literally tin pot dictator, but he was learning things, and the Doctor did so enjoy having an enquiring mind.

'What are you doing it for, Captain?' The Doctor adopted his Be Reasonable tone. Romana would have been surprised to discover the Doctor had conversational gambits, but he did. He even had a special set of them, kept polished and sharp for use in dungeons:

- There was his old friend Angry Bluster ('You'll never get away with this, you know.')
- There was Feckless Insouciance ('I say, is that a mind probe? How jolly.')
- There was Outright Mockery ('Is this going to take long, only I've forgotten to cancel the milk.')
- And there was the occasional Trojan Horse attempt at undermining his enemy through cunning disguised as candour ('All right, all right, I'll tell you what you want to know – only…')

The Be Reasonable tone was used to bring villains down to his level. The Doctor had noticed that, from Super Computers to Giant Prawns, if there was one thing a megalomaniac did not care for, it was being treated as an equal. It really did provoke them, while at the same time forcing them to reveal any insecurities. If they stopped stroking their beard and their eyes slid nervously towards a big red auto-destruct button, then it was a good day.

The Doctor pressed on with the Captain, Being Reasonable. 'I mean, what's it all for, eh? It doesn't make sense and you know it. I can understand the life of a full-blooded pirate, the thrill, the danger, the derring-do, but this?' The Doctor gestured with a strapped-down shoulder. 'No. Hiding away in your mountain retreat whilst you hop through space eating other people's perfectly good planets? Where's the derring-do in that?'

'Ah…' True to form, the Captain hesitated wistfully before shouting. 'Silence, I forbid you to talk of these things!'

'You just try to shut me up,' goaded the Doctor. 'You can't kill me whilst I'm lying here helpless, can you?'

'I can't?'

'You can't. You're a warrior at heart and it's against a warrior's instinct. You should have thought of that before you tied me up.' The Doctor winked at the Captain.

'By the Hounds of Hell!' The Doctor had a point, so the Captain windmilled his arms and smashed them into the slab. It was all very intimidating, but perfectly harmless behaviour. Well, so the Doctor hoped. He knew the Captain. In his right mind, he'd never shoot someone in the back, he'd never bludgeon a helpless opponent. The Captain would, instead, do something stupid and let the Doctor win. The Doctor wasn't quite sure how, not just yet, but he definitely would win.

'It's very difficult not to listen, isn't it Captain, when someone's touching a nerve?' The Doctor edged a little bit of extra chattiness into his Being Reasonable. 'Yes, yes, you're a warrior, aren't you? But what are you after here? It can't be the fantastic wealth you've accumulated, can it? You don't need it, you don't use it, what does it benefit you? I mean you've hardly developed much of a lifestyle up here on top of your mountain.

I bet you haven't even bought yourself a pair of skis. What devilment are you really up to?'

'I…' began the Captain. He looked as though he was trying to lick his lip.

The Doctor pressed home his advantage. 'I assume you don't want to take over the universe? No, you wouldn't know what to do with it, beyond shouting at it.'

There was a ghastly silence in the room.

The Doctor and the Captain glared at each other, and the Doctor knew that this time, his life really did hang in the balance. He tried to work out how much of his head would survive if the Captain started pulverising it with his metallic fist. Probably not enough to make soup.

The Captain gave a sudden snort. Was it a laugh or fury?

'Well?' demanded the Doctor.

The Captain strode over to the door of the Knowhere. 'Guard,' he called.

'Yes, sir?' came an anxious voice.

'Release the Doctor.'

'Sir?'

'He said,' the Doctor called out, unable to keep the deadly earnest from his tone, '"Release the Doctor."'

CHAPTER NINETEEN
MEMENTO MORI

The Captain led the Doctor into his gallery. It had started out as his Trophy Room and become something altogether more awesome in scale. It was a vast circular chamber, the marble flagstones echoing marvellously. Suspended at regular intervals were little cases. They were, at first glance, slightly twee. The kind of places you might keep swimming trophies, or little plates with painted kittens.

The Doctor leaned close. No. No painted kittens.

Each cabinet contained a small model of a planet, hovering in mid-air, glowing gently as it spun in a force field. At one level the artistry was exquisite; at another it was ghastly. It was like standing in a graveyard orrery.

The Doctor noticed that someone had taken the care to very neatly label each of the exhibits. In his experience, very neat labelling was the sure sign of a maniac. The Doctor was standing in front of a model of Bandraginus 5. So realistic it looked as though you could simply fly down onto it. But it was not real. It was simply a tombstone.

'Doctor.' The Captain was striding proudly around his gallery, his arms pointing from one cabinet to the next. 'You say I am a warrior, and so I am – a pirate warrior. But I would not want you to die, as die you shall, I promise you…'

'Why, thank you.' The Doctor bowed, trying not to look at a model of the planet Granados. He'd once spent a long weekend fishing there.

'No.' The Captain was almost nervously proud. 'First I shall allow you to comprehend the extent of my genius.' He gestured at the whole of the room and waited for a reaction.

'Ah,' coughed the Doctor. 'It's "I'm not just a pretty face" time, is it?'

'Silence,' the Captain almost chuckled. 'Or the Sky Demon plucks you where you stand. This is my Trophy Room, Doctor.'

The Captain clapped, and the trophy cabinets began the spin, the glass cages fading away as the planets themselves lit up, spinning in a slow, beautiful waltz around each other.

'Feast your eyes on this, for it is a sight and an achievement unparalleled in the universe.'

'What?' the Doctor sneered. 'You've spent your evenings whittling little models of all the worlds you've destroyed. What are these? Memorials? Is that something you're pretty proud of, then?'

'These…' The Captain shook his fist. 'These are the entire remains of the worlds themselves!'

'What?' The Doctor stared at the spheres bobbing past his head. 'You ghoulish fiend!'

The Doctor had not, it should be said, taken in exactly what the Captain had said. There was a penny still to drop. He was preoccupied with doing some magnificent shouting. 'You come in here on your evenings off for a good gloat over the wanton destruction you have wreaked on the universe! Is this what you wanted to show off?'

The Captain shook his head, slowly and sadly. 'No, Doctor. You mistake me. I come in here to dream of freedom.'

The Doctor should have been listening to this, but that penny had finally dropped with a bang, and the Doctor could only hear the explosion in his head. 'Excuse me, did you say these are the entire remains of the worlds themselves?'

'Yes, Doctor!' The Captain tapped a passing planet labelled Viskon Alpha. 'Each of these small spheres is the crushed remains of a world. Millions upon millions of tons of compressed rock held suspended here by forces beyond the limits of the imagination, forces that I have generated and harnessed.'

'But that's impossible!' Staring at the light show around him, the Doctor experienced a terrible urge to run away screaming. 'That amount of matter in that small a space would undergo instant gravitational collapse and form a black hole. The whole of Zanak should be disappearing into a gravitational whirlpool.' He frowned at the walls, expecting them to collapse at any moment.

'Precisely, Doctor.' Standing at the centre of his dancing constellation, the Captain was enjoying himself. 'And why doesn't it? Because the whole system is so perfectly aligned by the most exquisite exercise in gravitational geometry that every force is balanced out within the system!' He was roaring away now, but there was a new tone to his voice, that of a scientist. The Captain no longer sounded angry. He sounded smug. 'Which is why we can stand next to billions of tons of super-compressed matter and not even be aware of it.'

He stroked the surface of a world.

'With each new planet I acquire—'

'*Acquire?*' The Doctor's jaw fell open.

'– the forces of my exhibit are meticulously realigned, but the system remains stable.'

'If what you say is true—'

'Oh, it is.'

'Then,' whispered the Doctor, 'it is the most brilliant piece of astro-gravitational engineering I have ever seen… It's a staggering concept. Pointless, but staggering.'

'I am gratified that you appreciate it,' purred the Captain.

'Appreciate it? Appreciate it?' The Doctor got this far and then, just for once, was lost for words. He jabbed an accusing finger in the direction of poor Bandraginus 5. 'You commit mass destruction and murder on a scale that is almost inconceivable to the human mind and you ask me to appreciate it because you happen to have made a brilliantly conceived mathematical toy out of the mummified corpses of planets!'

'Devilstorms Doctor!' The Captain seemed annoyed, rather than angry. 'This is not a toy!'

'Then what is it for?' The Doctor was nearly screaming. 'What are you doing? What can possibly be worth all this?'

The Captain flung the Doctor up against a passing light cage. It was empty, all neatly labelled and waiting to hold its memento mori. It was labelled 'Calufrax'. The Doctor found his head rammed into a space meant to contain an entire world, the force field buzzing around his head, surrounding his thoughts and mind, getting ready to close in on him. The pain was exquisite.

The Captain leaned very close, his voice ever so soft. 'By the raging fury of the Sky Demon, Doctor, but you ask too many questions. You have seen! You have admired! But you have not thought. Soon you will die! Bother me no more.'

Furious, the Captain yanked the Doctor's head out of the cage. The Doctor fell gasping to the floor.

'No one understands me…' Muttering to himself, the Captain turned away.

Lying on the floor, the Doctor had the strange feeling that he had disappointed the Captain somehow. He looked up at the tortured remains of planets hanging above him.

'What am I missing?' he wondered.

*

K-9 was now faced with a problem. He was, after all, not a particularly agile hound. No leaping over walls or worrying postmen's knees for him. He did not want to admit that he was stuck. Not stuck per se. He was simply faced with an annoying complication. He could not get out of the air-car. He decided that he could try and rock the craft onto its side by the simple method of rapid motivation backwards and forwards.

Having checked that he was unobserved, he then began to race from side to side in the air-car. The ship tipped with him, but, due to its landing legs, did not quite tip over.

K-9 stopped rocking.

It had all been Mula's idea, Romana thought as she ducked. A diamond the size of a fist smacked into the wall above her.

Things had turned ugly, and they had not really been that beautiful to start with. Going door-to-door with a group of telepathic zombies had turned out to be a pretty awful way of winning public support.

Doors would open, and, before Pralix could even flash his ghost of a smile, they would be slammed shut again.

The people of Zanak were, thought Romana, unfriendly and incurious.

'How does the Captain talk to them?' she asked.

Mula looked at her. 'He shouts at them,' she said.

'He would.'

'Well, he sends his Guards to shout at them in the public squares. There's normally someone there, sifting through the piles of Prosperity in case there's something they've missed.'

'Right then,' Romana announced, although it was definitely not her idea. 'Then let's go and shout at them.'

At the approach of the Mourners, the people in the square stopped sorting through the rubble and started fleeing in panic. But the Mourners came into the square from all sides. This had seemed,

Romana thought, like a good way of getting people's attention but, in the final analysis, it simply appeared to cause panic.

Realising they were hemmed in, the people started picking up gemstones and throwing them. It got a little unpleasant. Shoved and trampled and with her head stinging from a lucky shot with an opal, Romana hastily dismissed the nagging thought that the Doctor would have done this better. No, she told herself firmly, he would simply have been luckier. That was how things were for him.

She staggered to her feet, looked around, and decided how she could bring things under control.

Which was when the shooting started.

Oh dear. How terribly unhelpful.

The Captain's Guards rushed into the square, penning the Mourners alongside the people, and firing at both pretty indiscriminately.

Romana was only just learning about guards. The Doctor spoke about them like flies, rats or tax returns – a baffling inconvenience of existence. They had guards at home, on Gallifrey. But they were of quite a different calibre. For one thing, on Gallifrey, if you wanted to stand still looking after a doorway, you had to be fiendishly overqualified. Some of Gallifrey's greatest philosophers were guards, people who really valued the chance to spend a few hundred years standing still and really thinking things through. They were people who, if you were lost, or simply confused about the meaning of existence, were always happy to offer advice, if not an answer.

So much for Gallifrey. Sadly, things were, Romana was realising, not quite the same in the rest of the universe.

The guards she had so far met on her extensive voyages (i.e. two), had proved intellectually limited and liked hitting and shooting things. She wondered how you became one. While dodging a rather well-aimed blaster shot, she speculated on the bits of physiognomy visible peeping between their leather helmets. The Captain's Guards were subtly genetically different from the people of Zanak, and therefore, she inferred, were most likely the descendants of the Captain's original crew. There was, and here she allowed herself a sidebar while leaping away from a melting golden fountain, a lot to be said for the irony of this. The Captain's Formidable Crew of Space Pirates, scourge of the spaceways, a symbol of all that was disorder, becoming instead the Captain's Guards, upholding the rule of law on Zanak. They didn't even seem that interested by the piles of wealth. They'd gone from being mildly romantic crusaders to bored colonial rulers, taking pot shots at citizens and occasionally (Romana ruefully remembered) thumping visiting aliens. They were to be pitied, more than anything. Well, once she'd done something about them.

She grabbed Mula by the hand, pulling her away from a toppling bronze statue. 'This is all getting out of hand,' she said.

Mula nodded, her face pale.

'I really think the problem is—'

'Less words,' growled Mula.

'The Mourners aren't fighting back.'

'They don't.'

'Well, it's about time they did,' snapped Romana and hared through the bullets to Pralix.

The Mourners were just standing there, being shot at, falling to the golden dirt.

The people of Zanak stared at them with hatred and fear, pelting them with gems. The Captain's Guards fired at them. And the Mourners just did nothing. No force wall. No fight back.

The old woman who had recently retired as Chief Mourner caught Romana's eye, her face so wide and sad. 'This is how it is for us,' she shrugged. A rock hit her forehead and she toppled to the ground.

Romana tried getting Pralix's attention. 'Do something,' she yelled, snapping her fingers.

Pralix shrugged painfully, and she realised he had been shot in the shoulder. 'Our sadness is confronted by the people's hatred. We do not wish to make them fear us more.'

'On this one occasion,' said Romana, 'perhaps we can make an exception.'

Pralix considered this. His consideration was helped by Mula, who ran up and kicked his shin.

'Oh Pralix,' she shouted. 'I finally thought you'd found a purpose in life. But look at you – you're just as useless as ever. I don't care what you are, do something.'

Pralix sighed.

And the rest of the Mourners sighed with him. A sigh that echoed through the city.

A great wave of sadness poured out across the square.

The Guards stopped shooting and staggered back, sobbing helplessly as they crouched on the floor, swatting at the air as they tried to fight off the misery of existence.

The crowd of people fell back, subdued by the awful sight.

Pralix hopped up onto the ruins of the fountain, using it as a plinth.

'People of the City, you must listen to me!'

The crowd glared back at him, uncertain.

'It's me – Pralix! Yes, I have become one of the Mourners. But I have learned that they are not to be feared.'

The crowd stared at him, dubious.

'Komnor, listen! Pitrov! don't go! Kala, Bagindal!' He picked out familiar faces in the crowd who were shying away from him. 'The Mourners are your friends. Listen, it is the Captain who is evil!'

The crowd glared at him. This seemed highly unlikely.

'He has been destroying worlds to make us rich. That's why the mines keep filling up. We're stealing from other worlds, crushing them. We must destroy the Captain. He is not a great benevolent leader, he's a murdering maniac!'

The people of the city had never heard a Mourner speak to them like this before. Actually, they'd never heard a Mourner speak. But that really wasn't helping Pralix's message go over. Romana had grown up delighting in telling people the truth. People did so prefer it. And yet, looking at this, she was not so sure that the truth really was so delightful. Her tutor had always seemed utterly charmed when she had told him what she thought of his marking. And yet, out on other planets, this did not exactly seem to be the same. Why weren't other worlds Gallifrey?

'Listen to me!' repeated Pralix. 'The Captain is a maniac who must be destroyed. All your wealth comes from the deaths of worlds!'

The people stared at him. As much as a crowd could ever be said to be mulling it over, they mulled it over. Then they started to run away.

'Don't run off!' pleaded Pralix, as the people shoved aside the whimpering Guards and vanished into the streets.

'Stay and listen, can't you?' he wailed.

Mula watched him trying. She felt so proud of him. She was certain that, had Kimus been here, he would have made a better speech, but here was Pralix, actually standing in a crowded square and leading the fight against the Captain. She was so proud of him. Even if the square was now deserted.

Pralix shrugged helplessly.

Mula looked around and sighed. 'It's no good. We can't overcome their basic fear of the Mourners, we can't make them listen.'

Romana looked at the square, empty apart from a few whining Guards crawling miserably away.

'Yes you can, actually.' She smiled tightly. 'Look, we really shouldn't do it like this, but I think we have to. It's wrong, terribly wrong, to compel people to act in any particular way, but it can't be wrong to compel them to listen… and –' she smiled winningly at Pralix – 'the Mourners can do that. Can't you? Just make the people come back.'

The Mourners stood there and looked at her.

'Oh,' said Pralix.

The Mourners reached out into the vast cloud of sadness, and channelled off a few top notes – the parts that yearned, that ached with loneliness.

Gradually, the people started to wander back into the square, looking dazed. The original crowd was joined by more, by a huge press of the people, crammed into the square and the streets beyond, all staring up at the small crowd of Mourners with a look of desperate longing. They were completely hypnotised.

'Whatever you do,' Romana whispered to Mula, 'don't tell the Doctor I did this.'

Pralix nodded to the crowd. He knelt down, scooping up a handful of diamond dust. He flung the dust up into the air, and it hung there, shimmering and slowly forming into the picture of a planet.

'My friends. I have a sad truth to tell you today. Many of you have never known it. Some of you have done your best to forget it. It is about how the Captain made you rich…'

K-9 was experimenting with velocity of movement and even with shifting his internal gravity in order to tip the air-car over. He paused, up against the far side of the seat, and noticed something which he had failed to observe before. He chided himself silently for this, quietly pleased that no one was around to comment on his failure. No one would ever know.

The air-car was balanced by a runner on each side. He simply extended his nose blaster and severed the runner nearest to him.

The air-car tipped over.

K-9 felt a brief moment of mild triumph, followed swiftly by alarm as he was thrown out of the air-car, landing upside down on the grass.

This had not gone according to plan. His tra
wheeled helplessly.

K-9 bleated one word unhappily.

'Master?'

The Doctor stood in the Trophy Room. He knew that he was missing something. The planets hung around him, and all he felt was a little dizzy.

The Captain stood a little distance away from him, watching him curiously.

The Doctor wondered again what he was missing.

The empty case hovering near him started to glow. A small sphere appeared inside it. The crushed remains of Calufrax.

The Doctor stared at the trophy glumly.

The lights around the other exhibits glowed and sparkled as the gravity fields recalibrated themselves. In a triumph of dimensional engineering this happened without causing anything more than a tiny vibration in the Doctor's kidneys. He stared at the display, as though daring it to implode. It really wasn't just a feat of engineering, it was quite a piece of performance art. Slowly, steadily, the planets began to dance again.

After a while, he realised the Captain was standing at his side expectantly, giving him one final chance.

The Doctor ruefully shook his head. He still wasn't getting it.

The Captain sighed, a surprisingly gentle noise, and opened his mouth, about to speak.

Mr Fibuli appeared at the edge of the gallery, waving a clipboard frantically as he flapped across the floor. 'Captain! Captain, sir!'

The Captain glared at him, and Mr Fibuli wondered if he was about to die.

'We've just had news! From the City. It's the Mourners. They are gathering!'

The Doctor tried not to beam delightedly.

Surprisingly, the Captain appeared to have abandoned his frustration. He threw back his head and roared. 'Excellent, Mr Fibuli, that is simply excellent.'

This was not quite what the Doctor had expected. The brightness dropped out of his face. He really had missed something quite important. Surely the Life Force feeding the Mourners was more than a match for anything the Captain had up his sleeve? A planet glided past his nose and the Doctor became more certain. The Captain had manufactured the means of his own destruction. How poetic.

The Captain swept away, Mr Fibuli trailing in his wake.

The Doctor realised that he had been completely forgotten. He couldn't help feeling terribly insulted.

The Doctor stood in the Trophy Room, taking one final, sad look at the spinning planets. He held up his fingers and thumbs, weaving them together so that he could perform a brief triangulation of their various positions. A vast and complicated balance... a system of unimaginable forces woven together... so delicately. But what would happen if that balance went wrong...?

Two Guards appeared at the Doctor's side and lifted him, almost gently, away.

'You know,' sighed the Doctor to the Guards. 'If he's such a genius, why does he sometimes pretend to be such a fool?' He caught his reflection in a cabinet and shrugged at it. 'Your boss. I've a feeling he's been trying to tell me something and I have completely failed to see what it was. Any ideas?'

Beyond clubbing him round the head, the Guards did not answer.

CHAPTER TWENTY
DOG FIGHT

Pralix talked and the people of the city listened. His voice echoed across the square and through the streets. The people looked up at him, slightly glazed. The young stared at him in adoration. The old, as much as they could, shook their heads, trying to close their eyes to the glowing light show.

'It all makes sense,' Pralix was pleading. 'That's why no one has ever been allowed to ask questions. That's why we are pampered with riches… That's why the Captain will shoot people before the Mourners can reach them. All these years we thought we were living in luxury… but we were being made accomplices to the Captain's crimes.'

He snapped his fingers and the dust drifted to the ground.

Mula stared up at her brother, and not because she had to, but because she adored him.

'Just look at him,' she breathed. She had forgotten what Pralix was like when he was normal. That thin, gaunt figure had always looked so sad, had always been either painfully quiet or raving like a madman. And now, here he was, stating his case simply and calmly.

'I do hope we're doing the right thing.' Romana was at her side, worrying at a fingernail. 'I mean that really is a captive audience.'

Mula looked at the sea of slightly empty faces. 'It's a lot to take in. They'll respond to it when they finally understand.'

'I hope so.' Romana speculated about how a world's population would take being bluntly told they'd been devouring planets.

'I mean, it's just so nice to hear it clearly stated.' Mula smiled sadly. 'It's been an undercurrent amongst the younger people – the sense that there's something seriously wrong and we're not being told about it…'

That, thought Romana, is the very definition of being young.

'And now,' Mula continued, 'we are all being told about it. The old, though, the old…' She glanced with disgust at some of the people in the crowd. 'They knew. Maybe not the full story, but they knew. It would have been passed down, hushed up, forgotten. The Captain bought their silence. But not… not any more.'

'We'll know how it goes over in a minute, when the Mourners release the people.'

Romana's eyes fell on an old man. Tears were streaming down his face. How sad, she thought. He looked so kindly. Then she noticed he was shaking, twisting as though trying to get free. He was in a terrible panic, and the Mourners had rooted him to the spot.

That was when Romana noticed the noise. A buzzing whine, a little like a distant air-car. Only it was in the square. It was the people. She could see it now, the people shaking and twitching, their eyes wild. She called out to the Mourners.

'Let them go! They can't take it, it's too much for them!'

One of the Mourners turned to stare at her, and she felt a wave of sadness wash over her. The man smiled slightly, and, just for a moment, she wondered if she was being hypnotised as well.

'Let them go!' she yelled again.

The Mourner looked away and breathed out.

All the Mourners breathed out.

As they did so, the buzzing faded as the crowd regained their senses, blinking as though they were all recovering from a dream.

There was an air of peace hovering over the square. A moment's perfect peace.

That went well, thought Romana.

Then the screaming started. People backed away from the Mourners in horror, crushing each other in their squabble to get away from them, from the square, from each other. They ran howling and screaming away. Some shouted that the Mourners were liars, some threw rocks, but most just ran.

The Mourners stood there. They did not retaliate, they did not reassert their power. They let the people react.

After a while the stampede was over. Reassuringly, the square was not empty. Most of the younger people had stood their ground. While the Mourners were placidly sad, they looked very angry. A few old people sat on benches, their heads in their hands.

'Well now,' Pralix addressed the crowd. 'Now you know the truth. What do you want to do about it?'

'Destroy the Captain!' they shouted, and it sounded mighty.

Romana beamed. This was her first ever revolution and it was actually going smashingly. 'Fantastic!' she giggled. Mula looked at her strangely. It was only then that Romana remembered that, actually, this was perhaps not an occasion for jumping up and down with delight. Which she definitely hadn't done. Much.

'So,' she coughed. 'Let's see if we can do something practical about it. Which should be fairly straightforward so long as the Doctor and Kimus have managed to break into the Engine Room without being caught.'

'Well, we're in trouble if they haven't,' Mula said.

'Don't worry.' Romana let her confidence run away with her and told an outright lie. 'The Doctor knows what he's doing.'

The Doctor was carried onto the Bridge. He turned to his guards.

'Would you care to put me down at all?' he asked.

They dropped him onto the floor. All around the Doctor was an air of bustle. He liked an air of bustle. Especially from the opposition. It usually told him they were about to lose.

The Captain sat at a desk, tinkering with a piece of equipment. He did not look up, although his robot parrot glared at him. The Captain was whistling while he worked, his parrot joining in. He worked with the precision of a watchmaker.

'My present commotion,' the Captain began genially, 'is being caused by your friends the Mourners, Doctor,' he chuckled. 'The poor misbegotten fools are going to attempt to storm the Citadel.'

'Oh good,' said the Doctor. 'That should be fun.'

'It will indeed Doctor,' muttered the Captain, soldering a component into place with a finger.

The door to the Bridge groaned open and an unconscious Kimus was dragged in. He was dropped to the floor next to the Doctor and simply lay there.

'Kimus? Are you all right?' the Doctor asked.

'Mmmmwwwwerrrr.'

'That's good,' the Doctor lied.

Kimus began to shake. He'd watched whole planets burn. It was a tough thing for anyone to go through.

The Doctor turned to the Guards. 'For heaven's sake, do untie him. The poor fellow's not going to be a threat to anyone ever again.'

The Captain shrugged his agreement. 'Do it. We will take them off and kill them in a moment.' His patience suddenly ended. He stabbed at a microphone. 'By the bursting suns of Banzar, Mr Fibuli, where are my crystals?'

'Coming, sir,' called the worried, wiry man, hurrying away with a clipboard. The set-up on the Bridge looked surprisingly efficient. The Doctor had been on several pirate ships and they normally had an air of lethal incompetence soused in rum.

Kimus stirred and looked about himself muzzily. 'Doctor?' he asked. 'Where are we?'

'We're on the Captain's Bridge. Nice, isn't it?'

'The Bridge!' Kimus did not react as though this was good news. Then his expression changed from alarm to horror. 'What is that?'

'Oh.' The Doctor lowered his voice. 'That is your beloved Captain.'

Kimus couldn't quite believe his eyes. It was one thing to say the Captain was a monster. It was another thing entirely to discover that he actually was. He couldn't take his eyes off the figure, the tiny bits of man jammed haphazardly into tin sheets. There were statues of the Captain all over the cities of Zanak. They looked nothing like this. And they didn't smell like that either. There was a strange odour – of meat cooking in a greasy oven.

'Oh, good grief, that really is obscene,' sighed Kimus.

'Yes,' agreed the Doctor. This was the most sensible thing Kimus had ever said.

'It goes to show that when my comrades—'

'Yes,' the Doctor whispered. 'The Mourners are on their way now.'

'But we haven't sabotaged the engines.'

'Well no, not yet,' the Doctor sighed. 'But on the other hand, we've taught the Mourners how to fight back, and the Captain has no defence against their psychic power.'

'Oh, good point,' said Kimus. 'What's that machine?'

'What, that?' The Doctor noticed the box the Captain was working on. A rather marvellous lash-up. Actually the level of detailing and finish elevated it way above lash-up. It was, thought the Doctor, such a neat job it was practically showing off. 'Oh.' He downplayed it. 'It just looks like a Psychic Interferometer.'

'A what?'

'Well,' the Doctor shrugged. 'It's just a sort of machine for neutralising psychic power...' He ground to a halt.

He and Kimus stared at each other in horror.

There was a chuckle.

'Quite.' The Captain leaned over them. 'Wag your tongue well, Doctor. It is the only weapon you have left. '

K-9 lay on his back and briefly contemplated issuing a Computer Distress Signal. In theory this would bring any nearby semi-sentient automated life form to his aid. But ever since landing on Zanak there had been a strange sensation pinging away in his wireless networks. The sense that there was something on this planet that... How curious. It was not within his operational parameters.

K-9 did not really deal in sensations. He would, if asked, reasonably and patiently (and only a little haughtily) explain that he did not possess feelings. Whether this was true or not, K-9 certainly did not believe in intuition. But there was something in his circuits that told him that there was something bad on this planet, and that he was much better off not trying to contact it. No, he would sort this out by himself.

Which was all very well, but he was lying on his back on the top of a mountain.

According to his computations, the Doctor-Master would be expecting him to provide a surprise rescue in 12.54 minutes' time. If he failed to provide this, he would, in all probability, remain on the mountain top until the elements damaged his components. Even then, his auto-repair systems would do their best. He could be here for quite some time. K-9 did not, of course, experience boredom. After all, he was only a robot and had no emotions.

But he certainly did not relish spending a hundred years upside down with nothing to do. That would be a waste of his operational capacity.

With slow patience, K-9 extended his probe. It came out of his forehead. The probe was a marvel of multi-functionality. For example it had recently formed a complicated interface with the air-car's circuitry. Right now he was using it to lever himself off the ground. He had managed to achieve an angle of thirteen degrees, which was really not at all promising. He was just working out what to do to increase this to a more viable level, when a Guard appeared and started shooting at him.

K-9 considered this latest input and drew the following conclusion: the present rotation around the binary star system was most unfavourable to his optimal operation. In other words he was having a bad day.

The Doctor was loudly pooh-poohing the Captain's Psychic Interferometer.

'Nonsense Captain. To make that machine work you would need a supply of some very rare crystals.' He adopted a lecturing tone. 'Such as Voolium and Madranite 1-5. And they only occur on one planet I know of, and that's… er… It'll come back to me…'

Mr Fibuli fussed over, triumphantly holding a small box. 'Captain, we have the crystals!'

The Doctor groaned. 'Calufrax… I think I must be at a low point of my biorhythms or something.'

The Captain laughed what was almost a good-natured laugh. He took the crystals one by one out of the box and plugged them into his device. Each crystal began to glow and the robot parrot clucked happily as the power grew within the Interferometer.

'Excellent Mr Fibuli, excellent.' The Captain leaned back in his chair and waved over at his Nurse. See, he appeared to be saying, I am relaxing.

The Nurse gave him a tight nod of approval.

'You see, Doctor?' said the Captain. 'Your friends are doomed. Now all we have to do is wait for them to die.'

He flicked a switch casually. 'All Guards to be fully armed and prepared to ambush the Mourners. They are coming, and they will be quite unable to harm you.' The Captain's tone, his entire demeanour appeared to have changed. 'And now Mr Fibuli, if you would care to take control of the device, I think this would be an excellent opportunity for me to take care of the Doctor and his incessantly wagging tongue.'

He stood up and strolled creakingly over to the Time Lord. The parrot on his shoulder cawed with delight.

K-9 had observed that the Doctor-Master would frequently turn an opponent's strengths against them. He had never congratulated the Doctor-Master on this fact, as that would have set a worrying precedent, but he had stored this in his memory banks.

Coming under heavy blaster fire from the Captain's Guard, K-9 retrieved this fact from his bubble memory and wondered how best to employ it.

The Guard helpfully demonstrated by missing, the blast impacting on the bank next to him and throwing K-9 onto his side.

K-9 hastily worked out a strategy to move things forward. He quickly calculated the firing pattern of the Guard, and how best to arrange it. He carefully established a complicated spread of ordnance which would drive the Guard into exactly the correct position in order for the Guard to take just the right shot at him, the blast from which would flip him the right way up. It was, he thought, quite a neat piece of computation, one which showed off both a good knowledge of aggressive humanoid psychology, probability, and physics.

'Kalaylee,' K-9 uttered his battle cry and went to war.

The Guard hastily dodged out of the way of the blasts from K-9's gun, desperately trying to take aim at the improbable assailant. He threw himself behind a bush, which burst into flames. He rolled back, pushing himself up, throwing himself to one side again, and, in mid-air, squeezing off a shot which was bound to destroy the robot.

A curious thing happened. A blast from the robot's gun met the Guard's shot and deflected it into the fuselage of the air-car.

There was a very loud explosion and a lot of smoke.

The Guard scrambled to his feet, puzzled as to what had just happened.

The smoke cleared, and a very smug robot dog rolled out of it.

'Most satisfactory,' K-9 announced, and shot the Guard.

Romana stood in the street and addressed the Mourners. Things had gone reasonably well in the city. True, they hadn't won over the whole population, but still, they had some followers.

'Well,' she began. 'All in all, we still have a bit of a mountain to climb,' she said.

So they climbed a mountain.

K-9 stood before the door. Sadly, he did not have a hairpin. The locking system behind the door was, indeed, worthy of commendation. Yet awarding prizes did not help.

His probe buzzed furiously but ineffectually against the lock.

K-9 turned his attention reluctantly to the Guard he had stunned. By his own calculations he had done a very thorough job, and the Guard would not be regaining consciousness for approximately eighty-seven minutes. So there would be no help there. K-9 deducted the points he had awarded himself for that. He examined the Guard's pockets. There did not seem to be something as practical as a key.

K-9 glided huffily back to the door and extended his probe again.

'You are a very stupid door,' he announced. 'I order you to open.'

The Captain loomed over the Doctor terribly excitedly.

He looked about to say something, but the Nurse materialised by his side, popping a thermometer into his mouth.

'Doctor—' he began.

He stopped. The Nurse was inflating the armband so that she could take his blood pressure.

'We need not delay—'

The Nurse's black box chirruped. The Nurse checked the readings on it.

The Captain rolled his eyes at the Doctor, half in apology, half in annoyance. The Doctor smiled back in a 'Well, what can you do?' way.

As if aware of them for the first time, the Nurse looked up, and blushed. 'Oh, do excuse me,' she said. 'The Captain does get so excited before an execution.' She checked the readings. 'Nearly there. Just a tick,' she nodded. 'Splendid.'

She unfastened the armband, pocketed the thermometer and vanished.

The Captain sighed.

The moment had, all agreed, been lost. But anyway. He drew himself up and declaimed, only a little flatly: 'Doctor, we need not delay your execution any longer.' Rallying a little, he roared, 'By the curled fangs of the Sky Demon, I have looked forward to this moment.'

'And I have looked forward to this moment, Captain,' cried Kimus. No longer whimpering, he was rushing forward, arms flailing, rage boiling in his no longer entirely sane face. 'Captain!' he snarled. 'Our great and benevolent leader. A hideous, deformed, murdering maniac!'

He grabbed hold of a chair and swung it against the Captain's body. There was a dull, empty clang. He swung it again, connecting with the shoulder. There was another thud.

Kimus beat the chair against the Captain again and again. The problem was there was so much of him to hit. And yet also, so very little. He couldn't quite reach the remains of the man's face, so ended up belabouring his legs.

The Doctor had once seen a cartoon series in which a mildly annoying dog gained a very annoying cousin. It reminded him, rather sadly, of that. Episodes would end with the surprise villain revealed, and the small, very annoying dog pedalling away at the villain's ankles. It was a pity, as the Doctor was really terribly fond of dogs. His mind wandered, as it so often did. He did so very much like cartoons, but where did this habit of giving perfectly reasonable heroes idiotic siblings come from? They'd even done the same to Godzilla, the poor thing trying to munch on a skyscraper while his nephew tripped over and a choir sang with ghastly saccharine cheer '… and Godzookie'. (Who were those singers? Did they sleep at nights?) On the whole, that cartoon had been the most perfect example of bathos he'd ever seen. Until he watched Kimus, the young rebel who'd spent much of his breath loudly promising to overthrow the Captain, finally having a go at it, and looking like he was poking him with a matchstick.

Kimus stopped hitting the Captain, awfully aware that his arms were aching and that the crew of the Bridge were watching him. Not with admiration or shock, but with a kind of mild, sneering amusement.

'Kimus…' the Doctor said gently.

'Finished?' the Captain asked, surprisingly mildly.

Kimus looked up at the Captain, his cheeks burning with shame. He had tried, tried so hard, and he had failed.

'Avatron.' The Captain reached up to pet the bird on his shoulder. 'Kill.'

The Avatron gave a happy little chirp and flew off the Captain's shoulder, before plunging down eagerly. The Doctor grabbed Kimus and pulled him out of the way, but the bird spun round, ready to swoop again. Its eyes were glowing, its talons buzzing with electricity, and there was a vengeful mania in its eyes that suggested it did not particularly care who it killed.

As the Doctor and Kimus threw themselves across the bridge, no one noticed the great door opening. This was far too much fun. The Captain's crew watched, jeering and placing bets as the bird feinted, swooped and pounced. It was playing with its prey.

The excitement with which the crew watched this was tempered, perhaps a little by a curious relief that, this time, it was not them being fed to the parrot.

The Doctor and Kimus scrambled frantically out of the way of another blast.

'I'm going to be killed by a robot parrot,' the Doctor thought, hurling himself through the air. What a way to go. He imagined the postcards winging their way over the Space-Time Telegraph. 'Have you heard?' the Dalek Supreme would coo. 'A parrot.'

'No! Really?' the Cyber Controller would reply. 'Fancy.'

Kimus cried out as a talon raked him, and a blast sizzled the edge of the Doctor's hair. He landed awkwardly in a heap, banging his shoulder against something. He felt it give slightly. He looked up, wondering what it was.

Peering over him was K-9.

'Master?' the dog enquired.

The Doctor considered his luck, for the very briefest of moments.

'K-9? Fetch.'

K-9 trundled rapidly forward. There were times, the Doctor admitted, when his robot dog made rather a meal of getting about. Give him a slightly sandy planet, or the mildest of marshes, and you could barely hear yourself thinking brilliantly over the rattling of gears. Sometimes it was a little like going for long country walks with a coffee grinder. But here they were, on the Bridge of the Captain's spaceship and the floors were lovely and level. More fool you, Captain, the Doctor thought as K-9 glided smoothly to attack.

The Polyphase Avatron paused mid-swoop. For a moment the robot dog and the robot parrot glared at each other. They sized each other up and picked a size that wasn't flattering.

So that, K-9 decided, was what had been interfering with his local area network. He was mildly put out. Really? He had tangled with super computers and thwarted psychic evils from the Dawn of Time. A robot parrot should present him with no problems.

The Polyphase Avatron had happily started composing the death song of the pathetic robot dog. It gloatingly trilled a few lines of it.

K-9 emitted a noise which sounded, just a little, like a growl.

A fully fledged battle began which sent virtually everyone else ducking hastily for cover. Only the Captain stood his ground, watching the combat around him and laughing.

The air sang with blaster fire.

There were scratch marks down K-9's flank.

A metal feather fell to the floor.

The desk the Doctor was hiding behind burst into flame.

The Doctor grabbed Kimus and darted through the smoke. If they could get to the Interferometer then there was a chance that the Mourners wouldn't walk into a starring role in a massacre. The problem was that there were three Guards standing around it, and they were all aiming at the Doctor.

'Plan B,' the Doctor yelled.

'Which is?'

'Scarper.'

The Doctor made for the door. As they went, a Guard fell past, smoke pouring from his back. As he died, his gun fell into Kimus's hands. Kimus stared at it. That, he thought, was fate. Another chance to prove himself. He really was a fighter now. He aimed a shot at the Captain, but the Doctor looped his scarf round his neck. 'Come on.'

They ran off into the Citadel.

K-9 squeezed off an expert shot at the ceiling, bringing a girder down. He fired backwards as he retreated, giving the parrot a challenging 'Are you coming?' glare, before zooming after the Doctor.

The parrot sang another verse of the Song of the Scrap Metal Dog and flew after him.

'Kill them! Kill them all, my pretty!' the Captain called after it.

The Polyphase Avatron trilled back that it would be only too happy to, and swooped out of sight.

Mr Fibuli fussed around with a fire extinguisher. Some Guards applied themselves to lifting the girder out of the way. It had sealed them in.

The Captain stood still, revelling in the chaos.

The Nurse, as unruffled as ever, came to stand by him.

'A minor setback,' he growled.

'But an amusing one,' she said.

'Hah,' the Captain snorted. 'They cannot escape from the Citadel. They are welcome to it.'

'Unless –' there was the slightest pause in the Nurse's voice – 'they penetrate the Inner Chamber.'

'And what if they do?' rumbled the Captain.

For a moment the Nurse looked at the Captain venomously.

'Don't worry,' he said. 'My Avatron will deal with them. Pity. I was looking forward to seeing them die. Never mind. The Ace of Death will still be played. I have all the cards I need.'

'Do you?' The Nurse, for once, seemed sardonic. She began a cursory examination of the Captain, checking to see if he had sustained any damage in Kimus's attack.

Putting out some smouldering paperwork, Mr Fibuli glanced over at the two of them. He sometimes wondered why the Captain didn't just fire her and find a Nurse he liked. But then again, maybe the Captain had had enough of cringing deference.

'I was just wondering…' The Nurse finished her examination but didn't go. 'Has the computer selected a death for the Doctor?'

'It has.' The Captain really didn't seem in the mood for small talk with the Nurse. And yet he shuffled over to the torture computer and tore off a printout.

He handed it to the Nurse. She read it and then giggled in a very pleasantly amused way, as if she'd been shown a picture of a friend of hers wearing a silly hat.

'Oh yes,' she smiled. 'I like that.'

CHAPTER TWENTY-ONE
A LEAP OF FAITH

After a while, the corridors of the Citadel became eerily empty.

This was mostly because the Avatron and K-9 were whirling in a fight to the death, and there were quite a few stray blasts. Any Guards around either found somewhere else to be or lay twitching on the floor.

The Doctor's elation at being rescued was mingled with rising alarm that he'd be shot by his own best friend. He wasn't sure either of them would ever forgive themselves for that one. The dogfight whipped past him and he pulled Kimus into a doorway.

For a moment he thought about calling on K-9 to calm down, but then he saw how much his dog's tail was wagging. He knew K-9 would not admit this to anyone, but the dog was clearly having a wonderful time being let off the leash. Well, good for him.

The Doctor winced as a blast took a chunk out of the ancient masonry of the Citadel. Well, that was someone else's hard luck. 'We have to find a way out,' he said.

Kimus waved his gun. Clearly he fancied carrying on the fight.

'No,' the Doctor said. 'Either we get to the Engine Room and disable them, or we warn the Mourners.'

'We should press home our advantage.'

'But Kimus, we don't have an advantage.' The Doctor rolled his eyes. 'We need to know more than our opponent, or we need to have turned his mighty engines into marmalade, or we need an army of homicidal telepaths on our side.'

'But I have a gun.' Kimus waved it, and the Doctor patted it away.

'Yes you do, and very nice it is. But it won't help. What will help is a door labelled "Engines This Way".'

They wandered along the corridors.

They found themselves in the Captain's Trophy Room.

Kimus stared at it.

The Doctor told him what it was.

Kimus stared at it some more. 'If the people knew... If the people knew about this...'

'About half of them would cough and look at their shoes and pretend they hadn't heard,' the Doctor muttered. 'The Captain's been very clever. He's enslaved you, but he's made you rich. Mind you...' He started to wander among the spinning cases, looking sadly at an exquisite depiction of the fjords of Atericus, the heart-shaped continents of Bibicorpus, the rings of Granados, the silver seas of Lowiteliom, the fire clouds of Temesis, and the dancing dusts of Tridentio III.

'People are funny,' sighed the Doctor. 'They get used to anything. I liberated people from the Dalek mines of Bedfordshire who promptly started complaining, "Now, you wouldn't get this under the Daleks" when the rabbit stew was late.'

'But this...' Kimus really wasn't listening to the Doctor. He started to make one of his speeches, and the Doctor returned the compliment by not listening to him. He watched the planets dance sadly past and he wondered, as all people have wondered about great works of art, 'Well, yes, very nice but what's it for?'

Then, absently, he whipped out an arm and threw a still gabbling Kimus to the floor.

The Avatron and K-9 tumbled into the Trophy Room, their blasts ricocheting off the force fields. The parrot whirled up among the promenade of planets, looping around Temesis like a giant bird going into orbit. K-9 zipped from one side of the room to the other, loosing off blasts with what even the Doctor was starting to consider gay abandon.

'Careful, K-9, you upset that balance and you'll turn us all into an instant black hole!'

K-9 fired another shot, which momentarily knocked Lowiteliom's orbit, sending the silver seas sloshing, and causing the tiniest shift of gravitational forces.

'I knew something was upsetting K-9 from the first moment we arrived on this lump. He could obviously sense that wretched bird. Hey ho.'

The Avatron flew out from behind the planet, and K-9 fired again, the blast bouncing off the planet's surface and smacking into a wall at the end of the chamber.

Curiously, the wall sprang open.

'Well done, that dog,' the Doctor yelled and dragged Kimus through into a very surprising room.

The chamber they stumbled into was very dark. At the centre of it was a little raised dais. No good, in the Doctor's experience, had ever come of a raised dais. People would leave thrones on them, for a start. As they had in this case.

From force of habit the Doctor ignored the figure on the throne and glanced back at the battle raging among the planets outside.

But Kimus, bless him, was transfixed by the raised dais. 'Doctor… look!'

The Doctor had heard that one before. Like a raised dais, it never ended well.

He grudgingly paid some attention to the figure on the throne. It was a very, very old woman. The face was crumpled like rotten fruit, the hair falling in rat tails over the features which time had reduced to gnarled lumps. There were traces, somewhere underneath it all, of great beauty. But this was also a cruel face. The cold grey eyes lacked any sparkle, and the area around the eyes and the mouth was smooth of laughter lines.

She appeared frozen in the middle of shaking her head at some bad news. It was not quite a statue, nor was it a waxwork. There was the tiniest suggestion that the figure was moving very slightly.

'Good grief,' the Doctor said.

'What is it?'

'Not what, who.'

'Who?' Kimus reached out to touch the figure, but the Doctor stayed his hand. Like the planets outside, this creature was off limits.

'Can't you guess?' he asked.

'No.' Kimus frowned at the creature. Yesterday life had seemed very certain. He had merely suspected the Captain was bad. Now he knew the Captain was a monster, one who ate planets, tortured people, and kept an old woman prisoner in his castle.

The Doctor pointed at the creature. 'I think we've found the final part of the jigsaw, but how does it fit in, eh? Was this what the Captain was trying to tell me?'

Unhelpfully, Kimus announced, 'Well, I think she's hideous. But she's dressed like a queen.'

'Exactly!' The Doctor nodded.

Kimus stared at the haughty figure of the ancient queen. And the penny finally dropped.

'That,' the Doctor intoned, 'is your beloved Queen Xanxia of Zxoxaxax.'

'But Queen Xanxia is dead!'

'Oh, I wouldn't say that, but she's certainly not very well.'

'Can she hear us?' Kimus stared up at the twisted, cruel old face. 'I mean, I just called her hideous.'

'No, I don't think so… not with those things round her.' The Doctor indicated two tall metal pillars on either side of her. Steady, patient pulses of energy flowed through them like the ticking of a clock.

'What are those things?' Kimus went to step past them.

'Don't go near her. I rather think they are Time Dams.'

'You've lost me, Doctor.'

'Time Dams,' the Doctor started to explain, and couldn't resist a slight bit of showing off. 'They're a primitive device, but effective. They actually hold back the flow of time in the area between them. Within that field, time decelerates exponentially, meaning that whilst time is still technically advancing, the next moment is never in fact reached.'

'The next moment…?'

'… In this case, her long-anticipated demise, I suspect. That's generally what they were used for. Either that or to torture people by boring them to death.' The Doctor prodded the time field, feeling the very tip of his finger slur in the air. 'Queen Xanxia's being held back within the last few seconds of her life. It's really a form of suspended animation, but with two important differences.' The Doctor was in full lecture mode now, all thought of imminent escape and sabotage abandoned for the chance to do some really quality showing off. 'Do you want to know what they are?'

Kimus hadn't fired his gun yet. He was very aware of this fact. 'Am I likely to understand?'

'No, but I'll tell you anyway. The first is that neural currents can still be directed round the cerebral cortex artificially…'

'You were right. I don't understand.'

'In other words she can still think. And the other difference…' The Doctor ground to a halt, glaring poisonously at the shrivelled dusty figure inside the time dams.

'Yes?' Kimus hoped it involved guns.

'Is that the process uses astronomical quantities of energy. The sort of quantities you'd have to ransack entire planets to find.'

Kimus shared the Doctor's look of hatred. He raised his gun. He knew the Doctor wouldn't let him fire it, but he raised it anyway. 'So everything that's happened on Zanak has been with the single purpose of keeping this monster alive?'

'Well, there's something more to it than that. But what? I mean, would you go to those sort of lengths just to stay alive?'

The Doctor and Kimus stared at the wizened, shrivelled form, trapped forever on its seat.

'Not in that revolting condition, no,' conceded Kimus.

'No, not in that condition... So, in what condition?'

The Doctor wandered around the chamber. It wasn't entirely empty. There was an instruction manual. Despite the rather jolly font on the cover, it was unread and remained so. The Doctor had better things to do with his time. He rifled among the other pieces of equipment, and found a display screen. 'Ah, now this gives me an idea.' The Doctor turned it on and gawped at the picture.

'Eureka. I've got it,' he said.

Kimus looked over his shoulder. 'But... but that's... Isn't that the Bridge?'

The Doctor nodded. 'From someone's point of view.' He jerked his hand over at the Queen, her head perpetually frozen mid-shake. 'One final mystery,' he said. 'Who do you think she's talking to?'

Kimus frowned. The Doctor was right. Xanxia's mind may have been elsewhere, but her body was what had changed. So very slightly. Her lips had moved, her head had shaken itself a fraction more.

'Intriguing, isn't it?'

Something was coming. The Doctor held up his hand.

The door to the chamber slid open again. There was an ominous whirr.

K-9 bumped unsteadily but triumphantly in, a very dead Polyphase Avatron clamped to his muzzle.

He ceremoniously dropped it at the Doctor's feet.

The Doctor tried to pick the bird up, but it was still hot. 'Well done, K-9, well done. Look at that, isn't that marvellous!'

'Your congratulations are un-un-unnecessary, Master,' K-9 stuttered proudly.

The Doctor noticed that his dog obviously wasn't in very good shape himself. 'Never mind, pooch. We'll patch you up in no time, when we get back to the TARDIS.'

'Well that's a relief,' said Kimus. 'But what do we do about the others? The Guards? How do we get out of here?'

'Easy.' The Doctor pointed to the end of the chamber. 'I spotted a service elevator over there. Must go down to the engines.'

'Why didn't you say so before?'

'I was busy finding things out.' The Doctor winked. 'Remember what I told you about needing an advantage? Knowledge, engines, Mourners? I think I've found a way to get all three.'

He ruffled K-9's battered ears. 'You deserve a rest, old fellow. Why don't you take Kimus with you down in the lift, find the Engine Room and sabotage the engines. All right, K-9?'

'Affirmative, Master.' The dog paused, just slightly.

'Kimus,' the Doctor said so calmly it almost didn't sound like a threat. 'Go easy on the dog. If his power packs run down, I shall be very cross.'

'Of course, Doctor,' vowed Kimus solemnly.

'Good boy, off you go, then.'

A little drunkenly, the robot dog weaved towards the elevator.

'But what about you?' demanded Kimus.

'Ah,' the Doctor drew himself up, ready for action. 'Now we have the upper hand, I'm going to deal with the Captain.' The Doctor sorted through the equipment. One thing looked vaguely familiar. He toyed with pocketing it on the grounds that it might come in handy, but instead jammed his hands in his pockets and grinned his most serious grin. 'Ready Captain?'

Two Guards had only just cleared the last of the debris away from the entrance when someone tapped them very politely on the shoulder.

'Ah gentlemen, good afternoon,' said the Doctor. 'How nice to see you. I'd like to see the Captain, please.'

The Doctor was led onto the Bridge by two bemused Guards.

An expectant hush fell across the crew. Mr Fibuli put down his clipboard.

The Captain creaked loudly to his feet, striding powerfully towards his enemy.

'Ah, Doctor! By the feet of the Sky Demon, I've been expecting you. Your execution awaits.' A confidential gloat. 'My computer has surpassed itself in devising your death.'

'I'm sure it has,' the Doctor hissed urgently into the Captain's ear. 'But, oddly enough, it wasn't that I wanted to see you about.'

'Doctor, it is precisely what I wanted to see you about.' The Captain shoved him back.

'Oh, must we?' The Doctor's face fell.

The Captain rubbed his hands together. 'I am pleased to see that you have survived. It would have been such a waste. Now, what about your friends?'

The Doctor made a dolorous shrug.

'Ah, my Avatron accounted for them, no doubt. Vicious little brute,' the Captain purred proudly.

'Well, now, that's a very sad story,' the Doctor coughed, awkwardly pulling something out of his pocket and dropping it with a clang to the floor. It was the twisted remains of the Polyphase Avatron.

The Captain stared at it in horror and something inside him seemed to break.

'Destroyed?' he gasped in the strangled voice of a little boy. He reached down, and scooped the bird up, cradling the twisted wings. Eventually he looked up, staring at the Doctor furiously. 'You shall pay for this. Guards!'

'Listen to me,' protested the Doctor, 'What I have to say is important.'

'No it isn't.' The Captain carried on stroking the bird.

'But—'

'Silence!'

The Captain pulled a lever on his desk, and, at the centre of the Bridge, a pit sprang open. It appeared to be overlooking a steep precipice. Projecting from the ledge was a plank.

The Captain twitched a ghastly grin across his face. 'Behold your death, Doctor!'

Well, thought the Doctor, at least this was novel.

The Captain strode out onto the plank. He waggled one foot over the abyss and then looked back at the Doctor. 'An ancient custom, from the very earliest days of piracy. The theory is quite simple – You walk along it, you fall off. I'm sorry there isn't an ocean to receive you, I'm afraid you'll have to make do with a very long drop.' He pointed down with his metal boot. 'That hole there takes you right down to the hollow centre of Zanak.'

The Captain bounced on the plank. It creaked alarmingly.

The Doctor stared at him in horror. 'Walking the plank? You can't be serious. Supposing I don't walk along the plank?'

The Captain roared with laughter, leaping back onto the Bridge. He slapped the Doctor on the back, with every indication that they were best friends. The slap pushed the Doctor a little bit further towards the edge.

'Oh, but you do want to, Doctor! By the beckoning finger of the Sky Demon, you do. That's what this is for.'

With a flourish he picked up a glittering cutlass.

'The plank, if you please, Doctor.'

The Doctor stared at the thin faces of the Nurse and Mr Fibuli. Mr Fibuli avoided his gaze. The Nurse favoured him with mock sympathy and a tut.

The Doctor placed one foot on the plank. It creaked. He looked down. There was an awful lot of down. He really had never had a head for heights. He took another step. The plank sagged.

'Listen.' The Doctor sensed he was losing his advantage. He spun round, hopping off the plank. 'I wonder if we could chat about this?'

The Captain prodded him with his cutlass and the Doctor edged reluctantly back onto the plank.

The Captain held his sword in one hand, cradling the remains of his parrot in the other.

'The time for talking is past, Doctor. Your only remaining function is to die.'

The Doctor balanced carefully on the plank and tried to work out how it had all gone so wrong. The terrible thing about the plank was that it was awfully bouncy. And became more so with every tenuous step. He was working out a really very elaborate and impressive method of escape using his scarf when the Captain jabbed him again.

'That's really not fair,' protested the Doctor. He took another wobbling step and worked out what the piece of equipment he'd picked up and then put down was.

It was a holographic ray projector. He really should have brought it with him. It would have been terribly handy. He could have used it to create a holographic him which he would really have much rather had bouncing on the plank right now.

The Captain jabbed him again and the Doctor cursed his own stupidity.

He held up a hand, desperate for another go at this.

But the Captain swept the cutlass through the air.

The Doctor ducked, missed his footing, and in a tangle of limbs and scarf, tumbled howling off the end of the plank, falling into the empty heart of Zanak.

Part Four

Tyger tyger, burning bright
In the forests of the night,
What immortal hand or eye
Could frame thy fearful symmetry?
William Blake, *The Tyger*

CHAPTER TWENTY-TWO
JOURNEY TO THE CENTRE OF THE EARTH

The Captain and the Nurse stood watching the Doctor fall into the planet until they could see him no more. It was done.

'Cooeee!' a voice rang out behind them.

The Doctor fell.

He had never fallen into the heart of a planet before and he would have found the whole experience fascinating if he hadn't been devoting quite so much of his time to screaming. The good news, if it could be called good, or even news, was that there was very little of Zanak to get in the way of his falling. The shaft he spun down was clearly some kind of ore intake chute, and it widened rapidly as the Doctor progressed down the mountain, through the thin crust of the planet and then into the nothingness beyond.

The really good news (and even then, the Doctor still wasn't certain if he wasn't pushing his luck a bit describing this as good) was that Calufrax was no longer in his way. Clearly, the poor planet had been pulped.

The Doctor had been in a lot of life-endangering situations, and had only lost a handful of times. The constant variety was actually not that refreshing. Of course he got tired of continually being held at gunpoint by people who were a little old for leather trousers. His idea of a refreshing change was getting through a week without someone pointing a weapon at him or uttering that tiresome conversational gambit of 'Kill him, kill him now.' And they never did. It really was the villainous equivalent of 'We must have a drink some time.'

Guns and so on he could cope with. Ever since the Guardian had turned up in his life, Death's Infinite Variety had been showing off. In the last couple of days he'd nearly been eaten by a monster, blown up by a warlord, had depressed telepaths and robot parrots thrown at him, and now this. This was ridiculous.

The interesting thing (and one which he really needed to phone a friendly physicist about) was working out what would happen when he hit the middle of Zanak. Would he hit a gravitational null point and slow down, floating miserably around until a planet materialised on top of him? Or would he sail on through to smear himself against the underside of Zanak's equator? It was fascinating, if by fascinating you meant 'completely unknown and frankly terrifying'.

The Doctor took a deep breath and screamed again. Given that the acoustics were so marvellous it would have been a shame not to.

It had been a long and exhausting climb up the mountain. Romana had found the journey there by air-car rather nippier, but that time she hadn't been joined by the Mourners and all the disaffected youth of the city. One of the most exhausting things about the climb was the disaffected youth, actually. They were all a bit Kimus. They kept saying how sickened and revolted they were by the true history of their planet, while at the same time being unable to hide how pleased they were. 'I thought so' and 'I knew it' were written all over their faces. Halfway up the mountain, they'd started to argue about whether they were a Resistance or a Movement. Someone had suggested they sit down for a breather. Someone else had asked if they'd packed any food. Romana had, there and then, nearly started crying.

But they'd finally made the plateau and the entrance to the Citadel.

At which point Pralix doubled over in pain.

Romana rushed to the Mourner's side. She noticed the other Mourners were also wincing.

'Pralix,' she asked. 'What is it?'

Pralix focused on her with difficulty. 'There is a new voice in the Mourning,' he said.

'Really?' said Romana. 'Whose?'

He told her.

'Oh, you're kidding.'

Unaware that his scream was reverberating on a psychic level, the Doctor carried on falling. He really should take notes. He did not, it had to be said, seem to be slowing down. Gravity was keeping out of his way, observing him with the same mild curiosity it has for cats. Thankfully he was not being crushed into a rather woolly lump of coal. At least, not yet. The situation was looking up. Even though the Doctor no longer had much of an idea of where up was.

'Look,' Romana sighed to the rebel forces. 'You wait here. I've just got to do a thing. Sorry about this. I'll be right back.'

And then she set off back down the mountain.

The Doctor carried on falling. Had he known that Romana was already trying to work out his velocity whilst also steering an air-car, he might have cheered up a bit. But not much. He had thought he might have got a little bit bored of falling by now, since he'd done so very much of it. Turned out not. He carried on his deep baritone yell.

Romana staggered into the TARDIS, ignoring the outraged shouts of the Guards she'd landed an air-car on top of. 'Sorry,' she called. 'Really no time to listen to a lecture on parking.'

The TARDIS vanished into the Time Vortex and Romana started doing some very hard sums.

She stared helplessly at the vast control panel and at the huge TARDIS manual, and she realised something very important. It was all very well to say you were going to 'do things by the book' but there was no book for what she was about to do. There wasn't even a title. If it did have a title, it'd probably include a rather weary exclamation mark.

She calculated the Doctor's rate of descent, the time taken so far, and the diameter of Zanak. Then she did it twice more, just to make sure.

Even for her, this would require precision. She tapped a switch on the TARDIS console gently. It fell off.

'Oh, good grief.'

For a terrible moment the Doctor realised he'd forgotten to scream. He wondered if he'd actually fallen asleep. It was, of course, more likely that he'd passed out, but he had a nagging suspicion he'd nodded off. Humans (who'd never really got the hang of it) described air-flight as boredom sandwiched between two slices of terror. The Doctor was steadily realising he was bored. Bored of falling.

The utter sensory deprivation did not help. For a while there had been some twinkly lights on the underside of the planet's surface. He did not know what they were for, but everyone loves a twinkly light. They'd got further and further away and then dimmed. There was no sign of any more coming along in the near future. So, when he did finally hit the ground again, he'd at least have no idea it was coming.

Actually, that was pretty chilling. It could happen at any moment. How long did it take to fall through a planet, even? He tried running some sums, but then the idea of the surface being inches away got the better of him and he started screaming again.

When Romana had first opened the TARDIS manual, a set of instructions for a teasmade had fallen out. That about summed up her luck with it.

The problem was that, viewed one way, the TARDIS was a terribly complicated, rather cautious meeting between science and fairy tale. A magical blue box that could go anywhere in time and space. Viewed another way, it was hopelessly obsolete. That was the problem she was trying to get her head around. Nowadays, TARDISes didn't even have control panels. They just had Thinkterfaces. You didn't have to set the coordinates, ramp up the waveform oscillators, disengage the Gravitic Anomaliser or even prime the Mandril Condensors. You just thought about where you wanted to go and your TARDIS took you there. A trifle smugly, perhaps, but it did the trick. Learning how to do things the old-fashioned way had a certain quirky feel, like baking your own bread, making your own candles, or doing your own painting. Everyone knew a computer would do a much better job, but it was jolly fun, wasn't it, to get your hands dirty and know how things were done?

Well, yes. In theory. Buttons and switches and circuits were all very well if you were doing something easy like telling a computer how to make a croissant. A little more fiddly if you were planning on plunging through the Space-Time Vortex.

It also did not help that the TARDIS was alive. No one knew exactly when TARDISes became sentient, but they were. There were several theories about this. One was that, at some point in the future, they'd started building sentient TARDISes and one had nipped back in time to tell the others what the trick was. Tempting as this theory of trans-temporal unionisation was, there was a much simpler explanation that Romana remembered sticking up for in front of her tutor.

'People treat things as if they're alive all the time. A TARDIS is simply smart enough to take the hint.'

They kept their sentience well hidden. But it was there. It had been measured (when it wasn't looking). Modern TARDIS interfaces were chatty, but you weren't talking to the real TARDIS. More like a footman, there to greet you, take your card, find you a nice seat, and then convey your message to the Lady of the House. (Everyone always assumed that TARDISes were female. Romana didn't know if that was intended as an insult or a compliment.)

TARDISes also became like their owners. Her tutor's TARDIS had arrived ponderously, carefully, clearing its throat before finally settling. Military TARDISes smacked themselves down on a planet's surface, did what needed to be done, and then stomped off elsewhere. The President's TARDIS famously always arrived late.

Then there was the Doctor's TARDIS. Romana had only taken two trips in it, and on both occasions there had been a resentful huff as it had roared off. Now it was under the control of the Tracer, it was expected to leave A and promptly arrive at B. And it did so. But with just the slightest roll of its non-existent eyes. 'Oh very well. If one has to. In order to save the universe. Again. But really…'

Of course, Romana could just have been imagining that. Her tutor had once told her, with a sly twinkle, that she had no imagination. She'd spent the next week imagining different things falling on him just to prove him wrong. But he had (as the old goat always did) a point. As a Time Lord you didn't really need an imagination. Their society did not, as a rule, encourage speculation, temporisation or even day-dreaming. For another thing, why bother imagining something when you could travel anywhere in space and time to see it?

The Doctor's TARDIS presented her with a problem that required all her ingenuity and imagination. Previously, whenever she had wanted to get her own way, she had simply argued her point. Eventually her tutor had given in. Sometimes with a wry shake of the head which said, 'Well, yes, but you'll learn.' Mostly he'd just surrendered to the cold inexorable sway of her logic. And her very firm stare.

The problem was that the TARDIS was as stubborn as she was. Making it land by the book had been one thing. Making it take off again was proving to be quite a different matter. This TARDIS did not do short trips. It did not pop in and out of the Time Vortex. It was used to taking the long way, the high road, to a potter and a saunter. The Doctor, having never really known how to fly it, had been happy to let her have her own way for far too long. This TARDIS was, simply put, spoilt.

Well, thought Romana, opening the manual crisply and firmly. We'll see about that.

The Doctor woke up again, hastily converting the yawn into a scream. 'He died in his sleep after all,' he thought to himself. He'd been falling for so long he wasn't sure if he was still falling. Maybe he'd landed. Landed on the underside of a grassy meadow. He'd have to dig his way out. That would take time. Romana would give him such a look when he finally turned up. Knowing her, she'd have overthrown the Captain, dismantled Xanxia's Time Dams, and located the Second Segment of the Key to Time. She had promise, that one. He wouldn't tell her, of course. And the ball gowns would definitely have to go.

But no. Romana was a good egg. With the potential of being a great one. If she didn't stick to the rules all the time. He imagined she'd rather enjoy rattling around the universe with K-9. Finding the segments. Handing them over to the White Guardian. And then what? Ah yes. And then what? Would she go back home, or would she wander off to save a few planets?

The Doctor found himself lost in speculation. He drew his coat around him. It was getting chilly. That was odd. Chilly and strangely hard to breathe. Was the air running out? What about… The Doctor drew out his yo-yo to test gravity. Or wind resistance. Or something. It seemed terribly sluggish and indecisive about the up-or-down question. The yo-yo just wrapped itself around his neck. Fancying a scream of frustration, the Doctor drew breath. He realised that something was wrong with the air. The air and the gravity.

He'd never actually been to the centre of a planet before. In some ways it was quite disappointing. No dinosaurs or Peter Cushing. In other ways it was simply, very simply, terrifying.

The Doctor managed another scream and was almost pleased at the sheer renewed vigour in it.

Romana slammed the manual shut and glowered at the TARDIS. The problem with doing things by the book was that there was nothing in the book about what she was planning on doing. The book, while curiously detailed on straw bedding, stayed stubbornly silent about plunging a TARDIS into the empty heart of a planet. A winking icon at the bottom of one of the pages suggested she consult the online help, but that was never any use. She hadn't been born yesterday.

Romana switched on the TARDIS's computer-based Index File, only to discover it was badly overdue a software update. She dreaded what would happen if she connected it back to Gallifrey. Probably have to mark off the next thousand years while it performed a series of vital updates before crashing halfway through and asking her where the warranty was.

A thought struck her. What if the TARDIS just wasn't working properly? Given how slapdash and generally hopeless the Doctor was, it wouldn't surprise her. She ran a finger along the console, looking for the Fault Locator circuit. Then she wondered. Well, on a TARDIS this old, the Fault Locator might be a bit bigger than a tiny read-out. Where was it? She looked round for something roughly the size of a book.

She'd never really noticed the large curtain drawn across one wall of the control room before. The very large and very dusty curtain. With a heavy sense of dread she tugged the curtain back, to be confronted by a whole other room. Through a filthy glass partition she could see banks of ancient equipment. She'd found the TARDIS Fault Locator. She pulled open the rusted door and trod on the mummified remains of a civilisation of spiders. Sweeping webs away and trying not to choke on the dust, she made her way over to the Fault Locator itself. Well, of course the Doctor had turned the Fault Locator off. He'd probably been delighted with it to start with, grown quickly bored, then forgotten about it entirely. That seemed like the Doctor.

Well. All that was about to change. Romana was going to fix this TARDIS, save the Doctor, and show him.

She turned the Fault Locator on. Rather as if it was catching up with several decades of a particularly grim soap opera, it immediately got very excited. All the bulbs on the vast machine lit up angrily. Then, just as quickly, they all went out. Except for one. Romana peered at it, wiped it, and then read the output. The Fault Locator told her that the Fault Locator was broken.

The Doctor had stopped screaming. This was a shame as he'd really got his scream on. There was just nothing left to scream with. There was no air. There was also rather a lot of gravity. Gravity that was simultaneously crushing him and pulling him on faster. The Doctor was running out of time. And he didn't have a clue what to do.

'Tonight, Matthew,' he thought, 'I'm going to be a singularity.'

*

Romana wiped the dust from her hands, pulled the curtain closed and marched over to the console. 'Right then,' she announced to the TARDIS and the universe in general. 'Don't do it by the book. Don't do it at all properly. Just do it like the Doctor. Push the first button that comes to hand.' She pushed one. 'And think of something.'

With a roar of approval the TARDIS pirouetted away into the Vortex.

As they tumbled, Romana felt her way across the controls in a mixture of instinct and blind panic. Calculations rushed through her head as she balanced the speed of the TARDIS with the velocity of the Doctor and the curiously argumentative interplay of the laws of physics you'd find at the heart of an empty planet. And somehow, things just fell into place. They simply happened.

She flicked on the TARDIS Tuner, using it to trace the Doctor's position. Her hands flew across the dials as she brought the TARDIS into sync with the Doctor's fall. Finding the dead centre of the planet was as easy as pi. Getting there at the exact same moment as the Doctor – well, that required translating a set of fairly dazzling improvisational maths into some deft flicks of some partly broken and slightly rusty knobs and dials. But she did it.

Romana and the TARDIS both honked in triumph as the machine began to materialise in the heart of Zanak.

At the last moment, Romana realised what she'd got horribly wrong. Of course she'd forgotten something. But why did it have to be the Gravitic Anomaliser? She'd forgotten to engage it, and without that, the Doctor would turn into mist the moment he arrived.

Romana howled in fury as she tried to reach it, but she couldn't. She watched in horror as the TARDIS materialised inside Zanak, wrapping itself around the Doctor. The ghost of him hung there for a moment, solidifying as the TARDIS pushed itself into reality.

Romana flinched. Any second now there was going to be a loud pop and an awful mess. She shut her eyes.

The TARDIS engines coughed to a halt.

'… aaaaaarg,' the Doctor gasped hoarsely as he fell to the floor.

Romana opened her eyes and gaped.

The Doctor was there. The Doctor was fine.

He sat up and beamed at her.

'Ah, you got here in the end, eh?' he croaked. 'Good old girls. Both of you—'

He was about to launch into one of his speeches, but Romana held up her hand.

'Don't,' she said. She went over and stared at the Gravitic Anomaliser.

It had somehow set itself.

The TARDIS departed the centre of Zanak, the mocking laughter of its engines echoing off the vast rock walls. Zanak was once again empty.

'So,' the Doctor said airily. 'How are things?'

'Not bad,' said Romana. 'Organising a revolution. About to storm the Citadel. You?'

'Oh well,' the Doctor shrugged. 'Same old, same old. Kimus and K-9 are sabotaging the engines. Should be there by now. There's a couple of things I need to take care of, but they shouldn't hold you up. Vive La Revolution and all that. I say…' He paused, terribly casually. 'You wouldn't mind dropping me off a couple of minutes early, would you?'

'Doctor—' began Romana, but he flashed her a grin, and she realised how much she'd missed him.

'Hush now, what happens in temporal flux stays in temporal flux.' The Doctor thought about telling Romana how proud he was of her, but settled for tapping her gently on the nose. 'And besides, I rather fancy making a big entrance.'

Chapter Twenty-Three
Playing the Queen

The Captain and the Nurse stood watching the Doctor fall into the planet until they could see him no more. It was done.

'Cooeee!' a voice rang out behind them.

They spun round. Lounging against a desk was the Doctor. He was juggling the crystals from the Captain's Psychic Interferometer.

'Hello everybody,' he said.

For a moment, nobody said anything. Mr Fibuli marvelled that there was somehow enough of the Captain's face left to gawp.

'But—' the pirate managed eventually.

'Do you know…' The Doctor thought about explaining but then decided they just didn't deserve it. 'I've got the most terrible head for heights. Hello again. Where were we?'

Mr Fibuli had never seen the Captain's jaw drop before. He wasn't sure he liked it. The Nurse thinned her lips into a tight moue of disapproval.

The Doctor was striding around the Bridge, tossing the crystals up into the air and catching them again, over and over.

He didn't care about all the guns trained on him. He rarely did, but especially not now. Why, what if a blast should shatter one of the crystals? That would be irksome. The Doctor enjoyed the way they caught the light as they spun in the air, enjoyed the look on everyone's faces, just enjoyed life in general.

'I've just discovered your embarrassing little secret,' he addressed the universe. 'We are not all quite as we seem to be, are we?' The universe shifted a little guiltily. The crystals vanished into the Doctor's pockets and out came a small box. 'This is a remote holographic generator.' There was one light winking steadily on it. The Doctor flicked a switch.

Suddenly there were two Doctors on the Bridge. The other one waved. 'It can project the image of a person. Like me. Hello, Doctor!'

The real Doctor waved back. 'Hello, Doctor. How are you?'

'Can't complain,' the fake Doctor beamed. 'Neat little machine, isn't it? The images it projects might almost be real.'

The hologram vanished. The Doctor had flicked a switch on the projector. A light on the side dimmed. But one light still remained.

'It's multi-channel. It's still projecting an image of a person. So, just as I was able to turn off that image of myself, I can turn off another apparently real person, can't I?'

Enjoying the tension creeping across the Bridge, the Doctor waved the device across the Bridge, watching people flinch. Then he flicked the switch. A little light on the projector went out. 'I wonder which of us will disappear this time? I wonder…'

It took a while for everyone to notice the Nurse vanish. But then again, that was the Nurse's way. One minute she was there, the next she wasn't. That was just how unobtrusive she was. Mr Fibuli had never noticed her come or go. He'd never really paid that much attention to her.

But all of a sudden, in front of everyone, the Nurse vanished.

Mr Fibuli stared at the empty space in bafflement. How had that happened? How had he missed that?

The Captain's reaction was surprising. He roared with laughter and slapped his thigh. There was an air of madness to his laugh.

The Nurse reappeared, standing on the plank, balancing on one leg. Her smile was even broader than the Doctor's. The Doctor glanced down at the box. The light had come back on. The Doctor, surprised, jiggled the switch. The image of the Nurse shimmered slightly but this time did not vanish. She stepped off the plank and strolled casually across the chasm.

There was a new air to her. The meekness had gone from her posture. The demure downcast of her lips had thinned into a cruel smirk. She nimbly bounced up towards the Doctor, throwing back her hair. She prodded the projector.

'You can try all you like Doctor. It won't work.' The Nurse's quiet simper now had a haughty sneer to it. She stretched out her arms and examined them slowly. 'My new body has almost attained fully corporeal form. It can no longer simply be turned off.' She snapped her fingers. 'Guards!'

A couple of Guards stiffened with surprise. Did she mean them? Who was she?

'Guards,' the Nurse repeated tersely. 'Seize him!'

Well, clearly she was serious. But still. The Guards looked over at the Captain, who, remarkably, had slumped down into a chair and was trying to make himself look very small indeed. When he spoke it was with a sulky mumble. 'Do as she says.'

The Guards shrugged.

The Nurse stamped her foot, which, confusingly, made no sound.

'Seize him, I say! He has the Interferometer crystals.'

Well, if she was going to say stuff like that, they'd better do something. The Guards pulled themselves together and moved towards the Doctor.

The Doctor gathered up the crystals and made to lob them into the pit. A gun smacked against his wrist and the crystals scattered across the floor.

The Nurse bent down and, smiling, slowly picked them up, one by one.

'That's better,' she simpered. 'Now, Captain, order everyone back to work.'

'Do as she says,' the Captain mumbled miserably. 'Everyone back to work.'

Once, so very long ago, the Captain had been looking forward to a glorious death. The *Vantarialis* (which really was the most impressive and terrifying ship in the entire pirate fleet) was in trouble, falling burning out of the sky.

As his crew had stood screaming helplessly around him, the Captain leaned back in his chair and laughed. After all, it had been a life of audacious risks, and the Devil of Agranjagzak had to win a round sooner or later. What better round than this to lose? His enemies crushed, their fleet in smithereens. Yes, yes, he was dying, yes, his crew was dying too, but were they not going to a glorious death?

He stood up, walking easily to the prow, staring out through the window, beyond the flaming hull, to a final glimpse of the stars. There was a planet coming into view. How wonderful, thought the Captain, if they could take that out? One last final, glorious gesture.

'It doesn't have to be that way,' said a very loud, very deep voice.
The Captain looked around. There was no one there.
He realised. 'The Sky Demon?'
The voice chuckled. 'If you like.'
'Ha!' The Captain snorted. 'I knew we would talk at the end.'
'Well,' the dark voice rumbled. 'That's just it. This doesn't have to be the end. I have a rather interesting proposition for you…'

*

292

Romana had been gone a couple of minutes. The Mourners and the young people looked nervously at each other. Neither group entirely trusted the other. Pralix and Mula had emerged as leaders of each faction, which did not, it turned out, make things easier.

'You're brother and sister,' mumbled one young man. 'You're just going to agree on everything.'

'And you're clearly an only child,' Mula said.

With a welcoming bellow, a small blue box pushed its way out of nowhere to arrive on the plateau.

The crowd stared at it in surprise.

The door opened and Romana stepped out.

'Now,' she said. 'Where were we?'

Mula frowned. 'What is that?'

'Spaceship,' offered Romana vaguely. 'Just had to go and check on the Doctor. He's got one or two little things to sort out, but he's on top of them. Our main priority –' she pointed at the entrance – 'is to get that door open.' She realised she should have borrowed the Doctor's sonic screwdriver. Then again…

'Do you think you can open it?' she asked the Mourners.

Pralix nodded, grimly. The Mourners focused their energies on the door. The complicated interlocking mechanism suddenly felt rather sorry for itself and the door sagged open.

Behind it was a squad of the Captain's Guards. They had been waiting for them.

They raised their guns and opened fire.

The crowd screamed, but the Mourners raised their hands, plucking the bolts from the air.

The Guards raised their guns to fire again, but the Mourners looked at them, looked at them with the full force of a dozen dead worlds. The Guards fell back, crumpling into miserable heaps, shaking and wailing.

Mula stared at Pralix in horror. 'Is that in your head all the time?' she asked.

He nodded, that tiny little wrong smile tugging down his lips. 'Yes.' He nodded, very slightly.

'I'm sorry.'

'It's been there for so long. You get used to it.' Again the sad smile. 'But there's so much of it, we are only too happy to share it.'

The Mourners turned back to the Guards, and a fresh wave of misery broke over them.

Back on the Bridge, the Nurse sat down in the Captain's Chair. She met the questioning looks of any of the Guards with a challenging glare. She stabbed a finger in the direction of the Psychic Interferometer.

The Captain creaked miserably towards it.

'Mr Fibuli!' the Nurse's voice rang out. 'Replace the crystals in the machine.'

The Captain stopped in his tracks.

Mr Fibuli, with little more than a wince of apology in the Captain's direction, sat down at the Interferometer and began to plug the crystals into the lattice.

'Madranite 1-5…' he said. The device began to glow.

The Battle was over. The Guards had last been seen running screaming down the mountain. The Mourners stood around, placidly, while various citizens slapped them on the backs and laughed.

Romana was becoming a little worried by the vaguely festive air. Then she noticed Mula rubbing her arm.

'Are you all right?'

'Yes, I think so, it's only my arm.' Mula made a determined attempt not to make a fuss. Her arm had been caught in the gunfire and, frankly, hurt an awful lot. But she didn't want to be the one to slow things down.

'Can you carry on?' Romana asked. Oh dear. She clearly should have set up a field hospital.

'Of course I can carry on, I've got another arm, haven't I?'

'Good.' Romana nodded approvingly, after a cursory examination.

Two Guards appeared above them on a ledge. Positioned as snipers, they opened fire on the crowd. Romana heard the screams and felt the rising panic.

She turned to Pralix, but he was standing open-mouthed.

'Do something!' she urged.

Four of the Mourners fell to the ground.

'What's the problem? Fight back!' Romana urged.

'We can't,' Pralix croaked. 'The Power's gone.'

The Mourners began to whimper and stagger.

Pralix had gone pale. 'The Life Force is still flowing into us – but the link has gone. We can't channel it out!' he wailed.

The Mourners shook their heads.

The snipers continued to blast at the crowd.

Mula leaned down and snatched up a fallen gun.

She fired twice.

The snipers fell to the ground in front of them.

'And that was my bad arm,' said Mula. 'My good arm's terrific.'

'Pralix? What's happened?' asked Romana.

'We cannot tell.' Pralix's voice was a confused whisper. 'The contact between us has gone… Our minds are buzzing, we cannot function.'

'Oh.' Romana refused to take it as a setback. What was needed was firm action before the crowd started to turn. She watched as those who could, picked themselves up. 'Oh well,' she announced firmly. 'So much for the paranormal. I suppose it's back to brute force. Find yourselves guns, everybody!'

Mr Fibuli wondered if the Nurse was going to kill him. This was, he reflected, a bit of a change. The Captain was no longer the most terrifying person in the room. He was still trying to get his head around who exactly this woman was. He was baffled.

She'd just been there. All his life, standing at the Captain's side, quiet, malicious, but also barely noticeable. Like the annoying rattle from the air-conditioning vent on Level 3. Just one more miserable thing in poor Mr Fibuli's life. Now, all of a sudden, she was terribly in charge of things. She wasn't even, if the Doctor was to be believed, entirely real. He wasn't too sure about that, but it would explain why she'd never aged. Funny, he'd never noticed that about her. He'd never noticed anything about her.

Now there was no ignoring the Nurse. The entire atmosphere of the Bridge had changed. She strode around it, utterly in command, both glaring at everyone and yet not meeting anyone in the eye. The Crew exchanged worried glances and occasionally muttered. Someone was very quietly running a sweepstake. Mr Fibuli ignored them. It was all a little bit complicated. There was so much to deal with in his life right now and it hadn't exactly been empty before. He noticed a pile of folders for his urgent attention had landed on the desk next to the Psychic Interferometer. He felt the urge to sweep them to the ground and scream. No. Perhaps best not. He sneaked a hand towards them, just to see what dooms they contained. The Nurse's hand slapped down on the folders.

'Well?' she snapped. 'Is it working, Fibuli?'

'Yes,' he said hurriedly, 'The Interferometer is at full power.'

'Good!' The Nurse stood back and clapped her hands together. Her face lit up with a weird, childish glee, and her voice gushed with enthusiasm. 'Now let's show these miserable zombies who really rules Zanak.'

The Doctor tried not to worry about what was going on. He'd returned from the dead, he'd produced a remarkable bit of denouncing, and all that had happened was that he'd been swept to one side while the unmasked villain got on with winning.

He didn't care for this one bit. He wasn't entirely sure whether 'this' referred to the wrong people winning, or to him being ignored.

'So…' He cleared his throat, and winked at the Captain. 'Queen Xanxia, the tyrant Queen of Zanak, ruler of Zxoxaxax. And yet… Well, those clothes. Hardly a very fitting get-up for a queen, is it? A nurse's tunic? I would expect something far more lavish.'

For an instant, Xanxia seemed annoyed at being interrupted and then dismissed it. She favoured the Doctor with a beam that was practically giddy. 'You wish to see a queen, do you, Doctor? Then you shall do so…!' She clapped her hands together, and the Nurse's outfit vanished, replaced with resplendent royal gowns. They were exact copies of the ones worn by the ancient figure behind the Time Dams, only lacking the dust. They were also covered in tiny sparkly jewels. The Doctor betted that, if he could be bothered to find out, each jewel would have come from another plundered planet. Xanxia stared at the Doctor, eager for praise.

'Oh very nice,' the Doctor clucked insincerely. 'But I've already seen a queen, thank you. The real you is the wizened old body pinned between the Time Dams. Why not wheel her out, eh? Bit of fresh air would do the old girl good.'

'That thing is not me!' Xanxia spat furiously. 'This is now me! Queen Xanxia reborn!'

'Well, not yet it isn't.' One of the Doctor's hobbies was failing to let tyrants down gently. 'I presume it's based on a cell-projection system, isn't it?'

'It is.' Xanxia rallied. 'A permanent regeneration based on cells from my old body.'

'Ah,' the Doctor tutted. 'That shiny new body of yours started out as a holographic projection, a three-dimensional blueprint of a body. The pattern fleshes itself out by degrees, pulling atoms and molecules out of the air and fitting them into the blueprint until the hologram becomes a solid living person. But you haven't achieved that yet, have you? You're still unstable, you're still dependent on the last few seconds of life which remain in your original body.'

Queen Xanxia regarded him regally. 'I am nearly complete Doctor. My molecular structure has nearly bound together... Very soon I shall be fully reborn. Xanxia shall live!'

'Well, yes and no,' the Doctor chided. 'It won't work. Believe me, I'm an old hand at regeneration. The Time Dams won't work – not for what you want them for. There isn't enough matter in the universe for what you're trying to do.'

'Doctor.' Now she had gowns, Xanxia was making the most of them for striding. 'I assure you the plan has worked before, it is working now and it shall work in the future. I have calculated every detail. Xanxia shall live for ever, the Eternal Queen!'

Oh lordy, the Doctor rolled his eyes. She really was off on one.

'Live for ever, what sort of dream is that?' He sounded reasonably bored.

'Eternal life,' the Queen sparkled. 'Why! It is the greatest dream of all, the greatest quest in all history, the secret of eternal life, eternal youth.'

'Poppycock, absolute poppycock.' The Doctor played to the crew. 'Do you know, I've never heard such drivel in all my life.'

The slap landed the Doctor on the floor. Interesting, he thought. Not good. Not good at all. The Queen's new body had a surprising amount of strength. She'd not been able to resist a few enhancements.

'Have a care, Doctor...' The Queen stood over him, examining her fingers gently.

Rather fearing for the state of his jaw, the Doctor pressed on with his attack. 'Piffle, hogwash, a waste of words. Eternal life? What kind of talk is that for a grown woman? What are you now? Six hundred, seven hundred? You really should know better at your age.'

'Life, Doctor, is the most precious thing in the universe. It is to be cherished, preserved... The continual reblossoming of life is the greatest dream a sentient being can have.'

Who doesn't love a despot with no sense of irony? 'You've been reading too many commercials, that's your trouble.'

'You dare to mock me, Doctor?' Queen Xanxia let off an annoying peal of sarcastic laughter. 'Oh, you shall die for your insolence!'

The Doctor thought she was going to hit him again. Instead her hand daintily stroked the little black box still slung around her shoulders.

For a moment nothing happened. Then the Captain stood up jerkily and lumbered towards the Doctor, a hook springing out of his mechanical arm and swiping the air menacingly. The Captain regarded the hook, and indeed his walking, with surprise and alarm. His flaccid human hand swatted at his legs until the robot arm reached over and pushed it out of the way. The lumbering steps continued, as inarticulate as a puppet being jerked along. The Captain looked up, and for the first time, the Doctor saw the man trapped inside. He could see the mouth twisting to call for help, but then realised. The Captain had given up hope of rescue long ago.

The Doctor felt nothing but pity for the creature lurching towards him. He was horrified that the pirate had been mummified alive. Then the hook glinted in the Captain's arm, and the Doctor's self-preservation kicked in.

'Xanxia, if you think turning the Captain into a toy is an acceptable way to treat a guest –' the Doctor backed away from the Captain with his most dignified shuffle – 'then that shows you've a pretty selective view of which particular life it is that's to be cherished and preserved, don't you think? Because you're going to have to end up being very selective indeed. You poor fool, don't you realise how the Time Dams work? Did you read the manual or just the pretty brochure?' He knew which he'd choose, but that was beside the point.

'You know nothing of the Time Dams!' roared the Queen, smirking as the Doctor hurled himself out of the way of the Captain's swiping hook.

'Oh no?' The Doctor tried to pant insouciantly and discovered it was tricky. 'Which of the outfits was it that got their claws into you? Forever You Eternity Incorporated? Tree of Life Enterprises?' He searched her eyes for a flicker of recognition, but saw only blazing fury. 'Most of their victims died in poverty and degradation, but then most of their victims didn't manage to get hold of someone like the Captain to do their dirty work for them, did they?'

At that moment, the Captain hoisted the Doctor up, pinning him against a bulkhead, his hook ready to fillet him. Staring death right in the face, the Doctor favoured the Captain with his most earnest grin. 'I really would listen to this, Captain, if you can. It very much concerns you.'

The glorious revolution had faltered, just a little.

'It is not the way of the Mourners to use guns,' said Pralix.

'Oh, really? Well you should have thought of that before you decided to have a mental block at the crucial moment.'

Romana was feeling waspish. The citizens weren't behaving much better. A couple had picked up the guns, looked at them, and wondered how they worked. Currently Romana's armed militia was Mula. The Mourners leaned against the doorway, their faces creased in abject misery.

'This was not something we decided,' croaked Pralix. 'Something is happening to us. Something is interfering with our thought power. Our minds won't project.'

This all seemed rather convenient for Romana's way of thinking. 'You're sure you haven't left the safety catch on or something? Come on, find yourself a gun and don't make a fuss. Perhaps your powers will come back again when it's all over. You could show us some card tricks.'

'You think we are frightened? You mock us because you think we are frightened?' Pralix frowned. It was a very simple frown, and it rather broke Romana's hearts.

'No, Pralix, I think I'm the one who is frightened.' For the first time in her life, Romana felt abashed. 'I'm sorry.'

'It is hard for us to explain what is happening.' Pralix grimaced.

Romana noticed the Mourners were no longer wearing the exact same expression, but were all displaying various symptoms of anguish.

'The sadness just continues to pour into us. And now we must carry our burdens alone.' Pralix slumped dejectedly against the door.

Mula stared at the crumpled figure. It was like the old Pralix had come back. The listless creature that would flop from sofa to sofa, sighing loudly, eager for attention. She wasn't putting up with that any more. Instead, she marched over to Romana and loudly changed the subject. 'Have you seen the Captain?'

'Yes, I have seen the Captain.'

'What is he like? None of the city people have ever seen him. At least, anyone who has hasn't lived long enough to come back and tell us. Perhaps… if you could tell the people what he's like, what he's really like… that might help.'

Romana considered. Maybe she could make him sound like a nightmare from a fairy tale. But they already had one of those – a Sky Demon who came to them in a whirling ball of flame. She thought this one through and then figured the plain and simple truth would do rather well. She stood on a rock and called them all to attention. Goodness me, she thought, this is what it's like being a tutor. Woe betide anyone who asked a question.

'The Captain,' she began. 'Let me tell you about the Captain. I've met him. And I've survived. He's not really a very ornamental sight. He's obviously undergone some pretty major spare-part surgery, because over half of his body is a robot.'

'Robot? What's a robot?' called someone and Romana's spirits fell.

'A robot is a machine man, an artificial being designed to obey the orders of a man.'

'What man, any man?' Mula asked.

Romana was about to dismiss this, when she stopped. The crowd stared at her. Confused.

'Do you know,' she said. 'That's what I've been wondering. Who controls the Captain?'

The crowd looked at her and muttered worriedly. Her rallying speech had not, perhaps, been a wild success. A few were casting glances at the walk down the mountain. I have somehow, Romana thought, lost them all.

Which was when the plateau echoed to the sound of a dozen guns powering up. Romana looked up at the cliff above them. A squad of the Captain's Guards were grinning down at them. Clearly they knew the Mourners' powers had been taken away. This was just a frightened bunch of people with nothing to do but be slaughtered.

But Pralix and the Mourners stared back up at the Guards. Each produced a gun from under their robes.

'We are all armed and ready,' Pralix called to the Guards with the smallest of smiles. 'Shall we proceed?'

'You've been used!' the Doctor proclaimed, and for a moment, it didn't seem entirely certain who this applied to. The Captain, hook mid-swipe, hesitated. The Doctor jabbed his brass shoulder. 'She's kept you alive just to do her dirty work. But what sort of a reward are you expecting? A new body? Eternal life for yourself?'

The Captain lowered his hook. He seemed about to say something, but did not.

The Doctor stepped out from underneath his arm, and stormed across the Bridge to Queen Xanxia.

'Shall I tell you all about your Time Dams?' he said. 'You may think you're special. But really, you're not even famous enough to have made the news reports about the scam. Imagine that. Everything you've inflicted on your people and the universe and you didn't even make it onto a list of celebrity victims.'

'You can't possibly know about the Time Dams!' she declared, but with a touch less giddy enthusiasm.

The Doctor brought his hands together in a ghoulish imitation of her clap. And then he spoke.

'Tree of Life Enterprises were a fly-by-night outfit, supposedly peddling the secrets of eternal life. And they knew how to pick their customers, oh yes. They weren't interested in all that "eternal reblossoming of youth" nonsense – that was just their sales pitch. The people they found were those who held life cheap, the murderers, the capricious rulers who herded their subjects out to die in pointless wars, those who saw death as their own personal toy to play with, because they're the ones who fear death the most, aren't they, Queen Xanxia? They are the ones who will eventually pay any price to avoid death happening to them. But they didn't tell you, did they, that the price gets higher and higher and higher?'

'They...' Queen Xanxia looked around the Bridge, and faltered. Like anyone caught out, she was nervous of admitting she'd been taken in. Especially in front of these people. 'They promised me when the process finished I would be free for ever.' She glared at him defiantly. 'The salesman was quite emphatic.' As she said the words, she seemed to realise how feeble they sounded.

'Oh, they hooked you good and proper, didn't they?' The Doctor nodded. 'Told you they knew how to pick their customers, didn't I? You don't believe that any more, though, do you? You know the truth. But what about him?' The Doctor jerked a thumb at the Captain. 'Does he know?'

The Queen tilted her chin up, her stare regal and defiant. 'Say your piece, Doctor. Time is running out for you.'

'Yes, but not nearly as fast as it's running out for you.'

Queen Xanxia looked worried.

CHAPTER TWENTY-FOUR
SMALL PRINT IS NOT FOR ETERNITY

Romana's first attempt at organising a rebellion was back on the road. After a brief shootout, the Mourners, looking increasingly grey about the gills, were leading the way into the Citadel. The people were following on behind. Mula, Romana and Pralix were at the front of the crowd. (Romana couldn't really call them a strike force, and her head kept offering her the word 'gaggle'.)

They paused at the inertia-less corridor. Crowds are not, as a rule, good with new concepts, especially not one as baffling as a path you have to switch on.

'What is this?' Mula asked.

'It's a very sophisticated transport system.'

Romana could just have left it at that. But she just couldn't resist the urge to make everyone in the room just that little bit smarter.

'You see, the main problem with trying to cover a long distance fast is that you have to spend as much time decelerating as you do accelerating because you have to overcome the body's inertia. In this corridor they seem to have found some way of cancelling out the force of inertia so you accelerate all the way and simply stop dead at the other end.'

She beamed at the crowd. No one beamed back.

'It's terribly clever, I expect I'll eventually be told to do a thesis on it or something. Come along.'

Romana herded them together at the start of the corridor and then switched it on. At this point she realised she should, instead of explaining the underlying principles, perhaps have spent a few moments reassuring everyone about what the experience would feel like.

Hurtling smoothly into the mountain, the crowd started to scream.

'It's terribly fast,' gasped Mula.

'Well that, roughly speaking, is the point, yes,' muttered Romana.

'Oh.'

'I'm sorry.' Romana frowned in genuine apology.

'What about?' Mula noted that regrets were one thing, but Romana had so far done nothing about actually slowing this thing down.

'Well,' said Romana candidly, ignoring the wind whipping past her face, 'the Doctor's always saying that sort of thing to me and it drives me mad. I'll ask a perfectly sensible question about why things are behaving unusually. Why a simple corridor has to be so fast, why he has a robot dog, or even why anyone would build a key to control the universe without building a door for it to go in. You know the sort of thing. And instead of even acknowledging that life is indeed bizarre, he'll simply act like I've been boring.' Romana frowned. 'I've got it!'

'He thinks you've got what?'

'The Nurse!'

'There's something you need a nurse for?' Mula looked around for something to hold on to. There really was nothing, so she gripped her gun even more tightly. Mula really hoped Romana wasn't going to be sick. It had been a long day, and she really wasn't sure what would happen at this speed.

'No, no.' Faced with a perfectly sensible question, Romana swatted it away. 'It's the Captain's Nurse. Strange, meek little thing. And yet she's always hovering around the Captain, fiddling with a little black box. I bet she has control of the robot side of his body! He must be completely in her power. Who'd have thought it?'

Suddenly, Mula's world, which had already had to adjust to very fast corridors and their Captain being some sort of machine, was now having to come to terms with their ruler being controlled by a quiet nurse with a little black box. Also, the corridor seemed to be getting even quicker. She reached out for Pralix's hand. Her brother squeezed back.

'Nurse? What nurse?' he asked.

'The Captain has a nurse, she's always hovering around him, and I've noticed that whenever anyone talks to him he shouts at them, and whenever she talks to him he just seethes, so she must have some power over him. Quite logical really.' And not a little clever, Romana admitted to herself. It was all a matter of basic psychology, which she was rather good at, if you could just ignore the wailing crowd behind her. 'I think that if the Captain's making this planet jump around the galaxy eating other planets it must be for her. I wonder who she is.'

'I don't know,' said Pralix. He had decided to close his eyes. The force of misery pouring into his head was not made any better by the sheer speed with which the corridor was whipping by. A nurse did not, at that precise moment, seem terribly important.

'Listen.' Romana was still talking. 'What was the name of that queen you said ruled for hundreds of years and drained the planet of everything it had?'

'Queen Xanxia,' Pralix said tightly.

'But it can't be her,' offered Mula. 'She's dead.'

'But how do you know that?' asked Romana.

'We don't,' said Mula. 'But no one can live that long.'

'That's not necessarily true, you know,' Romana retorted. Six hundred years was nothing. She knew people still working on their first thesis at that age.

'But the legend said she was destroyed!' Yesterday, Pralix had not thought the world could get any harder. And yet this young woman seemed determined to keep throwing impossibilities at him until he broke.

'Ah-hah-ha! But –' there she went again – 'supposing it happened this way? The Captain's pirate ship crashed on Zanak, and his body was terribly mutilated. We know that he must be an engineering genius just to have been able to rebuild Zanak into a planet-sized pirate ship, so it's quite possible that he had highly sophisticated medico-cybernetic equipment on the ship...'

'What?' asked Mula. The impossible corridor took a rather unwelcome sharp left turn.

'Well, if you're a pirate, you're always having bits lopped off you, aren't you?'

'Are you?'

'Yes,' said Romana firmly. 'Now supposing Xanxia rescued the Captain, and used that equipment to rebuild his body as best as she could, but she did it in such a way that she retained control over him. She would then have a brilliant criminal hyper-engineer as her slave, wouldn't she?'

'If you say so...' Pralix's voice was little more than a whimper.

'Is there anything in the legend which flatly contradicts that?' Romana was employing a tactic her tutor would have wearily recognised.

'No, but—'

'But what?' Romana pressed on.

'But nothing. Just… but…' bleated the telepath. Had he been there, Romana's tutor would have wandered over, put a friendly arm around his shoulder, and said, 'If you think that's bad, my boy, you just try explaining the Second Wave of Impossible Cancellation Vectors in the Blinovitch Limitation Effect to her. Spot of lunch?'

Romana suddenly jumped for joy. It was a good thing the corridor was programmed to deal with this, or the crowd would have been wearing her for the rest of the day. 'Do you know what? I bet the Doctor hasn't worked that out yet! Promise me you'll tell him I worked it all out by myself, won't you?' She seemed delighted.

'But why?' Mula found Romana's jubilation at unearthing the terrible survival of Queen Xanxia rather poor taste.

'Well,' beamed Romana, 'because the Doctor doesn't think I'm as clever as he is.'

'No.' Mula rounded on Romana. 'But why is she doing it? Why does she want Zanak to eat planets?'

Romana's pleased expression fell off. 'Er.' she said.

Romana would have been even more annoyed to know that, a few hundred feet above her, the Doctor was busy working it all out, if not exactly before her, then certainly at pretty much the same time.

'It's all about energy, you see!' he declared. 'Energy! The energy requirements of the Time Dams increase exponentially.' He screwed his hands up into a tight ball and then spread his arms out as wide as they could go until they seemed to fill the Bridge. 'Don't you see the progression? Don't you see where it's leading you? Tree of Life Enterprises sold you the Time Dams to slow down the flow of time over your original body… but that time flow has to get slower and slower and slower and slower, doesn't it? Because your body's point of death is only seconds away in real time.'

'You are lying, trying to save your worthless neck!' Xanxia shrugged. It was embarrassing having her problems aired in public by this fool, but she could always have the Captain execute them all afterwards. Anyway, the Doctor was wrong. 'It will no longer matter when this new body becomes fully corporeal...'

'Oh but it never will! Never, ever! That's the confidence trick you fell for, don't you understand?' The Doctor winked at her coaxingly. 'You do understand really, don't you, but you won't let yourself think about it.'

Xanxia stood up from her throne. 'But that's not what he promised. The guarantee says—'

'Guarantee!' The Doctor barked with laughter. 'Are you mad? Well, of course you are. Don't tell me about a guarantee from an organisation of confidence tricksters who were destroyed by the Time Lords five hundred years ago!'

The Nurse blinked. 'What?'

'Oh yes. Shut down, wrapped up and literally liquidated by experts,' the Doctor snorted. 'Why do you think they stopped coming round selling you more energy at extortionate prices? Why did you have to start ransacking Zanak for all the energy it contained? Why do you now have to reduce entire planets into energy... more and more planets, more and more energy to feed the Time Dams to make those last few seconds go slower and slower? Where can you go from here? Eh? Eh?' The Doctor paused for breath and just to make quite sure he had everyone's full attention.

'But my calculations—'

'Are wrong.'

'Impossible!' Queen Xanxia stamped her foot.

'Inevitable.' The Doctor flashed her the ghost of a grin. 'Because they're based on a false premise.'

'No! I've ransacked planets from Bandraginus to Calufrax! Do you think I'm going to stop now?'

'What's next on your awful list? Will you steal suns? Will you try and convert entire galaxies into energy? Because you'll have to eventually, you know.' The Doctor conjured them up with his hands and banished them. 'Phooey! Where does it end? There isn't enough energy in the universe to feed those Dams, and so in the end you will die. I don't think it's worth it, do you?' Lecture over, the Doctor jammed his hands in his pockets and waited for applause. He so rarely got it, it always seemed rather a shame. 'So what about you, Captain, what do you think? Is she worth eating the universe for?'

The Captain stood still.

'Captain?'

The Captain was still slumped, the hook hovering in the air. His one human eye was rolling furiously. The corner of his mouth was twitching. He seemed to be in terrible pain.

The Doctor glanced around, and noticed Xanxia twisting a dial on her box.

'The little black box?' He tutted, suddenly feeling very sorry for the Captain. 'So that's how you control him. Poor Queen Xanxia. No friends. Not even any allies. Just the broken remains of a genius who you torture until he obeys you. You poor fiend.'

Mr Fibuli very nearly cheered. He'd noticed the atmosphere on the Bridge shift. At first there'd been hidden smirks and winks, quiet amusement at seeing their old tartar being put in his place. Followed by even quieter outrage at being told what to do by the Nurse, of all people. Now the mood had changed, to sombre uncertainty and fear about what was going on here. And it was all down to this strange Doctor. Mr Fibuli stood there, and tried to catch the Doctor's eye. Look at me, he wanted to say to him, just ask me to help you and I will. We all will.

The Doctor started to turn towards him. And then alarms went off, ringing throughout the palace.

Mr Fibuli looked down, and automatically reached for the loudspeaker. 'Action stations! All Guards alert! Invaders in the Citadel! The Mourners have gained access to the Citadel!'

Queen Xanxia took her hand off the black box and pointed to the door. 'Captain! Deal with it!'

The Captain staggered, blinked, and took one halting step towards the door, before swinging round, lurching towards the Queen, murder in his eye. 'By all the—' he began.

Shrugging, the Queen twisted the dial again, and the Captain froze, sparks whirling around him. The air filled with a greasy, warm smell.

When the Queen spoke, it was with a return of her breezy calm. 'I said deal with it! So go on! Do!'

She released the button.

The Captain twisted away, throwing her a glare that contained all the savagery in the universe. 'I promise you, Xanxia, by all the blood of the Sky Demon, you shall die at my hand.'

She nodded casually. 'Well, we'll see about that, won't we?'

The Captain shuffled away from her. He didn't say anything. His back twitched, very slightly, his step faltered, but he kept going. He stood before Mr Fibuli, and, for once, looked cowed.

'Mr Fibuli,' the Captain began, hoarsely, his voice rising. 'Seal the Bridge.'

Mr Fibuli looked up at the tormented figure standing over him. 'Yes Captain, of course, Captain,' he said gently, and pulled a lever. Steel bulkheads slammed down across all the entries to the Bridge.

'Let them do what they like.' Queen Xanxia tossed her hair back and laughed. 'They won't get in here.'

If the inertia-less corridor hadn't been too much for the rebels, the invisible lift proved to be quite enough, thank you very much. The Mourners had managed to look even more miserable, and several people simply flailed around in mid-air shrieking.

Still, thought Romana, just a few more floors to go and then they'd be in the Citadel and they could begin the fight back. The Doctor would, at any moment, disable the jammer and retake control of the Engine Room. And then they could win. She knew this because she believed in the Doctor. She finally understood him, that impossible, wonderful man.

The lift stopped. Some of the rebels stepped out. A few crawled.

Romana looked around at them all and smiled her most warm and encouraging smile. 'Come on everybody!' She pointed to the door to the Bridge. 'This way!'

At this point, Guards stepped out from every doorway and fired on them. The Mourners started firing back, but they were being forced against the bulkhead to the Bridge.

Romana banged on it. It was firmly sealed shut.

'Oh,' sighed Romana. 'I get the feeling the Doctor's not in control here.'

The Doctor was reluctantly reaching the same conclusion.

It wasn't helped by Queen Xanxia summarising the situation. 'We are impregnable. The Mourners are powerless, the Guards will pick them off at will, I control the engines, the Captain, and the entire planet.' Yep, she was definitely a summariser. The Doctor did so hate a summariser with their 'May I remind you, Doctor, that my clone army' this and 'You seem to forget, Time Lord' that. Too much list-making when young, that was the problem.

Queen Xanxia snapped her fingers. 'Captain, is Calufrax now entirely rendered?'

The Captain reached for a control, and then paused. 'Mr Fibuli?' he called, his voice flat. 'Is Calufrax now entirely rendered?'

Mr Fibuli, dear Mr Fibuli, smiled up at him from a clipboard, and the Captain felt himself flush with shame. The First Mate's business-like voice was soft, as though trying to convey a sympathy under the works. 'Yes, sir, all the energy-reducible minerals have been mined, refined and stored. And the residue has been processed in the normal way, sir.'

'Thank you, Mr Fibuli!' Queen Xanxia replied before the Captain could, oozing delight. 'Then the mines are clear. And Captain, you have located a planet where we can find the mineral required to restore our engines to full working order, haven't you?'

'Mr Fibuli, have I?'

'Yes, you have.' Mr Fibuli bowed to both of them, his bow to the Queen perhaps a shade quicker. 'The mineral PJX18.'

'PJX18?' butted in the Doctor. 'That's quartz.'

Mr Fibuli consulted a star chart. 'It is found on the planet Terra in the star system Sol.'

'Captain, we will mine that planet immediately!' commanded the Queen. 'Prepare to jump.'

'The Earth?' This really was too much for the Doctor. 'You're going to plunder the Earth? Do you really mean to go on with this madness? This insanity? Don't you understand you can't win? Are you going to take everyone else with you? The Earth is an inhabited planet... billions of people. Are you really that insane? You're going to throw billions of good lives after bad?'

The Queen acted as though she hadn't heard. She was clapping her hands together. 'Jump immediately, Captain! I command you to jump!'

The Doctor had an absurd image of the Captain jumping. The Captain seemed similarly unimpressed. 'By all the moons of madness, do not molest me!' he rumbled sulkily. 'It will take ten minutes to set the coordinates.'

'Then do so!' the Queen declaimed.

'Mr Fibuli,' sighed the Captain drily. 'I suppose we'd better announce a new Golden Age of Prosperity.'

'But Captain, the last one was only yesterday.'

'Then the people are very lucky, Mr Fibuli,' the Captain growled, with some of his old energy.

'Of course, sir,' Mr Fibuli smiled back.

The Bridge started to bustle as the vast vessel made preparations for flight.

The Doctor couldn't help laughing at it all. 'You can't win. All that's between you and defeat is that bulkhead. The Mourners outside can destroy you with the mind power of dozens of dead planets. I should warn you, it's really quite something. Perhaps you shouldn't have destroyed so many planets.'

'No, no, Doctor,' chided the Queen. 'You are forgetting my Psychic Interferometer.'

'You mean this?' The Doctor edged across the Bridge, aware of all the eyes following his every move. 'Not likely to forget it when you've called it that, am I?' He made a sudden leap towards the device, causing Mr Fibuli and a small rush of Guards to block his way.

The feint allowed the Doctor to pirouette mid-leap and yank on the bulkhead lever. The great door swung up and the Doctor threw himself under it. As he slid across the floor, he aimed his sonic screwdriver at the lever. With a whirr and a bang, the lever fell back.

'Ha! Got you!' the Doctor laughed as the door slammed shut behind him.

'Oh, you're all such fools,' tutted Queen Xanxia.

For once, the Captain was philosophical. 'The Doctor can do no damage. The Engine Room is sealed. We dematerialise in nine minutes. What can he do in that time?'

'Exactly!' Queen Xanxia tapped the Captain on the nose. 'And then I'll live for ever! Won't that be fun!'

CHAPTER TWENTY-FIVE
NEWTON'S REVENGE

Romana was rather surprised to see the Doctor slide into the middle of her war. Surprised and not a little worried.

The Doctor sat up, seemingly oblivious to the crossfire sizzling around him. 'Hello everyone! Is this a revolution? How giddy!'

'Doctor!' she cried, dragging him behind a crate.

'Well, Romana, this is quite the party,' the Doctor beamed as blasts chipped away at their shelter. 'Just one question – where are Kimus and K-9?'

She noticed he'd swiftly followed his praise by making her responsible for the one thing he was supposed to be looking after. Hmmm.

'I don't know. I haven't seen them.'

'What?' The Doctor rolled his eyes. 'I sent them to try and sabotage the engines. I hope Kimus hasn't slowed K-9 down too much. This planet's about to jump again.'

'And,' Romana said as their shelter took another hit, 'we're fighting a losing battle here. The Mourners can't seem to get their psychokinetic powers to work any more. And, it turns out, they are pretty dreadful shots.'

'You armed them?' The Doctor stared at Romana in alarm. Whatever next? 'They're blocked because the Captain's installed a Psychic Interferometer on the Bridge. Oh look, here's Kimus!'

Kimus came running up to them, realised he'd wandered into a barrage of gunfire and flung himself to the ground. The crates they were sheltering behind took another battering.

'How is it going?' he asked Romana. She smiled at him, and he tried to work out if the smile was simply polite or deeply thrilled to see him.

'Kimus!' demanded the Doctor. 'Where's K-9?'

'It's no good, Doctor,' said Kimus. 'We couldn't get into the Engine Room, it's barricaded with steel inches thick.' He sounded a touch resentful, as though the thickness of the door was the Doctor's fault. It was also, the Doctor noticed, a politician's answer.

'Where's K-9?!' he demanded again.

Kimus looked a little sheepish. 'He's following behind slowly. He seems to be exhausted from trying to burn down the steel door.'

I'll bet he is, thought the Doctor grimly. He'd hardly had time to recharge from the battle with that pewter parrot, and I bet you kept him at that door after he'd said it was too much effort. 'I hope you realise K-9 is our only hope of setting up a counter-interference to the Psychic Interferometer,' he thundered.

'Right.' Kimus clearly didn't understand a word.

'Let me put it simply. If his batteries are depleted, we've no hope of doing anything.'

'You do rely on that dog for a lot of things, don't you?' said Kimus, a trifle sharply. He really had wanted to open that door. To achieve something.

He looked up and down the corridor. There were guns everywhere. There was smoke, the curious smell of singed electrons, and so much noise. Everyone was shouting, the guns were so loud, and wherever he looked there seemed to be someone curled up in pain. Kimus took it all in and wondered – is this really what a rebellion is like? In his head it had been a few speeches and some cheering. He turned to the Doctor, but he was already up and away.

'Kimus, stay there. Mula?'

'Yes Doctor?'

'Lovely shooting. I don't normally say this, but do some more of it. I need a spot of covering fire. Pralix?'

'Yes Doctor?' Pralix was crouched behind a crate, eyes squeezed tightly shut, hand shaking, his gun going everywhere.

'Tell your fellow Mourners they can breathe a sigh of relief and put down their guns. I'll need all of you at the engines. We've got a lot of thinking about a door to do. Romana, come with me.'

For a moment, Romana felt like telling the Doctor that, actually, she would rather be here, leading her rebel troops, but a slightly shaky Kimus had already stood up and was making a speech exhorting them to victory, while Mula got on with the hard work of shooting at people.

So much for politics, Romana thought, and raced after the Doctor.

She was very pleased to see him again. She wanted to say something that would tell him this. She opened her mouth and instead said, 'What are we going to do, Doctor?'

'I don't know,' the Doctor replied, breaking into a trot. 'But I can think, run and answer questions at the same time. Come on.'

K-9 was stalled in front of the Engine Room door. He tried raising his head at their approach, but the most he could manage was a feeble twitch of his tail.

'Master…' the dog whispered.

The Doctor sprang at the floor, patting the dog with genuine concern. 'K-9! Come on, old boy, we need you!'

Again, the tail twitched.

'Without you, we can't get into the Engine Room.'

The tail drooped. 'I have tried, Master...' Was Romana imagining things, or was there a trace of petulance in the dog's croak? 'Batteries... My... Exhausted... Nearly... Are...'

'Oh don't worry, old pooch, this is Plan B. Well, Plan... um...' The Doctor waved the precise letter away. 'This time you don't need to use your laser beam. Absolute promise. The Mourners can lift the door if you can set up counter-interference on the psychic plane. Wavelength 338.79 microbits. Can you do it?' The Doctor peered at his dog encouragingly. 'Can you? Just that little thing.'

'Negative... Master.'

'What a fine best friend you turned out to be,' the Doctor sighed.

The dog's head slumped forward and he whispered something in a pathetic electronic gurgle.

The Doctor bent forward to listen and then slumped back on his heels. The dog's lights went out and his tail fell.

'Oh, K-9,' the Doctor said sadly.

'What did he say?' asked Romana.

'He said...' The Doctor looked miserable. 'He said there's a power cable right behind me.'

'Oh.'

The Doctor sprang to his feet and started disconnecting a cable from where it had been doing a reasonable job of powering the air-conditioning.

'Open his inspection hatch,' the Doctor commanded. 'We'll be able to recharge him directly.'

'Right.' Romana started fiddling with the catches along the dog's side using a fingernail. It hurt, so she stopped. She really did need a screwdriver of her own. 'But doesn't it take a long time to recharge K-9?'

'Romana…' The Doctor was buried inside an inspection hatch, tugging at the cable. 'I assume you've already taught your grandmother all you know about egg-sucking or you wouldn't be standing around here with time on your hands. Open that dog!'

'Yes, Doctor,' Romana said, and got on with it. 'Doctor, are you cross with me?'

A better man with a bit less universe to save would have stopped right then and there and made a charming apology. Or, at the very least, congratulated Romana on raising a rebel army on only her second trip. Instead, the Doctor said:

'Cross with you? No. I'm cross with everything.' The Doctor finally pulled the cable free and, despite the urgency of things, ground to a halt, staring at the sparking end of it. 'Do you know what they're up to? Those maniacs up there are about to try and materialise Zanak around the planet Earth, and I swear that if I have to save that planet one more time I shall go stark staring mad.' He handed the cable to Romana. 'Plug the fellow in, would you? We're going to run him off the mains.'

The dog jolted and his head shot up, his eyes glowing a little too brightly. He made a low growling noise and lurched forward.

'Master?' said K-9, perhaps rather rapidly.

'Splendid!' The Doctor ignored the smell of burning wire. 'Now, K-9, can you divert any of this current into your frequency projectors?'

'That would be very difficult, Master,' K-9 ruminated. 'Much of my circuitry was damaged fighting the Polyphase Avatron.'

'That horrid parrot?' gasped Romana. 'Did you kill it, K-9?'

'Affirmative, Mistress,' the dog announced proudly.

'Oh, well done!' Romana patted the dog, and received a very small electric shock.

The Doctor, for once, had his eyes on the prize. 'Romana, billions of lives are at stake, can we chat about parrots later? How are we doing K-9?'

The dog considered. 'Master, the voltage supplied by the engines has dropped slightly.'

'Ah,' said the Doctor. 'Not entirely good news. That means that some of the pre-dematerialisation circuitry has already been activated. We're running out of time. Well, we're always running out of time.' He coaxed his dog. 'K-9, can you project any kind of counter-interference on that wavelength yet, however weakly?'

The dog barely even considered. 'Affirmative Master. Counter-oscillation is now running between wavelengths 338 and 339 microbits.'

What this meant was immediately explained by an almost joyous cry from Pralix. 'It's clearing! The buzzing is clearing!' The Mourners looked between each other, a shared half-smile spreading between them. 'We cannot yet project the Life Force out, but we can share it between ourselves. It is… bearable again.'

'Well done, K-9, keep it up boy!'

The dog growled happily. Romana tried to ignore the sparking halo forming around him.

Pralix reached over to the Doctor. 'Yes,' he sighed. 'We are thinking together now… Our minds are as one. But Doctor, it's very weak.'

'Ah, but is it enough to open a door?' The Doctor tapped the Engine Room door. 'Just a little, little door.' It was a very large door, actually.

'Brothers…' began Pralix.

The Mourners turned to stare at the door, trying to pour their energy into it.

Nothing happened. Resolutely.

The Doctor turned back to K-9. 'More projection, K-9!'

'I am projecting what I can, but I am very weak,' the dog retorted, snappily.

The Mourners leaned back against the walls, their faces creased with misery.

'We are not nearly strong enough to open it,' sighed Pralix.

'I have calculated that the required power will build slowly,' announced K-9. 'It will work in time.'

Romana had also had several goes at the calculations and didn't like the answer. 'Time is something we just don't have.'

The Doctor stared at the door and felt really very cross. He'd never been defeated by a door before. There was always a way round it. 'There must be something else we can do… It's nagging at the back of my mind.'

Well, that'd be one cluttered place, thought Romana. She dreaded to imagine what she'd find in there.

The Doctor grinned and patted K-9 with delight, and then sucked his burnt fingers. 'Wait! I've got it! Romana, do you remember what happened when we first tried to materialise on Calufrax?'

'Yes, we couldn't materialise, because Zanak was trying to materialise in the same place—'

'And if we couldn't materialise then neither could Zanak! Romana – we're about to do something revolutionary. We're going to get somewhere first!' He swept off down the corridor. 'Come on, we're going back to the TARDIS. K-9, keep building up your power.'

'Affirmative,' said the dog. It had calculated its survival options, and even fed the wavelengths into the I Ching (33: 'Withdrawal from a situation is progress' and 39: 'Trouble Ahead'). Imminent destruction seemed highly probable wherever he was located; he did not currently have sufficient battery power to make it back to the TARDIS, and also, the I Ching counselled, a wise old man from the South West shall bring benefits to persistent endeavour. K-9 was never entirely sure why the Doctor had installed that. The robot dog, faced with imminent destruction, looked up at the nearest thing it had to a wise old man, and nodded. He would do it.

'Good boy,' enthused the Doctor, handing out jobs and praise like he was running a village fete. Curiously, the Doctor had never run a village fete. The results would have been disastrous. 'Pralix, I've a little focusing test for you. Can you see inside my mind?'

Pralix frowned. 'What?'

'My mind! Can you read it? What am I thinking of?'

Pralix's frown intensified. The Mourners frowned too.

'I can see something... But...' He shuddered. 'It's green... glutinous...'

'Just the ticket!' the Doctor beamed. 'Now whatever you do, concentrate on my mind. I'm going to need a link with you lot when things get dicey. Dicier.'

Romana was right now finding the Doctor utterly baffling.

He nudged her fondly on the arm. 'Romana, stop standing around! We've got a planet to save!'

They ran back through the Citadel, towards the lift terminal.

There, Mula, Kimus and the rebels were still fighting a pitched battle against the Guards.

'Green and glutinous?' Romana asked as she threw herself under a barrage of laser beams.

'Yes!' The Doctor snatched his scarf out of the line of fire and started working on the lift door.

'Is your mind green and glutinous?' Romana picked up a stray gun and dropped a Guard.

'No, no.' The Doctor had the lift door open and pulled her in out of the way of a blast. 'I was thinking of a jelly baby.'

'When do you not?' Romana squeezed off one final shot.

The Doctor activated the lift.

Kimus's worried head appeared above them in the shaft.

'Romana, where are you going?' he asked.

'To save six billion people!' the Doctor replied.

'Right.' Kimus looked a little put out. 'Will you be back soon?'

'Hope so!'

The Doctor and Romana floated down the invisible lift, the sounds of battle receding. By rights, they should have been back there, she supposed, manning the barricades and leading the heroic charge. She tried to imagine the Doctor using a gun. Before today, she'd only ever really fired one at tafelshrews, and mostly missed. No, the battle for Zanak was best off in the hands of Mula and Kimus. Well, mostly Mula.

Romana looked casually down at the ground several hundred feet below them. 'Doctor, I've worked it out. Listen.'

The Doctor cupped a hand to his ear. 'I can't hear anything.'

'This is important, Doctor. I think you should know the Nurse is really Queen Xanxia.'

'Yes,' the Doctor nodded. 'I know.'

'And,' Romana continued, rallying. 'She has the Captain in her power.'

'Yes, I got that too,' said the Doctor.

Romana refused to be put out. He could just be making it up. 'She actually has control over the robot half of his body from that black box she carries.'

'Yes, I know that.' The Doctor sounded bored. 'I've seen her do it.' A thought suddenly struck him. 'How did you know?'

'Oh, I just worked it out.'

'What? Without seeing anything?' The Doctor raised both eyebrows. 'Do you know, that's really very clever of you!'

'Why, thank you, Doctor,' said Romana, thinking it was all, somehow, worthwhile.

People were handing Mr Fibuli reports like birthday cards. The Bridge was a hive of activity. None of the crew knew what was going on, who was in charge, why they were under attack, but they did know one thing. They knew how to start up the planet's engines, and they were throwing themselves into it.

'Captain, sir!' Fibuli called, looking up from his report.

For a moment, no one answered. The Queen sat on her throne, the Captain stood rigidly by her side. Mr Fibuli was unsure about royalty – did one address them directly? He went to the Captain's side and whispered to him. 'Captain, sir—'

'No!' rumbled the Captain gently. 'By the green eye of the Sky Demon, Mr Fibuli, do not speak to me.'

'But sir—'

The Queen looked up from her throne and glanced over at him. 'And what is it, dear Mr Fibuli? Good news? Do let it be good news!'

'Er…' Mr Fibuli looked between the two of them and then said 'Er' again.

'Speak, Mr Fibuli, to whichever one of us you choose,' sighed the Captain.

'But who am I to obey, sir?' wailed Mr Fibuli. He realised he'd spoken too loudly. His voice echoed across the Bridge. The crew fell silent. Mr Fibuli began to mutter and babble, until he realised the Captain was shaking his head slowly from side to side. Mr Fibuli stopped talking. This was it, I'm going to die now, he thought.

Instead, the Captain reached out with a solid metal arm, and rested it wearily on the First Mate's shoulder.

'Who have you always obeyed?' His voice was gentle, sad.

'Well, you, Captain, of course, but I simply wondered—'

'Wonder no more.' The Captain stepped away from the throne, addressing the entire Bridge. At first it seemed like there was something wrong with his voice. The crew leaned forward, straining to hear, and then realised that it was just that he wasn't shouting at them. He was simply talking to them at a normal volume. His tone was strange as well. Gone was the constant anger. In its place was a bitter shame. 'Every word I speak, every move I make has been monitored, checked and controlled from that devil woman's box.' He jabbed an arm at the Queen, who simply nodded and simpered as though he'd paid her a very great compliment indeed. 'Why else would I not have destroyed the hell hag in the Time Dams or even instructed one of you to? You have all obeyed her. All along.' The Captain looked them all in the eye – as many of them as would meet his eye. 'She is your true captain.'

The Queen stood up gracefully, and let her piercing gaze take in the entire room. 'And it's too late for any of you to think of destroying me now. The Time Dams are booby-trapped. The slighest disturbance in the Time Fields and the whole Bridge explodes. It has never been my intention to die. It is certainly not my intention to die alone.'

She watched that bit of news sink in, smiling at them, a cold, sparkling smile. Then, dismissing them all, she sat back down, spinning the chair round to admire the view out of the window. She could see the clouds beyond the prow begin to boil. It was all so thrilling.

'Dematerialisation in four minutes,' Mr Fibuli announced, rather sadly.

'Hurry!' urged Queen Xanxia.

The Doctor and Romana were zipping along the inertia-less corridor. Romana really had grown rather used to it as a way of travel, and looked forward to writing a little paper on its merits some day. She looked over her shoulder to check a pet theory about the effect of inertia on perspective. What she saw alarmed her.

'Doctor,' she cried. 'Look out!'

'I always hate it when people say that,' murmured the Doctor.

'Guards!' she shouted.

'I hate it when people say that too.'

The Guards started firing on them.

'Oh dear,' the Doctor said. 'We're sitting ducks in here.'

Romana watched the energy bolts heading towards them. Now, if there'd been any justice in the world, given the fantastic speeds at which they were travelling, the bolts would have stayed in their guns and blown the Guards up. Instead they headed towards them, a little faster than they were travelling. The Guards kept firing, which, Romana figured, was a bit of a mistake. The blasts were not going to reach them any faster. She added a cross little footnote to her paper on inertia-less travel.

'Quick.' She threw the Doctor down. 'Keep down, we'll present a smaller target.'

By lying as close to the floor as the corridor would allow, the blasts would eventually pass over their heads. But the sensation was quite disagreeable.

'I went surfing once,' the Doctor announced. 'I was a little too old to really appreciate it.'

As they neared the end, the Doctor pulled her up into a crouch. The blasts were crawling through the air behind them.

'Jump to one side,' the Doctor ordered.

At the end of the corridor, they did just that, flinging themselves sideways. The blasts left the corridor, and buried themselves into the wall beyond. The concentrated detonation was impressive.

The Doctor and Romana stood amongst the smoke. Romana tugged at his sleeve.

'Let's get out of here before the Guards reach us.'

The Guards were getting very near, their guns ready to fire again. One of them was smiling nastily at her.

'Well, we could,' began the Doctor, infuriatingly calm. He had spotted something on the wall and was opening it like a Christmas present. 'Ah yes, this'll be the Inertia Neutraliser. I think that the Conservation of Momentum is a very important law of physics, don't you?'

'It is indeed,' Romana nodded solemnly. The Guards were very close to the end of the corridor.

'And, you know, it's a law that I don't think should be broken, do you?'

'Frankly, no.'

'Good,' said the Doctor. He yanked out a wire from the Inertia Neutraliser.

At that precise moment, the two Guards reached the end of the corridor, and, instead of jerking to a halt, they carried on, sailing through the air and thudding impressively into the wall.

They slid down it slowly, groaned, and lay still.

'Newton's revenge,' said the Doctor.

The Doctor and Romana strolled out onto the plateau. The Doctor noticed the TARDIS was parked a few yards away and smiled at Romana again. How terribly thoughtful of her. She really was working out splendidly.

'So who's Newton?' Romana asked.

'Old Isaac?' The Doctor started the long slow walk across the plain. There'd been quite a battle here. 'He was a friend of mine on Earth, he discovered gravity. Well I say he discovered, he needed a bit of a prod in fact.'

'Which you gave him, I suppose.'

'Oh, yes.'

'What did you do?'

'I climbed up a tree and dropped an apple on his head.'

'And so he discovered gravity?' Romana was dubious about the entire tale.

'No no.' The Doctor waved it away. 'He got up and shouted at me to clear off out of his apple tree. I explained it all to him later over dinner.'

The Doctor was still laughing when the Guards came out from behind the TARDIS.

Mr Fibuli had a new problem. It might just mean the death of all of them.

'Captain, sir…'

'Yes?' cooed the Queen.

The Captain flinched. 'Devilstorms, Mr Fibuli, why do you torment me!'

Wringing his hands with embarrassment, Mr Fibuli gestured over to the Psychic Interferometer. 'Your device. It's buzzing slightly. There must be something counter-jamming it.'

'What?' The Captain swept over, plugging himself into the device. 'No! By all the banshees of Betelgeuse it must be stopped!' He thumbed a speaker. 'All Guards on alert! There is a Psychic Interferometer counter-jamming frequency projector in the Citadel! Find it and destroy it!'

'Captain, sir,' purred Mr Fibuli worriedly. 'Do you suppose any of the Guards know what a Psychic Interferometer counter-jamming frequency projector looks like?'

The Captain shrugged. It had been a long day. 'Guards! Destroy everything!' He turned back to Mr Fibuli with a 'There! Happy?' gleam of devilment in his eyes.

Queen Xanxia rolled her eyes. 'Captain! Enough of this! We must dematerialise instantly! We can waste no further time!'

'Dematerialisation in three minutes,' announced Mr Fibuli.

'Exactly,' thrilled the Queen. 'Only three minutes to go.'

'A lot can happen in three minutes,' the Captain said very quietly to himself.

There are a fair few ways of interpreting the command 'Destroy everything!'

The Guards engaged in the fight with Mula decided to start firing on the ceiling, bringing it down in chunks around the rebels.

'They're stepping up the attack,' Mula announced, springing up and loosing bolts into the cloud of debris. 'I don't know how much longer we can hold them –' she squeezed off another shot, and a Guard screamed and fell – 'but we will.'

Kimus blinked. This really wasn't the Mula he knew. She was something different, something rather marvellous, if a little frightening. She'd found her purpose in life and that purpose appeared to be shooting things. He looked at the gun he was holding in his hands and really, really didn't know what to do with it. The world was very odd. Kimus could understand if the impossibly glamorous Romana barely noticed him, but it was a bit of a blow to find out that his fall-back position of good old, reliable Mula was no longer such a safe bet. He really felt lost.

'We'd better be prepared to withdraw,' she said, snapping her fingers for a fresh gun. He passed his gun to her. 'Pralix... the Mourners must be guarded at all costs. They're the most important people on the planet right now. All of them.' She smiled, and it was a curious smile. The smile of someone who has finally solved one of the universe's greatest mysteries – what their brother is for. 'Kimus – go down to the Engine Room and warn them that things are hotting up.'

So, thought Kimus as he trudged down the corridor, that's all I'm really good for. I'm not the great leader. I'm the messenger boy.

The Mourners stood in front of the Engine Room door, pouring all their energies into it. It stayed exactly where it was.

Kimus ran out of the darkness. 'Brother Mourners!' he began. 'How are you doing in your brave and heroic struggle against...' He dried. 'Against the Captain's door?'

Pralix sighed, whether at Kimus or the door he didn't know. 'We are still far too weak to move the door. K-9 can't generate a strong enough counter-jamming field. The Life Force is getting stronger, but too slowly...'

With nothing else to do, Kimus joined them in staring very hard at the door.

Romana pulled the Doctor behind the wreckage of an air-car.

'There are Guards around the TARDIS!'

'Do you think they saw us?'

'Doesn't matter. We'll never get in!' Last time, she'd had the element of surprise on her side. And had landed an air-car on them. This time, they were pinned down.

331

'Never?' The Doctor looked hurt. 'Never say that to a Time Lord.'

'Never say what?'

'Never.'

'Never what?' asked Romana.

'Mind,' the Doctor sighed.

'What mind?'

'Never mind.'

'Never mind what?'

'What?' Now the Doctor was thoroughly confused.

'What?' Romana heartily hoped someone would shoot them. The Doctor first, though.

'Doesn't matter,' the Doctor said. 'We'll get in somehow.'

'We can't!'

'Never say that to a Time Lord,' the Doctor beamed.

'Oh, you're impossible.'

'No, just very, very improbable.'

Standing on the plateau guarding the strange blue box, the Guards tried to concentrate. First there'd been that distant explosion. Then they were fairly sure they'd seen something. But they weren't sure what. It didn't help that the entire mountain had started to throb with energy.

Suddenly, a strange man bobbed up out of nowhere, threw something at them, yelled, 'Get down!' and vanished.

The Guards stared at the object at their feet and then threw themselves away from it.

The Guards stared at the object, trying to work out what it was.

It didn't explode.

It still didn't explode.

One of them stood up, and then motioned to his subordinate to go and examine the device.

Nervously, the Guard got up and went over to it. He prodded it with his gun. It didn't explode.

He picked it up.

He stared at it, passing it to the other Guard.

He rifled in it and pulled out a tiny figure of a baby, carved in a soft orange material.

Both stared at the bag full of small statues in alarm.

They failed to notice anything until a small door closed behind them.

They pounded on the door.

Ignoring the hammering outside, the Doctor threw himself at the TARDIS console with such enthusiasm Romana was amazed it didn't squawk in alarm. He started tugging at levers and twisting switches seemingly at random. He stopped and barked with laughter.

'You know what this is?' His eyes were those of a madman. 'This is the most dangerous manoeuvre the TARDIS has ever done, and that's quite a list.' He leaned close to the console and whispered, 'Don't take it personally, old girl, just try and survive.'

Romana went over to the corner of the room and picked up the TARDIS manual. She thought about handing it to the Doctor, but then flicked open a page at random. The page was terribly knowledgeable about which barley gave your eggs a perfect yellow hue. Romana let the manual drop to the floor.

'Now, Earth coordinates... 5804-4684-884. Multi-loop stabiliser, synchronic feedback...' the Doctor was muttering happily.

'Doctor, if we're going to try and materialise at the same point at the same time as Zanak, how do we actually know exactly when to materialise? It only happened as a fluke before.'

The Doctor stopped muttering, and looked up at her. 'Very good point. Zanak could start dematerialising any second now... We've got to be spot on.' He shrugged sheepishly. 'If I was by myself, well, I'd just have taken pot luck. But I've got you. You're the expert in finicky manoeuvres. You'll have to monitor the warp oscilloscope and gravity dilation meters... they'll both peak when Zanak switches from dematerialisation mode to rematerialisation mode. And then...'

'Then?'

'Brace yourself.'

The Queen's forehead was pressed to the cool glass of the great viewing window.

'How soon, Captain, how soon?' she called back to him without looking up. 'This waiting is intolerable! We must jump, we simply must jump!' She clicked her fingers at him impatiently.

'By the twenty-three moons of madness, if she doesn't shut up, I shall commit bloody acts!' muttered the Captain to Mr Fibuli. Out loud he called, 'We are now ready.'

'Then jump! Come on! Jump instantly!'

The Captain heaved himself towards the controls, and tugged them into some kind of order. 'Planet Terra, star system Sol, galactic coordinates 5804-4684-884, surround jump commences in five seconds. Four... Three...'

As he counted down, the Queen watched fire dance up and down the mountain, pouring into the air around them and then boiling up into the sky. The funnel of light spread out across the sky, wrapping itself around the entire planet, before punching it into time-space.

On the streets of the city, the people fell quiet. Balaton looked up into the sky.

'Ah,' he said to himself. 'A New Golden Age of Prosperity.'

Maybe this one would be better.

CHAPTER TWENTY-SIX
A SPANNER IN THE WORKS

'Now, Doctor, dematerialise now!' Romana called.

The Doctor had a lot of levers he was fond of. But the dematerialisation switch was quite his favourite one.

With a delighted bellow, the strange blue box vanished from the mountainside, leaving behind two very startled Guards.

At almost, but not quite, the same time, gravity had to do some quick thinking. The Calufrax system – an intricate arrangement of seven bodies and two suns – wobbled as the entire planet of Zanak simply faded away. Of the planet Calufrax there was now nothing left.

There was a small fire on the console. The Doctor patted at it casually with the end of his scarf.

Romana marched over to a roundel in the wall, pulled out a fire extinguisher and squirted it.

The fire went out.

Romana put the extinguisher on the floor. 'I'll just keep this handy,' she said. 'Other than that, I think we're doing quite well so far.'

The Doctor gave Romana a look.

The entire ship was shuddering.

Mr Fibuli looked up from a screen, sucking at the end of a pen. 'Captain – there was a slight disturbance on the warp oscilloscope during dematerialisation.'

'Monitor it,' the Captain cautioned.

The Queen stood at the window, exulting in the view it gave of the dizzying whirl of stars above the planet's surface. Her back practically invited you to plunge a knife into it.

But there would be no point. Not yet.

The Captain reached over to a control and, with an expert's touch, tweaked it just a little.

'Prepare for rematerialisation. Surrounding Planet Terra in five seconds...'

Over at galactic coordinates 5804-4684-884, the Planet Earth was enjoying a splendid day. This was not in fact true – half the population was asleep, and the other half were reluctantly awake. But still, the sun was shining and they were alive. All that was about to change.

'Rematerialisation commence!' called Romana.

The Doctor did nothing.

'Now, Doctor!'

The Doctor looked up. 'Oh, right,' he said, and pulled his second favourite lever.

The TARDIS hurled itself out of the Space-Time Vortex.

Sometimes it referred to its occupants as pilots, sometimes as pets. Always wanting to go somewhere, always wanting to do something, always leaving a bit of a mess. But bless them. They were, by and large, fun.

The TARDIS knew exactly what its pilots were up to. Never a stickler for detail at the best of times, they were asking for it to materialise at a precise pinpoint in space and time, and at the exact same moment as another craft with significantly larger engines. Their basis for this outrageous feat of musical chairs was the simple fluke of having managed to do it once before by accident.

The TARDIS had mixed feelings about this. First there had been the installation of the Tracer for the Key to Time, which had been, just a little, like being fitted with a lead. Then there had been the New Girl who had first insisted on landing them by the manual, and then had, rather charmingly, thrown it all away in order to rescue the Doctor from certain doom. Now they were asking it to do a third taxing thing.

Still, thought the TARDIS, these things do come in threes. What it was being asked to do was at least novel, daunting and very, very dangerous. It also had the advantage of being utterly wrong.

TARDISes do not speak. Or, if they do, we live too quickly to listen.

But, as the TARDIS hurtled out of the Space-Time Vortex to save the planet Earth, it allowed itself to say one thing.

'Wheeeeeeeeeee!'

It is unlikely you've ever been to the planet Earth, but if you had, you'd have been surprised how often its inhabitants look at the skies, tut, and say, 'Not again'.

A shadow crept across the sun, a rippling, ominous darkness that spread across the fields, the trees, and the winding streets. People on their way to important jobs glanced up and realised those jobs were maybe not quite so important after all. Queues at bus stops wondered if it was going to make the bus even later. And people who had taken the day off wondered if they'd wasted their time.

A pity, because, in England at least, it had had the makings of a lovely summer's day.

A shadow wrapped itself around the world. The shadow began to squeeze.

And then, somewhere inside the darkness, a small blue box popped up. It was such a little thing, really. Especially if you were a shadow wrapping yourself around a planet. Barely even a dot.

But as soon as the dot arrived, really very bad things started to happen.

Mr Fibuli shook so hard he knew what was going to happen next. Any second, any second now, and I shall simply shake to death and it will all be over and that will be a mercy.

He could hear the screaming from the other control decks and knew that things were not going well. If they made it through all this alive, he would definitely have to kill himself as the paperwork would be lethal.

For some reason, the air-conditioning units had failed, and the atmosphere was acrid. He could smell smoke, he could see flames, but it was all so very hard as the air itself shook. The jelly in his eyeballs shook, his bones jarred against each other. He tried to keep pushing buttons, but he had no idea any more if he was even pushing the right buttons.

The Captain strode across his Bridge, sweeping people aside as he stabbed down on various controls. He was flying the entire planet single-handed, and he just didn't seem to care. He just seemed annoyed that something was interfering with his marvellous engines. 'Devilstorms, Mr Fibuli. It is happening again!'

Over at the window, Queen Xanxia turned around. The view out of the window showed the surface of Zanak shimmering into transparency. Through it peeped the planet Earth, a blue-green globe wearing a veil of cloud. The planet was ringed with a fierce red glow as Zanak tried to get a grip on it.

'What's happening, Captain? Stop it doing that simply immediately!'

The Captain did not even look up from the controls. He sounded weary. 'It's the Doctor's vessel. He's trying to materialise in the same space as us.'

Mr Fibuli managed to make sense of a readout and wished he hadn't. 'Every circuit's jamming. The whole of space-time is being torn apart!'

Romana had stopped putting out fires. The extinguisher was empty.

She'd never really known what the round things decorating the TARDIS walls were for. A few of them were cupboards, but most of them seemed purely decorative. If it had been up to her, she would have used the space to put up shelves, but then, that was her. Anyway, the round things were now flying out of the walls like dinner plates hurled in a restaurant fight. Smoke poured out of the circuitry behind them.

The floor had tipped to such an alarming angle that the ceiling seemed the best place to stand. Romana's grip on the console was mostly a very large lever that someone had sellotaped a note to. The note read: 'Please do not hold on to me in an emergency.'

Romana breathed in, judged the air to be poisonous, and immediately engaged her respiratory bypass system. She was in a whole world of trouble. She scrabbled around for the belt the Doctor had used earlier, but the panel was jammed shut.

She tried to read a dial, but the glass cracked and smoke dribbled from it.

'Doctor! There's no way we can survive this! We'll have to back off!'

Romana suddenly realised why the Doctor had a scarf. He'd looped it around the central column and was using it as a seatbelt. She'd never have told him this, but right now, he looked just a little magnificent.

'Romana,' he said in a tone that had made armies change their minds, 'the moment we back off, the Earth dies! We have to keep jamming!'

'But Doctor, it's getting worse!' Romana felt the lever she was clinging to bend a little and she really hoped it didn't do anything important.

'I know!' The Doctor, of all things, smiled at her. No one really smiled on the planet Gallifrey, and the Doctor's smile was quite the nicest thing Romana had ever seen. She just wished he wouldn't smile only when they were in absolutely mortal peril. 'And it'll carry on getting worse until one of us explodes... unless the Mourners get that door open!' The Doctor threw back his head and shrieked a single word:

'Pralix!'

'What are you doing?' cried Romana.

'Shhh!' the Doctor counselled. 'I'm trying to call Pralix.'

'Don't tell me – you're thinking of an orange jelly baby this time.'

Things were not calm outside the engine room. The good thing was that the Mourners were so crushed by a life of constant misery that being trapped at the epicentre of a multidimensional collision was really not that much worse.

The Mourners poured their souls into the engine room door, willing it to give way.

Pralix looked up, sensing another mind. A mind that smelled just slightly of sugar dusting the insides of a paper bag. He looked up, and he almost, almost smiled.

'Pralix! Can you hear me?' the Doctor's voice sang into his head from a long way away.

Pralix nodded. 'Brothers. The Doctor is trying to reach me. We must concentrate together. The voice is too faint for me to reply.'

Aboard the TARDIS the Doctor hit the side of his head several times.

'Pralix! Can you hear me? Over?'

A voice wandered faintly into the Doctor and Romana's heads.

'What? I can hardly hear you, Doctor!' the voice said and then washed away. There were more words, but they were hopelessly indistinct.

The Doctor shook his head, annoyed. 'There's just so much background noise,' he sighed.

'We could just turn the engines off,' suggested Romana facetiously, and then instantly regretted it.

'Romana!' the Doctor cried with delight.

'Yes?' she said weakly.

'We're going to turn off something else. We're going to turn off the TARDIS shields.'

Oh, now he'd gone too far. Far too far.

'What? Doctor, that's madness and you know it. The shields are the only protection we've got against this. Turn them off and we'll explode.'

'If we're lucky,' the Doctor agreed. 'All the same. Turn them off.'

Romana hesitated. Two days ago she'd had a bright future ahead of her – academic success, a thrilling mission to save the universe, and the possibility of collecting some fascinating subjects for her next thesis. She'd learned so much since then that it almost seemed a pity to throw it all away for a planet she'd never even heard of. Surely there was another way?

She reached over to the controls. 'It's been nice knowing you Doctor.'

'And you,' he replied.

Romana turned off the TARDIS shields. The noise and shaking instantly got worse. Circuits blew across the entire console. Smoke belched from the empty holes in the wall, and a vast crack shivered across the console.

But, in good news, Pralix's voice echoed much more clearly in their heads. So loud, you could barely hear the TARDIS's shrieks of alarm.

'Doctor,' said Pralix. 'Are you there? What's happening?'

With the TARDIS shields down, there was nothing to stop the arrival of Zanak. The pirate planet squeezed itself a little more into corporeality, the shadow around the Earth starting to solidify.

Some people looked up at the sky and thought, 'What now?' Quite a few people stood there screaming. And a few looked up and wondered if it would rain.

In theory, all Zanak's mighty engines had to do now was to crush the tiny little blue speck that stood between it and the Earth. Sensing their advantage, the planet's vast engines galvanised themselves and fought even harder to materialise.

There was a problem.

In theory, with the TARDIS shields down, all that Zanak would have to do was sweep through the little blue box and on to the Earth.

But, in practice, what occurred was quite a fascinating problem of multidimensional engineering. Put simply, a very irresistible force met an unexpectedly infinite object. The quasi-solid atoms of Zanak poured into the TARDIS. And kept on going.

The tiny little blue box swelled like a balloon, wrapping itself around Zanak until the atoms of both were hopelessly and miserably comingled.

The vast engines of Zanak roared.

At first the tiny blue box seemed to be screaming. And then, if you listened, you realised it was laughing.

*

Mr Fibuli could feel death, feel it so close. 'Captain! It's getting worse! We must back off!' he begged.

The crew had all been thrown to the floor. Queen Xanxia stood at the prow of the Bridge, staring into the maelstrom beyond the windows. Her hands were grasping the rail and the knuckles were white.

'Please,' Fibuli repeated, 'we must stop now.'

Only the Captain was still standing at the controls, working them with a single hand while his other steadied him against a chair.

It would have been so easy to let the Doctor win. To flick a switch and fling them off to the other end of the galaxy. But no. This was his last chance to finish what he'd worked so hard for. He just needed one more planet. And he resented the Doctor attacking his engines. Most of all, the Captain hated being told what to do.

'No, by the X-ray storms of Vega!' he roared. 'No! We shall never stop!'

Xanxia turned from the melting sky. 'More power, Captain!' she screamed. 'Let's have more power!'

The skies above the Earth shuddered as impossible shapes filled the skies.

Down on the planet's surface, day or night, everyone was now awake. Awake and running. But there was nowhere to go. And, as the sky churned, the air filled with a noise. A terrible noise. A sound that no one would ever forget.

A terrible wheezing, groaning sound...

The Doctor was trying to keep his voice calm. Realising he was clenching one of his hands, he jammed it casually in his coat pocket.

All around him, the TARDIS was melting as if it had been left too near Salvador Dali and a barbeque. The walls buckled and warped, the enormous control console wilted, and the floor sagged.

But there, hovering in the thick air in front of them, was the image of Pralix's head, frowning.

'Doctor,' it said. 'Are you all right?'

'Perfectly,' the Doctor replied hastily. From the corner of his eye, he saw that Romana was sprawled out, trying to stop falling through a gaping tear in the floor. 'Now, Pralix, please tell me you have enough power to lift that door?'

Pralix shook his holographic head. 'No, Doctor. The counter-jamming field is still too weak. Doctor, there are terrible noises coming from the planet's engines. Surely you can hear them?'

'Sadly, no.' Not over the terrible noises coming from my own engines.

'It would be fatal to enter!' protested Pralix.

'You must try! Six billion lives depend on you lifting that door!' Plus two time travellers and a rather distressed time machine.

'Doctor!' Pralix's face twisted with despair. 'Our minds are so weak we couldn't lift anything bigger than a spanner!'

'A spanner?' the Doctor boggled at the hologram. 'A spanner! That's it! Bung a spanner in the works.'

'What?'

'Pralix! Forget the door, can you project your minds past it?'

Pralix frowned. The Mourners frowned. They took their energy, the Life Force of dead worlds, and pushed their way past the great bulkhead, their minds' eyes floating beyond into the mighty Engine Room.

To one side, K-9 squeezed a little more power into his projectors and cast the I Ching Again: '99: One is held back but things are progressing nevertheless. There is potential for new resources, but they are not yet coming. Dense clouds, but no rain from the West.'

*

The vast engines of Zanak were deserted, filled with the pounding energy, the screaming of metal, and the howling of alarms. The crew had fled or were unconscious. The failure of the air-conditioning system had filled the space with choking fumes.

Vast cogs churned. A giant lead pendulum swung backwards and forwards, weaving between the various spokes and pistons that blurred into movement. The whole engine, so finely balanced, looked as though at any moment it could all fall apart. But it did not, because it was so precisely, indomitably made.

A force, somewhere between psychic, telepathic and terribly sad, prowled around these vast engines. Flinching away from them, as though at a memory of pain, but exploring steadily.

The TARDIS fell back into the Vortex, dragging Zanak with it. The fabric of Mutter's Spiral ripped as a planet managed to be neither in two places at the same time, nor entirely in time. The TARDIS, exhausted and shaking, howled once more and dragged Zanak further into the Vortex.

Romana had fallen to one side of the control room. With a crash, the curtain at the side tore down, revealing that enormous bank of switches and dials. The TARDIS's Fault Locator, so long neglected, was now fully operational, and completely lit up. The whole control room glowed with its angry red lights which burned brighter and brighter.

'Doctor!' yelled Romana. 'We really have to do something. Every major circuit is now way past critical. The TARDIS is about to explode.'

The figure at the console remained perfectly still. He didn't seem to have heard her.

'Doctor! Listen to me! We're going to explode!'

The Doctor looked up and held a finger to his lips.

When he spoke, his voice was terribly steady. 'Stay calm, Pralix,' he called. 'How are you doing?'

'Doctor! Our minds are now in the Engine Room. Can you see?'

The Doctor looked at the projection. A blurry picture of utter chaos. He squinted, and mentally re-walked his earlier tour of the room.

'I think,' he announced casually, 'that if you look over there on the right, you'll find a lovely spanner lying on the floor.'

As Romana watched, the picture focused in on a small spanner – the one the Doctor had left behind earlier. It twitched, and then lifted up into the air.

'Wonderful!' the Doctor said. The TARDIS controls he was gripping were now uncomfortably hot. But, from the genteel tone of his voice, he could have been having quite a nice picnic somewhere by a stream. 'Now then, where shall we go... Ah yes, on your left, you'll see a Macrovectoid particle analyser, go straight on past the omnimodular thermocron over there! And what do we have here on our third left? Why, it's the megaphoton discharge link! That'll do splendidly.'

'But what do we do?' asked Pralix.

The Doctor sighed. 'Hit it.'

The spanner hovered in mid-air, hesitant, curiously polite.

'Hit it!' the Doctor repeated.

The spanner fell, smashing down on the megaphoton discharge link.

A lever on top of the brass dome quivered. The quiver brought it into contact with a small cog, which in turn froze, causing it to jam against a larger cog, which rammed a piston down, which failed to release a valve, which pushed the vast pendulum crashing into the side of the mountain.

There was a small explosion. Little more than a pop. Then another one. A little bigger. Then another, bigger still.

And then the mighty engines of Zanak, the biggest warp engine the universe had ever known, blew up spectacularly.

CHAPTER TWENTY-SEVEN
MR FIBULI GETS HIS WISH

The explosion roared through the Citadel, blowing the top off the great mountain. Fire shot up into the air, and rubble began to fall from the sky. Not precious stones, metals or gems, but rocks and lava, falling in a burning, choking hail on the terrified people of Zanak.

Mr Fibuli screamed in terror as the blast hit the Bridge. The noise was terrifying. The shaft to the planet's empty heart blew open, a pillar of flame leaping up from it. The air filled with the shrieking of every single alarm as the view from the prow went from a whirling blue void to a strange, empty whiteness.

The Captain cried out – whether in fear or in rage at the death of his engines, Mr Fibuli never knew.

The Queen howled in fury, gripping the prow as the vast, glass window exploded around her. She held her ground, even as though the whole world seemed to tip forward, as the entire planet plunged into a nosedive. Mr Fibuli, dangling over a terrible drop, screamed and grabbed desperately at a strut.

All of a sudden, the world went quiet.

The alarms stopped.

The vast engines of Zanak stilled.

There was no sound, other than a vague creaking of metalwork and the feeble moans of the injured. The worst of it was over. The ceiling above their heads shifted but did not come crashing down.

Mr Fibuli, who had stared death in the face so many times, just this once, smiled back at it.

The silence persisted.

'It's bad,' Mr Fibuli said, tightening his grip on the strut, and looking the Captain jubilantly in the eye. 'But I'm all right. I'm actually going to live.'

Those were his last words.

The mighty engines of Zanak were no more. The mighty engines of Zanak, which had worked so hard to shift the planet away from the Calufrax system, to wrap it round the Earth, and to resist being pulled into the Vortex, were forever silent.

Zanak was, for just a moment, nowhere.

Unable to stabilise itself around the Earth, it had no choice but to be pulled further into the Vortex. And, with nowhere else for it to go, it rushed into the body of the tiny blue box.

Unfortunately, even infinite tiny blue boxes can only take so much.

The Doctor tore Romana away from the controls. The central column shattered, a dreadful light pouring from it as it burned like a candle. The ship's various complicated dimensions argued furiously about how to cope with the sudden, unstoppable inrush of planet and then just shrugged and gave up.

The bright light of the console flared and then died.

For a moment the only light in the TARDIS was the angry red glow of the Fault Locator.

And then every single light in the Fault Locator blew, and the TARDIS went dark.

Crammed to bursting point, the blue box gave up. Zanak, stretched through time and space like an elastic band, was let go. The tangled jumble of molecules leapt through space.

The people of planet Earth stopped looking at the heavens. Whatever it was, it had now gone. All they could see was the clear blue sky with a chance of rain later. Ah well, there were buses still to catch, shopping still to do, and newspapers still to read.

These things always seemed to sort themselves out, for some reason or other.

Some reason or other opened his eyes and blinked.

The Doctor essayed a cough.

Well, he was still alive and the voice sounded roughly the same. That was something. He did like that voice.

He sat up.

'You can never relax for a moment in this job,' he announced.

Romana was dangling over a chasm in the floor, holding on to a hat stand. She was staring at him in amazement. She hauled herself to safety.

The only light in the TARDIS control room came from the hole in the floor, which burned an angry red.

Romana tried picking some of the dust from her hair and then gave up.

'We've done it, Doctor.' She couldn't quite believe it. They'd destroyed the engines. They'd saved the planet... um, what was it? *Earth.* That was it. She must look it up some time. 'We've done it.'

'Yes, but the question is, will we ever be able to do anything else?' The Doctor kicked a lump of molten plastic that had once been… well, he'd never really known. He'd always avoided using it. Ah well, too late now.

The TARDIS had constantly hummed. Wherever they went, whatever they were doing, it had hummed away. Often contentedly, sometimes reprovingly. Like an aunt fussing around a kitchen.

But now the TARDIS was silent. Dead. It echoed.

Romana shivered at how cold it was.

The Doctor looped his scarf around her neck. At first she recoiled – Rassilon alone knew where it had been, let alone when it had last had a wash – but there was something about the scarf that was, in its own way, very comforting. She perched on the hat stand and watched the Doctor sort slowly through the shattered fragments of the console.

'Hmm,' he said eventually. It was not a promising hmm.

'Do you think you can repair the TARDIS?' Romana asked.

The Doctor laughed the sad laugh of a man who couldn't even fly it.

A large hexagonal light fitting had fallen from the roof, and the Doctor sadly heaved it away from the wreckage of the console. Some of the controls underneath were relatively undamaged. He squinted at them. 'Water pressure. Pah.' He moved around to the next panel, and sadly nudged a little bit of plastic caramel that had once been the dematerialisation switch. He toggled it sadly.

The TARDIS coughed.

'Oh,' gasped the Doctor. He flicked the switch again.

The TARDIS coughed once more.

'Life in the old girl yet.' The Doctor rubbed his hands together, and for a moment seemed like an entirely different man. 'Now then, let's just see if we can manage just one more materialisation…' He pulled out two wires and beamed at them. 'Tell me, Romana,

350

have you ever hotwired a Ford Cortina? We'll be flying blind, of course, but…' And then winked. 'That's how we like it.'

Zanak had arrived. The sky above it was unpromising, with just a single sun, but the planet was in one piece. For the moment. The stresses and strains of its recent contortion had pressed down on the thin crust. The great metal bulwarks underneath shivered and split. Cracks spread across the surface. Sand poured down through the gaps. The planet began to fall into itself.

The world was quiet. Even the great citadel was silent. Apart from in a single chamber, where a small blue box dragged itself painfully out of thin air.

'Good grief.' Romana wrinkled her nose in disgust.

Normally the TARDIS believed in making an entrance. It delighted in thundering out of nowhere, its arrivals a constant bellow of 'Here I am! Sorry I'm late, let's get on with it!'

Not this time.

The TARDIS had shuddered out of the Time Vortex, shaking itself down to land with a subdued croak.

When Romana had opened the doors they'd seemed flimsy. The Doctor had closed them gingerly and the box had wobbled like an old shed. The light on the top had gone out, and the usually absurd lettering around the top simply announced 'LICE BOX'.

The Doctor made to pat the ship and clearly thought better of it.

'We'd best make ourselves at home,' he'd sighed. 'I wonder where we are.'

Which was when Romana had seen the strange figure watching them.

The Doctor had turned at her yelp, and taken in the vast black chamber, the raised dais, and the two throbbing metal pillars at either side of her.

'Ah yes. Back on Zanak. Queen Xanxia's Throne Room. The TARDIS must have locked on to the temporal field.'

'Is that her?' Romana continued to stare at the repellently ancient figure shrivelled onto the chair.

'Oh yes, there she is. The old bat.'

Romana squinted. 'Is she talking to someone?'

'Maybe. Maybe she's just crazed. Locked off in a dreadful time stream of her own.'

The Doctor pulled a face at the ancient queen. She did not react. He pulled some more.

Romana, feeling impetuous, stuck her tongue out. Then she prodded one of the pillars. 'And so these are her Time Dams, are they? I see.' Clearly, she was not awarding high marks. 'Fascinating. Archaic but fascinating.'

'Romy,' the Doctor chided.

Romana pursed her lips.

'This is no time for indulging in industrial archaeology. We've got a job to do. Let's go and find the rebels.' The Doctor made a final face at Old Queen Xanxia and headed down to the engines.

Young Queen Xanxia should have been dead. She had been impaled by a heavy girder when the ceiling had collapsed, obliterating the Bridge. No matter. She simply rearranged the molecules of her new body, shifting to one side and standing up. The movement was a little awkward. She checked the black box, for a moment worried that it had been damaged. No. But the power levels of the Time Dams were running down.

That was bad. But not the end. Anyway, she knew that, if they did run down, if it all had to end for her, then so be it for everyone else.

Smiling a cruel smile, she arranged herself an entirely new set of garments and made to survey the wreckage.

The view from the shattered window showed only stars. A thin, cold wind swept in, sending shredded reports fluttering up into the air.

'Captain!' she called.

There was no reply.

'Captain?' she felt a moment's worry. Was everyone else dead?

Then she heard a strange noise. She edged her way past the shattered workings of the computer, and saw the Captain hunched on the floor dragging a tiny bundle from under a pile of rubble. The noise was coming from the Captain. He was crying.

'Mr Fibuli.' He pointed to the limp figure crushed under the ceiling. 'Dead. He was a good man.' With a sigh, he took Mr Fibuli's glasses off, and lifted the clipboard from his hands. For old time's sake, he glanced at it, and then placed it gently down over the man's face.

The Captain stood stiffly. His robotic arm flopped weakly to one side, fluid leaking from an elbow joint. His faceplate was dented, and his human eye was swollen almost shut. As he moved towards the Queen, his left leg dragged and rattled. With an effort, he focused his damaged eye on her.

'They're all dead,' he said, gesturing to the bodies scattered across the Bridge. 'My crew…'

Queen Xanxia snapped her fingers. 'Captain, pull yourself together. This is not the end. It is never the end. Come on!' She clapped her hands together firmly. 'We can still defeat that rabble out there.'

The Captain groaned. 'Somehow,' he muttered darkly. 'Somehow, Mr Fibuli, you shall be avenged.'

'Quite!' Queen Xanxia nodded. 'We shall crush the rebels, and, if he's still around, we shall destroy this Doctor once and for all.'

She swept away, not bothering to read the Captain's expression. Clearly, that was not quite what he had meant.

Slowly, painfully, the Captain dragged himself over to a control panel, placed Mr Fibuli's glasses on it, and began work.

CHAPTER TWENTY-EIGHT
THE HEART OF ZANAK

The Doctor and Romana wandered through the wreckage of the Citadel. Everywhere were the dead bodies of the Captain's Guards.

'Good shooting, Mula,' Romana said.

'You know, Romy, in general, I don't really approve of arming one's rebels.' The Doctor toed one of the Guards' bodies.

'Noted for future reference,' she said solemnly.

'Still,' the Doctor conceded. 'Not bad for a first attempt. Not bad at all.'

They found the rebels gathered together, more or less, outside the entrance to the Bridge.

The Mourners were slumped disconsolately against the walls.

Mula was cleaning a gun.

Kimus was delivering a speech to the young citizens. There was some sporadic cheering which, Romana suspected, was more a polite reflex than because he'd said anything particularly worthwhile.

Pralix stood up, greeting the Doctor wearily. 'The entrance to the Bridge is sealed,' he said. 'We were about to try and force it open.'

'I say leave it!' announced Kimus loudly, and to no one in particular. 'They're dead! And if not, then so much the better. Leave the bodies of the vile Captain and his hag bride shut up for ever! What harm can they do now?'

The crowd cheered. Clearly they'd had enough.

'Quite a lot of harm, actually,' the Doctor said. His voice could certainly carry, marvelled Romana. 'If there's one thing you lot should have learned, it's never to take anything at face value. The Captain is still a very dangerous man.'

Inside the Bridge, Queen Xanxia stared into the hole that led to the hollow centre of the planet. It had come unsealed in the final catastrophe. She looked down into the utter darkness and frowned. It reminded her of something. A voice from the shadows that haunted her dreams. She blinked, dismissing the stray thought, and straightened up. She crossed over to the prow, glaring out at the city below and the ruptured sky above. This was still her world. Somehow, somehow, it would keep her going. Or it would, obviously, perish. For what was life without her?

The cold wind tugged at her cloak and she shivered. It was good to feel the cold. It was good to feel again. It was, if anything, a sign that the Doctor was, of course, wrong. Her new body was very nearly finished. And then she would have no need of any of this, ever again. She could leave. She could start over. She had wealth. And there were a lot of planets out there. Ones which needed taking in hand. She sniffed the air, exulting in the fresh tang to it. It was good. She toyed with going out to say her last farewells to her old body. But she could not, would not. It upset her to see what she had once been. What she would never be again. Queen

Xanxia was now immortal. And she wouldn't waste a moment of it on these people.

She turned away, sweeping back towards the Captain. Her old pet clanked and hissed away. He seemed convinced he could bring life back to the engines, summon up some power. Just enough. People kept telling her there was never enough. But there always was. She kept going.

The Captain looked up at her, slowly, the human side of his face drooping. The poor old thing was falling apart. But then again, not everyone was like her. She was lucky. No one else got to be Queen Xanxia.

'Hurry, Captain! Do hurry!' she called over to him.

He put a circuit board down with a slam and glared at her.

She smiled back at him, tweaking her black box, just a little.

He picked the circuit up and resumed work.

'We are nearly finished,' he said.

The entire rebel army of Zanak was once again trying to open a door. It seemed to have become a habit.

'Come on, K-9,' the Doctor coaxed. 'It's time to see the Captain again.'

The Doctor had fetched K-9 to open the door to the Bridge, but the dog's tail sagged. 'Insufficient power to blast the door,' the dog had remarked testily. For once, K-9 had had enough of shooting things.

Mula raised her gun, but the Doctor waved it to one side with his sonic screwdriver. It whirred a little, and then he sighed and put it back in his pocket. 'No screws,' he sighed. 'Who builds a door without screws?'

There was a cough. The Doctor turned, fearful that Kimus was going to talk to the door.

Instead it was Pralix. Behind him stood the Mourners.

'We shall try and open it,' vowed Pralix.

The Mourners nodded. 'The flow of Life Force is increasing. This time we shall succeed.'

The Captain wired up one last circuit board and slotted it into place. The deck started to hum with power. The Captain smiled, his human hand stroking the remains of the Polyphase Avatron. He'd found it among the wreckage and placed it on the desk so that it could watch. Pretty Polly, he thought. She'd have liked this.

'Have you done it? Say you've done it!' Xanxia rushed over to him.

'Yes Xanxia.' The Captain turned around to face her. 'It is done. I am ready at last.' He leaned back in his chair, and concentrated on cleaning Mr Fibuli's spectacles.

Queen Xanxia paused. She never liked anyone's tone, but she suddenly and particularly disliked the Captain's.

A nagging question formed in her mind. And then she noticed the door to the Bridge. With a weary groan, it was opening. What now?

'Captain!' Xanxia screamed in alarm as the rebel army surged in. Rebels, on her bridge! 'Do something!'

'By the Sky Demon, I shall,' the Captain vowed. He surged up, grabbing for a large button on the desk. 'By his bones, I shall take you with me.'

He lunged for the button and Queen Xanxia had a suspicion about what he'd been doing these last few minutes. He'd not even touched the engines.

She gave the dial on her black box a vicious twist. The Captain froze, mid lunge, a horrid croak coming from his throat.

'You are a fool,' sneered Xanxia. 'You always were a failure. Fail one last time.'

The Captain's agonised eye rolled helplessly in his frozen body, twisting as first smoke and then fire guttered from the joints of his mighty frame. His remaining hand twitched helplessly, desperate to reach the console. But then his body vanished in flames.

For a moment, the figure of the Captain stood there, and then the burning figure toppled forward across the desk, coming to rest by the broken Polyphase Avatron.

Queen Xanxia brushed her hands together and turned to the rebels crowding the bridge. She faced them with a smirk and a raised eyebrow. 'Yes?' she said. 'Can I help you?'

Kimus stepped forward, holding a gun. 'In the name of a free Zanak, die traitor! Die!' He nodded to Mula.

They both fired, the energy from their weapons pouring into the Queen before the Doctor could stop them. Her body flickered, wobbled, and then solidified. She threw back her head and laughed.

'Thank you,' she said. 'You've finally done something useful. I think that was precisely the last thing I needed.' She strode towards the rebels. She would show them.

One of the badly dressed, shabby old Mourners blocked her path. Tiresome.

'Never again,' said Pralix to his queen.

The Mourners stepped forward and stared at Xanxia mournfully. Then they closed their eyes and breathed out. The Life Force, the combined sadness of so many worlds surged through them, pouring into Queen Xanxia.

She raised her arms up to protect herself, but this couldn't be warded away. The horror, the misery, the torment, everything she had done, the billions of lives she had swept away, the eternity of stolen sunsets and uprooted trees, the raging souls of a dozen dozen planets fell on Queen Xanxia and she backed away screaming.

'Never!' she shouted. 'I am immortal.'

Heedless of where she was going, she stumbled backwards into the shaft and fell to the centre of the planet with an endless cry.

The Mourners listened to the scream for a long time. And then, suddenly, they all broke into radiant grins.

Pralix turned to the Doctor and bowed. 'Zanak has a heart at last,' he said.

Then the Mourners turned around and left the Citadel.

CHAPTER TWENTY-NINE
THE CAPTAIN'S PLAN

The Doctor stood there with Romana, idly stroking the bent tin wings of the Captain's pet. Through the shattered glass of the prow, the long night was coming to a close, and the first shades of dawn were breaking through the sky.

'Hum,' he said. He was staring at the button the Captain was going to press. 'I always find buttons fascinating. Now, I wonder what that one does?'

He confounded Romana's expectations by not pressing it.

Kimus found the Doctor's sombre mood surprising. 'Come now, Doctor! The Captain and Xanxia are dead!'

'Dead?' the Doctor peered down into the shaft. 'The Captain, maybe. But I'm afraid we haven't finished with Xanxia yet.'

The Doctor took them to the Throne Room.

Kimus, with the air of a showman, called out to the rebels. 'Behold, citizens! Behold the monstrous parasite who has sucked us dry...'

There was more of this. While he talked, the people gave all their attention to the strange tiny figure beyond him. It was impossible to think that she was still somehow ruling all of them. They crowded in and pressed up against the humming barrier of the Time Dams. This little husk of a woman was now little more than a carnival curiosity.

The Doctor held up a hand.

'Kimus – I think it's time to let nature take its course. Would you like to turn the old queen off?'

There were cheers. Kimus turned to acknowledge them.

'Yes Doctor,' he said, half-turned towards him but still addressing the crowd. 'It will be a pleasure to rid Zanak of her.'

'Well, you can't,' said the Doctor. Kimus's face fell. 'The whole thing's booby-trapped. Otherwise the Captain or one of his men would have turned the old goat off years ago.'

Romana peered at the configurations and nodded grudgingly. 'Presumably the slightest disturbance in the Time Dam Field would trigger a massive explosion. As she's inside the field, Xanxia would remain completely unharmed. We're lucky it hasn't gone off already.'

'In that case –' the Doctor was chewing the end of his scarf and thinking, probably about listeria – 'the Captain must have had some other plan entirely. Something I've been quite overlooking.' The Doctor slapped his forehead. 'Of course! What a fool I am.' He turned to Kimus, opened his mouth, and then took hold of Mula. 'Mula, could you lead everyone off the mountain? I'm afraid it's pretty unstable here.'

'But…' began Kimus.

Mula shook her head gently, and smiled. 'Come on, everyone, this way,' she said. She paused in the doorway. 'Will you and Romana be all right?' she asked.

'I think,' the Doctor grinned slowly, 'we're going to be ridiculously good.'

*

The Doctor walked slowly into the room filled with slowly spinning planets.

'This is the Trophy Room, Romana. I knew it had to have some purpose.'

'Is this what I think it is?' Romana found the display both moving and intellectually impressive.

'Yes.' The Doctor waved a hand towards Bandraginus 5. 'This gallery contains the compressed remains of dozens of planets, and I think I've suddenly realised why. The Captain really was an unparalleled genius. Suspended round this gallery are billions of tons of super-compressed rock.'

'But surely, the gravity—'

'Oh yes.' The Doctor nodded. 'A perfectly balanced system. A masterpiece of gravitic geometry. All the forces cancel each other out. This —' he dabbled his fingers in the atmosphere of Qualactin – 'is sheer genius.'

'He never seemed like a genius to me,' Romana said tartly. 'He spent most of his time blustering and shouting at people.'

The Doctor winked at Romana. 'It was an act, to lull Xanxia into a false sense of security whilst he prepared this. She thought she'd broken him – in body and spirit. Why not let him have a hobby, eh? Just a Trophy Room. She'd let him build it, keep him out of mischief. But just think. Astronomical amounts of energy were generating that Time Field, and the slightest disturbance of it triggers an explosion which would finish off poor Zanak. The only way he could destroy her would be to get into the middle of that Time Field without breaching its perimeter. But again, it would require astronomical forces to achieve that. And here they are, dancing all about us, but at the moment perfectly balanced.'

The Doctor and Romana stood still, admiring the system spinning slowly past, and the brain that had created it.

'So…' Romana said. 'When the moment is right he slightly alters the balance?' She held up her hand, watching as Temesis neatly shifted its orbit around it. 'He creates a standing vortex right in the middle of the Time Field. Time there begins to proceed normally again.'

'And the ancient queen dies in a few seconds,' the Doctor said. He sucked a finger and jabbed it at a hole in the system. 'Poor old Earth was probably the last planet he needed. When he died he was going to try and trigger it without it. What an incredible mind.'

'So are you going to try it?'

'Sadly, no.' The Doctor poked Lowiteliom. 'Unfortunately it wouldn't have worked in the way he thought it would.'

'Why not?'

'Because –' the Doctor spun round in a gesture that was, even for him, elaborate – 'one of these planets is a fake.'

'Oh.'

The Doctor licked his finger, closed his eyes and pointed, seemingly at random. 'Calufrax,' he said.

'Who'd fake a planet?' Romana frowned.

'Calufrax is not a normal planet, it's an artificially matricised structure consisting of a substance with a variable atomic weight.'

'Oh, you're kidding.'

'No, I'm not.'

'The entire planet?'

'The entire planet. Calufrax was the second segment of the Key to Time.' The Doctor waved at it as it went past. 'Hello!'

'No wonder the Tracer kept going mad.' Romana wrinkled her nose. She tried to ignore the sick feeling in her stomach. 'But now it's a husk… Does that mean we're too late?'

'Don't think so.' The Doctor shrugged. 'Try the Tracer now. You have still got the Tracer?'

'Of course.' Romana patted her pockets and stopped. 'No. Doctor?'

The Doctor rummaged in his coat and pulled out the Tracer. 'There we are. You should be more careful with it, you know.'

Romana took it from him and waved it at Calufrax. There was a loud crackle.

'Don't hold it too close, not yet,' said the Doctor. 'Not before we do something immensely clever.'

'Of course,' sighed Romana. 'I should have guessed.'

'Sorry to interrupt, could you hold that for me? Thank you, your majesty.'

Deep inside the darkness of the Time Dams, Old Queen Xanxia blinked, and blinked very slowly. Who was this now? What had happened to the other voice?

She looked down. She was holding a wand.

She looked around, trying to see who had handed it to her.

She looked around for the figure who had been talking to her before.

But he had gone from the shadows.

There was no sign of anyone.

Everyone had gone.

Ah well.

'I do think that's cheating,' said Romana.

'Showmanship,' shrugged the Doctor.

They were stood in the Trophy Room. The Doctor was holding a keyboard in his hands. A very large wire snaked from it back to the Bridge.

K-9 was checking the components and advising against the feasibility of the plan.

'Everyone's a critic,' sighed the Doctor. 'How's Zanak doing?'

The dog considered his answer. By sheer fluke the planet had survived the voyage. The system it had arrived in hadn't immediately crushed it. Without the sustaining balance of the engines, and given the pounding it had been through, the planet's crust was weak. Seismic disturbances shivered across the surface and the continental shift was accelerating alarmingly. Zanak was collapsing rapidly.

'Oh,' the Doctor remarked on the silence. 'That bad, eh?'

Romana looked up from a small controller she'd brought from the TARDIS. 'Well, the hyperspatial field is established. We can use the massive power source of the planets themselves to trigger the two-stage operation. But I still don't see how we're going to get Calufrax back without a mighty cataclysm.'

'Hush,' said the Doctor. 'You're thinking by the book again. And you were doing so well.'

'Thank you, Doctor,' Romana said tartly.

'We should have sold tickets for this,' he said. 'Though I'm not sure there are that many people in the universe who'd understand this, and the few of them there are I probably wouldn't want watching. They'd be bound to send letters.'

'Relax, Doctor,' said Romana. 'It's been a long day.'

'Hasn't it just,' the Doctor smiled.

'Shall we?'

'Let's.'

They admired the horrid beauty of the gallery and its slowly spinning planets one final time.

Then the two Time Lords each pressed a button and stood well back.

The planets vanished and the Trophy Room was empty.

Old Queen Xanxia woke up.

She could sense time returning at a gallop. The sluggish haze of time was suddenly far, far too fast, far too much like living normally. No, no, she thought, not yet, I can't die, not yet. Is it complete, is my new body complete? She reached out to it, desperately wondering how many heartbeats she had left. It can't be over. It can't all be over.

She looked out beyond the throne at her Time Dams, and her Throne Room seemed so vast and so dark.

In the space beyond she could see so many planets, planets bowed down in worship before her. How right this is, she thought. This is my universe. This is how it should be.

Queen Xanxia smiled. She raised the wand someone had left in her hand and prepared to conduct the music of the spheres.

She heard someone screaming her name. Just how she liked it. This really was perfect.

There was someone else on the dais with her. She focused with difficulty. So many visitors. It was all so confusing. This one was a young woman, lying there, screaming. Ah well.

And then the old queen noticed something odd about the planets out there in the darkness. So many of them. Had she killed so many of them? Had that really been the plan?

The young woman stood up, staring at her, shouting her name. There was something about her, about her face, about the furious way she was using her name.

Oh no. No! Was this really how it ended?

The old queen and the young one stopped staring at each other, and turned instead to the planets. They were rushing towards them. They were coming so close.

Queen Xanxia threw up her hands, screaming as the planets swooped towards her, growing larger and larger. The darkness was lit up by a brilliant white glow. A fire that went on for ever.

The Doctor walked into the empty Throne Room. There on the dais was the Tracer and, nuzzled next to it, the Second Segment of the Key to Time. He polished it with his scarf.

He waited for his companion to ask him some questions, but for once Romana seemed perfectly contented.

'Well done Doctor,' he said to himself and then said out loud. 'We created a hyperspatial force shield around the shrunken planets and another around the Time Dams. Then with the exercise of a tiny bit of ingenuity, we dropped both into the centre of Zanak, let the interplay between the various force shields intermingle and invert and BANG the remains of the planets expanded in an instant to fill the hollow interior of Zanak, thus stabilising its core. Meanwhile, Calufrax was flung off back up here. Like doing cavity wall insulation with a magic wand. Bit fiddly, but not bad.'

'Actually, I'd say it's fantastic,' admitted Romana.

'That's what K-9 said as well, didn't you?'

'Negative.'

'Well Doctor –' Romana couldn't keep the admiring tone out of her voice – 'it's just magic.'

'Magic? It's hyper-science. Far more exciting. Hey ho.' The Doctor sauntered off back towards the TARDIS.

'But Doctor, what are you going to do about the Citadel?'

'Well, the encore is the *pièce de résistance* of the entire plan.'

'Why, what are we going to do?'

'Blow it up.'

The surviving Guards staggered down to the bottom of the mountain.

Standing at the edge of the city was a very tired-looking old man, his arms outstretched.

'Welcome,' said Balaton. 'You'll have quite a few changes to get used to. And believe me, no one likes that. But come in. There's a lot of clearing up to do.'

Getting the TARDIS to make the short hop had been, the Doctor claimed, like racing a milk float, but the little blue box eventually chugged into the City's Market Square. Gathered there was quite a crowd. The young, the old, the Mourners, and, standing slightly sheepishly beside Mula, was Kimus.

Mula stepped forward. 'Welcome Doctor,' she said. 'On behalf of—'

'Your people?' the Doctor said with a wink.

368

Mula considered her reply. 'On behalf of all of us, thank you.' She stopped, sheepish. 'That's as much of a speech as I could think of.'

'Doesn't matter,' said the Doctor. 'I've got something even better. Fireworks.'

He produced a remote-control detonator and pointed up to the Citadel.

'It's all up to you now. You've got a fair bit of work cut out for all of you to turn this dried-out world into something worth living in. At the moment all you've got is wealth, which as you've discovered doesn't help you very much. But this is quite a nice part of the galaxy for Zanak to settle in, reasonable sun, some quite convenient star systems nearby when you get around to normal space travel. The Mulfoonians of Bagras 111 are only three light years away, and they're quite a pleasant crowd, so I think you should be all right. Now then, who wants to blow up the mountain?'

Pralix stepped forward, leading the Mourners.

'We will Doctor. There is just enough Life Force left, I think, to push that button. It seems a fitting way to spend it.'

The crowd nodded.

The Mourners stood around the detonator. They seemed less pale, less gaunt, their faces almost unlined. They frowned, but it was a gentle, determined frown.

The satisfyingly big red button sank down.

A few seconds later the remains of the mountain, the mighty engines, the Citadel and the *Vantarialis*, the most feared pirate ship in the mighty fleets of Agranjagzak, all vanished in dust and flame.

The Mourners stood back and laughed.

The crowd applauded.

And, if no diamonds rained from the sky that day, no one minded.

EPILOGUE

Even if you were being kind, it was a mean little planet. The light from two suns made its way meekly through the frosty air, which somehow managed to be completely unromantic. Winds howled, and you would howl if this was the only planet you got to blow around. Meagre streams filtered their way through slushy wastes that were neither snow nor ice. The occasional shoot of greenery poked its way up through the mush and then wondered why it had bothered.

The dirty white plain overlooked a mucky white sea where bored ice floes bumped into each other with a sigh. It was a rail-replacement bus of a world.

Into all of this a small blue box arrived with a snort of derision.

A wooden door opened and a man strode gingerly out, wrapping his scarf tightly around himself. He produced matching gloves from a pocket, jammed them on, and got on with the happy business of making 'phoof' noises.

A moment later a woman in a dazzling white feather dress flowed out. She stopped.

'Oh,' she said.

'Well, I said Calufrax was a dull world,' the man answered.

'Even so.'

'Come on. And don't bring the Tracer,' the Doctor cautioned. 'Just in case you accidentally trip over and create the worst paradox in history.'

They trudged off through the slush.

'How are you doing that?' the Doctor was slipping and sliding and making unsteady progress. 'How are you getting anywhere?'

'Ah,' said Romana, hitching up her dress just a little. 'I found them in a cupboard. Wellington boots.'

'Very sensible,' the Doctor nodded and fell over.

They made their way to the top of a hill, which did little more than tell them how far they'd come from the TARDIS.

'Doctor, why are we here?' asked Romana.

'Good question,' the Doctor pondered. 'Oh – here? On Calufrax? Well, we've got nothing better to do while the TARDIS repairs itself. So I thought we'd pop back and have a look round. Pay our last respects.'

'I see.' The Time Lady pulled the feathers of her cloak more tightly around her.

'Poor old Calufrax.' The Doctor kicked a puddle of slush. 'Imagine that. The Segment could have hidden itself away as anything. Instead it made itself one of the most boring planets imaginable.' He gestured around at the wastes. 'How very clever. Make it dangerous and hostile and adventurous types would be turning up all the time. Make it nice and you'd get holidaymakers taking photographs. But make yourself dull enough and you can sit out eternity undisturbed.'

'I see,' said Romana.

'It's why hardly anyone bothers invading Gallifrey.' The Doctor chuckled and wandered down to the meagre beach, where a sluggish sea dragged itself onto the shore, eventually changed its mind, and then came back for something it had forgotten. He picked up a pebble and tried to skim it across the waves. It sank without trace.

Another pebble bounced effortlessly after it, skipping away into the distance.

The Doctor turned. Romana was standing beside him. She smiled.

'Very good,' the Doctor said.

They carried on looking out to sea.

'Well, yes,' the Doctor admitted. 'It is rather boring. But coming here seemed like a good idea.'

'No, no.' Romana nodded, thoughtfully. 'It was the right thing to do.'

The sea carried on in its own way, and the sky began to grow dark.

'Night falls quickly here,' said Romana.

The Doctor looked up. 'Actually, that's Zanak arriving. Come on. We should go.' He took one last look around before they trudged back to the TARDIS.

'Goodbye, Calufrax. I am sorry.'

The man sat in the deckchair and admired the peacocks strolling across the lawn.

Yes, he thought, it was all going very well, very well indeed.

So far, the Doctor had collected two segments of the Key to Time. The First had been a lump of Jethrik ore smuggled to the planet of Ribos by a thief from Hackney. The Second had been the planet Calufrax. Now, what lay ahead of him?

The man steepled his fingers and smiled. It was not a nice smile. Ah yes. The Third Segment was currently standing in a stone circle on Earth. The Fourth Segment lay forgotten on the feudal planet of Tara. The Fifth Segment was worshipped as a god on the third moon of Delta Magna. And the Sixth and final segment – ah yes, now there was a challenge. Would the Doctor dare go through with it?

The man settled back in the deckchair and pondered. Why go to all the bother of collecting the segments yourself when you could just ask the Doctor to go and do it for you? A little nudge here, a prod there, and these things all fell into place. All he had to do was wait a bit, and then turn up and collect his prize. If there was one thing the Guardian excelled at, it was waiting.

The man yawned, spending a moment enjoying the darkness of the shade. It really was a lovely spot.

And then, at the edge of the garden, a door opened.

So the man stood up and went elsewhere.

The Doctor opened a door and marvelled as a breath of fresh air rushed over him.

'Well, this is all wonderfully unexpected,' he said, stepping into a large open conservatory, filled with lush plants. Small fountains trickled and tiny birds chittered from plant to plant.

Romana took one final look at the chilly surface of Calufrax and then closed the door firmly behind her.

'What is this place?' she asked. The air was humid, the cool marble of the floor stretching ahead to large French windows apparently looking out at a pleasant sunny garden.

'This?' The Doctor smiled, crossing to a stone sundial placed, curiously, in the middle of the conservatory. He ran his hands over it, and lights began to wink over its surface. He pressed one of the lights, and the doors sealed. He pressed another and the central part of the sundial rose up and, with a grating noise, began to rotate.

'Hah!' he cried with delight. 'How lovely.'

Romana had been expecting the charred remains of the old control room.

'This is a temporary control room. That's one of the advantages of these old Type 40 TARDISes,' the Doctor explained, examining the fruit on a strawberry bush. 'Lots of spares. I suspect the old one will be back in a few hours. But in the meantime this will do marvellously.' He popped a strawberry in his mouth and strolled out into the garden.

Bewildered, Romana followed him. The garden was peaceful, with a scrupulously mown lawn. Old trees carefully provided lots of shade. The gentle humming of the TARDIS had become the slow drone of summer, the air filled with birdsong. In the distance, K-9 could be glimpsed, chasing a peacock. She had the slight sense that something had just moved in the shadows, but when she looked, nothing was there.

The Doctor made his way to an iron table, on which afternoon tea had been set out. Curiously, a cup of tea appeared to have already been drunk. How odd. He poured himself a fresh cup, and went to sit in one of the deckchairs.

'What's the model for all this?' asked Romana, trying to work out how to switch the deckchair on.

'Oh, this is England. A long summer's afternoon with jam for tea. Perfect!' The Doctor reached for a scone. 'We really should go some time.'

'Hmm,' said Romana, blinking with surprise as the Doctor handed her a cup balanced on a saucer.

'Milk?'

'What's that?'

'It comes from cows.'

'Oh. No thank you.'

The Doctor sprawled in his deckchair. Romana perched on the edge of hers and wondered how to take her wellington boots off. It did not seem possible. She sipped her tea and decided she liked it.

'What do we do with all of this?'

'I think we should enjoy it while it lasts.' The Doctor favoured the entire world with a smile. He fished under the chair, and found a copy of the TARDIS manual. He pushed it across the lawn to Romana. 'Here. If you're bored, you could always keep some chickens.'

Romana nudged the manual away with her boot. 'I think I'm done with manuals,' she declared.

'Good for you,' the Doctor laughed and settled back into his chair. 'I may even have a doze.'

'But Doctor,' Romana said. 'We have a universe to save.'

'Absolutely.' The Doctor's eyelids drifted gently closed. 'Later.'

'It was just a thought,' muttered Romana, sipping her tea.

'"A green thought in a green shade".' The Doctor settled back in his chair to enjoy a nap.

And the TARDIS flew on to further adventures.

AFTERWORD

Before I could start work on *The Pirate Planet*, I needed to solve a mystery.

When working on a book (*The Doctor: His Lives and Times*) in 2013, I'd kept coming across intriguing quotes about *The Pirate Planet*...

That was [Douglas Adams's] first television credit. I had heard about *The Hitchhiker's Guide to the Galaxy*, which was being prepared for Radio Four at that time, and I think in fact [previous Script Editor] Bob Holmes had come across this and passed the thought on. I picked it up and read it and thought, 'Now here's a guy who obviously has a very lively imagination. He could be very valuable and give us a whole new dimension to *Doctor Who*.' I was very taken with him. Ideas were sparking off him.

The problem was harnessing him to the format, because he had a tendency to go off in his own directions. In the end it worked extremely well.

The first draft was way over the top and looked as though it was unworkable. [Producer] Graham Williams was away at the time, and at that point [BBC Head of Drama] Graham McDonald saw the initial scripts and said, 'This isn't going to work.' I said, 'Don't worry, we will make it work.' The director Pennant Roberts went in with me and said he could shoot it. So we managed to calm him down.

Anthony Read, *Doctor Who* Script Editor
(speaking to *TV Zone* magazine)

The original idea for *Pirate Planet* was just the basic concept of a hollow planet, Graham was interested in Space Pirates, so we just married the two. The original storyline was of a planet being mined by the Time Lords. The plot was so complicated, I remember reading a synopsis of it to Graham, after which he sank into his chair, mumbling that now he knew how Stanley Kubrick felt.

The whole adventure trod a narrow line between being dramatic and being outright funny, which I think is the most interesting area to work in, as I think humour plays a very important part in *Doctor Who*.

I felt that I had caused so many problems that I would be lucky to get anywhere else, but everyone seemed very happy with the script.

Douglas Adams
(speaking to *TARDIS* magazine)

I wondered how much of this was true. After all, good stuff always gets cut. This happens because, if life is cruel, television is more so.

When I was novelising *City of Death*, I'd been lucky enough to be sent the original rehearsal scripts for that story, which had contained a joyous amount of extra material – totalling a few extra lines here and there, the occasional entire page. So I wondered, with *The Pirate Planet*, if all this talk of extra material was true, or simply pleasant anecdotage? How detailed were these original outlines? Did a 'way over the top' first draft still exist? Had it ever existed?

If it did exist, I knew just where to find it. Jem Roberts had just written *The Frood*, a biography of Douglas Adams, and had had access to the Douglas Adams Archive at St John's College, Cambridge. I knew that, if extra material existed, I should look there.

Luckily, the estate consented, and I was put in touch with Douglas Adams's archivist, the splendid and splendidly named Miss Marvin. She replied to my email of enquiry:

> I did think that you might be in pursuit of *The Pirate Planet* and am happy to say that we do in fact have some material that should help you a bit.

Naturally, I wondered what 'some material' could mean.

It's been twenty years since I've been inside a college, and the whole experience was gratifyingly strange. Yes, the porters magically knew who I was before I stepped through the gate, and yes, I did get to sit in a Gothic building full of impossibly precious books. If you thought you had your sock drawer neatly filed, you have nothing on the archives at St John's College.

'Now,' said Miss Marvin, 'would you like to see *The Pirate Planet*?' She pointed to some grey boxes.

The Adams Archive has little on *City of Death*. Famously written over a weekend, there really isn't much beyond the script. But *The Pirate Planet* was composed over a long, arduous summer, by a man twisting from *Doctor Who* to *Hitchhiker's* and back, fizzing with ideas he was desperate to find the right home for.

I'd always wanted to write comedy sci-fi, ever since the early days of *Doctor Who* and Dan Dare in *The Eagle*. I sent the first episode of *Hitchhiker's Guide to the Galaxy* in to *Doctor Who* – hoping that they would then want me to write for the show. I was then commissioned for both shows at once, so was deluged with masses of work.

Douglas Adams
(interviewed in *TARDIS* magazine)

Miss Marvin carefully, slowly, and with quiet delight showed me the evolution of *The Pirate Planet*. We had paper jottings, doodles, notes taken during meetings, typewritten attempts at a treatment which suddenly stopped crossly, a short thesis about the Key to Time, and then, finally…

A complete treatment for 'Doctor Who and the Perfect Planet'. What?

I know.

I stared at that.

A lot.

Douglas Adams hadn't just had an idea for a hollow planet, he'd developed it as an almost completely different story. To summarise 'The Perfect Planet', the Doctor arrives on a world where life is perfect, and he becomes immediately annoyed. No invaders to thwart, no villainy. Something must be wrong because nothing is wrong. You'll be delighted to hear that the treatment follows in a few pages. It's full of striking images and scenes, a few of which made the long journey into *The Pirate Planet*; some others may make you question how involved Douglas Adams was in the last two episodes of *The Armageddon Factor*.

There were more notes, more treatments, more ideas, and then, in a box all by itself, the very first draft of *The Pirate Planet*. Perhaps a little snow-blind from the sheer amount of archive, I nearly discounted it. Formatted like a radio script, it seemed to be very like the rehearsal scripts occupying the next box. This was a little hard to tell, as centuries of experience of muddled papers and even more muddled dons have taught the archivists to issue one document at a time. But the two drafts seemed pretty identical. Someone had simply taken Douglas's weirdly formatted typescript and turned it into a proper television script.

About two pages in, that theory fell apart. The first draft of *The Pirate Planet* was extraordinarily different and very, very long. Each episode ran to nearly forty densely typed pages. Forty densely typed and very, very funny pages.

So, in order to novelise *The Pirate Planet*, I now had a wealth of sources to choose from. Not only did I have the final televised version, but I had Douglas Adams's notes, his treatment for 'The Perfect Planet', his treatments for *The Pirate Planet*, a rehearsal script and the very long, very different first draft.

Over the next few pages I'll bore you with how it all slots together...

THE FIRST DRAFT vs THE REHEARSAL SCRIPT
vs THE FINISHED VERSION

It would be so much easier if Douglas Adams had submitted a draft script, which was then cut down into the rehearsal script, which was then cut down still further to make the televised version.

The real story is much more complicated, and joyously so. At every stage, Adams revised his own dialogue, or went off on tangents, or picked up the pieces after his work had been thrown into the thresher of the BBC rehearsal room.

A peculiar example takes place in Part Two, when Romana meets the Captain. The first draft contains TWO very different versions of this scene. The rehearsal script is different again.

First Draft Version 1

SCENE ELEVEN

THE BRIDGE. ROMANA FACES THE CAPTAIN.

CAPTAIN: Speak girl! Who are you that you dare to intrude upon my ship?

ROMANA: Ship? You mean this mountain is your ship?

CAPTAIN: By the mountains of hell I will not ask you again, but obliterate you where you stand! Your name girl!

ROMANA: Romanadvoratrelundar. Well, you did ask. My friends call me Romana, but I think you're probably going to have to call me Romanadvoratrelundar though, from the look of you.

CAPTAIN: Silence! Or the silence of death descends upon you in the winking of an eye!

THE POLYPHASE AVITRON SNAPS OPEN ITS LASER EYE.

CAPTAIN: Now, how come you to this planet?

ROMANA: By Tardis. I'm a sort of Time Lord you see. Not actually a proper Time Lord yet because I've still got some exams to take, and all the dinners as well which are terribly dull, but…

CAPTAIN: By the Alpha storms of Cignus, plain speaking! For by the mealymouthed prophet of Agranjagzak, obliteration is at hand!

ROMANA: Sorry, yes, plain speaking. Well, I, as a Time Lord, or a nearly Time Lord, travel around in space…

CAPTAIN: Ah, just a common space urchin. You will die.

ROMANA: And of course Time, hence Time Lord.

CAPTAIN: Time? Travel in time? How is this possible?

***

First Draft Version 2

SCENE ELEVEN

THE BRIDGE. ROMANA FACES THE CAPTAIN.

CAPTAIN: Speak girl! Who are you that you dare to intrude upon my ship?

ROMANA: Ship? What ship? I don't understand...

CAPTAIN: By the mountains of hell I will not ask you again, but obliterate you where you stand! Your name girl!

ROMANA: My name? Romanadvoratrelundar...

CAPTAIN: You jest with me!

ROMANA: No, really, it is...

CAPTAIN: Silence! Or the silence of death descends on you in the winking of an eye!

THE POLYPHASE AVITRON SNAPS OPEN ITS LASER EYE.

CAPTAIN: How come you to this planet?

ROMANA: That's my business.

A BEAM FROM THE AVITRON BLASTS SOMETHING VERY CLOSE TO ROMANA.

CAPTAIN: By the fangs of the Sky Demon what happens on my ship is my business!

ROMANA: Ship? You mean this mountain? This mountain is your ship?

CAPTAIN: How came you here? Speak or die!

ROMANA: By Tardis.

CAPTAIN: Tardis? What is this Tardis? By the ninety names of hell!

ROMANA: It's a sort of space time machine. I'm travelling round the Universe in it. I'm a Time Lord you see.

CAPTAIN: Time Lord? What is this?

ROMANA: Well not actually a proper Time Lord yet because I haven't done all the exams yet, but…

CAPTAIN: By the Alpha storms of Cygnus, plain speaking! For by the mealymouthed prophet of Agranjagzak obliteration is at hand! What is your function?

ROMANA: Well at the moment I'm just travelling around in space…

CAPTAIN: Ah, just a common space urchin. Good, you will die.

ROMANA: …and of course Time, hence Time Lord, whilst I'm learning…

CAPTAIN: (CONTEMPTUOUS) Bah! Time Travel!

***

REHEARSAL SCRIPT: SCENE 12. INT. BRIDGE. DAY

(ROMANA FACES THE CAPTAIN)

CAPTAIN: Speak girl! Who are you that you dare to intrude upon my ship?

ROMANA: Ship? You call this mountain your ship? Bit cumbersome isn't it?

CAPTAIN: Your name girl!

ROMANA: Romanadvoratrelundar. Tell me, have you had an accident?

CAPTAIN: Silence!

ROMANA: I only ask because whoever patched you up obviously didn't know much about the new developments in cyboneutraulics. Do you get a squeak when you move your arm like this…?

CAPTAIN: Silence! Or the silence of death descends on you in the winking of an eye!

(THE POLYPHASE AVITRON SNAPS OPEN ITS LASER EYE)

Now, how have you come to this planet?

ROMANA: By Tardis. I'm a Time Lord you see… or at least I will be soon, I've still got a couple of qualifying exams to take, and all the dinners to eat as well which is terribly dull, but…

CAPTAIN: By the mealy mouthed prophet of Agranjagzak, speak plainly. Obliteration is at hand!

(HE GESTURES VIOLENTLY WITH HIS ROBOT ARM)

ROMANA: See, it does squeak doesn't it. The new frictionless bearings…

CAPTAIN: I will not ask you again! What is your function?

Finally, the televised version begins at the line 'What is your function?'

Again, marvel at Part Three, as Romana goes off to lead a rebellion. In the draft script we touch on exactly what the story is about for Adams, with Romana and Mula and Pralix having impassioned speeches, exploring themes of guilt and responsibility and free will, and the power of the younger generation to wash away the sins of the old. In the finished version, this rebellion is told through two short silent film segments of Mary Tamm striding through a wet field with some men in orange cloaks.

THE ORIGINAL SEGMENT

One fascinating sidebar is Douglas Adams's speculation on the nature of the Key to Time. Having extensively debated what his segment of the Key could be (see endpapers), Adams's notes seem to settle on Africa:

Africa – the Key from Earth. The Africa we know was a substitute, specially designed. The Doctor was actually involved in the operation of putting it there, during which Atlantis was accidentally submerged. The original Africa is now stowed in the hold of the Tardis.

When they try to reach the Earth in order to retrieve the Africa key they can't land, something is stopping them, so they materialise in orbit…

The Forges of Bethsalamin. Ancient. Deserted. Bloody enormous.

When the substitute Africa was put there, alien power was embedded in it secretly for the benefit of the Witch Doctor who is a renegade in hiding who managed to blackmail one of the Bethsalamin into building the continent in this way.

The Doctor has to go to Bethsalamin, revive the sleeping giants, and get a new Africa made at Time Lord expense.

They went into suspended animation when the bottom fell out of the continent market – waiting for the economic recovery of the Galaxy.

Their revival switches are geared to the Galactic stock market index.

Weight-conscious hitchhikers will encounter a planet called Bethselamin elsewhere in Adams's work. Curiously, at the bottom of Adams's original typewritten document on segments of the Key he has added a single handwritten word. The word is 'Mice'.

THE VILLAIN

Right from the start of development of *The Pirate Planet*, Adams is determined on a female villain:

'… Cleopatra? No. Who is the archetypal spoilt evil woman? (other than Jackie Onassis)

Why the Earth? What's the reason, other than wanting to collect beautiful planets?

Nero? But how and why? …

We think it's Nero. In fact… oh blah blah blah. Stop this rubbish.

If she's the Master's daughter, she is collecting the planets which witnessed his defeat. Because she loved him… or hated him?

The idea continues to evolve, until:

> If she's going to do Gallifrey instead of the Earth, then why
> not just say straight out that she's the Master – no further
> problems about motive.

STORY DEVELOPMENT

Preserved in the Archives are the steady progression of the
various treatments. Several ideas are worked on ceaselessly that
don't make it through to the final production. The Captain's
torture chamber is agonised over by Adams – what would be in
there? How would it be defeated? Sometimes it is a menacing,
yet ineffectual Dalek. At one point it is sand. At another, Adams
doodles the Doctor drowning. The placement of this segment
varies – in many breakdowns it is in Part Two. And yet, if you
look at the finished Part Three, is there an odd remainder of it, as
the Captain brings a (possibly tortured) Doctor and Kimus back
from unconsciousness?

Another key element, carried from 'The Perfect Planet', is the
Doctor falling into the centre of the planet. *The Pirate Planet* is
immaculately structured (Adams even uses quadrant diagrams to
illustrate the impacts of various themes on his characters). Just as
the Doctor and the Captain are shadows of each other, there are
originally three big uses of the TARDIS. Firstly, Romana makes a
simple landing by the book. Then she has to make the TARDIS do
the impossible to rescue the Doctor, and finally, the Doctor has to
outdo even her in order to save the Earth.

Responsibility and Guilt are a key theme to Adams's
development of the story. (They even get one of Adams's quadrant
diagrams showing how guilty each group of characters feels.)
It's not just about a cannibal planet – it's a fable about a world
where refusing to face up to past sins brings down society. The
Mourners are an unfocused force of guilt, the hidden conscience
of the people of Zanak. Adams is clear that the older generations

knew, or suspected, the terrible source of their pointless wealth. With each generation, the young are shown as becoming more questioning, more powerful until, finally, Pralix emerges, someone from an innocent generation who can finally use that power to win back the soul of their planet. On TV the mysterious cult are called the Mentiads, but I've gone with Adams's original name of the Mourners – it seems more evocative of what he was trying to convey.

THE TIME LADY GRAVITY

Douglas Adams started work on *The Pirate Planet* while the new companion was still being developed. In 'The Perfect Planet', the Doctor's companion is a nameless Time Lord referred to as X. He becomes Komnor, who becomes Gravity (sex unknown), before finally arriving as the Romana we know and love. Sort of.

The Romana of the first draft has, not surprisingly, been written before Mary Tamm has been cast. Yet she's still amazing – she's aloof, she sends the Doctor up rotten (try and imagine Mary Tamm standing on one leg and clucking sarcastically. Yes. That image will stay with you all day), and she knows everything. Jem Roberts's biography of Adams, *The Frood*, touches on the author's worry that he didn't write strong enough female characters. Arguably he writes nothing but strong women when he writes *Doctor Who*. His Romana is a gun-toting, evil-genius-thwarting Time Lady, who is never afraid to open her mouth, whether it's to say something brilliant or talk witheringly about her tutor.

The first draft has a few odd moments that vanish in later versions. The Doctor constantly refers to her throughout as 'silly girl', 'wretched girl' and once, gloriously, as having the brains of a goose. 'Just because I'm a woman he thinks that I'm not as clever as he is,' Romana laments quite fairly. It doesn't fit the characters we see on screen. Imagine Tom Baker's Doctor calling Mary Tamm's Romana 'you silly girl' – he'd have been wandering around the story with rather more than a bruised lip.

Mind you, this Doctor still occasionally refers to Romana as 'Romy', a pet name which clearly didn't find favour.

THE CURSE OF THE SKY DEMON

Novelisers have a strange life. Gareth Roberts had the joy of finding an entire unused scene for *Shada*. For *City of Death*, I had two extra pages by Douglas Adams, and that was a delight. For *The Pirate Planet*, not only did I have a plethora of unused scenes – I ended up leaving some of them out. Adams makes a lot out of Pralix's family – Balaton and Kimus have endless discussions like characters from a Greek comedy. I reproduced it all faithfully, and found my eyes skipping over it when I re-read it. So did an early reader. Consequently, their material in Part One has been substantially reduced – there's still a vast amount more of it than even makes it to the rehearsal script, mostly to do with whether or not to throw Pralix out into the street. I feel bad about leaving it out, but I hope I've kept as much as I can of it without making you grind your teeth.

I think the problem is that Adams's Doctor and Romana are so engaging that when you're not reading about them, you're twiddling your mind thumbs.

Talking of which, the Captain's swearing has been reduced. Again, we still have lots more of it than on screen. It's all great stuff, and would have been a joy to hear performed, but on the printed page the Captain came across as that friend we all have who still texts in caps.

K-9

Fans of K-9 will be delighted to discover that Adams loves him as much as we do. Not only does he get a cascade of extra lines, he also gets an entire extra subplot, in which K-9 has to rescue himself from a crashed air-car, repair it, and then fly to the Captain's Citadel. Adams is clearly having a whale of a time – he perfectly conveys K-9 landing on his back by typing a pathetic 'Master?'

upside down. Surprisingly tricksy on a twenty-first-century word processor, Adams simply rolled the page out of his typewriter, put it back in upside down, and typed, no doubt laughing.

PART FOUR

Structurally, Adams works hard at getting Part Four in the right order through the various drafts. In the scripts, much more is made of Xanxia's tyranny. Of the Nurse's true identity, the crew are innocent (as much as a bunch of planet-murdering pirates can be), which begs all sorts of questions that Adams does not, for once, answer. He's rightly more fascinated by the idea of Queen Xanxia, a typical supervillain, being taken in by a sales brochure. There's so much to explain that in the first draft Mr Fibuli lives to the end, so that he can explain a bit more. Meanwhile, Adams is having fun depicting the assault on the planet Earth, in scenes eerily familiar from the TV version of *Hitchhiker*, as startled commuters watch the skies darken.

The shooting of Queen Xanxia is quite odd. In the first draft she is symbolically shot by Kimus and Mulov. In the first draft, Mulov was Pralix's brother. He's shown as practical where Pralix is spiritual. Kimus was always the vaguely hopeless rebel leader, but it is Mulov who does the heavy lifting of actually organising a rebellion. By the rehearsal script, Mulov has become Pralix's sister Mula, which avoids Zanak having a reproduction-troubling all-male population. Given Mula / Mulov and Kimus's journeys through Adams's script – from wanting to do something to leading a rebellion – they've earned their shot at the evil Queen. By the time this reaches the screen, however, you may be a bit baffled as to why Kimus fires a gun at her and she just dies. Why has no one else thought of this? And why just Kimus? Poor Mula stands on the side lines.

A possible explanation is a copy of the rehearsal draft of the script lodged in the archives. It includes some curious handwritten alterations, clearly by someone with a tin ear for the humour of

Douglas Adams. For example, the Doctor's final speech goes from 'This is quite a good part of the universe for Zanak to settle in. Reasonable sun, good neighbours, some quite convenient stars…' to 'Reasonable sun, good neighbours in the next star system.' It's a painful example of the gradual shaping that *The Pirate Planet* underwent to take it from a brilliant outpouring of ideas to four episodes of broadcastable *Doctor Who*.

THE BLACK GUARDIAN

By the end of the Key to Time season, Douglas Adams was already in place as Script Editor, and was assigned the job of writing the last half of the final episode – the epic confrontation between the Doctor, Romana and the Black Guardian. The Key to Time has been reassembled, the fate of the universe is in the Doctor's hands… and Adams put his own spin on it.

What if, he argued, the Doctor had been doing the Black Guardian's work all along? Had he ever even met the White Guardian, or had he simply been conned into collecting something that was never supposed to be found? Adams's revolutionary take on the concept of the series was watered down by the time it reached the screen, but the final scripts still credit the raging figure who appears on the TARDIS screen simply as 'the Guardian'. So, given this reading of the Doctor's quest, it seemed appropriate to drop in a few hints that the Black Guardian is standing behind the scenes of *The Pirate Planet*, nudging events gently along.

A NEW CONTROL ROOM

At the end of the treatment for *The Pirate Planet*, I found an intriguing note. Whereas the television version ends with the Doctor and Romana walking off laughing, there's a curious final scene:

> The Doctor and Gravity make their farewells and go back to the Tardis, rather worried about what sort of state it's going

to be in inside. As they enter a breath of fresh air brushes past them and they discover a totally new interior – a large open conservatory with plants and small fountains and large French windows apparently looking out on to a pleasant English Garden. In the centre is a large stone sundial. The Doctor walks up to it and runs his hand over it. Lights wink on over its surface. He presses one and the doors close, he presses another and the central part of the sundial rises up. The Doctor is delighted…

It's clear from the treatment and the scripts that the TARDIS control room is pretty much destroyed. (On screen we get a puff of smoke.) Experienced fans know that an old TARDIS control room set had been pressed back into service for the previous season – could this paragraph be a hint that producer Graham Williams was determined to put his stamp on the show and try and create a control room of his own? As an abandoned idea it's intriguing – as a potential end to a book, it's irresistible.

AND FINALLY

The final, mystifying words will be left to Part Three's rehearsal script, where at the bottom of page 41 is a small typed note: '(No Page 42)'. And the typist is quite right. There isn't.

DOCTOR WHO BLANKET THEME: THE SIX KEYS

Notes by Douglas Adams

The Doctor has to find the six keys which are hidden in different parts of the Universe. In each case they may be something fairly large and significant (eg Great Pyramid of Cheops) which once taken revert to their original form. The problem in each case is that the object plays some significant role in the life of the planet on which it is located, either for good or evil, and the Doctor has to consider how its removal will affect life on that planet.

A) Africa.
B) Person. (Apparently a person, though the Doctor knows him to be a robot, or rather android)
C) Piece of rubbish, like empty tin, bit of string. But it must be something he uses conspicuously. Tin that he puts his jelly babies in, dog lead for K-9, hat band. Something he hangs round his neck and annoys his companion with.

Here's a thought. If his companion is the undergraduate Time Lord who is actually causing the Doctor a certain amount of embarrassment by showing him up rather too often then this could be a ploy of the Doctor's to get his own back. Therefore by getting hold of and displaying the key very obviously from the beginning he is scoring some fairly good points.

Now, clearly whatever it is that the Doctor pretends to look for must have some ulterior purpose. He must have some reason for wanting to move it from where it is.

(May be the undergraduate Time Lord is actually a baddy…?)

So the object they are removing must either

a) have some significance in the Doctor's relationship with the Time Lord (i.e. because the Time Lord knows that they are searching for a key)

or b) be something that the inhabitants of the planet on which it is located would only be prepared to give up if they knew that it was one of the six keys.

If b) then why?

1) Because everyone knows of the search for the Six Keys and is anxious to help. No, unlikely, difficult and boring.

2) Because they are in some sense special and in a privileged position in the galactic hierarchy. Not actually Time Lords but perhaps not too far removed from them in importance. Now if whatever it is that they give up is in some way a source of malignant power which they use (perhaps not overtly malignant, but let's say oppressive) and is either a person, a computer or a powerful crystal, then they must believe that the utilisation of the key will in some way be to their positive advantage. Perhaps this serves to make the Doctor suspicious at the end of the 'God' in a white hat.

3) The undergraduate Time Lord, being young and earnest and keen to do things by the book would not interfere in a bad situation unless he was forced to. Therefore the Doctor leads him (and of course us) into believing that the computer or whatever is the key simply so that he can get rid of it without the Time Lord protesting… and then casually mentions at the end that he's got the key all the time. Egg on the face of the u.g. T.L.

OTHER POSSIBLE KEYS

The Doctor himself. That of course puts another slant on his decision not to go through with it, which may be a problem.

Similarly if it's the Tardis.

But how about the Atlantic Ocean?

Buckingham Palace?

Stonehenge?

BUCKINGHAM PALACE

Set it in the future by a good few years so that you can't actually recognise the incumbent, thought possibly make him/her Windsorish.

Problems with that I expect. But how about a Stately Home?

Nice location work.

The Sun?

Any of our planets.

THE MOON!

Phobos, the Moon that doesn't make sense.

If it's our own moon, there could be a nice scene with the Doctor examining the footprints and debris left by the Apollo astronauts.

Mice -

DOCTOR WHO AND THE PERFECT PLANET

Original Treatment by Douglas Adams

The Doctor.

The Student Time Lord, whom for the moment we shall call Komnor.

Komnor is obviously very bright and anxious to learn from the Doctor. But he takes everything to do with being a Time Lord very seriously, and is frequently outraged by the Doctor's flippancy, and his habit of flouting Time Lord convention and going his own way. Obviously since Komnor is going to be a Time Lord it is in his own interest he thinks to do everything he can to enhance the power and prestige of the Time Lords. By and large they get on reasonably well, but are inclined to over-react to each other at times.

Komnor sees these missions as being simple clear cut jobs – simply fetching the keys. He disapproves of the Doctor's insatiable curiosity and thinks he should simply stick within his brief and otherwise leave well alone.

The Tardis lands on the planet of Jetral, which in the distant past was the Time Lords' major source of a crystal used in Tardis construction. The Doctor is curious to notice that it seems to have several more moons than are recorded on the ancient star charts. Because of his curiosity he refuses to tell Komnor immediately exactly what they are looking for.

The planet appears to be almost unbelievably peaceful and pleasant, the people charming and polite almost to the point of absurdity. This is embarrassing to the Doctor who rather enjoys being rude to people occasionally, and he finds it hard to cope with people who won't take offence.

A feast is held in honour of the visitors. The Doctor quite deliberately behaves disgracefully, to the fury of Komnor. When a toast is proposed from a fabulous ornamental stirrup cup, the Doctor prefers to drink from an old tin mug he has found lying by the side of the road, after which he hands out some totally gratuitous insults and leaves. He wanders about outside deep in thought.

Later that evening Komnor finds him sitting alone staring at a moon. 'There is something here which is very very wrong' says the Doctor. Komnor, still furious, says that the Doctor simply doesn't know a good thing when he sees it – he's an incurable meddler, why can't he simply recognise and accept the beneficent influence of the Time Lords on this planet?

'What influence?' demands the Doctor.

Komnor explains that he has been taken to see a large square in the city which has an enormously tall totem-pole-like statue of a Time Lord in it, which appears to be the centre of the planet's religion.

The Doctor becomes very agitated and demands to go and see it.

The statue is very impressive. It seems to be radiating some sort of power. It is clearly treated with enormous devotion and awe by the people of the planet, and there seems to be some connection between the power of the statue and the tranquillity of the people. That makes Komnor very proud and the Doctor very worried.

Komnor demands to know what the key is that they've come to get.

The Doctor says 'What's cylindrical, metal, and forty metres high?' and turns to stare at the statue.

Komnor is horrified. How can they possibly take that from the people of this, the perfect planet?

The Doctor consults Galactic records in the Tardis computer, and discovers that in the time when the Time Lords used to mine this planet, many millions of years ago, the inhabitants were brilliant, excitable, emotional and politically unstable people. This was a constant problem for the Time Lords, who even had to prevent a full scale nuclear war at one point. They decided as a temporary measure to impose a new religion on the planet, the worship of the Time Lord totem. The totem in fact generated a hypno-ray which drained all aggression, hatred and evil from the mind taking with it a significant proportion of the mind's intelligence as well. When the Time Lords perfected a process for producing the crystal artificially they despatched a Lord to go and disconnect the hypno-ray. He never returned, but the Time Lords had gratefully lost interest in the planet and failed to follow the incident up. The Doctor is very worried to know what happened to the missing Lord.

Suddenly a hideous voice rings through the Tardis. 'So the Time Lords have come to find me at last have they? You are too late. Far too late! Far far far too late!'

The Doctor and Komnor decide it's time they went to investigate the statue. They find their way in by means of a concealed entrance, and are immediately captured by some strange shadowy forms, and led along a series of underground passages. They manage to escape and find their way into a chamber from which the ancient Time Lord mining equipment was operated. The Doctor is staggered to discover that it is still operating, not only because it hasn't worn out, but... how can you possibly mine the same planet for millions of years? There'd be nothing left...

They are recaptured and taken to see... Malchios, the lost Time Lord!

He is an indescribably hideous travesty of a Time Lord, the embodiment of everything evil, he sits gaping at them in the middle of a pool of boiling yellow mud. Cackling monstrously, he tells his story.

He had arrived on Jetral to disconnect the machine generating the hypno-ray. Something went wrong and he accidentally wired himself into the machine, so that all the aggression and evil intelligence that was being drained from the population of an entire planet was being pumped into his own mind. He was totally trapped, and as the centuries passed he became more and more evil and more and more intelligent – the dark alter ego of a million billion artificially contented people. And as his evil mental powers grew he learned the power of telekinesis to overcome his physical immobility, and with this tool he began to formulate his gigantic plan of revenge on the Time Lords.

He continued mining the planet for crystal, and when all the crystal was found he continued mining anyway.

But what was he mining for? demands the Doctor. And if he'd been mining at the same rate for millions of years, where on earth was all the debris?

Suddenly he realises… the Moons! Gigantic slag heaps in space! But why, why why?

He manages to escape again, runs back down the corridors to the chamber where the mining equipment was controlled, and reads off some figures. Hearing sounds of pursuit he leaves the chamber again and goes off into another passage running deeper, whilst doing some rapid calculations in his mind. He works out exactly how big the planet is, exactly how much has been mined, how big the moons are. Hearing the sounds of pursuit gaining on him he comes across a large plate let into the floor and begins to prise it open. As he is doing so, he suddenly realises the significance of his calculations. Over three quarters of the interior of the planet has been removed and is now circling the planet in the form of moons. The planet must be entirely hollow! At that moment the plate comes up and the Doctor finds himself staring down into the interior of the planet, billions of cubic miles of nothingness.

He hears the voice of Malchios howling with laughter down the corridors.

'That's right Doctor, it's completely hollow!'

The Doctor twists round to evade capture by the shadows pursuing him, and falls straight down the hole… into nothingness.

The Doctor falls through nothingness for miles and miles and miles – he will not stop till he reaches the precise gravitational centre of the planet.

Komnor, hearing what has happened to the Doctor, also manages to escape and finds his way back to the outside world and the Tardis. He has never flown a Tardis before but knows the general principles. He also knows that his only chance of saving the Doctor is to try and make the Tardis materialise round him – at the precise gravitational centre of the planet.

Amazingly enough, he manages to do this, and the Doctor is rescued. They return to the surface. The Doctor is puzzled; he has computed the total mass of material that has been removed from the centre of the planet, and the figure seems oddly familiar. But he still doesn't know what it is that Malchios is up to so they have to go and find him again.

They re-enter the labyrinth beneath the statue, are re-captured by the shadows, and are taken once more to Malchios. He is in a gloating mood, and talks wildly of his terrible revenge on the Time Lords for having allowed him to stay buried underground for these millions of years.

The hour of his revenge is almost come.

The Doctor demands to know what he is going to do.

'Can't you guess?' screams Malchios. 'See if this will help you'

A door flies up revealing a chamber full of immensely sophisticated equipment. It seems very familiar to the Doctor, but he can't quite place it. Another door flies up revealing a chamber full of time crystal.

The Doctor is stunned: it takes one piece of crystal the size of a finger to run the Tardis, yet here is nearly a thousand tons of the stuff wired together. There's enough there to make an entire planet jump through space...

'Exactly,' cries Malchios.

But why a hollow planet? Why scoop out the centre of the planet, leaving a hole the size of... a hole the size of Gallifrey...!

The Doctor, horrorstruck, finally understands the bizarre immensity of Malchios's plan. The planet Jetral is going to jump through space like the Tardis and materialise round Gallifrey.

The entire planet of Gallifrey is going to be buried alive inside Jetral!

Malchios howls in triumph that the Time Lords will be buried alive for eternity whilst he harnesses the power of Gallifrey to take over the Universe. And nothing the Doctor can do will stop him.

But the Doctor suddenly produces a device he has brought from the Tardis, and clamps it round his head. He has realised that the shadows which captured him and Komnor were just Malchios's thought projections. This device is a thought shield which should give him some protection from them. He starts to make a run for it, back down the passages. The shadows are ineffectual against him, but Malchios has other tricks up his sleeve – using his telekinetic power he starts to make objects fly through the air at the Doctor. Twisting and turning, the Doctor reaches the end of the passage. He can hear a familiar noise starting – the asthmatic grinding of a Tardis engine. He reaches the surface of the planet again. The cylindrical Time Lord statue is beginning to pump up and down like the central column of the Tardis – the entire planet is preparing to dematerialise. He races towards his own Tardis brushing aside some of the local people who still want to give him baskets of fruit and maybe sing the odd song together.

Inside the Tardis he sets the controls for Gallifrey in the hope that by trying to materialise in the same point in space as Jetral they will simply jam each other, and neither will be able to materialise.

Gigantic shock waves pass through the Tardis and Jetral. We see the night sky above the planet disappear and a new one begin to appear but as the Tardis sets up its space jam the two night skies begin to oscillate – the planet can't materialise.

Malchios is totally occupied in trying to materialise the planet and Komnor finds himself left unobserved. He finds his way into the chamber containing the space jump controls, and tries to find his way round them. He dithers terribly because he can't work out which controls what. Eventually he just picks up a large piece of equipment and takes a swing at the control panel. All hell breaks loose, but the mechanism slows down, the grinding dies away and the planet rematerialises in its own space.

Malchios howls in rage and sends his shades to capture the unprotected Komnor.

He is about to put him to death when the Doctor bursts in and severs the lifeline which feeds Malchios with the mindpower drained from the hypno-ray. Malchios shrivels away with a dreadful shriek.

The Doctor sets about sabotaging the hypno-ray mechanism and he and Komnor then race back to the surface of the planet as a series of muffled detonations break out behind them.

They reach the surface. Komnor reminds the Doctor that they have to take the key with them, i.e. the statue. The Doctor says oh yes he'd forgotten about that, and at that moment the statue explodes. The people who have been gathered in peaceful adoration around it suddenly appear to wake up, their faces fill with anger, and they turn against the Doctor and Komnor, who have destroyed their idol. Chase back to the Tardis – they only just make it.

As they prepare to take off, Komnor is appalled that the key they came to find is not only left behind, but totally destroyed. The Doctor, rather to Komnor's astonishment, says everything is under control, he's got the key with him, and produces the old tin mug he found by the roadside. Komnor demands to know why he had told him that it was the statue.

'But I didn't,' insists the Doctor. 'I set you a riddle. What's metal, cylindrical, and forty metres high?'

'But that's never forty metres high,' protests Komnor.

'Yes I know,' says the Doctor, 'but you're an intelligent lad and I didn't want to insult you by making it too easy. I lied about the forty metres.' He explains that he was convinced there was something wrong with the planet, that the statue was something to do with it, and the only way he could overcome Komnor's reluctance to meddle in Time Lord affairs was to mislead him.

'But never mind, you did save Gallifrey as a result of it, so that's worth at least three out of ten for effort.'

ACKNOWLEDGEMENTS

The Pirate Planet would not have been possible without the help and encouragement of the Douglas Adams Estate, and the Archivists of St John's College, Cambridge – Mrs Kathryn McKee, Special Collections Librarian, and Miss Mandy Marvin, Manuscripts Cataloguer. I'm grateful to Lee Binding who made this book less boring and more funny. Any remaining boring bits are my fault.

Material from the Douglas Adams Archive appears by permission of the Master and Fellows of St John's College, Cambridge.

BBC

DOCTOR WHO

City of Death

Douglas Adams and James Goss

ISBN 9781849906753

'You're tinkering with time. That's always a bad idea unless you know what you're doing.'

The Doctor takes Romana for a holiday in Paris – a city which, like a fine wine, has a bouquet all of its own. Especially if you visit during one of the vintage years. But the TARDIS takes them to the 1979, a table-wine year, a year whose vintage is soured by cracks – not in their wine glasses but in the very fabric of time itself.

Soon the Time Lords are embroiled in an audacious alien scheme which encompasses home-made time machines, the theft of *Mona Lisa*, the resurrection of the much-feared Jagaroth race and the beginning (and quite possibly the end) of all life on Earth.

Aided by British private detective Duggan, whose speciality is thumping people, the Doctor and Romana must thwart the machinations of the suave, mysterious Count Scarlioni – all twelve of him – if the human race has any chance of survival.

But then, the Doctor's holidays tend to turn out a bit like this.